Hearts and Diamonds

Anchor and the Moon, Volume 2

Maxx Victor

Published by Maxx Victor, 2022.

This is a work of fiction. Similarities to real people, places, or events are entirely coincidental.

HEARTS AND DIAMONDS

First edition. October 31, 2022.

Copyright © 2022 Maxx Victor.

Written by Maxx Victor.

Cover design by: Paul Mah

Prologue

Three weary travellers move through a calm, starry night. A pair of conical beams illuminate two lanes of meandering bitumen, ever stretching out into the blackness ahead. Majestic trees loom on both sides, stretching leafy arms towards each other, creating a botanical archway. The dense greenery moves slowly towards them at first, then zooms past their peripherals, disappearing into the darkness behind. Keeping one hand firmly on the steering wheel, the driver tweaks the rear-view mirror and adjusts his posture to gain a better vantage of the occupants in the back seat. As a newlywed, he would watch his young bride as she slept, believing nothing could be more beautiful. Then his children came; first, his amazing baby boy, then the precious daughter that he could now see framed in his mirror. The angelic delight of his heart, with his eyes and her mother's hair, lay sleeping peacefully, wrapped in an embrace only achievable by the familiar and trusted arms of a loving mother. Mother and daughter slept, trusting they would be home when they again opened their eyes.

The proud father had more experience with magic than most, but nothing cast a spell over him quite like watching his children sleep; warm floods of future dreams intermingled with the bittersweet sting of nostalgia. If only this joyful moment was to be his last. Unfortunately, the last few moments as his soul lost its grip on his body were to be filled with terror and fear.

With the crack of towering timber, something large and bright flashes in the headlights. Glass, metal, and wood, popping and exploding on impact. Leaves and shards of glass pepper his face as he feels his seatbelt straining to keep him from falling towards the roof. The sudden and sharp meeting of head and steering wheel bringing darkness.

Regaining consciousness, he slowly becomes aware of a set of powerful hands trying unsuccessfully and painfully to pull him free. Petrol fumes waft through the twisted, metal frame where the windscreen had been, intermingling with the reek of hot rubber and burning oil. The forbidding bouquet bites at his nose and stings his eyes.

'I'll get you out.' An unknown woman's voice says reassuringly.

'No!' the driver implores. 'Save Katie, save my daughter!'

. . . .

Thirteen years later, only a few hundred metres north of the events of that night, horror is heard echoing once again through the dark forest. A woman screams in terror as a large hairy creature drags her boyfriend from their tent.

'Tyrone!' she screams out his name, but he does not answer. He can no longer answer. She sits in the horrifying silence and darkness; gripping her sleeping bag around her. 'Tyrone?' she pleads in a whisper.

A set of heavy footsteps breaks the silence. She closes her eyes and holds her breath as the footsteps grow louder.

'Please answer me.' She tries to speak, but her words are hardly audible.

'Are you hurt, lass?' a deep voice asks. 'You're safe now.'

'Where's Tyrone?'

'He's gone. Sorry. I was too slow.'

Chapter 1
Red in the Morning

A storm builds, builds in strength and in might.
Is it strong enough to blow you back home tonight?

• • • •

That sound? Cinder's emerald green eyes shot open. She looked with sleep-blurred eyes at the tall, muscular man sitting next to her in the bed they now shared. His dark hair and eyes, midnight black in the dim morning light. These features had earned him the nickname Black, but he had many titles. Angus, surfer, warrior, leader, farmer, Nephelium, but what was he now to Cinder? Lover? Boyfriend? They had simply just become a single entity, Cinder and Black.

'Are you okay?' he asked.

'Yes, I just thought I heard something.' Cinder said sleepily. Angus tried to listen, but could only hear the rhythmic drops of rain against the windowpane. Cinder's breathing fell into tempo with the pitter-patter beat. He watched longingly as her freckled shoulders rose and fell beneath her long auburn locks.

'What can you hear?' he asked, running his hand along the flesh of her back until it curved up onto her hip. Moving his hand to her thigh, he kissed the top of her head, breathing her in – his heart lightening with her scent.

'Mmm. I'm not sure,' Cinder answered, moving her warm body closer to his and pulling his hand up onto her chest. Angus squeezed her tight, feeling her heart beating firmly. Cinder turned her head slightly to face him.

'What are you thinking about?' she asked.

'Dom.' Angus answered, before kissing her shoulder.

'Really?' Cinder asked, raising an eyebrow, sounding suddenly awake. Releasing his hand and pulling the covers up over her body, she sat up to face him. 'Do you usually think about your friends when you're touching a naked woman?'

Angus's dark eyes twinkled as an embarrassed smile spread across his stubbled face. 'Sorry. I mean, I was thinking about him before you woke up,' he explained. Cinder smiled and pushed his shoulder playfully.

'It's alright, I miss him too.' She rested her head on his knee and looked up into his strong, but sad, face. 'Still no news?'

Angus stretched out his long arm, stroking his fingers across Cinder's silky hair; his large anchor tattoo stretched out over his broad forearm. The words *Pride Before Your Pride* dancing as the muscles and tendons moved under his pale skin. 'Nothing real for six months, just rumours. I don't think he even knows that Tor is alive. As far as I know, he is still crazy with vengeance, chasing your stepmother somewhere around the world.'

'We're not calling her stepmother. Remember? 'Louvelle' will do, or 'She-devil' works for me, too.' Cinder said, her face hardening. Angus nodded in agreement.

'What about *the She-devil*? Have you heard anything?'

'Marraine says she's in Europe somewhere.'

A sudden flash of light filled the room, illuminating the dim of the overcast morning. Moments later, thunder rumbled and rolled along the coast and up through the hills, rattling the window next to Angus's head. Pulling the covers up around her, Cinder leaned across him and stared out of the window.

'You're not afraid of a little lightning, are you?' Angus teased.

'No, there's something else.' She replied, holding her finger to her lips 'Listen. Can you hear that? I think it's a siren.' A shiver ran its way slowly down the length of Cinder's spine. Angus felt her shift against him.

'What is it?' he asked, wrapping his warm arms around her.

'I don't often hear sirens around here, and the times I have, I'd rather forget.'

The wooden framed windowed creaked as Angus's large hand glided slowly across the pane, wiping away the condensation. As he watched the storm clouds forming over the distant ocean, a different light flashed across the glass, momentarily turning the droplets running down the window blood red.

Outside, the rhythm of raindrops on the roof and windows of the farmhouse slowed. Cold eddies blew and swirled along a path, cut into the side of a hill generations ago. The breeze whistled its way through a rusty iron gate, rattling its hinges. A sign, that because of decades of corrosion and weather was no longer legible, rattled against a sun-paled grey stump. Beyond, rolling green pastures stretched off to the horizon, the occasional sunlight glistening with moist, grey stones that dotted the landscape. A serpentine, orange gravel road, twisted its way slowly down an oak-lined laneway, through the patchwork of green fields. Down below, perched above the weedy dunes, rested the sleepy beach town of Heathcote. A plastic bag, caught by a gust of wind, danced unseen down the esplanade before rising amongst the wisps of smoke from half a dozen red brick chimneys. Grey wispy clouds meandered across the winter sun, casting grey shadows over the ocean. The waves lapped gently on the beach, empty, save for a few hungry gulls braving the cold, inquisitively circling something that had washed up on the shore.

Red and blue lights reflected off the ocean and the wet sand and rocks. Two Seagulls fighting over something on the beach took flight, startled by the approach of people in uniforms. Seeing something drop from the mouth of one of the birds, a dark-skinned man in a blue suit and a disposable yellow plastic raincoat, hurried to inspect the jettisoned package. Crouching down on the sand, he pulled a zip-lock bag and plastic gloves from his pocket. Without placing it on his wet hands, he used the plastic glove to pick up the sandy, moist object. With a contortion of his brow and a long, drawn-out sigh, he confirmed his suspicions.

'Well, Henry, our day just got more interesting,' he said to the uniformed police officer behind him, but keeping his eyes fixed on the dark pile at the edge of the water.

'What you got there, detective?' the officer asked.

'This Henry,' said the dark-skinned man, holding up the object, 'is an emancipated human eye.'

• • • •

A horn blasted angrily as someone walked arrogantly through the oncoming traffic in the fading light of a Bucharest afternoon. A dark-blue Roman truck rumbled its way past tall white buildings. Plumes of soil drifted from its rusting trailer as it crossed the Dâmbovița River and turned into the streets of the Jewish neighbourhood. Its aging engine groaned and protested under the weight of its load and released a cloud of dark smoke. A solitary pedestrian emerged from the cloud – a tall, slim man in a dark suit that was almost the same colour as his sunken eyes. With his hands in his pockets, he moved quicker and more confidently than his advanced years would predict. Once the air cleared and the grumbles of the engine died off in the distance, the man's expensive leather shoes returned to their echoing along the empty street. Without breaking his stride, the man crossed the road, continuing towards the river. His pace slowed as his long fingers exited his pocket, adjusting his white hair. His eyes darted left and right before glancing back over his shoulder. Nothing. The only movement in the street was a pamphlet offering two-for-one coffees, flapping against the gutter at the side of the road. His wrinkled face contorted into a grin, exposing greying teeth. Cracking his knuckles, he continued forward, quickening his pace once more. A dozen steps later, with great speed and dexterity, the old man vaulted an iron gate and disappeared down a cobblestone alley.

On the rooftops above, a dark figure moved swiftly and silently from shadow to shadow. Its form was human, but its movement as it jumped from rooftop to rooftop was more resemblant of an enormous cat. Reaching the alley that the old man has just entered, it dropped silently into the shadows below.

Recognizing the woman that now blocked his path, the old man froze. She walked forward, so that she was standing in a patch of sunlight.

'Hello, Patru. You are getting slow.' She said calmly.

'Hello to you. What are they calling you here now? Red Banshee?'

'We have been called worse, have we not?'

'Do you intend to kill me then, Banshee?' the man said, taking a step back.

'I warned you to stay away from my family.'

'Family? Ha!' Patru scoffed. 'What do you know of family?'

'Perhaps you are right, Patru,' she said, nodding her head slowly. 'I know little of family. But what I do know, is that I am bored with this conversation.' With incredible speed, she lunged forward, taking hold of his neck. Patru struggled helplessly as she pulled him out of the shadows. He blinked his dark eyes as the sunlight fell across his pale face. Pulling up his left sleeve, she revealed the tell-tale pallid outline, where until recently, a watch had been.

'Freci meta.' Patru said with a laugh. 'You are too late. I signed everything over to my Postea this morning.'

'Well, you won't need this then.'

Ripping open his silk shirt, she reached in and pulled out a silver pendant and chain, wrenching it aggressively away from his neck. With a shove, the red-haired woman forced the old man into the sunlight. Small dark areas appeared on Patru's face as he winced in pain. The dark areas grew, smoke rising from their centres.

'You are too late!' he yelled, as his head erupted in flames.

Chapter 2
Raining in Baltimore

His money had run out almost two weeks ago, but Dom's anger was still in ample supply. A casual acquaintance may not have recognised him as the same man from six months earlier. His hair had grown long and wild and a thick beard covered his slimmed down, tanned face. His rage had kept him busy and distracted, but he always gravitated towards a beach.

In the quiet moments, Dom would sit with his feet gently pushing aside the sand; watching the waves roll slowly up onto the shore, reaching out to touch his feet before reluctantly retreating in a swirl of water and sand. It was in those times, when a salty breeze swirled around his thick mop of dark hair, that his thoughts drifted back to the little beach town of Heathcote and the farm. And his family. But most of all, his sister.

He was far from the beach now, he thought, looking around the large bedroom that he now sat in. He decided this was also the furthest he had ever been from home. So much had happened since the night he saw his sister lying lifeless in their father's arms. Dom hardly recognised it as his life.

The night that his sister's murderer, Louvelle, had escaped, her step-daughter Cinder had left him on the beach holding Angus, his best friend, as he slipped in and out of consciousness. As Dom watched the lights of the yacht slowly drift away towards the next town along the coast, Tallo's Bluff, Cinder ran, disappearing into the dunes. Half propping Angus up, half dragging him, he managed to get his semi-conscious friend to the hospital, where if he had gone inside, Dom might have seen his sister in the emergency department clinging to life. After stealing a boat and tracking down Louvelle's yacht, he realised he had no wallet and no phone. *Who would I call anyway?* He thought to himself.

Louvelle's yacht was empty and there was no sign of where she had gone next. In his anger and annoyance, Dom found his way to a local bar. After dealing with some drunk fishermen that were breaking glass and making unwelcome comments about the female bar staff, the owners offered him some food and drink and a place to stay the night. After talking and drinking all night with the owners, he accepted their offer to stay on and help around the bar in exchange for food and lodging. This was as good a place as any to stay, he thought, until he decided where to go next. Over the next few months, he washed dishes, swept floors, and ejected undesirable patrons. Most importantly, he listened to conversations and made friends with locals and visitors; people who knew how things worked. When he had heard the same rumours enough times and had enough people to confirm them, he determined that Louvelle had taken a private jet from an airstrip inland of Tallo's Bluff and was now somewhere in Europe. Early in his stay at the bar, he had become friendly with the captain and crew of a container ship from the Central African Republic. When the crew returned and he discovered they were leaving for Rotterdam at the end of the week, Dom made a wager that he could beat all of them in an arm wrestle. This time there was no Marraine to whisper distractions in his ear, so he won the bet easily. He said goodbye to his friends at the bar and left to spend the next two months working as a deckhand. Just in time too, he thought, because a girl that worked behind the bar had begun referring to him as 'her boyfriend'.

Now, almost six months to the day since he left home, Dom found himself pulling his mess of dark hair out of his sleep-puffed eyes. Contemplating how long his hair has grown, he ran an admiring hand along the pure white sheets between him and the owner of the bed he occupied. He had never been sure what people meant by the term thread count, but he decided that these must be the highest possible. Dom smiled to himself as he reflected on the contrast to the old swag that had been his bed for the past few months; a swag that now lay hidden behind some rocks on the Marina surf beach on the coast of the Black sea. Following rumours of Louvelle's movements all over Europe, had brought him finally to Constanta, Romania.

As far as Dom knew, they had already buried Torry; his family and friends would all have been standing around at her funeral saying stupid things through their tears, like 'Where is Dom?' and 'He should be here.' *Where I am*, he thought to himself as he pulled back the expensive white sheets to reveal the arm of a middle-aged woman draped across his waist. *Where I am is here, being the only one doing what needs to be done. Well, maybe not this exactly*, he thought to himself as he considered the curvaceous body that was at the end of the arm. This wasn't part of the plan. This was simply a pleasant accident.

Dom had become friendly with a group of surfers from California. They had nicknamed him 'Wild Dom, the beach bum' when they discovered him sleeping in the dunes one morning. Last night, they had invited Dom to have some drinks with them at a local bar. Dom had declined, saying that his money had run out. The surfers then explained that their parents had been some early investors in a ridiculously successful online company that Dom didn't really understand anything about. When the surfers told Dom that their parent's American Express was paying for everything, he understood and accepted their invitation.

Slipping himself quietly out from under the arm, Dom recovered his clothing from the floor. He pulled on his underwear and tiptoed to the door, turning to look back one more time at the bed and realising with guilt that he had no recollection of the occupant's name. Dom did, however, remember one name from last night - Victoria.

Victoria was one of those girls, who always looked like she was standing in good lighting, always had her own gust of wind through her thick dark hair, and made any off-the-rack outfit look like a designer had crafted it for her personally. If Dom had seen a photo of Victoria, he would not have believed that she looked like that in real life, but she did. Dom was sitting at the bar, only half listening to a joke about the rain in Baltimore, when he noticed her gliding through the crowd; long, shiny hair flowing, dark brown eyes glistening with laughter. Dom's eyes widened, tracking her across the room as he laughed at what he hoped was the punchline. Rows of warm-white downlights glittered off her sparkling gold dress, perfectly at home against the golden art déco styled trims on the black walls. Victoria's smile filled the room with an angelic glow that moved towards him. Dom's body twisted involuntarily towards her, but someone new suddenly obstructed the glow.

'Prea tanar!' the voice of the person blocking Dom's view said aggressively.

'Excuse me?' asked Dom, noticing for the first time that the voice was coming from a middle-aged woman who looked remarkably like Victoria.

'Too young for you!' the woman replied.

'Who?' Dom pretended not to know to whom she was referring.

'My daughter. She 17. Too young.' she pointed at Victoria. Dom nodded in agreement.

'Yes, yes, far too young.'

'Then why you look?'

'Oh, I wasn't looking at her.' Dom continued the lie. The woman appeared even more agitated.

'I know when a man looks with, with eyes of desire.'

'Of course you do,' Dom answered calmly.

'Then you admit you have the desire,' she said, pointing at his chest. Dom rose from his chair and stood closer to the woman.

'Yes, I definitely have the desire. Just not for your daughter. Although, she is very beautiful.'

The middle-aged woman was wearing tall-heeled boots, but her face was still only level with Dom's broad chest.

'Then why you look?' she asked, looking up into his warm eyes. 'No one else with her, just me.'

'Yes, exactly.' Dom replied with a wink and a cheesy smile.

'Oh?' the woman responded, pointing at herself. Dom nodded in reply.

'Hello, I'm Dominic.' he said, extending his right hand. The woman accepted his handshake as her pale cheeks and décolletage flashed crimson. Dom recalled joining Victoria and her mother for a few drinks. As a few drinks became many, he began to share his story. Victoria hung on every word with wide-eyed awe, but her mother laughed the whole thing off as the ramblings of a drunk. Dom recalled dancing with mother and daughter and his American friends, but his recollection of the remainder of the evening was fussy.

Opening the bedroom door as quietly as the old hinges would allow, Dom slipped out into a long, dark hallway. Turning one last time to look at the bed before leaving, he whispered, 'Goodbye, Victoria's mum,' before pulling the door slowly closed with a click.

Pale green walls stretch up to a high ceiling, lit only by the early morning light escaping under eight identical doorways; four on either side of the hallway. The symmetry of the hallway and the fact that it stretched off in roughly the same distance in both directions made it even more difficult for him to remember which way he had come last night. The throbbing at the back of his head, was not helping either. *Okay then*, he thought to himself while pulling on the rest of his clothes, *Right it is*. He turned left and tiptoed to the end of the hall. Reaching the top of a stairway that led down, his stomach rumbled. So loud was the noise in the otherwise silence, that Dom began running down the stairs, fearful that he might wake someone. The stairs led him down into a large kitchen area. Along one wall was a long shelf stacked with an assortment of jars containing flour, sugar, pasta, and other items he didn't recognise. Another shelf below held fresh fruit and vegetables.

'Jackpot' Dom said quietly to himself as his stomach once more rumbled in agreement.

Dom pulled out the bottom of his t-shirt to create a makeshift basket and began filling it with pears, green apples, and carrots. The soft padding and shuffling of bare feet on the slate floor alerted him to the fact that someone else had entered the room. Dom swivelled his head around to see Victoria, looking just as angelic with her messy bed hair and her black silk pyjamas, as she did the night before. Victoria smiled and held out her hand. Thinking that she wanted him to give back the food, he sheepishly passed her one of the pears. Victoria giggled and placed the pear back in his t-shirt basket. Taking him by his wrist, she led him out of the room to another set of stairs. As they descended, there was a noticeable drop in temperature. Dom needed to duck his head under a curved stone roof as she led him down into darkness. The reverberation of his boots on the steps gave the impression that there was a large open space beyond the foot of the tunnel, but Dom's eyes had not yet attuned to the dimness. With a click and a splutter, a set of four florescent lights hummed to life. Blinking as his eyes adjusted to the light, Dom looked around in excitement and satisfaction.

Victoria jogged forward mischievously, pulling Dom with her, then dropped his hand. Dom stood looking around a large cellar, with his toned abdomen exposed, still holding the bottom of his t-shirt up to contain the pilfered food. Wine racks and large barrels lined the walls. All kinds of meats, cheeses, and bread hung from metal racks that ran down the centre of the curved stone ceiling.

'Is this heaven?' he asked. 'I died last night, right? You're an angel and this is heaven.' Victoria just laughed and scampered deeper in to the cellar, returning a moment later with a large canvas backpack.

'Here, put those in this.' She said, taking some of the fruit out of his t-shirt. 'Go collect what you want.'

After enthusiastically emptying the rest of the food into the backpack, Dom moved dazed and delightedly around the food.

'It smells amazing in here.' he called out, his mouth salivating at the notes of garlic, yeast, mustard, curry, and olive oil. Shuttling back and forth with handfuls of booty, Dom quickly filled the pack. When the weight had become too much, Victoria needed to sit the plunder on the floor. She placed her hand on Dom's shoulder as he squeezed one last wedge of vintage cheddar into the pack.

'You will need all this for your trip.' She said, running her thumb along his prominent deltoid.

'Thank you, Victoria,' he beamed, standing and swinging the pack over his shoulder. 'What trip do you mean?'

'You need to go to Hoia Baciu Forest,' Victoria answered, busying herself with tightening the straps so that the pack sat more comfortably on Dom's back.

'I don't know what that is. Why would I go there?' Dom was very confused. *But that's usual*, he thought to himself.

'I know the one you seek,' Victoria said. 'The Babau Vanator, the monster that other monsters fear. Some say she is a witch, others say she is a shapeshifter. Sometimes a red-haired woman, sometimes a bear, other times a wolf.'

'Why didn't you tell me about this last night?' Dom asked in surprise.

'My mother doesn't like me to talk about these things. She says they are stupid superstitions.'

'Can you tell me how to get there?'

'It is all here.' Victoria explained, unzipping a pocket at the front of the backpack and showing Dom a map and some money that she had put in there earlier. Dom took hold of Victoria's hands.

'You really are my angel,' he said. Blushing and smiling coyly, Victoria slipped the map and money back into the pocket, then quickly took hold of Dom's face in both hands. Before he could realise what was happening, Victoria's soft lips were moving forcefully against his.

'You must go now.' She said, as she pulled her face away. 'Before my father gets home.'

Chapter 3
Good Morgan

Bushy black and white eyebrows twitched as a reluctant eye bobbed open and tried to focus. A heavy, old eyelid rolled slowly shut, like a garage door, convincing the eye to return to its pleasant darkness.

Once again, the noise that woke Dom's aged father Gunn from his afternoon shut-eye, forced his wrinkled forehead to lift his large caterpillar-like eyebrows. It was not until the noise came a third time that Gunn registered it as a knock on the solid wooden door of the farmhouse. It was as much an unwelcome sound as an unfamiliar one. Almost all visitors to the farm were family members with keys, or neighbours, who would announce their arrival with an 'Anybody home?'

Gunn had spent the previous evening drinking with his brother Dand. Dand and his three sons had left early that morning, heading north to spend some much-anticipated time with their wife and mother. Gunn sat for a moment, his head pounding, hoping that he had simply imagined the knock as part of a daydream, but once more, the knocking came. Four knocks; slow, firm, and deliberate. Armchair and knees creaked in protest as Gunn pushed himself to his feet. He retrieved a large hunting knife from between the cushion and the arm of his chair; tucking it out of sight but not out of reach, into the back of his jeans before covering it with his flannelette shirt.

'I'm coming, coming' he called, walking stiffly to the front door and rubbing the sleep out of his weather warn face.

With one hand readied behind his back, Gunn pulled open the solid door to reveal a very serious-looking young man in a well fitted but functional dark blue suit. His pressed shirt appeared pristine white against his dark complexion.

'Good afternoon Mr Kinnard.' The new arrival said, as Gunn notice his thick dark hair, cut very short and seriously against his scalp. He was a thin man with long arms and legs, but Gunn noticed he had the confident stance of a fit man who knew how to handle himself. He stood straight and still, with his hands behind his back, chest pushed proudly forward.

'How can I help you there, lad?' Gunn asked. The visitor moved his hand inside his jacket, instinctively Gunn's hand found the handle of his knife.

'Mr Kinnard, I'm Detective Peter Morgan of the Heathcote police.' The detective showed Gunn his identification. 'Excuse the interruption. I just have some inquiries that I hope you can assist me with today.'

Gunn released the grip on his weapon and concealed it once more under his shirt.

'Certainly lad. Come in, come.' Gunn took a step back and gestured with his now free hand for Detective Morgan to enter. 'We are always more than happy to help out the boys in blue.'

Stepping inside onto the slate floored entrance of the farmhouse, Detective Morgan ran a discerning eye over the family room on his left and the dining and kitchen to his right. Warm was the word that sprung to mind - both physically and aesthetically. His mind wandered momentarily, childhood nostalgia evoked by the scent of tobacco, grease, and freshly cooked bread. A fire crackled invitingly in the fireplace. The flames were low, but the coals were red and bright. A collection of books stacked on the mantle caught the detective's attention. He made a mental note to research the titles later. In the kitchen, Gunn's teenage daughter, Torry, was busying herself making a ham, cheese, and pineapple sandwich. She pulled a set of wireless buds from her ears and smiled politely when their eyes met.

'Can I offer you a drink, Detective? I was just about to boil the kettle.' Gunn said, closing the door behind him. Detective Morgan waved away the offer with his left hand and then placed it behind his back again.

'No, thank you.'

Torry sat at the kitchen table, positioning herself where she had the best view of the living room. Gunn stepped back towards his armchair. 'Would you like a seat, detective?' He asked, motioning towards the other armchair.

'No thank you sir, I don't intend to take up very much of your time. Just a few questions.' The police detective said, looking around the room again.

'Well, suit yourself, but I'm going to rest my old legs.' Gunn sat down and looked the detective up and down. 'You look very young for a detective,' he said in an inquiring tone. Detective Morgan's serious face grew sterner.

'I assure you I'm old enough to do my job, sir,' he said. Gunn sent a smile Torry's way.

'I meant no offence, detective. I know better than many how capable young people can be.'

'Yes, but capable of what I wonder?' asked the detective, turning to look at Torry as a piece of pineapple dropped from the corner of her mouth onto her plate. Torry, embarrassed, smiled and swallowed a mouth full of food. Gunn stared at the young police man, his large eyebrows set low over his blue eyes.

'I have great respect for the young and for those who uphold the law. However, young man, if you continue with that accusatory tone, you will see the stubbornness that men of my vintage are famous for.' Gunn said, slowly. His voice low and gruff. Detective Morgan's puffed-up chest deflated slightly.

'I apologise, sir. I'm not pointing the finger at anyone, just trying to get answers.'

'We are honest people here, and we will try to answer your questions as best we can. You just need to make sure you're asking the right questions.' Gunn said, crossing his arms over his broad chest.

'Very well, sir.' Detective Morgan continued. 'My question is, do you know the whereabouts of a Mr Duncan Craig? He was in your employ, I believe.'

Gunn pulled his spectacles from his pocket, cleaning them with the bottom of his shirt. 'We've not seen Duncan for months now. I'm sure you have seen the missing person's report detective.'

'Yes. I read it again recently. I found the timing of his disappearance very convenient.' Detective Morgan said, removing a tattered black notebook from his vest and scribbled some notes. Gunn put on his spectacles and stared at him.

'Convenient? How's that?' he asked, raising one of his large eyebrows. The detective flicked through his notebook.

'There were some significant events that took place around the time of his disappearance. Some to do with your own family.'

'I don't see what was convenient about losing one of my best workers the same week my son went overseas, and my daughter ended up in hospital. I actually found the whole thing mighty inconvenient.' Gunn crossed his arms again. Detective Morgan nodded slowly and turned another page.

'And Mr Blair Abernethy, who was also in your employ, was fatally injured. More convenient for Mr Craig perhaps, than for you, sir?' he asked rhetorically, flicking back through his notes. 'Your daughter had an accident, is that correct?' He looked at Torry again. Torry pulled her hair forward over the scars on the side of her face. Gunn coughed to regain the detective's attention.

'Yes, unfortunately, farms can be dangerous places,' he said. Detective Morgan scribbled some more notes in his book.

'Some more than others, it would seem.' He looked up from his notes, waiting for a response from Gunn. Beside his armchair, a used cup and saucer sat atop a three-legged side table. A silver, tea-stained spoon rested on the saucer. Gunn's time-worn and smoke-blackened pipe sat next to the used crockery. He reached over and picked up the pipe.

'Was there a question there?' he asked, cleaning out his pipe with the handle of the teaspoon. Both men stared into each other's faces.

'Do you own dogs, Mr Kinnard?' Detective Morgan asked after a moment's silence.

'Dogs?' Gunn taped his pipe on his ashtray.

'Yes, dogs. Perhaps you have working dogs - large ones.' Detective Morgan jotted down the names of the books on the self. Torry's elbow hit against her plate, sending it twirling and rattling against the wooden table.

'No.' Gunn replied. 'We ain't too keen on dogs round here.' He placed his pipe down and looked up at the young man. 'Not to tell you how to do your job lad, but your questions seem to be all over the shop.' Undaunted by Gunn's remarks, the young detective continued his questioning.

'I believe Mr Craig and Mr Abernethy were close. Is that correct?'

'They was poofters.' Gunn answered matter of factually. Torry coughed, choking on her sandwich.

'Dad! I told you not to use that word.'

'I don't mean no offence, princess!' Gunn called out in the direction of the kitchen. 'I'm happy for anyone that finds love. That's just what they asked me to call them,' Gunn clarified.

'Thank you, sir, that's interesting.' Detective Morgan said, writing enthusiastically.

'How's that?' Gunn asked.

'Unfortunately, sir, homophobia is often a motive for violence and hatred.'

'Well, you won't find no homophobic dogs 'ere.' Gunn Joked. Torry giggled. The detective's face remained stern.

'We are still trying to track down the whereabouts of almost a dozen other people who went missing around the same time as your family's *accident*. My job is to try to piece together the connection,' he said. Gunn rubbed the black and white stubble on his chin.

'Well, I don't know nothing 'bout anyone else's business. I stick to my own. And as for the connecting, well, that's like you said, your job. Ain't it?' This made Detective Morgan smile. He placed his notebook back inside his breast pocket.

'I do apologise, sir. I am just trying to get a clear picture of what happened here earlier this year. All I have to go on so far is some poorly collected evidence and a bunch of monster stories from the locals. I'm just trying to separate reality from fantasy, in a town where fantasy is what keeps the tourist dollars flowing in.' Detective Morgan straightened his jacket. Gunn laughed to himself. He could see Torry doing the same.

'Well, like I said, we will tell you the truth of things; you won't be getting any fairy tales here lad.'

'I appreciate that, sir. If you think of anything else that might help, please call me.' He reached inside his other pocket and pulled out a small white card. 'This is my direct number. Oh, and it's not all bad news Mr Kinnard, we have had a possible sighting of Mr Craig just recently.' he said, handing the card to Gunn. Gunn raised his large eyebrows.

'That is good news. He owes me some money.'

Detective Morgan took the opportunity to have another look at the books on the mantle and a framed black-and-white photograph on the wall. 'Yes. Unfortunately, we had the body of a young man, a tourist, wash up on the beach two weeks ago. The young woman that was camping with him the night he went missing claims that a man matching Mr Craig's description helped her.'

'Helped her how?' Torry called out. The police detective turned and opened the door.

'He chased off a large dog, apparently,' he said, moving into the doorway. 'Convenience and coincidence, once again, it would seem. Thank you again for your time.' He exited swiftly and pulled to door shut behind him.

Torry picked up her plate and the remainder of her sandwich and carried them to the living room entrance, leaning against the timber archway. Gunn looked at his daughter and smiled 'So, what do we think of our new police detective?' Torry finished her mouthful before answering.

'I like him. He seems smart.'

'Yes, very clever I would say. Unfortunately.' Gunn agreed. Torry finished her meal and dusted some crumbs from her chest.

'I'm not sure he's ready for what he's getting himself into. He looked very young.'

'Yes, very young.' Gunn looked away, thoughtfully.

'And kind of cute.' Torry added. Gunn's large shoulders bobbed up and down with a laugh.

'I'll take your word for that. Now have you finished lunch?'

'Yep.' Torry showed him her empty plate. 'How come?' She asked, returning her plate to the kitchen and placing it in the dishwasher.

'I think you should go find Cinder and Black and tell them about our new detective.' Gunn said. Torry jogged back to her father and kissed him on the head.

'I'm on it!' she said with a salute.

· · · ·

Cinder sat with her cheek pushed against the cold glass of the passenger side door of a 1971 VW station wagon that was the property of their friend Blair before he died in the summer. Sunlight breaking through open spaces between the trees causing her wide eyes to blink intermittently, as the car wound its way noisily up through the forest. Angus sat tall and serious in the driver's seat, trying unsuccessfully to reassure Cinder with over enthusiastic smiles. After trying to think of something to say for what felt like the longest five minutes of his life, he decided instead to turn on the radio. A very serious sounding female was talking about an animal attack victim found on the beach. Cinder moved uncomfortably in her seat and crossed her arms around her chest, shooting Angus a sideways look. Angus understood immediately, his hand already on the dial, turning frantically to find some music. The reassuring sound of a four-four beat and a guitar solo filled the vehicle as Angus took the last bend.

With her heart rate already elevated, the sound of the gravel driveway and the smell of the rose gardens as they turned in through the familiar gateway hit Cinder harder than she expected. She took a succession of deep breaths to calm the pounding in her chest. And then there it was. The Big House rising impressively and monstrously out of the forest. Sitting high and proud on its hilltop perch. A grand multi-story structure boasting impressive iron work and mid-19th-century architecture. Until recently, The Big House had been the only home that Cinder had ever known. Her eyes becoming glassy, Cinder reached out and took hold of Angus's leg. This was the first time she had been back in months. She tried to speak, but all she produced was nervous laughter.

Cinder's friend, Bob, and her godmother, Marraine, had been taking care of the day-to-day running of the house in Cinder's absence. Marraine stood on the front steps waving to the car. Seeing her godmother looking as confident and beautiful as always gave Cinder some reassurance. Angus pulled the car up parallel with the front entrance, facing Cinder's door to the house. Bob appeared from somewhere and ran to open the door for her. 'Oh, thank you.' Cinder said as Bob offered his hand to help her out.

'My pleasure, my lady.' Bob said with a small bow. Cinder pulled her hand away in shock.

'What? What did you call me?' Bob looked from Cinder to Marraine, too afraid to answer.

'Just go, Bob.' Marraine waved him away and came down the steps to give her Goddaughter a hug. 'Sorry about that, sweetie.' She whispered in her ear. 'We will have to work on that.' She stood back but kept her hands on Cinder's shoulders, looking her up and down. 'How are you going?' she asked, already making her own assumptions from Cinder's body language. Cinder wiped the corner of her eye with the heel of her palm and forced a large, comical looking smile.

'I'm fine.' she exclaimed, stepping up towards the entrance to The Big House. Someone had propped open the large double doors. The familiar echo of her feet on the polished timber floors flooded her head with memories. A broad hardwood staircase rose directly in front of her to a head-height landing. From there, it split into two cases, one running left, one right, curving up the convex rear wall to the first floor. Cinder remembered the feeling of her father holding her safe and tight as she slid down the balustrade. A large circular chandelier hung from the first-floor ceiling high above her; the long crystal pendants twinkled and tinkled together with every minute change in the airflow. The bright warm light danced off the clean white walls and the polished timber of the floors, steps, and railings. Directly to the left of the staircase, a hallway led off to the sitting room. The same hallway that as a teenager, Cinder's stepmother marched her down to be paraded in front of her associates. As much as she was trying to stay calm, Cinder could feel herself breathing deeply. Angus could see the tension in her face. 'We can go back to the farm if this is too hard for you,' he said, taking her hand. Cinder squeezed his hand gently.

'No, I will be okay. This is my home, and it was my parent's home before Louvelle. Besides, with the police sniffing around the farm, I think we would be better off here.' She looked around. Everything was just as it was when she left months ago. 'It might be time to do some redecorating.'

Entering the sitting room, Cinder notice that someone had replaced the window. Cinder had thrown her stepmother's bodyguard through it last summer. Other than that, the room appeared just as she had left it. Then she noticed him standing there; Tibult, the very person who she had lifted above her head in rage and hurtled through the glass into the night. 'Why is he here?' she turned and whispered to Marraine, rage stirring again.

'It's okay, sweetie.' Marraine placed a reassuring hand on her shoulder. 'Just relax. We have only just had the window replaced. Can we keep Tibult inside the house, please?'

'I will relax as soon as someone gives me an explanation as to why he is here,' Cinder replied, loud enough for everyone to hear. Angus moved slowly, but deliberately, between Cinder and Tibult.

'Please, lady Cinder...' Tibult began to answer in his deep rhythmical voice.

'No, not you!' Cinder interrupted, holding her index finger up in Tibult's direction but refusing to look at him. Marraine stepped forward into the sitting room.

Tibult has joined us, joined you,' she said, then motioned towards Tibult. 'Apparently, he was very impressed by how you dealt with him that night. He has actually been very useful in helping me track down Dom for you.'

'You know where Dom is?' Angus asked, taking a step towards Tibult.

'Just rumours at the moment.' Marraine replied. Cinder flinched as quick footsteps echoed up the hallway and Bob ran into the sitting room. He paused, catching his breath before whispering something into Marraine's ear.

'It appears we have a visitor.' Marraine announced. 'Someone has just pulled into the yard on a motorcycle.'

'But who else knows we are here?' Cinder asked, her eyes widening anxiously. Marraine placed her hand on Cinder's shoulder.

'You wait here. I'll go see who it is.'

Moments later, Marraine returned, accompanied by a slim young man with dark features and dark clothing. Marraine cleared her throat with a cough and gestured towards the visitor. 'Everyone, this is our newest member of the Heathcote police. Detective... Morgan, was it?'

'Yes, thank you.' Detective Morgan gave a slight nod towards Marraine before turning to address the rest of the room. 'Please forgive the interruption. I was just hoping to have a word with Mrs Louvelle Delacourt. I believe she also goes by the name Gevaudan.'

'She's away on business, unfortunately.' Cinder said, holding her hands behind her back to stop them shaking. Detective Morgan retrieved his notebook from inside his jacket.

'Oh, that is unfortunate,' he said, looking at all the faces of the people standing around the living room. Just over Tibult's left shoulder, he could see scaffolding outside the window.

'Is there something we could help you with?' Marraine interjected.

'Possibly.' Detective Morgan continued, thumbing through his notebook. 'I did also want to talk to her daughter.' He stopped and looked up at Cinder. 'Miss Cinder Delacourt, I presume?'

'Yes.' Cinder responded uncomfortably. 'But she's not my mother. I mean, I'm her stepdaughter.'

'Noted.' The detective scribbled something in his notebook, the corner of his mouth turning up in smug satisfaction.

'How can I be of help?' Cinder asked, doing a remarkable job of not letting her inward fury show on her face.

'I am just following up on the vandalism that took place at the marina during the summer.' Detective Morgan slid his notebook and pen back into his inside breast pocket. 'It appears,' he went on, 'that your stepmother's yacht was the only vessel that went out that night, and as yet, has not returned. There was never a report of theft. I guess I am just wondering if you know the whereabouts of that vessel. *Lady-two*, I believe it's called.'

'I won't be much help, sorry.' Cinder offered apologetically. 'Lady Gevaudan doesn't share much of her business dealings with me.'

'If *Lady-two* was stolen, Louvelle would probably have her private security look in to it,' Marraine added.

'Ah yes, the staff.' Detective Morgan said, tapping the notebook at his breast and taking a few meandering steps into the sitting room. 'I did want to ask if your step-mother had any enemies. Some disgruntled employees, maybe?' He looked Tibult up and down.

'I am sure we can find a staff list around here somewhere.' Marraine said, motioning for Bob to follower her.

'Please don't trouble yourself.' Detective Morgan called to them, pulling out his notebook again. 'I just need the names of anyone she may have had a disagreement with.' Marraine continued walking, her heels tapping on the tiles and echoing around the large foyer.

'Oh, you will need all their names then.' She said, smiling at Bob. Angus laughed to himself, catching the detective's attention.

'And you, sir, are?' he asked.

'Black.'

'Black?'

'Yes, my name's Black.'

'Oh, I see. You know?' Detective Morgan paused, holding his chin and tapping his upper lip with his index finger. 'You actually fit the description of a Mr. umm.' He flicked back through his notes.

'Mr Dominic Kinnard. Do you know him?' he asked. Angus stared calmly at the detective.

'I've surfed with Dom a few times. Sure, I know him.'

'You wouldn't know anything about his whereabouts, would you?'

'No sorry, I haven't seen him for months.' Angus said dismissively. Detective Morgan made some more scribblings in his book.

'How many months would you say?' he asked without looking up from his notes. Angus glanced from Cinder back to the detective.

'Six months, I guess.'

'You guess?' Peter Morgan looked up. Angus shrugged his shoulders.

'Sure, six months.'

'Are you doing some renovations?' Detective Morgan shifted his attention from Angus and pointed his pen towards the scaffolding outside.

'No, no, just some repairs.' Cinder responded, looking out to the foyer, impatient for Marraine to return.

'So… Black, was it?' Detective Morgan continued as he walked past Tibult to the window. 'Are you a local?' Angus sat down on the arm of the large, white leather sofa, crossing his muscular arms across his chest.

'Not originally, but I'm here now.' He offered, disinclined to give more information.

'Interesting. Where were you before here?'

'All over really.' Angus rubbed the stubble on his chin. 'We moved around a lot.'

'Were your parents in the military?' The detective persisted; more notes scribbled down.

'No.' Angus countered, sending a mischievous wink Cinder's way.

Detective Morgan stopped and looked out of the window. No one spoke for several seconds. Marraine returned carrying a manila folder that could just as well have been a knife for how she cut through the tension in the room.

'This should help you.' She said, striding through the sitting room and handing the folder to the detective. 'A list of everyone who works here.'

'Thank you.' Detective Morgan slipped his notebook away and took the folder. 'Do you have your employer's permission to share this?'

'Oh, I don't work for her.' Marraine answered, taking a seat on the other arm of the sofa.

'No?'

'Good heavens, no.' Marraine made no attempt to hide the tone of disgust in her voice.

'I'm not sure that it's appropriate for me to have this then.' Detective Morgan said, looking down with concern at the folder.

'It's fine.' Marraine assured him. 'Cinder is in charge now, anyway. This is, after all, her house.'

'Is that correct, Miss Delacourt?'

'Well, um, yes.' Cinder responded, unconvincingly. Detective Morgan looked from Cinder to Marraine to Angus, then flicked through the pages inside the folder.

'This should give me somewhere to start. Thank you for your time, Miss Delacourt. You have a very beautiful home here.' Detective Morgan placed the folder under his arm and walked towards the foyer.

'I will see you out.' Marraine offered, standing and walking with him.

'You know,' Detective Morgan said, turning once more as he walked past Angus almost seeing eye to eye with him, even though Angus was sitting, 'I recently saw a photo of a man with the nickname Black. Black-Angus the giant, they called him. A fascinating character; you should look him up.'

'I'll be sure to do that.' Angus replied, smiling politely. Marraine walked their unexpected guest to the door.

'Well, so much for being here to avoid the police investigating.' Angus said, as Marraine closed the large door behind the detective.

'It's okay. We'll just go with Plan B.' Marraine responded, as she returned to the sitting room

'What's Plan B?' Cinder asked.

'That's up to you, sweetie. You're in charge now.'

'Oh, am I?'

'This is your home, your domicile. These are your pack.' Marraine motioned around the room with a sweep of her hand.

'Okay then.' Cinder flopped down on the sofa and rested her head on Angus's lap. 'I guess I need to work out a Plan B then.'

• • • •

Detective Morgan had parked his motorcycle at the front gates of The Big House. Other than the sounds of the ocean crashing against the rocks below and his boots rhythmically crunching on the gravel road, he walked in silent contemplation, flicking through his notes. Placing the manila folder in a brown leather saddle bag on the back of his ride, he lifted his helmet, making to place it on his head, but stopped and lowered it to his chest. A nagging thought collected in his mind. Placing the helmet back on his motorcycle, the young detective walked back towards the side of The Big House.

A tradesperson with a ginger beard and thinning blond hair pulled back in a ponytail, stood halfway up a tall scaffold. 'How you doin', mate?' he greeted the new arrival, a paint tin in one hand and a brush in the other.

'Good afternoon.' The young detective replied, removing his notebook. 'Are they just doing some maintenance here?' he asked.

'No, mate. Finishing up some repairs. They had a tree come through the window,' the man said pointing a paint-stained finger towards the window. Detective Morgan came closer, running his fingers along the glass. He could just make out the movements of shadowy figures inside.

'So, a tree did this?' he said, referring to the repairs on the window. The tradesperson continued touching up areas of the paintwork around the new window frame.

'That's what they tell me. It was all cleared away before I got here.'

Detective Morgan ran a discerning eye along the tree line. 'I see,' he said, walking next to the scaffold and placing his back against the wall of The Big House. Taking estimated strides, he stepped-out the distance from the wall to the tree line. Just over sixteen strides, he made notes. 'They did a good job of cleaning it up. I can't even tell where it would have fallen from,' he said to himself, but loud enough to regain the tradesperson's attention,

'Can I help you with something, mate?' he asked, with an air of annoyance in his voice.

'Sorry, I didn't introduce myself.' Detective Morgan said in a loud, confident voice, strolling along the edge of the forest. 'Detective Morgan, Heathcote Police.'

'Oh? Well, Jock's my name, Jock Stevens.'

Something on the ground caught the detective's attention. 'I do have another question. Have you noticed anything strange or out of the ordinary while you have been working here?' he asked, kneeling to inspect the object further. Jock laughed.

'You're not from around here, are you?' Detective Morgan could see an indentation in the ground that looked like a large animal print. He lay his pen next to the print and snapped half a dozen photos with his phone.

'No, but what makes you say that?' he asked.

'Welcome to Heathcote, mate.' Jock said. 'Everything's strange and out of the ordinary. How long you been workin' here?'

'Three weeks.' Detective Morgan replied, turning on his flash and taking another photo. The light reflected off something shiny at the bottom of the print. Placing his phone down and retrieving a zip-lock bag and a latex glove from his jacket pocket, he used the glove to pull a shard of glass out of the ground. 'Ha,' he said to himself, turning the glass over in his fingers. Jock laughed again.

'Three weeks hay? You haven't even been here for the full moon yet.'

Chapter 4
Only Fools Rush in Where Angels Fear to Tread.

Two ancient trees, twisted and gnarled by weather and time, stood at each side of an ancient path. Overhead, their moss and vine covered limbs, curled and reached across the divide, entwined together like two lovers' fingers, frozen in a time, until one becomes the other. Dom ducked slightly as he stepped through the natural archway, treading carefully on the roots warn smooth from the centuries of travellers. The scent of life and death in its continual cycle of renewal grew stronger and the mist thicker. Beech, oak, and conifers grew tall, old, and dark on all sides. Thick roots, overlaid with clover and lichen, disappeared beneath the dark, moist soil. The stumps of long deceased giants, slowly decomposing, sprouted the occasional orange fungi that reminded Dom of tiny beach umbrellas. He thought about the forest at home. The vegetation and the air here were different, but the feeling and the play of the moonlight in the leafy canopy were the same. The quieter his mind became, the louder the creatures in the dark grew. A rhythmic ballad. From the deep rumblings of frogs to the almost inaudible squeaks of bats and everything in between. Dom's quickening heartbeat kept the time. The path wound down and away to his left and, just as Dom thought he might lose his way in the dense growth, the canopy above thinned. Moonlight flooded in, revealing a very different area of the forest. The ground was flat and leafy and void of undergrowth. What made Dom stop and look around in amazement, however, was the strange growth of the trees. Their tops were long, thin, straight and ordinary; the trunks were anything but ordinary. From about two metres up, the tree trunks curved out in almost perfect semi-circles all the way to the ground. They resembled giant inverted question marks. Dom walked slowly towards the closest tree, running his hand along the curve, as if to confirm that his eyes weren't lying.

Now that Dom had stopped moving, he became aware of sounds on the track behind him that were very human. Footsteps, breathing, and yes, a man's cough. Squinting to see back into the darker part of the forest, he could make out the flicker of torchlight.

'Hello there,' he called out. The light stopped moving, but there was no response, just some indecipherable murmurs. The lights came closer and Dom tried to make contact again. 'Hello there, friends. Nice night for a walk, isn't it?' A beam of light came out of the dark and shone directly into Dom's eyes.

'Not a nice night for you. Friend.' Came a gruff voice from behind the light. Dom lifted his arm above his face to shade his eyes.

'Do I know you?'

'No, we have never had the pleasure, but you did meet my wife and my daughter Victoria a few nights ago.'

'Oh.'

'Yes - oh. You screwed my wife and robbed me. My turn to screw YOU and rob YOU!'

'I'm not sure that's going to work out for you, mate.' A mischievous grin crept across Dom's face.

'I think *my* mates might disagree, mate!' Four men walked forward. Dom could see an unknown number of others behind them. 'These are my brothers and Elena's brothers,' the front man said.

'Elena?' Dom asked.

'Yes Elena, my wife!' the husband spat.

'Oh, that's her name. I remember now. Ha!' Dom laughed to himself, removing his coat. He stopped halfway, a cold shiver running over him as a woman's laugh echoed through the forest.

'Still good at making friends, I see, Dominic,' the woman called from somewhere in the darkness.

'Well, well,' the husband called out. 'You have a friend. Maybe we could have some fun with her when we finish with you. Dominic.' The crowd of men laughed. Dom looked around as he finished removing his coat.

'She's not with me,' he said, hanging his coat on a branch and removing a large knife from a leather sheath on his hip. 'I think you should leave now, boys. This is not the kind of fun you were looking for.'

'What do you mean, leave?' The husband asked. 'Things are just getting exciting.'

'Oh, I agree,' said Dom 'the excitement is just about to start, but shit's about to get real. Tell-your-grandkids real, wake-up-in-the-night-screaming... real.'

The husband handed his torch to one of his companions and retrieved a long-handled hammer from another.

'Okay Mr Funny Man, we have heard enough. Time we shut that pretty mouth of yours.' As the husband walked forward, Dom could see him properly for the first time. He wasn't a large man, but what Dom had in height, this man had in width. He must have been almost half as tall as Dom. His round stomach, broad shoulders and legs made him appear almost square. His bald head, large wide nose, and thick beard reminded Dom of Dwarfs from books Angus used to read when they were kids. Three gold rings on his hands and a large gold chain around his neck advertised his wealth; the only reason, Dom thought, a woman Like Elena would be with this man.

'Find the woman,' he called to his companions, as he walked towards Dom, slapping the hammerhead against the palm of his left hand.

'Just... wait!' Dom called out, putting up his hand 'I just have one question.'

'What?' the husband asked through gritted teeth. Dom tapped his knife on his chin, his face puzzled.

'How? I mean... Is Victoria really your daughter?'

The anger that was already evident in the husband's face twisted into pure rage. His short but powerful legs hurtled him forward with surprising pace. Dom stepped to the side as the hammer swung past his head, crashing with an echoing thud against one of the oddly curved tree trunks. Grabbing the hammer's handle in his right hand, Dom swung his left elbow into the husband's wide nose, then down sharply into his arms, breaking his grip on the handle. The husband stumbled back in shock and pain, as blood dripped from his moustache onto his lips. Dom threw the hammer far behind him and snatched his coat from its hanger. Collecting himself, the husband swung a furious fist towards Dom's chin. Slapping his attacker's hand away, Dom flung his coat over the man's face before pushing him firmly in the chest. The husband stumbled backwards, gasping for breath. Dom Circled behind him, pulling the coat tight around his face. He pinned the husband's head against a tree, tying the coat-arms together. Muffled yells that Dom assumed were swearwords, came frantically from inside. Dom patted the husband's bald head.

'I told you this wouldn't go your way.'

Cracking of branches and twigs announced the rush forward of the other men. A multitude of white torch light beams flickered and danced wildly through the darkness, sending light rushing across the tree trunks and the canopy. One beam flashed across Dom's face, sending a play of purple dots across his eyes. Blinking to clear his vision, Dom ran at the closest of his attackers. Something metallic flashed in his obscured peripherals, and he brought the broad side of his knife up to meet it, supporting the blade with the palm of his left hand. The sound of metal on metal rang in Dom's ears as the heavy, round implement stopped inches from his face. Dom could now see a large metal bar in the hands of his attacker. He turned his knife and pushed the bar away firmly, before thrusting at where he hoped the man's shoulder was. Dom found something solid and fleshy; the scream of pain followed by the thud of metal on the ground was proof enough for Dom. He made ready to face his next opponent, but froze. Another scream rang out further back in the group. A third scream followed immediately, then a fourth. Dom strained his eyes, searching the darkness. A flash of fear and anger shot through his body when he saw it: a female figure moving impossibly fast through the frantic searching of the torchlights, red hair flowing behind it.

'Strigoi!' yelled one of Dom's attackers as he dropped his torch and ran. The man had only made a few stumbling steps, crashing through the undergrowth, before something stopped him. 'Strigoi!' He screamed again before something sent him flying backwards. He landed in a crumpled, terrified heap, a short distance from Dom. Whimpering and crawling on all fours, the petrified man scampered away into the depths of the forest. Another of the men tried to run away through the forest. Dom could hear his yells of fear, pain, and confusion amongst the sounds of cracking and snapping branches, as he smashed his way through the undergrowth. He made it a few metres before slipping on a moist log and falling to the ground with a thud. His flashlight fell from his grip and went twirling through the air. Another flash of red hair and he was dragged, kicking and screaming into the darkness, before falling suddenly silent.

Many times in Dom's life he had, and would again, run into a situation completely unprepared, letting his anger get the better of him. It was at these times he would often think *I wish Black was here.* This was one such moment. For months, revenge had driven him to find Louvelle and kill her; he was so full of anger that he had not really considered if he could do it without help. Watching the blur of the movements of a woman, moving violently through the night and listening to the screams of fear from a group of full-grown men being tossed around like a dog's plaything, it dawned on him that this plan was a bad idea.

Dom braced himself, planting his feet firmly on the ground and lowering his centre of gravity, eyes and ears alert. The surrounding forest grew quiet. A handful of discarded torches lay motionless, illuminating the forest floor and casting shadows of the twisted trunks and low-hanging branches. The jealous husband, who had finally freed himself from Dom's restraints, walked silently past Dom. Blood still dripped from his chin as his wide eyes searched the forest. Without a word, he reached out a trembling hand, giving Dom back his coat, and walked away as quietly as his large body would allow him.

Dom watched as the husband disappeared into the darkness. Hearing the crackle of twigs underfoot behind him, he turned slowly to see a dark figure moving amongst the trees.

'You were either very brave or very stupid to come here tonight, Dominic.' The woman said, darting into the shadows.

'You're forgetting 'very angry', Dom said, clenching his fists. A blaze of red hair flashed past the torchlight to his left. 'Come out where I can see you!' he yelled.

'I'm right here,' a gentle voice whispered in his ear. Dom spun around to see a tall woman in dark clothes standing right behind him, her red hair glistening like fire in the glow of the discarded torches. Dom took a few stumbling steps backwards. His mouth opened, but at first, no sound came out. Then he said, 'Great holy mother father. It's you!'

Chapter 5
Mother's Home

Torry pulled her hair into a ponytail and watched her breath condensing as it hit the icy morning air. Sunlight glistened off the blanket of dew on the green hills and played colourfully in spider webs that hung heavily on the old stone fences. Frost crushed under her well-worn work boots as she slipped her hair through the back of her trucker's cap and made her way across an open, grassy field. Blowing warm air into her hands, she listened to the familiar morning chorus of birdcalls, the ocean's soft rumble and the sleepy beach town of Heathcote waking. Spearmint toothpaste and coffee made an odd but familiar combination to fill her nostrils. Behind her, the farmhouse stood still and dark in the long shadows of two giant oak trees. A thin ribbon of grey smoke, rising lethargically to the clouds, was the only sign of the life within.

In the distance, Torry could just make out the sound of music over the rumble of the machinery and protests of the cows as Angus finished up with the morning milking. This morning, however, she could also hear an unfamiliar sound. At first, Torry thought it was just the sound of some of the local teens on their dirt-bikes. It was odd for them to be out this early, but not unheard of. As the sound came closer, Torry recognised it as something different to a dirt-bike. She turned her left ear towards the sound. The hearing in her right ear had not been the same since her run in with Cinder's stepmother. She walked away from the milking shed, climbing over a wire fence, making her way uphill towards the sound. The closer she got, the more convinced she was that the sound was from a road-bike not a dirt-bike. The sound of the motorcycle grew louder for a time, but soon dropped to a low rumble before stopping completely. Torry continued to the crest of the hill. The ground flattened, joining up with a gravel road that wound its way along the boundary of the forest and the farm. Torry could see most of the road that led away downhill. Further up, the road disappeared behind a large rocky outcrop. Holding up her hand to block the glare of the morning sun's reflection off the dew-covered rocks, Torry looked for any signs of the motorcycle and thought she spotted a helmeted head move behind the outcrop.

Making her way quietly around the rocks, Torry could tell by the smell of burning four-stroke still hanging in the air that she was close. Staying close to the rocks and treading carefully to avoid slipping on the moist moss under her feet, she peered around the corner.

A thinly built man in dark jeans and black jacket fiddled with the strap of his white helmet. Next to him, a vintage motorcycle stood, its headlight and chrome work, glistening proudly in the crisp morning air. Three red stripes ran down the centre-line of the Alaskan-white tank. Two thin stripes flanking one broad stripe. The rider removed his helmet and placed it on the handlebars. Torry took a moment to recognise the rider. He was far more casually dressed than when she had met him before.

'Nice ride,' she said, moving out from behind the rocks. 'Is it 60s or 70s?' she asked, eyeing the vehicle admiringly. Detective Morgan looked around, surprised to see someone else; but he smiled when he recognised Torry

'It's a 1966 Bonneville Roadster.'

'It's beautiful.'

'Oh, thank you, I've done some of the restoration myself, but it came to me in great condition.'

Torry made a lap of the motorcycle, nodding approvingly. 'So...' she said, crossing her arms and staring at Detective Morgan 'Are you here to spy on us?'

'I have a few places of interest that I am making regular checks on,' he answered, looking out over the farm that stretched below them.

'Don't you need a warrant or something?' Torry asked.

'A warrant? No. This is a fire access track. Police and emergency vehicles can access this at any time. Legally, your property finishes at this track, Miss Kinnard.'

'You can call me Torry. And since when have 1966 Triumphs been emergency vehicles?' she asked. Peter Morgan smiled again.

'No, she isn't exactly police issue,' he placed an admiring hand on the seat of his motorcycle. 'But believe me, it is perfectly legal for me to be here.'

'Well, legal or not, you can bring *her* around here anytime.' Torry said, also placing a hand on the seat. She turned and looked out over her home. 'Can you see anything illegal? We have some shifty look-ing cows. I could point them out for you.'

'No,' the detective said, casting a discerning eye over the property again. 'It all looks quite picturesque, actually. It is a beautiful part of the world.' He turned and looked at Torry. 'My people were from here originally, you know. This is our country. That's why I was sent here. I think they thought I might smoke some magical pipe and dance around a fire until I found the answer to all the local myths and legends.' He glanced at the forest on the opposite side of the fire track, still and silent in the frosty morning. Pale sunlight illuminated the mist and glistened off dewdrops as it shone through the branches in shafts and lit up patches of the damp leafy ground.

'Have you found the magical answers?' Torry asked with a laugh in her voice.

'No, Miss Kinnard - Torry - I am a man of science and evidence. All I have proven, unfortunately, is that racism is still alive and well in the police force.'

'What do you mean?'

'I mean, when my superiors look at me, they don't see my hard work and impeccable record, they still see an Indigenous man.'

'I'm sure that isn't true.' Torry said, putting the toe of her boot on the rocks behind her and sitting on her heel. Peter Morgan removed his notebook from his jacket pocket.

'It doesn't matter, anyway. I am still here to do a job and that's what I will do. I am glad you're here, actually,' he said, changing the subject. 'I wanted to ask you about your accident. You have some interesting scarring.' He looked at Torry. Torry looked down and turned her face away.

'I meant no offence,' Peter Morgan said apologetically. 'I think people should wear their scars with pride. They show character and a story of how you have lived your life. Here, look.' He placed his notebook on the seat of his motorcycle and sat his boot on a rock next to Torry. 'I came off my bike a few years back.' He continued as he untied his laces and removed his boot. 'My foot got caught under the bike and dragged along the road. The friction burnt right through my boot and took two of my toes with it.' He removed his sock to show he only had three toes on his left foot. The two outside toes were missing.

'Oh my God!' Torry exclaimed. 'Does it feel weird?' Peter wriggled his remaining toes.

'No, not anymore. At first, I could still feel my toes there. That was a little strange.' He pulled his sock and boot back on 'Do your scars still hurt?' he asked, as he tied his laces. Torry put her hand over the four thick lines that started between her right ear and chin and ran down her neck to her shoulder.

'No, not anymore. Not physically, anyway,' she said. Peter Morgan pulled the leg of his jeans down over his boot and collected his notebook.

'I know it was an accident on your quad-bike, but I was wondering what made those four lines?' he asked. Subconsciously, Torry ran her fingers down the scars.

'I fell on a barbed-wire fence,' she lied, shaking images of claws and teeth from her thoughts. 'So, what are you looking for, anyway?' She asked to change the subject. Peter Morgan finished making some more notes in his notebook before he answered.

'Dogs, or something bigger.'

'Why do you think we have dogs?' Torry asked. 'My dad told you we don't have any.'

'Well, before your family moved here,' he said, surveying the rolling patchwork of green fields. 'There was an abnormally large amount of animal attacks and disappearances in this area.' He slid his notebook back inside his jacket. 'Then there was a period for a few years when things got very quiet here. Until six months ago, right around the time of your accident, actually, when in the space of two days the Heathcote Police had to deal with a half a dozen missing people, gang violence, some drownings, property damage and three suspicious deaths.' Torry stood up, crossing her arms over her chest, and kicking at a rock sticking out of the side of the road.

'What's that got to do with dogs?'

Detective Morgan picked up his helmet and slid it back on to his head.

'The evidence I have to go on is very small and poorly collected. The only thing that seems to link all these things together so far are some photographs of animal prints collected from the scenes of the different incidents. So, either someone has some dangerous animals that they're keeping from me or there really are monsters roaming these woods.' He motioned with his head towards the forest. Torry glanced anxiously into the shadowy tree line.

'You don't seem like someone who believes in monsters?'

'I believe in evidence,' Peter Morgan said, making ready to get back on his motorcycle, 'and until I find something concrete, I find it helps to keep my mind open to all possibilities. I can't afford to let the truth be clouded by my own perception of it.'

'I guess you have heard all the stories then?' Torry laughed nervously.

'Yes, and if I have to hear about Mr Woo's chickens one more time...'

'It's Mr Loo.'

'What?'

'It's Mr Loo not Mr Woo. Be careful – you don't want to sound racist.' Torry punched his shoulder playfully. Peter Morgan looked at where she had just hit him.

'Careful – you don't want to get yourself arrested for assaulting a police officer.'

'I better make it worth it then.' Torry joked, putting up her fists.

'Miss Kinnard, please be serious.'

'What's wrong? Scared of a little girl?' Torry said, lowering her hands. Detective Morgan mounted his motorcycle.

'Not scared no, but from the profile I am building up of your family I definitely have a... let's call it a healthy respect.' He took the helmet from the handlebars while Torry tried to read his face. If he was joking, she couldn't say. His face remained unreadable and resolute.

'Well, I have a healthy respect for the police, too.' Torry replied with a cheeky grin. 'Especially when they have such a nice ride.' She nodded her head towards his motorcycle. Peter Morgan started the engine, and it spluttered to life. 'Are you leaving already?' Torry called out over the sound.

'Yes!' he called back. 'Thank you, you have been very helpful.' His rear tire skidded in the loose gravel at the side of the track. A trail of dust billowed behind him as he disappeared down the road. Torry stood alone, a little confused and concerned about what she might have said that was considered helpful.

• • • •

An ice cube dropped gently from a pair of silver tongs, clinking and rattling against crystal, a second one joining soon after. An unmistakable pop announced the removal of a whisky decanter stopper. Large hands poured viscous, brown liquid over the ice cubes, sending them frolicking and tinkling once more.

'Here you are, my lady,' Lysander said, replacing the lid of the decanter. Louvelle lifted the glass, swirling it three times, watching the liquid slide down the sides.

'Thank you, dear,' she said.

Mozart's Requiem in D minor played as Louvelle sat down in a high-backed green leather chair and crossed her legs. She hummed thoughtfully as she sipped. Lysander stood with his hands crossed behind his back, ever silent, ever alert. Next to him, bottles of various shapes, sizes, and colours, sat on a set of black, mirrored-glass shelves, twinkling under bright down lights. Louvelle shifted her weight in the chair and cleared her throat.

'I wonder, dear, could you ask your brother to come in here?' She said, tapping her long nails against the glass. The movement of Lysander's chin would have been undetectable to most, but to Louvelle it was a tell-tale sign of his discomfort.

'I am afraid that won't be possible, Lady Gevaudan,' he said in his deep Haitian accent. Louvelle's lips tightened as she took another sip.

'And why is that?' she asked.

'Tibult is not with us, my lady.'

'Not with us?' She held the glass to her lips and raised her eyebrows.

'No, my lady,' a single drop of sweat formed on the back of Lysander's bald head.

'Will he be with us tomorrow?' Louvelle probed, lowering her glass and crossing her legs the opposite way, so that she was now side on to Lysander.

'I'm afraid he won't be with us again, Lady Gevaudan,' he said, adjusting his shoulders. Louvelle swirled the ice in her glass, making a rhythmic tinkling.

'And why, may I inquire, is that?' she asked, almost whispering.

'My brother has left your service.'

'I am his queen! What do you mean, he has left my service?' A blue vein became visible on the side of Louvelle's temple.

'Tibult has joined a new queen,' Lysander said, trying to remain calm. Louvelle took a long, deep breath through her nose.

'Which queen?' she asked.

'Queen Cinder, my lady.'

An uncomfortable silence hung heavy in the small room. Then Louvelle's glass flew across the room, smashing into an antique record player. Mozart's requiem scratched to a stop with a crash and shattering of glass. 50-year-old single malt scotch dripped from the walls and flicked off the black vinyl as it continued to spin silently. Louvelle adjusted the hem of her dress and readjusted her posture, sitting up straight.

'She is not a queen; she is a spoilt, ungrateful little brat. What possessed your brother to make such a ridiculous decision?'

'He believes that she is the more powerful queen,' Lysander answered. 'More powerful and more compassionate – he called her the Queen of Hearts.'

'Compassionate! Ha.' Louvelle scoffed. 'Am I not compassionate? I took her in when she had no one else.'

'Yes, my lady.'

'This is all because of that bitch, Marraine. I should have dealt with her years ago.' Louvelle pointed towards the bar. Lysander understood and began preparing her another drink. 'You see?' she continued, 'I was compassionate. I let her live. Now look where that got me.' Louvelle rose slowly and walked towards Lysander. His body becoming rigid at her approach. 'Are you going to leave me too, my dear?' she asked, playing with buttons on his black silk shirt.

'No, Lady Gevaudan. I will remain with you and serve my queen,' he said, handing her the fresh glass of scotch.

'Thank you dear,' she said, taking the glass. 'I knew I could rely on you.' Lysander bowed his head in response.

Louvelle took a sip from her glass and strolled towards a tinted glass door at the other end of the room. She slid the door open and stepped out into the cool of the evening. Traffic hummed along the street several floors below. Her heels clicked against the tiles of the balcony as she walked forward and leaned against the balustrade.

'Marraine is probably in my house right now, drinking my wine,' she said, lifting her head to survey the view. Directly below her, a young couple exited a taxi and made their way along a concrete path that meandered its way through an undulating area of lawn. Beyond that, the ocean, illuminated by streetlights and the comings and goings of busy suburbia, stretched out towards the horizon. A collection of vessels of different shapes and sizes bobbed up and down in their moorings. Tall masts swayed back and forth like pendulums showing the timeless movement of the waves. Far off in the distance, glittering like a beacon on top of a hill, were the lights of The Big House. The shape of Louvelle's pupils slowly changed from circles to long oval-shaped slits. 'It's time,' she said, turning and looking back at Lysander.

'I want Marraine dead. Do it yourself. Bring me her pendant.'

'As you wish,' Lysander replied with another bow of his head.

Chapter 6
Leaving

Cinder stepped out of the double glass doors of the atrium, into the gardens of The Big House, pulling on a black, fleece-lined coat. The cool afternoon was now showing signs of being a very cold night. A breeze rattled the glass windows and wafted the scent of roses, violets, and chamomile. The chill on Cinder's neck encouraged her to zip her coat and fold the collar up towards her ears. It was far quieter in the gardens than inside the house. Out here, the only thing breaking the silence was the rhythmic crash of the ocean on the rocks far below. Inside, there was always cleaning to be done and meals to be decided, prepared, and eaten. That, of course, meant more cleaning. Worst of all, Cinder thought, was all the talking. Everyone seemed to have a request, a question, or some opinion to share.

Following the curved line of one of the garden beds, Cinder made her way towards an open patch of grass that gradually inclined its way down to the western boundary of the property. Beyond the grass, the edge of the hill fell away rocky and steep. A few small shrubs were all that grew amongst the rocks, affording an uninterrupted view of the ocean. Small, orange, and somnolent, the sun sat just above the horizon, doing its best to give one last bit of warmth to the world before the moon took over the night shift. The grass felt thick and soft under Cinder's feet as she moved further down, studying the sky as she went. Long wisps of translucent cloud drifted along slowly through shades of orange, magenta and pink.

'Red at night, shepherd's delight,' Cinder said to herself. It was something her father would always say on an evening like this; it warmed her from within, to think of his voice. Walking around the end of one more garden bed, she found who she was looking for. Marraine sat on a small, dark marble bench, a pink blanket wrapped around her shoulders and tucked under her backside to shield from the cold of the bench. She clasped the blanket around her neck with her left hand. Her right hand embraced a two-thirds full champagne flute. The remainder of the bottle occupied the seat next to her. Cinder coughed to announce her arrival.

'Is that Louvelle's blanket and her champagne?'

Marraine turned and smiled, taking a long sip.

'Well, she's not using them.' She looked admiringly at the liquid in her glass. 'I can't stand the woman, but I have to admit she does have good taste.'

'This is a good spot you have here.' Cinder said, appraising the sunset.

'This was our spot. Your mother and I would often sit out here on a night like this.' Marraine's gaze shifted from the glass to a point of no significance a few metres in front of her. Warm memories of innocent and less complicated days played across her mind. Cinder placed a loving hand on her shoulder.

'I wanted to ask you about what you said the other day, about me being in charge. Why is it so important?' she asked. Marraine placed the glass between her knees and picked up the bottle from beside her.

'I think we need another glass for this, sweetie.' She filled her glass, sat the bottle down, and then handed the full glass to Cinder.

'Oh, but that's your glass.'

'Don't worry about me,' Marraine said, picking up the bottle again taking a swig 'this is not the first time I have drunk from the bottle, nor will it be the last.'

'I could have the bottle.' Cinder offered.

'No, no, you are the lady of the house now.' Marraine held her hand up towards The Big House and bowed. Cinder took a long look at the house, then sat down close to Marraine, resting her head on her shoulder.

'That's what I mean. I don't know what it means to be in charge.'

'It just means that you need to know what kind of person you want to be. If you are true to yourself, everything else will fall into line.'

'Can't you just do it? You would be a good queen.'

'It doesn't work like that, sweetie. They have chosen you. You're their 'Queen of Hearts', remember?' Marraine chuckled to herself. Cinder took a big sip of her drink.

'How could I forget?' She swirled the bubbling liquid around in her glass, watching it reflect the colours of the sky. 'Can't I just order them to follow you?' Marraine adjusted the blanket so that it could wrap around both of them.

'I will always be around to help with the decision making and the day to day running of things, but it's more complicated than that and here's where I get serious.' She placed the bottle down, taking hold of Cinder's hand, interlocking their fingers. 'When we – you and I – take on our animal form, we are still in control. We can still think normally, still make decisions. For the men, it's different. Instinct takes over and they become irrational and often don't even know what they are doing. Like a dog without a master. But as a queen you become their master, your emotions become their reality.'

Cinder lifted her head off Marraine's shoulder and sat up so she could look in her eyes. 'What do you mean?'

'Well,' Marraine continued, 'if you're hungry, they will try to find food. If you're sleepy, they might just curl up somewhere. If you're feeling frisky, they might go out and hump the trees. Your mood and your beliefs give them their motivation.'

'Oh my God!' Cinder exclaimed, pulling away her hand and placing it over her mouth, her eyes wide with concern.

'What's wrong, sweetie?'

'It's my fault that people are getting hurt, and someone died'

'No, no, sweetie' Marraine tried to comfort her but Cinder continued.

'And the night Angus got hurt… I was angry with him. He still has the scars on his back. Did I do that too?' Marraine wrapped her arms around her.

'No, sweetie,' she whispered in her ear. 'None of this is your fault. It's your parents', Louvelle's, and even mine. It's the fault of all of us who have left you so unprepared.'

'But what if I was? What if I had stepped up as Queen six months ago? Would that tourist still be alive?'

'Honestly,' Marraine said, sitting back to look Cinder in the face 'it's impossible to say. These things are never black and white. Maybe your anger at Louvelle could have made things worse. In my ever so humble opinion, you not wanting power makes you the perfect candidate for having it.'

'But I can't do this.' Cinder pleaded. Marraine squeezed Cinder's shoulder.

'Yes, you can. You have all the skills you need to be a great queen, and you have people who love you. Hell, you have already brokered a peace treaty. There hasn't been a queen in five hundred years who managed that.' Cinder smiled.

'That doesn't count. I'm sleeping with the enemy.'

'Hey, no judgement here, sister.' Marraine smiled back. 'I've been known to dabble in some bedroom diplomacy from time to time.' Picking up the bottle and stroking it seductively, she took another drink.

Heavy footsteps behind them announced the approach of someone else. Turning their heads in unison, they saw Angus strolling tall, strong, and confident towards them. His thick hair, deep black in the dying light. When he spotted Cinder and Marraine cuddled together on the bench, he smiled widely, the setting sun twinkling in the corners of his dark brown eyes. Marraine let out a sigh.

'I bet he looks amazing naked.' She said as she took another sip from her bottle. Cinder slapped her on the side of her leg.

'Behave yourself.'

'Forgive me, Your Majesty.' Marraine teased. 'But does he?' she asked. Cinder tried to look angry, but her eyes twinkled mischievously above her reddening cheeks. Angus positioned himself behind Cinder and looked out to the horizon.

'Good evening, ladies,' he said, placing his large hands on Cinder's shoulders.

'It's better now you're here.' Marraine said, with a wink and a flutter of her long eyelashes. Cinder reached up and squeezed Angus's hand.

'Ignore her. She's been drinking.'

'It's okay,' Angus laughed. 'I kind of liked it.'

'Don't encourage her,' Cinder said, squeezing his hand harder. Marraine sat the bottle down next to her again slowly begun unbuttoning the top few buttons of her shirt.

'I am incorrigible.'

'Umm?' Cinder raised an eyebrow as the black lace trim of Marraine's bra appeared.

'Don't get excited, sweetie,' she said, pulling something metallic from her cleavage. 'I am just giving you this.' Marraine held a pendant and chain in her hand. 'It's okay,' she said, reading the expression on Cinder's face. 'I have a spare.'

There were three main parts of the pendant. A silver loop, just smaller than Marraine's palm. A tree made from seven gold strands intertwined, the roots wrapped around the bottom of the loop and spreading out into seven swirling branches at the top. The third part was a full moon. Carved from a blue sapphire nestled in the tree's branches. One almost identical to this belonged to Cinder. The only difference being that Cinder's pendant, the Red Queen's pendant, contained a red garnet. Her stepmother Louvelle had stolen that one from her last year. These centuries-old items of jewellery were imbued with the power to hold a Lycan in their human form, even when they were exposed to moonlight.

Marraine stood up and ran her hand over Angus's shoulder.

'Of course, you always know where my room is,' she said to Angus, as she picked up the bottle and undid another button. 'If you should ever need something.'

'I need something!' Cinder interrupted.

'What's that, sweetie?'

'I need you to stop giving away all of Victoria's secrets to my boyfriend.' Cinder replied, trying to look serious. Marraine flicked her third from last button open and seductively ran her finger down the inside of her shirt, bending down to give Cinder the pendant. Cinder blushed and turned her head to avoid staring straight down Marraine's open shirt.

'Why do I need this?' she asked, taking hold of the pendant.

'Well,' Marraine sauntered behind Angus, running her long, red nails across his back. 'It's a full moon tonight, and while I'm sure your *boyfriend* likes you to be an animal in bed, I'm guessing that's probably not literally.' She studied Angus's face 'I picture you more as a 'naughty nurse' or 'dirty cop' kind of guy.'

'Marraine!' Cinder cringed.

'Yes, sweetie?'

'Weren't you leaving?'

'Yes, yes, I'm going now.' Marraine began walking away, doing up her buttons. 'I would say don't do anything I wouldn't do, but that doesn't leave you with many options.' Cinder motioned for Angus to sit next to her.

'Good night, Marraine.'

'Good night, lovers.' Marraine waved and walked up the slope. Shortly after, she disappeared around a corner of The Big House.

'Sorry about her.' Cinder said as Angus sat down close to her. His cheeky grin glowed in what remained of the sunset.

'Yeah, that was terrible.'

'Yes, you look positively distraught, you poor thing.' Cinder joked, raising one eyebrow. She turned Marraine's pendant over in her fingers 'The moon won't be up for a few hours yet. I don't know what she thinks we will be doing out here 'til then.'

'I know what she thinks we will be doing.' Angus laughed. 'She's not very subtle.'

'No, not subtle.'

'No, she's sexy, seductive, sweet, sophisticated-'

'Shovel?' Cinder interrupted him.

'She's a shovel?' Angus asked.

'No, but you might need one to help you keep digging that hole.' Cinder said, finishing her drink. Angus flashed a cheeky smile again.

'So how does that work if it's not yours?' he asked, gesturing towards the pendant Cinder was still holding in her hand. Cinder held up the pendant so that the pink and orange light danced across the golden branches of the tree.

'I think it just works the same as mine. I can stay out in the moonlight and not change. And you know about the midnight and full moon part.' Angus reached out to touch the pendant, but withdrew his hand hesitantly.

'I wanted to ask you about that,' he said, putting his hands in his pockets. 'How long?' he asked.

'What do you mean?'

'I mean, it doesn't stay midnight forever, so does it last for an hour or the rest of the night?'

'Oh, I see.' Cinder said. 'Nice way to change the subject, by the way.' Angus pretended to dig into the ground with an imaginary shovel. Cinder continued. 'Marraine explained to me that it would probably last a shorter time for me because I am more powerful... I don't know.' Angus thought this over, then asked.

'How does she know you're more powerful than her?'

'Apparently, the She-Devil has made sure of that. The more we change, the stronger we get, and she made me change on every possible night of my life, and she made me change in the double moon too.'

'The what?' Angus looked confused. 'Double moon?'

'Yes, the double moon,' Cinder replied. 'The way Marraine explained it was that the moon's light is usually absorbed by the ground and the trees,' she pointed out to the sunset lit water. 'But here, by the ocean, the reflection off the ocean doubles the effect of the moon's rays. That's why we live near the ocean, even though most of us hate the water.' Cinder gazed intently out to the horizon, where a semi-circle-sun sat casting speckles of orange light on the tips of the darkening waves. Angus looked out along the coastline, collecting his thoughts.

'So, I have you 'til midnight then?'

'If you want to still be up with me after that, then you had better be like'n the Lycan.' Cinder said, turning to smile at him.

'I don't know. You've never really let me see you like that. Are you still you?' Angus asked. Cinder slid the pendant's chain over her head, then pulled her long red hair out through it.

'I still think the same, feel the same. I remember everything,' she said. Angus caught a waft of her shampoo as her hair fell against her neck and shoulders.

'How many buttons do *you* need to undo to put it on?'

'Down boy.'

'Well, if you are still you,' Angus continued, 'then what's not to like?' he kissed her cold cheek. Cinder smiled.

'There is one small issue.'

'What's that?'

'Well...' Cinder said, unzipping her coat slowly. 'I need to get out of these clothes before I change.'

'Oh?' Angus's eyes opened wide. He leaned in and kissed her, his lips warm against hers. 'What do you want to do to pass the time until midnight, then?' he asked. Cinder placed the pendant inside her coat and kissed him back. Moving her lips from his mouth to his cheek, then cradling his earlobe between her teeth. Her hand moved up his leg, cold and thrilling against the warmth of his inner thigh.

'You know what I really want?' She whispered.

'Mmm, what's that?'

'I want to talk about Dom.'

'What?' Angus sat up straight. Cinder giggled, her face mischievous with glee.

'I've decided I want us to go find Dom. You and me. I was already thinking about it, and now that the police are asking questions again, it might be a good time for us to leave.' Angus place his hands in his pockets to ward off the growing cold.

'Wow, okay. Where would we start?'

'Marraine has heard rumours, we can start there.' Cinder placed her hand on Angus's chest 'You want to find him, don't you?'

'Yes, of course I do.' he answered, taking his hands out again to hold hers. 'It will be expensive. We could be gone for months.' Cinder kissed his hand.

'I'm Queen now. I'm rich.' She said with a grin.

'What?'

'I never knew, but my father set up a trust fund for me for when I turned 21. I always thought that Louvelle had spent all of my parent's money, but my father was wise enough to protect some of it for me. Actually, *some* is not the right word. He kept a lot for me.'

'Wow. That's... wow.' Angus didn't know what else to say. 'How large is this trust fund?'

'*Large!*' Cinder said, smiling. Angus shuffled his body, pushing his broad chest out as if he suddenly had a weight lifted from his shoulders.

'How large?' he asked.

'Think large and then times that by ten,' Cinder said. Angus stood up and loosened his shoulders.

'Alright then, I guess we start making plans, book some flights.' He said as he paced back and forth in front of Cinder.

'Oh,' Cinder said, 'didn't I tell you? When I became Queen, I got control of everything that was my parent's. It's not just the house and the staff.' She looked over her shoulder at The Big House, then stood and put her hands on Angus's shoulders. 'I own an airstrip now and I have a private jet.'

Angus looked into her large green eyes, silently staring for a few seconds. Turning finally to watch as the last of the sun dropped away, he said.

'Hell yeah, that's cool.'

Chapter 7

Fallen Sparrow

Cinder sat a piece of chalk on the windowsill next to her telescope, rubbing her hands together to remove the dust. She took a step back from the wall, admiring her work before flopping down on her bed next to a vintage Louis Vuitton suitcase. She lay back and looked up at the lacy curtains of her white four-poster. Earlier that week, she had unceremoniously removed the pink silk sheets and fluffy cushions that Louvelle had inflicted on her bedroom. They now sat discarded in a pile in the hallway. Cinder rolled over and ran her hand across the white cotton sheets that were their replacement. She slid to the side that Angus had been sleeping in and snuggled into his pillow, breathing in his scent.

Someone knocked at her door. Sitting up in surprise, Cinder straightened her hair and the pillows before she invited them in. 'Come in.'

'Are you ready to go, Cin?' Angus asked, entering her room.

'Yes, all set,' she said, picking up her suitcase.

'I'll get that for you,' Angus said, reaching for the handles.

'I can carry my own bag. I'm a big girl.'

'I know, but I want to take it for you,' Angus explained.

'Okay then. Knock yourself out,' Cinder said, handing him the bag. Angus inspected her luggage, then glanced at the dark green duffle bag he had slung over his shoulder.

'This is fancy,' he said, holding her bag up in front of him.

'I don't own any grown-up luggage,' Cinder said, holding the door as he went out. 'It's one of... hers.'

'Oh?' Angus raised his eyebrows.

'I know, I know,' she said. 'It's just what it is.'

• • • •

Marraine was waiting with a taxi at the front of The Big House. As Cinder opened the large front door, light from the bright foyer flooded across Marraine's face, glistening off a single tear on her left cheek.

'Are you crying?' Cinder asked.

'Yes, I am.' Marraine said, wiping the back of her hand across her cheek. 'But these are happy tears. I'm glad that I am getting rid of you two. I'll finally get some time to myself.'

'It's all yours,' Cinder said, walking down the steps and kissing her on her moist cheek. 'Even the wine cellar.'

'Oh, I know,' Marraine answered, trying to smile while she wiped her cheek again. She pulled Cinder close and hugged her tightly. 'Be safe and don't take anyone's rubbish, okay?' she whispered into her ear.

'I will and I won't,' Cinder whispered back.

Angus carried the bags to the taxi, and the driver helped put them in the trunk.

'Bob should be helping you with that,' Marraine said. 'Where is that man?'

'I don't know,' Angus said, looking around.

'It's fine, we're fine,' Cinder said, taking Marraine by the hand and walking to the taxi. 'Are you ready to go, Black?' she called.

Angus didn't answer. He was still looking around. He took a few steps towards the tree line at the south-west corner of the property.

'Hey pretty boy, time to go,' Cinder called out again.

'Yep, sorry,' Angus said. 'I'm coming.'

After saying their last goodbyes, Cinder and Angus left for Cinder's private airstrip that was just outside of Tallo's Bluff. As they made their way out of the long driveway, Cinder could tell that something was distracting Angus.

'Are you okay?' she asked, as they exited through the gates.

'I just thought I saw something moving in the dark.'

'I'm sure it was nothing,' Cinder said, placing her hand on his shoulder.

'Yeah, you're right. I'm just being paranoid. Old habits.'

As the taxi wound its way down the hill, they both turned and searched the dark forest for any signs of movement.

'Bob, Bob?' Marraine called, as she closed the large front door of The Big House behind her. 'Bob!' she called again, her voice echoing off the high ceilings of the foyer.

'I'm here,' came a man's voice from the top of the stairs.

'Where have you been? Come down here.'

'I have been preparing everyone, like you asked.' Bob appeared at the top of the stairs.

'Thank you, sweetie,' Marraine said. 'Now come down here and take this.' She held up her phone. 'I don't want anyone to disturb me.'

'Are you sure?' Bob asked, jogging down the stairs.

'Yes, it's what needs to happen.' Marraine handed him the phone.

'Okay, but you know where to find me, if you need me.' Bob said, slipping her phone into his back pocket.

'I won't need you.' Marraine smiled and patted him on his chest. Bob took hold of her hand, looking her in the eyes.

'Okay then. Goodnight,' he said, before turning and making his way slowly back up the stairs.

Bob had prepared a fire earlier in the evening. It now burned bright and warm in the sitting room. The crackling orange flames and red coals were the only source of light in the room. Marraine sat, a champagne flute in hand, watching as the animated shadows flickered and frolicked over Louvelle's priceless rubbish. Marraine had organised some applewood logs to combat Louvelle's stench. The sweet, fruity aroma was helping, but there was just too much of Cinder's step-mother still in the room.

'Here's to the lady of the house,' she said to herself, sticking her middle finger up in the air and taking a drink with her other hand. Slipping off her shoes, she lay herself sideways along the sofa and finished her drink.

Leaning over the edge of the sofa to retrieve a champagne bottle from the floor, Marraine realised that both her glass, and the bottle were empty. Slumping her shoulders forward and dropping her bottom lip, she threw the empty champagne flute at the fire. 'Oops,' she said, as glass exploded and rattled across the hearth. 'You can stop lurking in the shadows,' she called out. 'I've finished the bottle now, anyway.'

Lysander, who had been standing hidden in the shadows at the entrance to the sitting room, stepped out into the glow of the fire.

'Hello Lysander, dear,' Marraine said. 'To what do I owe the pleasure of your company, so late in the evening?'

'The pleasure of your death, I am afraid, Ms Marraine.'

'Well, I'm not sure that will be very pleasurable for me, Lysander,' she said, sitting up.

'Then perhaps the pleasure will be all mine,' he said, moving towards her.

'Oh Lysander, no pillow talk? Do you just want to get right to it, you kinky old thing?' Marraine said, standing up on the sofa. 'If I'm going out, I'm not going out quietly.' She threw the champagne bottle, knocking a jade-monkey ornament from a shelf.

'Must you?' Lysander asked, closing the double doors of the sitting room behind him.

'Yes, I really must.'

Marraine jumped from the sofa, pulling a painting from the wall. Lysander ran forward and took her by the neck, lifting her feet off the floor and pinning her to the wall. Marraine slammed the painting down on his head, ripping the canvas and leaving the frame hanging about his neck, like an ill-fitting dog collar. Lysander gave a low growl.

'That was a Monet,' he said, fangs growing in his mouth.

'It's okay,' Marraine said, laughing. 'It's a forgery. The real one's been hanging in my apartment for the past six years.'

Lysander pulled her towards him, then pushed her back into the wall with a thud, cracks appearing in the plasterboard.

'Come on!' Marraine said. 'You can do better than that,' and she slammed her elbow through the wall. 'Full disclosure. I have been drinking,' she said, as a chunk of plaster and dust fell to the floor. 'You had better not take advantage of me.' She tugged playfully at the frame around his neck.

'It's time,' Lysander said, retrieving a long hunting knife from behind his back.

'It's so big. I hope you brought protection.'

Marraine grabbed hold of his arm, watching the blade glint in the firelight. The knife moved slowly down and across her forearms. Marraine screamed in pain but watched with sadistic satisfaction as her blood ran down Lysander's arm and dripped onto Louvelle's eggshell-white carpet.

Chapter 8
Darkness Brings Illumination

The engine of the 1966 Triumph Bonneville revved in agreement under the familiar control of Detective Peter Morgan. There was little that he enjoyed about his new posting in Heathcote, but any motorcycling enthusiast would have to agree that this part of the world had some great roads. He smiled as he snaked his way down through tall centuries-old trees and giant vine-draped ferns. Occasional gaps in the forest allowed peaks of deep-greens and blues of the ocean. He pulled off onto a wide, bluestone covered shoulder. Late afternoon sun shone down through the gap carved in the canopy by the road, but the air down in the shadows was cold and moist. Peter Morgan felt the chill against his face as he removed his helmet. He shrugged out of one of the shoulder straps of a backpack he was carrying. Looking around, he unzipped the pack and rummaged inside. He pulled out a thick, black woollen beanie and a Glock 22 semi-automatic pistol. Laying the Glock carefully down on the petrol tank, he slipped the beanie over his head, pulling it down over his ears. After dismounting his motorcycle, he slipped his sidearm carefully into a holster on his belt, clipping it in firmly. He didn't for a moment believe the stories his colleagues had told him about the creatures roaming these forests, but that didn't mean there weren't other *real* dangerous lurking about.

A grown-over walking track led off to his right, past a large stump that was blackened by fire, in the not-too-distant past. The recent rain had made the path slippery and formed puddles in some of the flat areas. Peter Morgan's sturdy leather boots offered some protection from the wet, but he still slipped and stumbled a handful of times. One of those times, he fell and knocked his hip against the trunk of a tree-fern, sending droplets of icy water showering down over his head and back. He was still wiping water from his shoulders and arms when he came to the clearing he was looking for.

Ducking under the blue and white chequered tape that surrounded the area, Peter Morgan retrieved his notebook and pen from inside his coat. A green and grey, four-person dome tent sat abandoned in one corner, the torn door flapping gently in the breeze. Charred wood and wet ash, circled by rocks, evidenced a recent but now extinguished campfire. Walking around the border, he treaded lightly, careful to not create many new footprints as he looked for existing ones. 'I work with idiots,' he said as he noticed just how much coming and going there had been. Giving up on the well-trodden perimeter, he moved closer to the tent.

There were signs of a commotion at the entrance of the tent and down the left side, closest to the forest. Deep tracks of disturbed dirt and grass spoke to something large being dragged into the trees. Finding a patch of intact ground, Detective Morgan crouched down to survey the scene. To his surprise, he quickly found what he was looking for. About a metre to the right of the fireplace, pushed firmly into the soft earth, was a large animal print. Pulling his phone from his pocket, he flicked through to find the photos he had taken a few days earlier at Berkley's Manor (the official name for The Big House). He scratched the back of his head under the beanie. The print here and the one in the photo were similar enough for him to call them a match. *What did that mean?* Resting his chin in his hand, he spent a few minutes looking around, connecting the puzzle pieces in his mind.

He took a photo of the new animal-print and slipped his phone back in his pocket. Images filled his mind – screaming victims, ripping fabric, panic, confusion, a body being pulled through the mud. He ran different scenarios through his mind. He could see the night when an unsuspecting tourist had been taken from his bed, stolen away into the night by man or beasts or both. Peter Morgan could feel the panic, hear the cries, and smell the campfire smoke. *The campfire smoke? Was he imagining that or was it real?* He stood up and sniffed the air as he moved around the abandoned campsite. The smell appeared to be stronger to the east, downhill from where he was, towards the ocean. Quietly and cautiously, he set off in the smoke's direction, his left hand unconsciously resting on top of his holstered sidearm.

Pushing aside the branch of a large fern and sniffing the air, Peter Morgan thought he heard the indistinct murmur of voices. He stopped and turned his head from side to side to gauge the direction of the sound. He moved on more cautiously, thoughtful of where and on what his feet were treading. The murmuring became louder and clearer and although he wasn't able to make out what was being said he thought he could pick out at least two separate voices. The setting sun sent beams of light through the smoke-filled air, making it difficult for him to see. He stopped, crouching behind a mossy log, peering through the ghostly translucent shafts of grey. Two shadowy figures sat beside a flickering fire. Close enough now to hear the crackle of the flames, Peter Morgan strained his ears to understand their conversation.

'Stupid, I tell ya. Stupid,' one of them said.

'You might be right,' the other voice said, 'but...' The owner of the second voice stood up and looked around. 'Hello,' she said loudly. 'Who's back there? You can come out, it's okay.'

Detective Morgan backtracked a few metres before entering the clearing, making sure the sun was behind him.

'Detective Morgan, Heathcote Police,' he announced, as he walked slowly into what appeared to be a well-equipped and well-used campsite. 'Good evening Miss Kinnard and Mr Duncan Craig, I believe.'

Duncan made an intimidating image, with the twilight sun reflecting off his bald head and thick, glossy beard. He sat on a makeshift wooded bench, next to a fire with low flames and red-hot coals. He was sitting, but his impressive height meant that he was eye to eye with the intruder. His expansive shoulders twitched as he poked a stick into the fire with his muscular arms. Behind him, a large canvas tent, held up in four corners by thick timber polls and ropes, flapped gently in the breeze. A shallow stream flowed behind the tent, rambling gently over time-smoothed rocks and pebbles. Someone had formed a circle around the fireplace with some of the larger rocks. Steam rose from a fire-blackened billy, dangling from the apex of an iron tripod that straddled the campfire. Torry stood looking back and forward between Duncan and the detective.

'Good evening, Detective. Would you like a cup of tea? I just boiled the water,' Duncan said, lifting a tin mug of hot liquid in his hand.

'No, thank you, Mr Craig,' Peter Morgan said, looking around. 'Do you have your dog tied up somewhere?' he asked, his hand resting on his holster again. Duncan laughed.

'No dogs round here, mate,' he said, before taking a drink of his tea. 'Tell him Tor.' 'It's true, Peter,' Torry said. 'No dogs here.'

'In that case,' Peter Morgan said, removing a set of handcuffs from the side pocket of his bag. 'When you have finished your drink, you will need to accompany me back to the road. From there, you will be transported to Heathcote station for questioning in relation to the deaths or disappearances of a dozen people, including your friend Mr Blair Abernethy.' Duncan's jaw tightened and his nostrils flared.

'But I've just got the fire burning nicely,' he said, throwing the rest of his drink on the grass. 'Why don't you take a seat, and we can talk here?'

'You can have my seat,' Torry said, motioning towards a stump sat near the fire. 'I was just leaving, anyway.' Torry moved away, but Peter Morgan held up his hand to stop her.

'I'm afraid you will need to come too, Miss Kinnard.'

'Why me?'

'You provided false testimony in an ongoing investigation.'

'What?'

'You lied to me, Miss Kinnard.'

'Oh, yes, sorry about that,' Torry said, sitting back down on the log.

'Now, if you would be so kind to both make your way back up to the road, I will organise your transport.' Detective Morgan took his phone from his jacket pocket and quickly typed a message, making sure to keep an eye on Duncan. Duncan smiled and stroked his beard.

'Nope, sorry,' he said. 'I got things I need to do here.' He stood up and walked to the fire, dipping his cup into the boiling billy water. He tipped his head to the side, looking the detective up and down. The firelight glowed on his bald head and large biceps as he swirled the water in his cup. Turning to smile at Torry, he threw the water at Peter Morgan's feet and sat down again.

Peter Morgan took a step forward and unclipped the strap at the top of his holster. 'It's my duty to inform you, Mr Craig, that you are under arrest,' he said in a formal and practised tone. 'Do you understand what I'm saying?'

'Yes..., Detective,' Duncan replied, sitting with his massive legs spread wide, his head tilted sideways, and his beard jutting forward.

'I would ask you at this time for you to remain seated and place both hands behind your back,' Peter Morgan instructed.

'It's okay Duncan, do it,' Torry added, standing up again.

'Please stand back, Miss Kinnard.'

'Okay.' Torry said, putting up her hands and taking a step back.

Duncan turned and looked at the fire. After resting his cup on the ground, he slowly placed his hands behind his back, one at a time. Peter Morgan opened his handcuffs and circled behind him, careful not to turn his back on Torry. Duncan smiled at Torry and, as he felt the first touch of cold metal on his wrist, he sprung up and spun around. Before Peter Morgan could react, Duncan had placed the second cuff on his wrist, cuffing them together. 'How's that? The first time I've met the man, and he's already giving me jewellery,' Duncan said, then pulled his arm up so that Peter Morgan lifted off the ground, dangling with one arm in the air.

'Put me down,' he ordered, reaching for his weapon but finding Torry's hand on top of his holster. He looked at Torry in alarm, but she was looking up at Duncan.

'Put him down, Duncan,' she yelled. Duncan took hold of the handcuff chain.

'If you say so,' Duncan said. He placed his large hand around the chain hanging from his wrist and snapped one of the links.

As Peter Morgan dropped to the ground, Duncan fled into the trees. The young detective regained his composure and made to follow him.

'Wait!' Torry said, stepping in his way and holding her hands against his chest.

'Get out of the way, Torry,' he yelled, moving forward and forcing Torry to walk backwards.

'I'm not trying to stop you,' she said. 'I'm trying to warn you, it's getting dark, it's not safe.'

'Stay here,' he said, ignoring her warning and pushing past her. 'I'll be back to get you soon.'

'I won't be here. Not after dark.'

• • • •

The quickly fading light made it difficult for him to see where he was going. Peter Morgan was relying more on listening to the sounds of Duncan's large body crashing through the undergrowth and his size 20 boots stomping on the twigs and dry leaves of the forest floor.

He kept track of him easily enough at first, seeing his shadowy figure moving between the trees many times. Shortly, however, the terrain changed, and the sound of the ocean grew louder. His heels sank and his feet slid as the ground became sandy and less solid. The tall trees, with their thick and well space trunks, were soon replaced by dense, spindly tea-trees. The branches snagged on his backpack and scratched at his exposed skin. Gnarled roots twisted their way out of the sandy soil, catching at his feet. Eventually, he could no longer see or hear Duncan. Cursing his own stupidity, he continued to search for signs of where Duncan had gone, but as the night creeped in, he conceded defeat. The best course of action, he decided, was to make his way down to the beach and gain his bearings from there.

As he made his way downhill, the ground became more sand than soil. Just as he spotted the ocean over the top of the trees, he slipped on a patch of green pigface. Falling heavily to his left, his shoulder thumped against one of the larger tea-tree roots. Pins and needles danced down his left arm and tingled at the end of his fingers. Gritting his teeth and moaning, he felt at a rip in his jacket. His right hand came away damp with blood. Although it was numb, he could still move his left arm freely. *Nothing broken,* he thought. He slid the rest of the way down the hill on his backside. Dusting himself off and checking again that all his fingers could move, he stood and looked around. The ocean rumbled and crashed close by, but he could no longer see it beyond the tall dunes around him.

'Are you okay?' Duncan's deep voice said from behind him. Peter Morgan spun around, drawing his weapon.

'Get down on your knees,' Detective Morgan ordered.

'Are you bleeding?'

'Yes, but I'm fine, down on your knees.'

'You might want to save those bullets then,' Duncan said, looking up at the waning moon. Peter Morgan held the Glock 22 firmly in both hands.

'Down,' he said, motioning with the barrel.

'Shhh,' Duncan held his finger up to his lips and reached behind his back.

'Hands where I can see them!' Detective Morgan yelled. Ignoring him, Duncan turned and faced the opposite direction. He pulled a large hunting knife from a sheath mounted on the back of his belt. Detective Morgan's eyes widened as he recognized the glint of metal in the moonlight.

'Drop the weapon!'

'Will you shut up, man?' Duncan hissed, turning his head and staring into the bushes, searching. Peter Morgan was about to yell again, but something about the look in Duncan's eyes made him stop. Now he could hear what Duncan was listening to, a rustle of branches and a snapping of twigs. There was something else as well, something low, rhythmic, and raspy. Breathing?

With a heart-jolting growl, something large and dark leaped from the shadows behind the detective. Peter Morgan instinctively spun around, releasing two shots. A great pain flashed through his left shoulder again. The force of the large object hitting him sent him crashing to the ground, pain exploding up his tailbone. The Glock tumbled from his grip. Lifting his head, he could see Duncan running at him. He searched the dark, sandy ground frantically for his weapon, but just as his fingertips brushed against the barrel, something pulled him backwards and sent him flying. The injured detective lay motionless on the ground, aware of scuffling, yelling, and growling around him. Cold perspiration beaded on his face as he struggled to catch his breath. Then he drifted into darkness.

Chapter 9
Arrivals and Departures

'Ding'. The fasten seatbelts sign illuminated. 'Sorry ma'am, we are coming up on a rough patch of weather and we're expecting some turbulence,' the captain's voice said over the cabin speakers. 'Please remain seated until further notice.' Cinder gripped the armrests of her seat as the aircraft shuddered, left and right, and up and down. Air rushed and roared violently over the wings and sheets of water washed over the windows. A flash of lightning illuminated the darkness outside.

'Oh my god,' she said, turning to look at Angus, 'Did you see that? The wing was shaking all over the place.'

'I'm sure it will be fine,' Angus replied, flicking through a magazine. The aircraft rattled, then dropped. The inertia of her body made Cinder feel weightless for a moment before pushing her down hard into her seat. Across the aisle, Angus chuckled.

'Aren't you scared?' Cinder asked, her voice shaky and shrill.

'Hey, I'm just along for the ride,' Angus replied, without looking up from his magazine.

Lightning flashed again, accompanied by rumbling thunder, shaking the aeroplane violently. Something orange flickered outside of Cinder's window. Bang! The flicker exploded into a huge fireball. Ribbons of orange, red, and blue flames trailed out of the wing, flooding the side of the aircraft with an orange glow.

'Oh my God, we need to tell the pilot,' Cinder screamed.

'But we can't,' Angus replied, looking more annoyed than alarmed. 'The fasten seatbelts sign is still on. We need to stay in our seats.'

'Can't you see that the wing is on fire?' Cinder yelled, her hands desperately fumbling with her seat belt.

'What do you want me to do about it?' Angus went back to reading the magazine.

Cinder threw her seat belt open and got cautiously to her feet. The cabin shook and wobbled. She pushed her face against the glass of the window to better gauge the damage outside. As she pulled away to talk to Angus again, a second flash of lightning struck the aircraft just below her window. Cringing, she held her ears against the deafening clap. A crack appeared in the window next to her. Cinder watched in horror as it grew and branched off into a network of dozens of smaller cracks. She tried to back away, but in an instant the window was gone, exploding out into the darkness with a whooshing pop. Air rushed and squealed around her, forcing her forward. Her head smacked into the overhead compartment as the suction pinned her against the wall, her stomach acting like a plug in the empty window cavity. The pain was immense. Trying as hard as she could, her arm muscles were no match for the force holding her in place.

'Black!' she screamed frantically to Angus. 'Please help me.' Angus looked over at her.

'I told you not to get out of your seat,' he said. 'You're on your own now.'

'What?' she yelled in disgust.

Moving herself painfully around against the wall, Cinder was able to see out of one of the other windows. The fire had grown larger and more violent, spitting flames up into the air. Blood was trickling from a wound just above her eye, obscuring her vision. She was just able to make out her stomach. The rushing air had ripped away her shirt, leaving a bulbous, fleshy mound that was growing more spherical as she watched. Something further out near the fire caught her eye. She struggled to clear the blood from her vision. A dark mass was zig-zagging back and forth on the wing, silhouetted against the glow of the flames. The dark figure came closer. Cinder watched as it took on the form of a person.

'Someone's out there!' She yelled. 'There's someone on the wing.'

'Good, maybe they can help you.' Angus said, looking up briefly from his magazine. Suddenly, there was silence, an unnatural silence. No rushing of wind, pelting rain, or roar of engines. Even the thumping of Cinder's heart that had been pounding in her head was gone. The face of the person came close enough for her to see. His smile, his beard, his eyes. He held his hand on her stomach and looked into her eyes. His expression was a familiar mix of power, intelligence, and love.

'Daddy please.' Cinder said, sniffing back the tears. Her father held his finger to his lips.

'Shhh,' he said, leaning down to kiss her stomach. 'She's coming.' He smiled warmly and turned away, moving towards the flame.

'No, no, no!' Cinder called out, banging against the wall. 'I need you.' But her father continued towards and then into the flames. The fire enveloped his body, swirling and twisting around him. From within the heart of the fire, a blue light grew and pulse before busting into a blinding green glow. Cinder fell to the floor.

'Are you okay?' Angus asked, holding Cinder's hand.

'I am now, no thanks to you.' Cinder said, pushing his hand away and struggling to open her eyes. Slowly, Cinder began to piece together the reality of her surroundings. She was sitting in her seat. The plane was intact and flying smoothly through a clear, star-filled sky. 'Sorry I was dreaming,' she said, rubbing the sleep from her eyes.

'Yes,' Angus said, standing and placing a reassuring hand on her shoulder. 'I could tell. Was it bad?'

'It's always bad,' she replied, looking around the cabin and placing her hand on her stomach. 'At least it was something different this time.'

'How do you mean?'

'It was still my dad, but he said something, something new.'

'What did he say?' Angus asked, taking his seat again. Cinder strained to remember the nightmare images; they were already drifting away like smoke on the breeze.

'She's coming, I think. Something like that anyway.'

'Maybe you are just worried about seeing your step-mother again.'

'Maybe.' Cinder lay her head back and closed her eyes. The cabin fell silent except for the background hum of the engine and the rushing of the air over the fuselage as they hurtled through the quiet night.

'I can't sleep now,' Cinder said a few minutes later. 'Can you tell me a story?'

Angus reached across the walkway and stroked her hair. She felt warm against his skin.

'Okay then,' Angus said, smiling to himself. 'Have I ever told you the story of Milo of Kronos?' he asked, moving a lock of her hair between his thumb and index finger. Cinder took his hand and kissed it.

'No, you haven't,' she said, closing her eyes again. Angus ran his fingers down her arm as he pulled his hand back. Then began his story.

'Milo of Croton was a Greek wrestler in the 6th-century. He had a very successful wrestling career and won many victories in the most important athletic festivals in Ancient Greece. One tale tells how he carried a bull on his shoulders. It was also said that he could burst a band around his brow by inflating the veins of his temples.'

'The story goes that one day the great Greek philosopher and mathematician Pythagoras, was staying at an inn near his home. Milo wanted to meet the man whose intelligence matched his own physical strength. When he came to the inn, however, there was a fire, and Pythagoras was trapped under a fallen roof. Milo rushed into the building, lifted the giant roof beams, and saved the philosopher's life.

The wise man and the strong man became best friends and Milo even married Pythagoras's daughter.'

'Pythagoras found a way to use Milo's blood, mixed with the blood of animals, to increase the strength and healing ability of others. The Lycan queen, Morrvela, grew uneasy with the strength and influence of Milo, Pythagoras, and their followers. She challenged Milo to pull apart a tree that had been partially split in two by lightning. When his hands were inside the tree, she forced the two halves back together, trapping his hands. Struggling with all his might, Milo could not free himself from the trap. When night fell, the Lycan crept from the shadows and devoured him.'

Angus finished his story and looked very proud of his effort at telling it. Cinder, on the other hand, looked very unimpressed. 'That was a terrible story,' she said, shaking her head.

'What do you mean?' Angus asked.

'I mean, the evil Lycan woman kills the strong manly hero. Am I the evil woman? Is that how you see me?'

'No, of course not. It's just a story.'

'Your heroes are always men and the women are the villains. Where are all your stories of strong women?' Cinder asked. 'How about a historically inaccurate musing about Joan of Arc or a cautionary tale involving Amelia Earhart? Perhaps an amusing anecdote from the life of Rosa Parks?'

'I don't know who Rosa Parks is.'

'Of course you don't,' Cinder snapped angrily, pulling off her jacket and throwing it down on the seat next to her. 'Is it getting hot in here?' she asked, fanning her face with her hands. Angus noticed beads of sweat appearing around her hairline.

'Are you okay?'

'I'm fine.' Cinder snapped at him again. 'I just need some more air.' She reached up and fiddled aggressively with the air vents in the roof panel. 'Arrgh.' She grumbled, hitting the roof and flopping back in her seat. The sweat began slowly running down her forehead and the colour disappeared from her cheeks.

'Are you sure you are okay?' Angus asked again, getting up to help her. Cinder raised her hand to stop him.

'Umm, I'm not, I don't...' She got up quickly, walking at first, then running to the toilet. She closed the folding door shut behind her with a thump.

• • • •

'Good morning Detective Morgan. Good to see you up and about.' Said Heathcote police officer Rebecca O'Bearn – Beccy, as she was known.

'How you doing, boss?' asked her counterpart, Henry Burket. The two uniformed officers entered the small, white-walled room. They removed their hats, tucking them into their armpits. Peter Morgan sat on a tall, metal framed bed. Next to his head, a blue box on a wheeled stand beeped and flashed as it had been doing all night. He had been wishing for hours now that someone would wheel it away so that he could think. Unfortunately, he was connected intravenously to the machine as it pumped clear liquid into his arm.

Beccy and Henry were the last two people on Earth that he wanted to see at that moment, but he greeted them with a polite smile. His two colleagues were very different in appearance. Rebecca O'Bearn had dark hair tied back in a tight bun. She was exceptionally tall for a woman and had been a local basketball star in her youth, still playing every weekend with the same ferocity, if not the same mobility. Even now she moved around the room, bouncing on the balls of her feet with her legs slightly spread, knees bent, and hands forward as if she was ready to receive a pass at any time. Henry Burket was short, with wispy blond hair strategically combed in an unsuccessful attempt to conceal his receding hairline. Henry still maintained the look of a man who had been fit and toned in his youth, but over the past few years, his waistline had increased faster than his uniform could accommodate. From the wrong vantage point, you could spy dark curly hairs through the gaps between his straining shirt buttons. As for their personalities, they were as similar as two people could be. O'Bearn and Burket had been friends since high school and had been working as partners for so long that the locals knew them as one entity: 'O'Burket'.

Henry picked up a blue folder that was hanging on the end of the bed, flicking through the pages, pretending that he understood what they showed.

'When are they letting you out, boss?' he asked.

'I'm being discharged this afternoon,' Peter Morgan answered, sitting up straight. Trying to maintain some semblance of authority in his backless hospital robe. 'They just wanted to monitor me overnight and get my fluids back up.' He lifted his arm to show them the tubing that held him captive to the infuriating machine. 'Did you find my bike?' he asked.

'Yep,' Beccy answered, picking up an apple that was sitting on a cupboard next to the bed. 'It's safe at the station. The Kinnard girl brought it back for you.'

'Did you arrest her?' Peter Morgan asked. The two members of O'Burket laughed.

'For returning you bike?' Beccy asked.

'Yes, she isn't licensed to ride on the roads.' Peter Morgan said. Henry and Beccy looked at each other.

'We will get right onto that.' Henry said, returning the folder to its place. 'While we're at it, do you want us to bring the tree that you hit your head on in for questioning?'

'I'm serious,' Peter Morgan said, becoming impatient with the lax attitude of his co-workers. 'I think we have a group of white su-premacist, red-necks running around the countryside with hunting dogs attacking people and possibly a family of vigilantes fighting a turf war with them.'

'Come on, boss,' Beccy said, polishing the apple on the crotch of her pants. 'We have had a few incidents, but I don't think they're related.'

Two deep lines appeared on Peter Morgan's forehead as he looked from Beccy to Henry.

'Honestly?' he asked. 'You can't see a connection here?'

'No.' Beccy said

'No.' Henry mimicked her, shrugging.

'In the past six months,' Peter Morgan continued, 'you've had the head of an unknown Asian man, turn up next to the body of Mr Blair Abernethy, a homosexual man.' He held his left thumb up as a count of one.

'Miss Jill Malain, a young woman of Japanese descent, disappeared from Tallo's Bluff.' Index finger up.

'Most recently, a Jewish couple vacationing here was attacked while sleeping in their tent.' Third finger.

'And Mr Woo, a former Chinese national, has had people terrorising his chickens for decades.' Four fingers.

'Oh yes,' he said, pointing towards the window with his free hand, his finger wagging in the air. 'There is a woman living in that giant house on the hill who seems to have two men of colour working as her slaves, for God's sake!' he added, raising his last finger. 'And somehow, the Kinnard girl and her family are all mixed up in it.'

'Hang on,' Henry said, holding his palms up towards Peter Morgan. 'Torry Kinnard was in a nasty accident the night of Blair Abernethy's incident. Are you trying to say that a 16-year-old girl was responsible for the murder and disappearance of half a dozen grown men, and then she faked an accident so convincingly that they needed to place her in a coma?'

'The girl died and had to be resuscitated! Twice!' Beccy added and took a bite of the apple. 'Oh, did you want this?' She asked with her mouth full, noticing Peter Morgan's raised eyebrows.

'No, that's yours now,' he answered, then continued. 'I'm not saying that she did all those things by herself. I just think she is involved and knows more than she is letting on.' Beccy waved the apple in Peter Morgan's direction and swallowed her mouthful.

'If you think it's all a big conspiracy,' she said, taking another bite. 'Here's another one for you. There was a woman at the station asking about the girl who bought your bike back.'

'And who was she?' Peter Morgan asked, his eyes bright and focused.

'That's the strange bit. She didn't give us her name but Henry there,' she motioned towards her partner with the half-eaten apple. 'He says she was the spitting image of a lady that died in a crash here about a decade ago.' Peter Morgan's shoulders dropped.

'So, it's not just monsters now, Henry? We've got ghosts too. What's next, aliens?' he asked.

'I saw a UFO once out over Vivien's Ridge.' Henry said. 'I was out there, smoking pot with Molly Prendergast. Remember Molly?'

'Who could forget Molly?' Beccy replied.

'I'd like to forget Molly.' Peter Morgan interrupted.

'Hey, don't you want to hear the rest of my story?' Henry asked, looking deflated.

'No, I don't want to know about your illegal drug activities or you taking advantage of Molly Penright.'

'It's Molly Prendergast.'

'No, her name is Molly I-don't-give-a-shit!' Peter Morgan said, his dark cheeks flashing with colour, 'I want to know about the apparently unknown woman who is making enquires of the police about people of interest in an ongoing case.' Henry and Beccy looked at each other and shrugged. A young man in dark blue, loose fitting cotton pants and shirt entered the room.

'Sorry, officers, but I need the room. It's time for me to check on Peter,' he said, retrieving the folder from the end of the bed. He smiled as he watched the two officers put on their hats and leave the room.

'Thank you for that.' Peter Morgan said. 'Your timing was perfect.' The young man collected a stethoscope that was draped over his shoulders.

'How is it working with Heathcote's finest?' he asked.

'You know that suppository they gave me earlier?' Peter Morgan asked.

'Yes.'

'It's very much like that.'

Peter Morgan looked out of the window as the nurse checked his charts. 'Can I ask you about a patient?' he asked, turning back from the window. 'The Kinnard girl who spent some time here last summer.'

'Super-girl?' the nurse asked.

'Super-girl?'

'Yes, that's what we all call her around here.'

'Why is that?'

'Most people wouldn't have survived her injuries, let alone recover from them as quickly as she did.'

'It must have been a very serious accident then.' Peter Morgan said. The young nurse made a noise at the back of his throat and his head bobbed up and down. 'It was a motorcycle accident, wasn't it?' Peter Morgan asked. The nurse looked around to see that no one was listening.

'We get dozens of kids in here that have come off their bikes. I would bet my next pay check that was no motorcycle accident.'

'What makes you say that?'

'Usually, kids will throw out an arm to stop themselves and break a wrist or a collarbone or dislocate a shoulder. There was nothing like that.' The nurse flicked through the pages in the blue folder, running an eye over Peter Morgan's charts. 'And we would also usually be pulling out splinters and stones from their scrapes for days afterwards. There were no stones, no splinters. Not even fragments of metal in the cuts that were supposedly made by a fence.'

'What do you think caused her injuries then?' Detective Morgan sat himself up straight. The nurse hung the folder back on the foot of the bed.

'I grew up here, you know,' he said, coming closer. 'I've seen one of them, you know, from a distance.'

'Seen what?'

'I don't know, but I'm sure the Kinnard girl could tell you. I'm sure she's seen one of them up close. Too close.'

Chapter 10
When in Rome

Hold me in the summertime, hold me in the rain.
Hold me to my promises, hold me through the pain.
Hold me like a child who has run away from home.
Hold me like you did that night we watched the lights of Rome.

• • • •

Crash! The wardrobe door rattled on its hinges, under the pressure of the large body forced against it. Cinder cowered in the darkness, holding a trembling hand over her mouth, desperate to contain the screams climbing their way vehemently out of her lungs. Four bloodied claws slashed through the door. Cinder blinked as shafts of early morning light broke through the openings. Fighting back her fear, she crept forward, chancing a peek through the fresh fissures. Her father, haggard and pale, lay in a mess of fur and blood. Distressed breaths rattling around his fluid filled lungs. His chest reluctantly continued to rise and fall. Holding his attacker, frothing and flaying violently in his powerful arms. He turned his head to look at the terrified green eyes peering through the cracks. Forcing in a deep breath, he yelled: 'Wake up, Cinder. The new mother is coming.'

'Wake up, Cinder.' Angus whispered, gently stroking her hair away from her moist, contorted brow. Her eyes shot open, staring with fear and dilated intensity at the fading residue of the nightmares playing out on the ceiling. 'Cinder.' Angus said again. 'Are you awake?' Blinking slowly as her eyes drifted back into focus, Cinder turned to look at his concerned but gentle face.

'Yes, I'm awake.' Cinder's voice sounded rattly, stifled, and embarrassed. She propped her head up with her elbow, looking around the room to regain her bearings. Sitting up, she stretched and yawned. Flopping her feet down beside the bed, she retrieved a t-shirt from the floor. Sleepily, she struggled her way into her top as she stood and walked to the kitchen, carefully negotiating her way across the dark, unfamiliar hotel room. When she reached the kitchen bench, she pulled her hair out from the t-shirt's collar, ruffling it as she poured herself a glass of water.

'Are you okay?' Angus asked, watching her sip the water.

'Yes, I'm feeling better now, thanks. Still a little bit embarrassed, actually,' she said. 'I just feel bad for you. It's your first time abroad, and you have had to stay here with me. All you have seen of Rome so far is the airport and the inside of this room.' She took another sip. 'I don't remember ever getting air-sick when I was a kid, but I guess people change.'

'Well, you're not a kid anymore, are you?' Angus said, appraising her long, bare legs.

'Are you checking me out?' she asked.

'Always.' Angus smiled. 'What were you dreaming about?'

'My father, I think he was trying to warn me about something.'

'What do you mean?'

'He said something about a mother coming,' she said, placing the glass on the bench and trying to remember as the dream floated out of her memory like wispy clouds on a warm summer breeze. Angus got out of the bed and walked to the window.

'Like I said on the plane, it sounds like you are just worried about seeing your step-mother again,' he said.

'She has been on my mind,' Cinder agreed. Angus rested his arm against the windowpane and leaned his forehead against his hand. Stretched out before him were the domes, spires, twisting streets, and twinkling lights of Rome. Many floors below, traffic hummed and the laughter of two lovers echoed around the unfamiliar shapes and colours of the city.

'Are you well enough to go out today?' he asked.

'Yes, I think so,' Cinder said, walking to join him.

'Let's go then.' He wrapped his arm around her. 'Let's go explore. We're in Rome for God's sake. Let's be in Rome.'

'But it's the middle of the night. What would we do?' Cinder asked, resting her head on his shoulder. Angus took her hand and held it against his face.

'Whatever you want,' he said, kissing her wrist.

'I want breakfast.'

'Let's go have breakfast then,' Angus said. Cinder looked at her naked legs and at Angus wearing nothing but a pair of black, Calvin Klein boxer-shorts she had bought him for his birthday.

'Do you think we should get dressed first?'

'Do you want me to cover up?'

'I didn't say that,' she said, running her finger down his torso and hooking it in the waistband of his underwear.

• • • •

Cinder and Angus were staying at the Hotel de la Ville, a renovated 18th-century palazzo at the top of the Spanish steps. After getting dressed, they crept quietly from their room. Hand-in hand, they ran through the central courtyard. Greenery draped from white stone walls and obelisks flashed by in their peripherals. Soft lighting flickered off the black and gold décor, evoking a feeling of an ancient candle-lit courtyard.

'Hold up,' Angus called, as Cinder pulled him out through a stone archway onto the street. 'Where are we going?'

'I don't know,' Cinder said, laughing and pulling him towards the Spanish Steps. 'Does it matter?'

'I guess not. As long as I'm with you, I don't care.'

Their shoes pounded loudly on the ancient stone steps. Angus let go of Cinder's hand and jumped down four steps in one leap. Turning to look at Cinder in smug satisfaction, he saw her stop and think. She placed her hands on her knees and crouched. Then, with a grunt, she launched herself into the air and landed at the bottom of the steps. 'Show off,' Angus called, trying but failing to look unimpressed. He ran down the remaining steps and lifted her up into his arms.

The Barcaccia fountain sat at the bottom of the steps. A historical and romantic pool of water set just below the street line, fed by water flowing from the sides of a half-sunken stone boat. Water flowed from two circular fountains at the bow, splashing loudly into the rippling pool. Angus held Cinder over a low handrail, dangling her over the water. The lights of the ancient city played on the ever-turbulent surface. Cinder held him tightly around the neck.

'Angus MacAskill! If I so much as feel a drop of water touch me, you are dead,' she said. 'You know I can do it,' she added, pointing her index finger at his face.'

'Okay, Your Majesty.' Angus said, taking a step back from the water.

'Oh, shut up.' She whacked his chest. Angus looked into one emerald eye and then the other. Pulling her close, he kissed her lips, softly, slowly, and deeply.

'I love you,' he said, pulling away. Cinder smiled and blushed.

'That's the first time you've said that.'

'Really?'

'Yes.'

'It's not the first time I've felt it.'

'Good,' Cinder said, running her hands through the hair at the back of his head and kissing him again. She pulled her lips away but touched the end of her nose against his.

'I love you too, Black.'

'Let's find breakfast,' Angus said, letting her down. Cinder ran to the fountain and splashed a handful of water over him.

'Yep, let's go,' she yelled, running off.

As beautiful as Rome was in the early hours of the morning, it could have been a ghost town for how quiet and still its ancient streets were. Cinder and Angus wandered hand-in-hand, happy to be out of their room, but finding somewhere to eat was proving to be difficult. Their footsteps and laughter echoed down the empty streets and the darkened windows gave no evidence of life or movement within.

'We could just go back to our room and order room service.' Angus said.

'No,' Cinder protested. 'We've been doing that for days. I want to sit at a table and see people, smell the food as it's cooking.'

'I do too, but look around.' Angus lifted her hand and twirled her. 'There's nothing open. We've been wandering around for more than an hour. I don't know how to even get back to the hotel now.'

'Do you need to know?'

'Eventually, yes.'

'Well, when we find somewhere to eat, we can ask for directions. Relax,' Cinder said, ruffling his thick black hair. Angus smiled and smoothed his hair back into place.

'Alright then, we'll keep looking. Someone has to open eventually, I guess.'

Cinder pulled her phone from her back pocket.

'Here's somewhere,' she announced excitedly, after searching for a few moments. 'La Base. It says it's open now and only about twenty minutes from here.' She stood looking at her phone a moment longer.

'What's up? Angus asked, seeing the troubled look on her face.

'It's just that...' Cinder typed a message 'I haven't heard from Marraine yet.'

'Is that normal?'

'She does disappear from time to time,' Cinder said, slipping her phone back into her pocket. 'I just thought she might have checked in by now. Come on,' she said, jogging and pulling Angus with her.

'Do you even know where you're going?'

'More or less.'

'Is it more or is it less?'

'Probably less,' Cinder said with a grin, shrugging and pulling Angus forward again.

. . . .

Shattered artwork and glass lay strewn across the sitting room floor of The Big House – a painful reminder of Lysander's handiwork. Bob tried not to look at the bloodstains as he picked wineglass shards out of the fireplace and dropped them into a cardboard box. Marraine's phone buzzed on the side-table, making him jump. As he picked it up, the screen flashed a notification. Cinder had sent a message. Bob was about to read it when the large front door creaked open. Bob slid the phone in his pocket and hurried towards the foyer.

'Welcome back, m'lady,' he said, seeing Louvelle enter. Louvelle turned to face him. An icy shiver ran up and down his body, following the motion of her eyes as she appraised him; her face unreadable.

'Get my things from the car, would you?' she said, continuing past him into the sitting room.

'It's still a mess in there, sorry,' Bob called behind him as he hurried to the car. Louvelle placed her purse on the side-table, clicking her tongue.

'This will all have to be replaced,' she said, circling a kidney-shaped crimson spot on her white carpet.

Lysander entered the sitting room in his usual black suit and tie. He stood with his legs spread and his hands held behind his back.

'My apologies,' he said. 'I have already made arrangements for the repairs.' Louvelle crouched low and ran her hand across the stain, then sniffed her fingers.

'No need to apologise, my dear,' she said, standing up. 'Sometimes we need to make one mess to clean up another.'

'You are a wise and generous queen,' Lysander bowed.

'Thank you, dear,' Louvelle said, inspecting the Marraine shaped impression in the wall. 'Now, I think you have something for me.' She held out her hand. Lysander approached and retrieved something from his inside breast pocket. Louvelle's dark red lips curled into a smile as Lysander handed her Marraine's moon pendant.

'You've done very well,' she offered as she ran her thumb across the smooth gemstone. 'I hope you took your time. I hope she felt every bit of my rage.'

'Yes, my lady,' Lysander replied.

Outside, Marraine's phone vibrated in Bob's pocket. He sat Louvelle's suitcase down in the driveway and pulled the phone from his pocket. *Everything is ok*, he typed in response to Cinder's message. *Sweetie*, he added.

Chapter 11
The Games We Play

Louvelle moved a soft brush in precise strokes along the top of her cheekbone, flicking it towards her ear. She sat cross-legged on a cushioned, four-legged stool. Her legs sat to the side, like a noble woman mounted side-saddle on her trusty steed. She turned her head from side-to-side to appraise her handiwork in a gold-framed, oval mirror. Placing the brush down on her handmade French-colonial dressing table, she undid the top two buttons of her white silk shirt. Finding some undesirable lines on her neck, she pulled at the skin around her jawline, then continued un-buttoning, revealing the pendant around her neck. Bright light from the lamps on either side of the dressing table sparkled off the golden tree branches and the red garnet moon.

Sliding open the top dresser drawer, she retrieved a similar pendant to the one she was wearing. This pendant had adorned the neck of many people in its life-time, but most recently had found a home nestled on Marraine's décolletage. She sat the pendant on the dresser, slowly lowering the gold chain in concentric circles around the outside. Winding her long auburn hair on top of her head and holding it in place with a bejewelled hairpin, Louvelle removed the pendant from her neck and replaced it with the one formally owned by Marraine. Again, she turned slowly from side-to-side, admiring herself in the mirror with smug satisfaction.

There was a knock at the door. Louvelle placed her pendant in a draw, locking it before buttoning her shirt.

'Come,' she said. Lysander entered.

'Please excuse the interruption, but there is a police detective here, my lady.'

'I assume it is our new Detective Morgan?' Louvelle asked, turning to look at Lysander

'Yes, my lady.'

'He has arrived earlier than I estimated. We will have to keep an eye on him, I think.'

'Yes, my lady.'

'Please inform the detective that I will be with him momentarily,' Louvelle said, checking her hair in the mirror. 'Then I would like you to go and collect our guest. We have little use for the cellar at present. I think perhaps he would be more comfortable down there.'

'Yes, my lady,' Lysander said a third time. 'As you wish.'

• • • •

Detective Morgan's motorcycle stood in the driveway of The Big House. The detective himself stood waiting patiently at the entrance, his hands held casually behind his back. The night air began to chill his face, but he remained still and composed. Light and warmth from the foyer flooded the steps where he was standing as Lysander returned and opened to door.

'Lady Gevaudan will be with you momentarily.' Lysander said, standing in the open doorway. Peter Morgan's eyebrows raised at the mention of the word *lady*.

'Thank you,' he said, reaching into his jacket pocket and retrieving his notebook. He busied himself with scribbling notes. Lysander looked on, silent and impassive.

'Good evening, Detective Morgan.' Louvelle twittered as she arrived and ushered Lysander away with a wave of her hand. 'Let me begin by saying it is a pleasure to finally meet our new detective. I have heard many good reports.'

'Thank you, Lady Gevaudan,' Peter Morgan said, consulting his notes and watching Lysander walk to a waiting car. 'I hope I pronounced that properly?' he asked, placing his notebook and pen back in his pocket. Louvelle nodded.

'Please excuse the late interruption,' he continued. 'I was just out following up some things when I heard that you were back. I didn't want to miss my opportunity to come and introduce myself.'

'I am always delighted to meet new members of our little community,' Louvelle said. 'I must apologise for not inviting you in, but with the ongoing renovations, things are in quite a mess.' The tail-lights of Lysander's car cast a red illumination on Louvelle's face as it calmly pulled away from The Big House and made its way out through the front gate.

'Yes, I did notice the renovations on my previous visit,' Peter Morgan said. Louvelle raised one of her sculpted eyebrows.

'Your last visit?' she inquired.

'That's right,' he said, making a mental catalogue of Louvelle's body language. 'I spoke to your daughter and her friends. Apparently, you were away on business.' Peter Morgan said, noting a twitch in Louvelle's left cheek.

'I was not informed of your visit, sorry. I hope you were treated well,' she said.

'Yes, everyone was very helpful,' he assured her.

Peter Morgan thought himself an excellent judge of people, but Louvelle was difficult to read. Most times, when he made house calls, the occupants appeared nervous and concerned. Louvelle appeared relaxed and confident. In fact, Peter Morgan felt that she might see him as something trivial or annoying.

'Speaking of your daughter,' he continued. 'I was hoping I might be able to have a word with her again this evening.'

'Well, when you find her, I also have some things I would like to speak with her about.' Louvelle said, watching as the white glow of the moon appeared from behind the clouds. Peter Morgan followed her gaze and glanced at the sky.

'You don't know her whereabouts?' he asked.

'Do you have children, Detective Morgan?'

'No, I don't.'

'I don't recommend it,' Louvelle said. 'She has her boyfriend now. She doesn't need me anymore.'

'Boyfriend?' Detective Morgan asked, reaching for his notebook. 'Black, is that his name?'

'Yes, that's the one,' Louvelle confirmed. 'Angus MacAskill is his real name. I'm sure you know all about him and his friends.'

'I see,' Peter Morgan said, scribbling in his notepad. 'That does clear some things up, thank you.'

'The two of them took my jet and disappeared somewhere,' Louvelle said with a flick of her wrist. As she did, her hand swept through the moonlight. She felt a familiar but unexpected tingle in her fingers. Quickly, but nonchalantly, she placed her hand behind her back. Her nail-polish cracked as her fingernails lengthened, becoming thick, dark, and pointed. Coarse orange-brown hair pushed its way out of the follicles on the back of her hand as it pulsed and swelled. Peter Morgan finished his notes, apparently unaware of the transformation creeping up Louvelle's arm.

'Well, I won't take up anymore of your time,' he said, closing his notebook. 'I'm sure you are very busy.'

'Yes, I really should check on my staff,' Louvelle said, placing her free hand on the door and taking a step back.

'Thank you again for your time.' Peter Morgan turned and walked to his motorcycle. Louvelle watched him collect his helmet.

'It was a pleasure to meet you. Please feel free to come again,' she said as she closed the door.

Chapter 12
Something Rotten

Gunn swatted a fly away from his face for the third time in as many minutes. His chin rested on the curved wooden end of a long-handled shovel. A squawk from above, sent his blue-grey eyes skyward. Three circling crows called to each other excitedly, their dark feathers glistening in the early morning sun. Torry came and stood next to her father. She had her nose buried in the elbow of her shirt. 'It smells so bad,' she complained, looking at the disturbing scene in front of them.

The grizzly remains of a cow's hind legs lay twisted and ripped on a patch of disturbed muddy ground. Flies buzzed and swarmed over the rotting, torn flesh, and dried blood.

'Yep.' Gunn grumped, swatting again. 'It's been here for a few days, I'd say.'

They were standing in a tree-lined valley at the northern-most end of their property. It was a marshy area far from the house that they would only visit if they needed to check the fences.

'Do you want me to get the digger?' Torry asked, taking a breath before covering her face again. Gunn looked around and kicked his heel into the moist earth.

'No, sorry love. I think it will just get bogged. We will have to do it by hand.' He handed Torry the shovel. Her shoulders slumped.

'Do I have to go near it?' she asked

'No, just dig the hole here. I'll get a rope to drag it over. You start and I'll be back in a bit to take over.' Gunn turned and started walking back towards the house.

'They haven't attacked like this in a long time.' Torry said, stabbing the shovel into the soft, brown earth. 'What does this mean, dad?' Gunn paused and glanced in the direction of The Big House.

'It means that I hope everyone comes home soon.'

. . . .

Louvelle's heels clip-clopped aggressively on the tiled floor as she walked down the hallway; the Red Queen pendant held firmly in her fist. In the kitchen, the staff busied themselves preparing the evening meals. Good-humoured banter mixed with the clatter of plates and pans and the sizzle of simmering dishes. Bob sat on the stainless-steel bench-top talking to an elderly woman in food splattered whites.

The conversation came to an abrupt halt as Louvelle entered the kitchen. Bob slipped nervously from the bench and tried to look like he had something to do. Louvelle appraised him as one might look at something a sick dog had coughed up on the carpet.

'Take your clothes off,' she ordered, standing behind Bob's right shoulder.

'What?' Bob asked, swallowing hard and turning around.

'Take off your clothes,' Louvelle repeated. Bob looked around for some assistance, but the others had turned their backs on him and returned to their jobs. His sweaty hands trembled as he unbuttoned his shirt and placed it on the bench.

'And the rest,' Louvelle ordered, looking with distaste at his pale, hairy torso. Bob slipped off his shoes and removed his trousers. He placed the trousers with his shirt and stood in the bright lights of the kitchen wearing grey socks and baggy white underpants.

Louvelle grabbed what was remaining of the hair on the back of Bob's head, pulling him violently across the room. Bob squealed and stumbled backwards, grabbing hold of her wrist with both hands.

'What is it? What's wrong, my lady?' he pleaded. Dragging him from the kitchen and down the hallway to the foyer, Louvelle ripped open the front door. Bob, in his semi-nakedness, was hurled out into the cold of the night. Shivering, he started to sprout a covering of thick black hair. His nose and mouth elongated into a sharp-toothed snout. Claws formed at the end of his fingers and toes as they grew longer and darker. Louvelle walked towards the cowering Lycan. Retrieving Marraine's pendant and chain from her pocket, she hung it swaying in front of Bob's face. Fear and recognition flashed in his large, dark eyes. Louvelle flung the pendant at him. Fumbling at first with his oversized, clawed hands, Bob held the jewellery to his chest. Louvelle circled him, her nostrils flaring as her heels crunched slowly and menacingly on the gravel driveway. Seeing that nothing happened, and that Bob stayed in his Lycan form, she lurched forward and snatched the pendant from his hands. Shoving the pendant back in her pocket, she kicked Bob hard in his ribs. He yelped and scurried away into the forest. Louvelle stormed back into The Big House, slamming the door with such force that she rattled the chandelier on the ceiling high above.

Chapter 13
Rumours and Stories

Navy blue curtains with small white polka-dots swayed gently in the warm afternoon breeze. Beams of soft white light refracted through fine particles floating lazily in the sweet-smelling air. Outside, the sound of children's laughter mingled with birdcalls and the distant hum of a lawn mower. Cinder untied a frilly white apron that was protecting her pink summer dress. Placing the apron down next to a tray of home baked chocolate-chip cookies, Cinder inhaled the steam rising from a freshly brewed cup of coffee. Gliding over to the window, she placed the hot beverage on a small wooden coffee table and looked out onto a lush green lawn. Her two children were running under a hose as Angus flicked the water up and down in a slow, wavelike motion.

'There you go, pop,' Cinder said, placing her hand on her father's shoulder. Her father turned in his recliner and looked up with love and pride at his daughter.

'Thanks, Love,' he said, 'You had better take this little bundle of joy.' He held up a small, swaddled baby girl and Cinder took the child, holding it close.

'Time to come to mum,' she said in a soft, high-pitched voice, kissing the baby's face.

Angus appeared beside her. He too, kissed their daughter and then Cinder. Her heart flooded with love and joy.

'Time to wake up, Cinder.' Angus said.

'What?'

'Time to wake up.'

Cinder opened one eye and stretched her arms above her head. 'Did you have to wake me?' she mumbled. 'I was having such a nice dream.'

'I'm sorry,' Angus said, 'but I thought you would want to see this.'

Calm blue-green water stretched out in front of them. A wide pier jutted out from a sandy coastline on their left. On their right, a collection of yachts floated peacefully in their moorings. But the view that Angus was referring to was directly in front of them. Nestled amongst a scattering of terracotta roofed white buildings was a first century Limestone Roman amphitheatre. It rose into the skyline, dazzlingly white against a row of greenery in the foreground.

'It's beautiful,' Cinder said, as she pictured leather-clad gladiators battling starving lions with nets and tridents.

'Yes, it is,' Angus agreed. 'I never knew this was here.'

Cinder cuddled up close to Angus, breathing in the crisp sea air. She watched as the breeze ruffled and tossed his thick black hair and the sun's reflection off the waves danced in his kind but sharp eyes. At times like this, it was easy to forget that they had come away together to find their friend. They had spent the last few months exploring the sights and sounds of new places. Cities and streets pulsing with history and charm. They roamed freely, away from prying eyes and expectations, meeting new people and tasting the food and culture. And the nights... the nights! Wrapped in each other's ecstasy, there were weeks they spent less time in their clothes than out. It is easy to neglect your responsibilities when you're teetering on the edge of bliss. Unfortunately, there was always the realisation that getting closer to finding Dom could also bring them closer to Louvelle. The last time they confronted Cinder's stepmother, they were both lucky to escape with their lives. The thought of seeing her again sat like one of her manicured fingernails, pushing against the elastic but tenuous skin of their love bubble.

After following their leads from dead end to dead end, they had decided to look into the stories of some kind of red-headed witch who lived in the forests of Romania. They had caught an early morning ferry from Venice to Pula, Croatia. Cinder had rested her head on Angus's lap to watch the white sand and rocky coastline of Italy fade into the blue waters as they departed. Eventually, the gentle rocking during the three-and-a-half-hour trip had lulled her to sleep.

'I was having a nice dream,' she said again with a yawn as they pulled into the dock at Pula.

'Wow, that's different,' Angus said, looking down at her.

'Yes, it doesn't happen often.'

'I'm sorry I woke you then.'

'It's okay. I'm glad you did. This view is amazing. I'm glad I got to share it with you.' The ferry's engines stopped for a moment before roaring into reverse. Churning water lapped against the underside of the ferry, slamming and splashing aggressively against the wall of the pier.

After arranging for their luggage to go ahead of them to their accommodation, they disembarked and made the short walk to the ancient roman structure. It impressed Angus to see that the first century arena was still a meeting place for the people of Pula. They had set rows of portable seating up in the centre of the elliptical stone wall. They had also erected a large screen for people to watch the latest blockbuster movies or their favourite classics in the warm summer night. He marvelled at how well-preserved and intact the amphitheatre was. Cinder strolled the perimeter, looking up at the sunlight falling through the windows. Two rows of stone arches and a top row of square openings. They reminded her of a television program she watched as a child. She stopped to take a photograph and her stomach rumbled.

'Let's go and find some brunch,' she called out to Angus, who was running his hands along one of the cold stone walls.

'Okay, just hold on. I want to get a photo of us.' Angus said. He had just convinced some other tourists, an elderly couple with grey hair and matching polo shirts, to take a photo of the two of them. He handed them his phone and stood next to Cinder.

'But I look terrible,' Cinder protested.

'Never,' Angus said with a grin.

After posing for a few photos, they collected Angus's phone and thanked the couple for their help.

'No problem at all,' the old man said. 'I'm Robert and this is my wife, Carol.' He gestured to his partner.

'Nice to meet you, Robert... Carol,' Angus said as he shook their hands in turn. 'I'm Angus and this is Cinder.'

'Hello,' Cinder said with a smile.

'Are you two honeymooners?' Carol asked, placing her hand on Angus's arm. Cinder blushed.

'No, no, we're not married, just vacationing,' she said.

'You should put a ring on that one before someone else snaps her up,' Carol said, punching Angus in the chest.'

'Oh, Carol, leave them be.' Robert interrupted. Angus blushed too and laughed.

'I'll think about that, Carol. Thanks,' he said, smiling at Cinder. Carol walked over to Cinder, taking her hand.

'You just make sure he does,' she whispered.

'Okay, I will,' Cinder whispered back.

'Oh!' Carol said, tapping Cinder's hand and turning back to her embarrassed husband. 'These two should go to the market. Tell them, Robby.'

'Yes, yes,' Robert exclaimed, excited to have an opportunity to change the subject. 'You should definitely go to the market.'

'Oh, a market,' Cinder said, her interest sparked.

'Yes, yes,' Robert said again. 'It's the Pula Green Market, and it's not far. Two young things like you should be able to walk there.' Robert pulled a map from his pocket and began giving Angus some directions. When Angus was confident that he knew where to go, he and Cinder thanked the elderly couple again. They took one more look around the amphitheatre and left for the market.

• • • •

Cinder nuzzled under Angus's arm as they walked along a cobbled street. Red and yellow canvas roofs flapped in the swirling afternoon breeze. Beneath the makeshift shelters, sardine-packed stalls walled the busy walkway as customers weaved in and out amongst the marketplaces. Produce and bric-à-brac of all shapes and sizes covered card tables, trestles, crates, or anything that could be used to form a flat surface. Vendors' hands busied with money exchanges as multilingual, rehearsed sales pitches flowed with deep chested gusto from their smiling mouths. Cinder and Angus joined the flow of other busy shoppers moving into the marketplace. People chatted excitedly as they moved in and out of the current of flowing bodies, lugging paper bags of newfound treasures.

'Oh my goodness,' Cinder said, pulling Angus forward towards a table of fruit and vegetables. 'Look at the size of these apples, and the colour!' But Angus moved on in the flow of traffic to the next stall. The lady behind the table offered Cinder a glistening apple of deep crimson.

'Beautiful red fruit for the beautiful red lady,' the stall owner said.

'How much?' Cinder asked, reaching for her purse. The lady waved her hands dismissively.

'No, no, no, you have. Is yours.'

'Thank you,' Cinder said, holding the apple to her chest. Skipping up behind Angus, she waved the apple under his nose. A table full of second-hand books and magazines had captured Angus's interest. Packed tightly, spine up, in repurposed fruit crates. Angus searched for signs of authors or titles he recognised.

'Look at this,' Cinder said, trying once more to gain his attention. Angus opened his mouth as if to bite the apple. 'Hey, no,' Cinder pulled the apple away. 'Get your own apple,' she said, stowing the fruit in her backpack.

'I'd rather get one of these. Look how old some of these are,' he said, flicking carefully through the time-yellowed pages of a dark green hard-covered book.

'Look,' Cinder said, picking up a small paperback. 'This one is about you and me.' She showed him the cover that depicted a scantily dressed red-haired woman draped seductively around a bare-chested man with long, dark hair. Angus swapped books with Cinder. She flashed him a questioning smile. 'What are you doing?'

'I'm buying this,' he said with a grin. Turning the book over to read the blurb, he continued. 'I just simply need to know what happens to Constance and her mysterious Latin lover.'

'It is intriguing,' Cinder agreed, studying the book in her hand, *Venezia La Bella* the title read. The text was in French. She could understand some words, but not enough to read it. 'I think your father would have liked this,' she said, turning the old book over carefully. Angus nodded and smiled, then paid the stall holder for the paperback romance.

'I didn't think you were serious,' Cinder said, whacking his arm playfully.

'Deadly serious.' Angus Joked as he placed the book in his pack.

A group of young men were studying a piece of fruit on a table two stalls away. Cinder could hear them laughing and arguing in their American southern-west-coast accents. 'You eat it.' One of them exclaimed.

'No-way man, it smells like your feet, you eat it,' his friend replied.

'I bet Dom the Beach Bum would eat it,' a third American said. 'He would eat anything.'

'Did you hear that?' Cinder said, poking Angus with her elbow. 'They were talking about someone called Dom.'

'That could be anyone.' Angus said.

'It can't hurt to ask.' Cinder said, putting down the book and weaving her way through the crowd towards the young men. Angus followed.

'Excuse me,' Cinder said, placing her hand on one of the men's shoulders. Much shorter than Cinder, he showed the signs of a life in the summer. Shoulder length sun-bleached hair draped in thickets around his ruddy, tanned and freckled face.

'Hey there,' he said, looking please by the attention from a young woman. His two friends were more taken with Angus.

'Sorry to interrupt,' Cinder continued, 'But I, we, overheard you talking about a Dom. We are actually looking for our friend, Dom. I know it's a long shot, but is the Dom you are talking about called Dom Kinnard?' The three men looked at each other, shrugging.

'Sorry,' the man next to Cinder said. 'We never found out his last name.'

'Can you tell us anything about him?' Angus asked. One of the others, a thin man with dreadlocks and long, sharp features, spoke up.

'He looked and sounded a bit like you, brother,' he said, pointing a tanned finger at Angus. Cinder looked at Angus, eyes wide.

'That sounds promising. Can you tell us anything else?' she asked. The three men looked at each other and sniggered.

'What?' Angus asked.

'The last we heard, he was hiding out in the forest back in Romania.' The first man said. 'Apparently, he had a ménage et tois with a local crime boss's wife and his teenage daughter.'

'Oh,' Cinder said, biting her lip to hold in a giggle. Angus place his head in his palm, shaking it from side to side.

'It sounds like we're heading in the right direction then,' he said.

Chapter 14
Fairest of Them All

Dim winter sunlight flashed gold and silver as the metallic object travelled its concentric path. A chain, holding it in orbit, pulled gently on Louvelle's manicured hand.

'Is he here yet?' she asked no one in particular, as she let the detested object fall to her palm. She had a clear view from the sitting-room window, now that someone had removed the scaffolding. A malicious ocean breeze pushed its invisible fingers up and through the evergreens. The less robust branches bent and swayed, bobbing and protesting at undesirable angles. Fissures in the blanket of green pulsed open and shut, revealing grey skies and turbulent turquoise waters. A dark-suited figure in the shadowed corner of the room reached his left hand to a concealed device in this ear. He cleared his throat.

'The car has just arrived.' he said. Louvelle squeezed the object in her fist and turned on her heel.

'Thank you,' she said, looking at the news-giver, with no recollection of his name. 'Make sure he finds his way in here.' The man in the dark suit offered an obedient bow and exited. He returned a moment later with Lysander.

Daylight stretched out in four long rectangles along the floor of the sitting room. Lysander stood with the toes of his polished black shoes, kissing the border between light and shadow. With his feet and shoulders set wide and his hands behind his back, he traced a discerning look around the perimeter of the room. Six men, in identical clothes to his own, stood nervous and attentive around the walls. Two of them he knew well, but the rest were strangers.

'There are some new faces here today, my lady,' he said, sizing up the new arrivals.

'Yes,' Louvelle said with a practiced smile, walking to the fire-place. 'I seem to be needing to change many things at the moment.' She ran her hand across the freshly painted walls. 'Have you been taking care of our guest?' she asked, turning to look at Lysander.

'Yes, my lady,' he replied.

'Then where is he?'

'I thought you may have liked him to stay where he is,' Lysander said. Louvelle clenched her fists.

'You thought?' she asked. 'Since when has thinking been a part of your job description?' She turned away, focussing her attention once more on the wall. Lysander, assuming that the question was rhetorical, remained quiet. 'Here,' Louvelle said, tossing Lysander, the object that was still squished inside her fist. Lysander snatched it out of the air. A gold chain hung from his hand, swaying backward and forward. 'While you're thinking,' Louvelle said. 'Why don't you have a think about what that is and what that means?'

Lysander opened his hand to reveal a pendant. He studied the bent and mangled silver loop around the outside. A full moon carved from blue stone sat nestled in the branches of a tree.

'Have I been a good queen, Lysander?' Louvelle asked.

'You are a strong and wise leader, my lady'

'But do you love your queen?'

'I have known little of love in my life, Lady Gevaudan, but I serve my queen with whatever strength I have.' Lysander glanced at one of the strangers moving in his peripheries. Louvelle strolled forward, plucked the pendant from his hand, tossing it into the fireplace. The blue stone came free as the jewellery smashed against the fire-black-ened bricks.

'I have been betrayed. Betrayed by the ones to whom I have shown love.' Louvelle said, turning to look out of the window again. 'They say love makes us blind and I am beginning to understand just how blind I have been. I have chosen to not have children of my own, so that I could be the best possible queen for all of you. But being a compassionate queen, I took in a child that was not mine, caring for her and instructing her like she was my own. My compassion has made me blind to many things, but now I am looking at the world again with my eyes wide open. Therefore, I ask you Lysander to be honest with me now for I will see through your lies.'

She turned back to Lysander, her lips pushed thin and tight. Lysander held his hands behind his back and stood tall.

'I have always been a man of truth and will continue to be so.'

'I thank you for that, and ask which queen is Lysander bound to?'

'Lysander's queen was Queen Marishka the wise. Marishka no longer lives, so Lysander is bound to no queen. Lysander chooses to follow the most powerful queen.'

'And who is the most powerful queen?'

'The Red Queen, my lady' Lysander adjusted his footing. Louvelle paused and admired the polish on her fingernails.

'What is the name of the queen you serve, Lysander?' she asked, so quietly it was almost a whisper.

'Cinder,' Lysander answered, swallowing hard. 'Am I to be killed now?'

'No. why would I kill you when you are only being honest? As I said, I am a compassionate queen. If she is your queen, then you should go to her. Go collect your things. Leave tonight.' Louvelle waved him away dismissively. Lysander adjusted his jacket, eyeing the occupants of the room as he backed out of the doorway.

Louvelle listened for the sound of Lysander's footsteps to trail off. Turning to one of the others, she indicated with her finger for him to approach.

'Follow him. When you find my daughter, bring her to me, alive. Kill the rest and bring me the head of the bitch, Marraine. I have let this all go on too long. Time to clean up a mess.'

The afternoon sun peeked its lazy head over the flat tiled roofs of harsh angled grey buildings. Cinder held up her hand to shadow her eyes as she looked around. Their search of Romania was now stretching into the third week. They had made their way to the Hoia Forest but could find no sign of Dom or the mythical red-haired woman. There was one rumour from a nearby village that sounded promising. A strong, red-headed woman who lived with a man named Dominic. Unfortunately, when they went to investigate, they discovered that the woman and the man named Dominic were one and the same. A local man spent his Friday evenings dressed in heels and a long, red wig, arm-wrestling drunken tourists for money.

Discouraged by their lack of progress and ignoring the warnings from the staff at their hotel, Cinder and Angus had now ventured into the backstreets of Constanta. Cinder strolled along a gravel road with a pack slung over one shoulder. Decades of traffic had worn two ruts into the narrow path, but at that moment, the road was empty.

A remarkably small woman sat with her back against a paint-chipped and use-worn red door, taking advantage of the shadowed entrance way. Her three-legged wooden stool groaned and creaked disagreeably as she nattered to herself. Hands, bent and calloused with time, still moved needle and thread with the dexterity of an artisan. Cinder dropped her backpack to the ground, rummaging to find her water bottle.

'Good afternoon,' she said, noticing the lady. Dozens of deep lines creased around the woman's grey eyes.

'Allo, allo,' she said, proudly showing off her five remaining teeth. Cinder smiled, drank, and waited for Angus. They had paused in an alleyway to admire some street art. Angus was taking some photos to send to Torry.

The old woman in the doorway fell silent. Cinder noticed her eyes dart towards two figures further up the street and the slightest of head shakes. As the lady went back to her sewing and nattering, Cinder moved her feet wider and positioned her head so that she had the two figures at one edge of her view and the alleyway at the other edge.

Two stocky men in tall lace-up leather boots and grey, woollen flat-caps approached Cinder with a quickening pace. The elder of the two had a split lip and a yellowing bruise around his left eye. He raised his hand in greeting.

'Buna ziua,' he said with a wide grin.

'Hello,' Cinder replied with apprehension. The younger man jogged ahead and began to sing loudly. Cinder watched him go by, but felt the other man close to her. Swivelling her head around, she spotted the first man's hand on her backpack.

'Hey!' she yelled, and stood on the shoulder strap, just as he lifted the pack off the ground. A jack-knife blade sprung out in the man's hand and he made to cut the strap. Cinder grabbed his wrist and smashed her drink bottle into his nose. He yelled and stumbled back. Blood and tears trickling down his stupefied face. The second man ran to help his accomplice, but a flying three-legged stool collided with his left eye. Still holding his wrist, Cinder flicked the older man's arm, like she was cracking a whip. With an audible pop-crack of his shoulder, the knife fell, rattling on the road. The second man took hold of Cinder's shoulders. With a growl, she turned to glare at her attacker, her eyes large, wild, cat-like.

'Strigoi!' the younger man murmured, his face turning pale and clammy. His arms fell limply by his side. Cinder picked him up by his shirtfront and threw him across the street. Strigoi! He called out in terror again before crashing through the red door and disappearing into the darkness inside. Cursing loudly, the old lady approached the older assailant. Kicking him in the leg and spitting on him.

'Strigoi, femeie cu parul rosu, Strigoi,' he muttered pitifully as he painfully shuffled along the road away from Cinder. Hearing boots stomping on the road, moving quickly towards her, Cinder spun around. She was relieved to see it was just Angus coming to help her.

'What happened?' he exclaimed, inspecting the damaged door and eyeing the injured man on the road.

'They tried to rob me,' Cinder explained as she picked up her bag, hugging it to her chest.

'Well, I bet they're regretting that now,' he said with a smile. 'What is he saying?'

'I'm not sure,' Cinder said, turning to the lady. 'Do you speak English?'

'Yes, yes, English,' the lady replied enthusiastically.

'Can you tell us what he is saying?' Cinder asked, looking at the man who was still muttering to himself on the ground, holding his shoulder.

'He says you are Strigoi. The red-lady, monster lady,' the old woman said before spitting on him again. 'They fear the red lady and the man.'

'Please, can you tell us about the man?' Cinder asked.

'They say he is sorcerer. Bewitched a man's wife and daughter, yes. He found Red Lady, the Banshee. The men followed, but he turned the red lady to a great beast, a Strigoi.'

Angus picked the injured man up from the road and held him off the ground. His face contorted in fear, anger, and pain.

'English?' Angus asked, shaking the broken and bloody man.

'Yes,' the man said between moans of agony.

'Tell us where the man is now, the man with the Banshee?' Angus demanded.

'Piss off!' the man yelled. The younger of the two would-be robbers stumbled out of the entrance to the old lady's home. Dazed and dusty, with blood flowing freely from a cut above his left eye. He looked from Cinder to Angus and ran limping down the street, disappearing into an alleyway. Still holding the man off the ground with one hand, Angus placed his other hand on the man's dislocated shoulder.

'Where is he?' he asked, squeezing. The man punched wildly at Angus, with as much effect as a disobedient infant trying to push away an unperturbed parent. Angus swatted away the attack and slapped the man's face. 'Where is he?' he asked again.

'He was staying in Constanta,' the man answer, conceding defeat. 'He was here with the Red Lady. With her.' He pointed at Cinder. 'He was seen weeks ago in the Bellagio club, but has not been seen since. People say he left Constanta. We hoped the Banshee had gone with him.' Cinder stepped close to the man and flashed her sharp teeth in his face.

'You see this lady?' she pointed to the old woman who was collecting her stool.

'Yes, yes,' the terrified man said.

'This lady is my grandmother. She is protected by the Red Lady. You let everyone know that.' Cinder pulled some money from her bag and gave it to the old woman. 'For your door,' she said. Flashing her limited teeth again, the woman took the money and kissed Cinder's hand. When she counted the notes, she tried to give some of them back to Cinder, but Cinder refused. She turned back to the man, still being held aloft by Angus.

'Protected, understand?' she said, pointing at him. Looking wide eyed at her hair, he nodded. 'Okay, put him down.' Angus dropped him and he stumbled backwards. Cinder waved him away, and he scurried off as best he could with his injured shoulder and injured pride.

'Did you hear what he said about Dom being with the redheaded woman?' Angus asked.

'Yes, but I'm sure he's okay,' Cinder said, putting her arm around him.

'I'm not so sure. It sounds like they have already left. I think it's time to go home,' he said, his bottom lip pushed forward, and fingers interlocked behind his head.

'Yes, I think so,' Cinder agreed, running her ponytail through her hands. 'But there is something I need to do first.'

Chapter 16
The Watch

In the back streets of Bucharest, a black car with dark tinted windows cruised to the side of the street and stopped. A grey stone wall adorned with multi-coloured tags of generations of street artists cast a long shadow over the vehicle and across the bitumen. The driver emerged, adjusting his grey flat-cap and driving gloves before opening the rear door for his employer.

A short, wide man with a baldhead, large nose, and thick beard, slid with difficulty from the rear seat. The manoeuvre made even more difficult by the fact that his left arm was in a cast, held in place by a sling. With his good arm, he reached into the car, grunting as he pulled out a long black coat. His driver helped him drape the coat over his shoulders to hide the cast and closed the door behind him. Two men in similar long coats and dark sunglasses also emerged from the vehicle. They stood tall with the confidence of men who knew how to handle themselves, their broad shoulders set back and their hands ready at their sides. They shadowed the short man as he strolled across the narrow street.

The short man entered a shadowed doorway of an old pub. Grumbling to himself about his arm, he made his way down a spiralling staircase. He had difficulty navigating his wide body down the narrow corridor. His cast caught several times on the decades of posters plastered haphazardly on the walls, one on top of another. Torn and tattered corners fell away from the wall to reveal mildewed and tobacco-browned paintwork below. This patchwork of flyers advertising entertainers, who had gone on to bigger and better things or disappeared into oblivion, were possibly the only thing holding together the cracked and dented walls. Although the short man tried not to think why his Italian leather boots stuck to the carpet, the smell of stale alcohol, coffee, and bodily fluids offered their own advertisements.

The sticky staircase wound its way down to a dimly lit, windowless subterranean room. Tattered grey carpet covered the majority of the long rectangular-shaped floor, save for an area of chipped, brown tiles that haloed the bar. Walls that had once been green but were now a patchy and faded shade of brown, groped upwards to a low ceiling.

In a darkened corner booth, a young man in a slim-fitting dark-grey Zegna suit, sat turning a whiskey glass in his left hand. His right arm rested casually across the top of the booth's backrest. He had his right ankle propped on his left knee. The short man grunted as he slid his large girth into the chair opposite the young man. The two men with him remained standing, eyeing the stranger as he continued to turn his whiskey glass between his fingers.

'You picked an interesting place to meet,' the short man said, as he caught his breath and looked around the room. He would never bring his wife to a dive like this, and if he ever caught his daughter Victoria in one of these places, he would slap her into next Tuesday. As much as he liked to think he had moved up in the world enough to not frequent these bars, he knew they had their benefits. A place like this was ideal for his off-the-book business dealings. In a place like this, people knew not to glance into the dark corners, to not make eye contact or ask questions. In a place like this, people came to forget, not to remember or be remembered.

'We have history, this place and I,' the young man said, looking around the room.

'History?' the short man scoffed. 'You barely look old enough to drink. How much history could you have with a place like this?'

'Looks can be deceiving, Mr Schmidt.'

'I've made my living out of reading people,' Mr Schmidt replied, looking him up and down. His tailored woollen suit, shoes, and the glint of gold from under the cuff of his jacket reeked of money. Even the way his whiskey hung on the sides of his glass showed that he must have ordered something special that was kept in the back room. The young man finished his drink and sat his empty glass down on the table with a clunk.

'Would you like a seat, gentlemen?' he asked, looking the two other men up and down.

'They're fine,' Mr Schmidt said.

'Very well, then. Thank you for joining me,' the young man said.

'Did you bring the money?' Mr Schmidt asked sharply, bumping the table with his large stomach, rattling the empty glass. Across the table, the young man reached inside his jacket pocket and retrieved a brown leather wallet. Unfolding and opening it, he withdrew ten blue notes. After returning the wallet to his pocket, he placed the notes on the table and sat the whiskey glass on top. With his good arm, Mr Schmidt reached for the money, but the owner of the money placed his hand on top of the whiskey glass.

'Information first,' he said. The older man's two companions pulled back their long coats to reveal revolver handles protruding from their waistbands. An arrogant grin twisted the corners of the young man's lips. Mr Schmidt held up his uninjured hand as a sign for his companions to stand down. When they had resumed their position with their hands held together in front of them, he lowered his hand and turned his attention back to the young man.

'So, you want to know about the red-haired woman and her friend?' he asked.

'The Red Lady, yes. I could care less about her friend.'

'I can tell you where they are, but I would warn you to be careful,' Mr Schmidt said, lifting his cast. The young man took his hand from his glass.

'I can handle myself,' he said with a wink towards the two men standing. Mr Schmidt laughed, wobbling the table and jiggling the glass again. His two companions followed his lead, joining in laughing.

'You see this?' He pointed to his cast with his good hand. 'This is what they did to me. The doctor tells me I might never get feeling back in my left hand. And I'm the lucky one. You should see what some of my friends look like.'

'I look forward to meeting this red banshee then,' the young man said, bringing his right arm down from the backrest and sitting it on his knee.

'He's got a death wish, this one,' Mr Schmidt said, turning to his companions. 'Two of my associates had the misfortune of running into the red woman a second time. They tell me she is staying at the Concorde, here in Bucharest. But we have heard rumours that she leaves soon. Arrangements have been made for her to fly out before month's end.' The young man leaned forward and lifted his glass, nodding towards the money. Mr Schmidt's eyes sparkled at the money and the gold band that twinkled on the young man's wrist.

'The son of a bitch with her, put his hands all over my wife and daughter, stole from me and then set his witch on me,' he said, placing the notes in the fingers protruding from the cast, licking his good thumb and counting the money.

'Not a witch, no.' the young man said, flashing his pure-white teeth. 'You say your fingers are numb? A witch wouldn't leave you numb. They would make sure you feel everything. No, Mr Schmidt, this red woman is something very different.'

Satisfied that all the money was there, Mr Schmidt, the man whose wife had invited Dom into her marital bed, the father of the beautiful young woman Victoria, the victim of the red banshee, slid the notes into his chest pocket and signalled to his companions. The two large men pulled their long coats to the side and took a step closer to the table.

'Seeing as though I've given you information and a warning, my price has gone up,' Mr Schmidt said with a grin. The young man leaned back in his chair casually.

'You have been most helpful, but unfortunately I don't have any more cash on me,' he said, reaching forward and running his finger around the rim of the glass. Mr Schmidt reached forward with one of his podgy hands and pulled back the young man's sleeve.

'This will do nicely.' he said.

The pulled back sleeve had revealed an antique gold watch. Set in the face behind the hands was a blue gemstone that resembled the full moon.

'Take your hands off me, Mr Schmidt,' the young man said in a calm but direct voice. 'You only have one good one left.' One of Mr Schmidt's companions reached for his gun. In an action that appeared to be nothing more than a flick of the wrist, the young man sent the empty glass hurtling across the room, smashing into the forehead of a man who had his gun halfway out of his waistband. Blood and glass exploded across the room as the man fell to the floor. His companion reach for his own weapon, only to find that the young man who only a second before was sitting across the table from his employer was now right behind him, holding the gun to the back of his head. His eyes wide with fear and confusion, he slowly raised his hands in surrender.

'Have you lost something?' The young man asked, as he slammed the man's weapon down on top of his head, knocking him out cold. 'This watch has been in my family for generations,' he said, pointing the gun towards Mr Schmidt as he sat speechless at the table. The colour had drained from his wide podgy face, increasing his resemblance to a large marshmallow with wide eyes and gaping mouth. The young man stepped slowly towards the table, the barrel of the gun fixed on the petrified man's head.

'I'll be leaving now, and I will be taking my watch with me. Thank you for your assistance,' he said, placing the gun casually on the table before turning and strolling out of the bar.

• • • •

Delicate fingertips traced the line of scar tissue, now almost invisible to the eye but still creating a trench along the sinew and muscle.

'Isn't age tiresome?' Louvelle said, running her hand up her leg. 'Once upon a time, my scars would just disappear.' She unscrewed the lid of a pastel-pink container, dipping her fingers into the creamy white substance. After rubbing a small amount of it between her thumb and index finger, she dipped her hand back in and applied a larger amount to her hands. 'Now my youth comes in small containers,' she said, taking another large portion of the solution and applying it in long, careful streaks up her legs.

'Excuse the interruption, my lady. The moon is out. We are ready to go. Would you like someone to stay behind with you?' A large man in a dark suit asked.

'No, that's fine. I have my insurance policy,' she said, flicking lotion at a man that was bound to a chair in front of her. The lotion splatter against the black hood that covered his drooping head. Louvelle admired her handiwork, then went back to applying the lotion to her legs.

'Very well, my lady.' The man bowed and left Louvelle alone with the hooded figure.

'You look a little dry,' she said, getting to her feet and strolling towards her captive. Wiping a clump of lotion off the hood, she placed her free hand on the prisoner's shoulder. 'I do so enjoy our little chats.' She said, massaging the creamy liquid into his muscular arms. 'I feel you're the only one here that really listens to me.'

Under the hood, the man made a muffled protest through his gag.

'No, no, dear,' Louvelle said, patting him. 'No need to thank me,' she said, rubbing lotion into his other arm. 'We're friends now, and friends help each other. You are doing an important job for me, so this is the least I can do.'

Chapter 17
Disturbing the Peace

Stepping out of the wagon, Detective Peter Morgan placed his sleeve against his nostrils to block the smell of burning flesh. The remnants of a fire, coals and smouldering wood, could still be seen under the grizzly, charred body. Bubbled, black skin intertwined with the remnants of clothing, smouldered and smoked. Party music pumped loudly through a portable sound system; it was the reason they were here – investigating a noise complaint. Someone's phone sat on top of the sound system. Detective Morgan removed a latex glove from his pocket and used it to turn the music off. Beccy O'Bearn stood at the edge of the scene, a clearing in the forest.

'It must have been one hell of a party,' she said, setting up a set of spotlights on a stand. 'This one is completely naked.' As she turned the spotlight onto the charred remains, her partner Henry started making a retching noise beside her, as if he was about to vomit.

Detective Morgan hurried over to inspect the body next to them. As Beccy had said, he was completely naked, lying face down in the long grass. A halo of dark red surrounded a smashed beer bottle protruding from his neck. 'I recognise this man.' Detective Morgan said, shining his flashlight on the dead man's face.

'Yeah,' Beccy said. 'That's Jock Stevens.'

'He was working at Berkley's Manor. I spoke to him.'

'Jock does a lot of work at The Big House,' Beccy said.

'*Did* a lot of work,' Henry corrected her.

'So, he's a local?' Detective Morgan interrupted them. 'What about the others? Do you recognise the rest of them?' Henry made the retching noise again.

'I'll go look then, shall I?' Beccy said, watching the colour drain from her partner's face.

'Could you? I'll look around for evidence.' Henry said, trying to look busy.

There were six other bodies scattered around the clearing. Two tangled in ripped and bent camp chairs. One with her hand in a blood splattered and upturned icebox. The body in the fireplace and two more closer to Jock's naked body, who looked like they had been trying to run away. Beccy crouched down at each one in turn, flashlight in hand.

'I can't tell with the burnt one,' she said, walking back to Jock's body. 'But I don't recognise any of them. They must all be tourists.'

'So why would this local end up naked at a party of strangers?' Detective Morgan asked, surveying the destruction. He turned his flashlight towards the ground, looking around the naked body.

'What are you looking for, boss?' Beccy asked.

'This,' Detective Morgan said, finding something. Blood from the naked man was still trickling from his ruptured jugular, soaking into the soil and pooling in an indent in the ground. 'I'm looking for a paw print,' he said, kneeling for a closer look and removing his phone from his jacket.

'A paw print?' Henry asked, edging closer.

'Yes, just like this one.' Peter Morgan said, taking a photo of the print. Henry crouched next to him.

'I didn't think you believed in the stories of Heathcote's beasts?'

'No, I don't.' Peter Morgan slipped the phone back in his pocket and moved his beam of light along the ground to see a trail of prints.

'But you think these are animal prints, right?' Henry asked, turning on his own flashlight. Peter Morgan thought about the question for a moment before answering.

'No, I don't,' he said again.

'That doesn't make any sense.'

'On the contrary,' Peter Morgan said, placing his hand on Henry's shoulder. 'It's the only thing that does make sense of everything.

Unfortunately.' Standing and shining his light into the forest, he looked back over his shoulder at the distant glow of The Big House. 'What's south of here?' he asked, looking back at the trail of prints.

'Not much, just the forest then farmland,' Beccy answered.

'Who's farm?' Peter Morgan asked, already moving briskly back to the vehicles, confident that he would know the answer. Beccy and Henry exchanged glances, shrugging.

'Should we follow him?' Henry asked, standing up and watching Peter Morgan leave.

'The Kinnard farm!' Beccy called out as he got to the road.

Chapter 18
Unwelcome Guests

The floorboards creaked and groaned. A regular night-time sound for the farmhouse as the temperature dropped. Again, the timbers complained, but not enough to disturb Torry's sleep. She remained in deep slumber; her quilt bunched up around her ears as rhythmic breaths vaporised on the cold air. One hand draped across her forehead, the other sandwiched between her pillows. Quietly turning a doorknob is a difficult task when you have oversized, clawed hands, but that was what the unwelcome visitor did. Sniffing the air, a bulky figure entered her room. Saliva ran from its jowls, dripping on a pile of discarded clothes on Torry's bedroom floor.

The viscous, moist substance hung like two glistening elastic bands, stretching to breaking point as the beast's jaws slowly spread apart. Some of the putrid liquid fell, splattering just above Torry's left eye. Her eyes shot open as the saliva slithered down to her hairline.

Awake, Torry screamed and covered her face against the attack. The Lycan roared, its teeth sharp, grey and wet, inches from Torry's flesh. Something silver and metallic exploded from the beast's throat, forcing its head to lurch backwards. Grabbing at its throat, the Lycan let out a horrible, gurgling howl as the blade retracted. A second later, the same blade, dripping with blood and gore, crashed down on the unwelcome guest's skull. Two large hands forced the knife deep into the fresh opening just above the Lycan's right eye. A twist of the blade tore apart bone and flesh, exposing the purple gore of brain and sinew. Gunn emerged, blood splattered and stern.

'Get up, princess, we got wolves in the henhouse!' he yelled, lifting the Lycan's arm and forcing his blade into its chest.

Torry flew from her bed in a whirlwind of sheets, quilt, and pillows. Down on her knees, she searched frantically for her hidden weapon amongst the slats of her bed. The putrid, ruptured head of her unwanted night-time visitor fell to the bed. Something moist and solid hit her cheek, making her flinch and dry retch.

'Dad!' she wiped her face with the hem of her pyjama top. 'Why did you put it on my bed?' she complained, standing, a long-handled, clawed hammer in her fist.

'I didn't mean it, princess, that's just where the bastard fell.'

'It's gross. There's brains and shit all over my sheets.'

'Hey! Mind your mouth.' Gunn said. But there was little time for them to worry about Torry's dirty sheets or her dirty mouth. A second Lycan rushed in through her bedroom door. Moonlight sneaking through the cracks at the edges of Torry's bedroom blinds flashed off the whites of the Lycan's eyes. Torry struck the side of its head with her elbow as it threw its hairy body at her. Her blow sent the beast tumbling into Gunn. After a brief tussle, man and beast tumbled out of the window in an eruption of shattering glass and the metallic crackle-snap of aluminium venetians.

Torry watched as their four flaying legs slid over the windowsill and disappeared. The chilly night air rushed into Torry's room. *Now I'm really awake,* she thought to herself. Ripping her broken blind to the floor with a crash, Torry used her weapon to smash out the remaining shards of glass. Sliding the hammer into the waistband of her blue and yellow striped flannelette pyjamas, Torry took a few steps back, before running and leaping arms first out of the window. Tucking her head under her arms, she landed on her left shoulder and rolled over into a crouch.

Glinting in the moonlight, Gunn's blade swept back and forth, deflecting the blows of deadly claws. Each blow forced the old man back. He knew this terrain better than anyone, but the experienced fighter knew that moving backwards in the dark was inviting errors.

'Get back, you mangy mongrel!' he yelled. Hammer back in hand, Torry ran to help her father. Barefoot on the grass, she moved quickly and quietly. Before the Lycan had time to register her approach, Torry jumped, swinging her hammer in a large arc towards its head. The beast flinched at the last moment, but too late. The blunt end of the hammerhead connected with a thud just below its right ear. Yelping and stumbling, the Lycan clawed at the side of its own head as if it could scratch the pain away. It turned a full circle before it fell, writhing and howling on the ground.

A throaty growl announced the approach of two more Lycan, running with pace on all fours around the corner of the farmhouse. Cracking his neck and setting his shoulders back, Gunn positioned himself between them and Torry.

'Run and get help,' he told Torry.

'I'm not going anywhere, Dad,' she said, moving beside him. Gunn grumbled in disagreement, but eyed her with pride.

The faster of the two, an imposing beast with silver streaks through its shaggy grey hair and an open cut above his left eye, was on them in three long strides, its dark-haired companion soon after. Father and daughter stepped apart to avoid the first assailant. The second had time to adjust its trajectory and collided with Gunn in full stride. Gunn tumbled to the ground with a grunt but managed to roll over and shove himself free of the dark-haired Lycan. He had kept hold of his knife, but when he tried to stand, pain shot up the outside of his leg and he fell to his knees. Realising its mistake, the grey-haired Lycan skidded to a stop and turned on Torry. Swinging her hammer, Torry connected with the Lycan's left shoulder, hard enough to force the beast off balance but not inflict any significant damage. The Lycan stumbled but continued towards her. Torry tried to get to her father, but the harder she tried, the further the Lycan's attack pushed her back. Gunn had managed to get behind his attacker. Still on one knee, he held the Lycan's lower jaw, forcing its head back as it flayed its arms wildly, trying to connect with his flesh. Tiring, Torry was forced farther and farther away from Gunn. The swipes of her hammer connected with their target, but none of them seemed to make any impact on its approach.

Even from his low position, Gunn had gained the upper hand. He slashed at the Lycan's legs. As the beast fell face forward into the dirt, Gunn gave one last swing of his mighty arm. His blade plunging deep and true into its thick hairy neck. Rolling over onto his back, struggling to catch his breath, he looked around desperately for his daughter. She was holding her own, but Torry was now a long way away from him. Gunn tried to get to his feet once more, but his leg just wouldn't hold his weight.

From out of the shadowed tree-line, several metres behind Tory, a third Lycan appeared. Gunn called out to warn Torry. With her damaged left ear facing towards him, she couldn't hear Gunn's voice over the growling and grunting. Yelling and waving his arms, Gunn tried desperately to hobble on his good leg. His injured leg kept wanting to fall under him. He was too slow. The Lycan would get to Torry first, and she had not even seen it approaching. Suddenly, blood exploded from the side of the third Lycan's head. A split second later, a gunshot rang out, echoing across the farm. With a howl, the remaining Lycan turned in fear and ran on all fours to the safety of the dark forest.

Peter Morgan advanced slowly from the corner of the farmhouse. He held his Glock 22 firmly in both hands, stretched out in front. His eyes were wide and his dark face looked a few shades paler than usual. Approaching the body of the monstrous creature lying next to Gunn, he kicked it cautiously. Taking one hand from his weapon but keeping it pointed at the body, he offered Gunn his hand, helping him hobble over to Torry.

'Are you both okay? Peter Morgan asked, looking around cautiously.

'We are now,' Gunn answered. Peter Morgan lowered his weapon, keeping his eyes trained on the tree line where the creature had disappeared.

'Is that one dead?' he motioned behind him. Gunn nodded in agreement. 'And this one too?' Peter Morgan asked, inspecting his handiwork as he and Gunn got closer to the second slain beast.

'Looks pretty dead to me,' Torry said, puffing and wiping blood from her face. 'I think I might've been in trouble if you didn't turn up.' She flopped down on the ground with her legs spread out in front, digging in the dirt with the claw of her hammer.

'Yes, you've done us a solid here, my boy,' Gunn said, patting the detective's back. 'But why are you here?'

'We had a disturbance on the other side of town, and I guessed that this lot were on their way here.' Peter Morgan studied the dead body next to him and wonder if it was his imagination or that it had grown smaller.

'Well, you guessed right lad,' Gunn said, testing some of his weight on his injured leg. 'We're mighty thankful for ya.'

'It's a good thing I purchased some silver bullets too,' Peter Morgan added, tapping his belt with the barrel of his gun. Gunn and Torry looked at each other and laughed.

'They are werewolves, aren't they?' Peter Morgan asked. 'I thought silver bullets were the right thing.'

'You got him right in the brains there, my lad,' Gunn said. 'I dare say you could've killed him with a solid bit of caramel toffee with a shot that good, but yeah, silver did the job.'

'That's just a myth,' Torry said.

'Up until a few moments ago, Miss Kinnard, I thought werewolves were a myth. That is what they are?' Peter Morgan asked.

'Sure are,' Torry said. 'But why did you have silver bullets if you didn't believe in them?'

'Because, Miss Kinnard, I was just following the evidence.'

'You saved my life, you can call me Torry now... Peter. I hope you didn't pay too much for those bullets.'

'I had them custom made by someone in Brookesmarsh.' Peter Morgan said, releasing the clip from his weapon and inspecting the remaining cartridges.

'Well, silver bullets do the trick. But you could have saved yourself some coin, son,' Gunn said, patting Peter Morgan on the back again. Torry stood up and stretched.

'Thank you,' she said, following her father's lead and contributing her own appreciative back patting.

Peter Morgan watched as the lifeless body slowly turned back into its human form. 'Does that always happen?' he asked.

'Yes,' Gunn said, removing his coat and laying it over the body. 'It takes some getting used to.'

'I've never shot someone before,' Peter Morgan said, holstering his weapon with a trembling hand. 'I didn't really think about them being a person.'

'That takes some getting used to as well, lad.' Gunn placed his hand on the young detective's shoulder. 'Are you going to be okay?'

'Yes, I think so. I just don't know how I'm going to explain all this.' Peter Morgan said, looking down at his shaking hands.

'Let's worry about that later.' Gunn said, limping away. 'Right now, I think we could all do with a nice cup of tea.'

Chapter 19

Lost and Found

A firm canvas strap squeaked against the metal rings that held it attached to a heavy satchel. The carry bag bulged and hung weightily under the arduous task of transporting Dom's worldly possessions. Although few, his clothing, black-market identification, and various keepsakes of his travels were more than enough for his one item of luggage. He looked well, much like his old self. He had found much more than he expected that night in the forests near Transylvania. The one the locals called Red Banshee had also treated him far better than he had expected, far better than he deserved, seeing as though he had gone there to kill her. Dom had spent the last week sleeping on crisp clean linen, dining on the finest cuisine of his choosing and enjoying a no expenses spared taste of Romania's exclusive nightlife pleasures. Compared to the life he had been living for the rest of his time away from home, it felt like he had fallen into someone else's life or someone else's dream.

With his new clothes, new shoes, new haircut, and designer sunglasses on his cleanly shaven face, Dom strutted along the streets of Constanta, turning the heads of more than one admiring onlooker. As he approached the Aeroportul International Constanta with its distinct semicircular roofed terminal, he felt a throng of emotions about his return home. And as he always seemed to in times of emotional turmoil, Dom spotted a beautiful woman.

Tall and athletic, a woman with long, toned legs stood next to a shuttle bus. She searched in her bag as travellers and drivers mingled amongst suitcases. A mischievous breeze danced over the sun warmed asphalt and flirted with the woman's summer dress and her long blonde locks. *I have time before the flight*, Dom thought to himself.

With the swagger of a skilled and powerful lion circling his pride, Dom approached the young woman. Stopping a few feet behind her, he checked for signs of attachment. No ring, only one suitcase. She appeared to be alone. He moved in for the kill, standing side on with the woman in the summer dress. As she turned to look at him, he opened his mouth to deliver one of his tried and tested lines. With his new look, how could the poor girl stand a chance? But just as he was about to speak, something about her eyes stopped him. They were green, deep luminous green. They were familiar. They were Cinder's.

'Dom?' Cinder said, frozen on the spot. 'Dom!' she yelled again gleefully, pouncing on him and embracing him to the point of suffocation.

'Hey! Okay, okay, ease up a little,' he said, tapping her on the shoulder.

'Sorry,' she let him go and held onto his hand.

'Hi,' Dom said, lifting his sunglasses to the top of his head and rubbing the back of his neck.

'Hi,' Cinder laughed. 'I can't believe you're here. We were just about to give up looking for you.'

After waiting for a few minutes for an English-speaking assistant at the information desk, Angus now had the departure details for Cinder's jet. Because of a holdup with a previous flight, there would be an hour delay for their flight home. It did not displease Angus to get this news. The longer he could spend with Cinder away from the demands of life back home, the better. He noted the information in his phone and collected his suitcase, wheeling it out of the automatic front doors to where Cinder was waiting for him. The bright afternoon sunlight dazzled his eyes, making it difficult to pick Cinder out in the hustle and bustle. He was also still not used to her blonde hair. On finding her, a sharp flash of jealousy rushed over him. Who was the tall dark stranger in the fancy clothes? And why was Cinder holding his hand with such affection? Realising who the stranger was, Angus let go of his suitcase, dropping it to the ground with a thwack of the extended handle. Leaving the case to fend for itself, he ran towards Dom and Cinder.

A young man in a dark suit stepped in front of Angus. Angus tried to stop, but they collided. The young man was much smaller than Angus, most people were, but he must have seen him coming at the last moment because he was able to step back and lessen the impact.

'Sorry about that, mate,' Angus said, checking that the young man was alright.

'That's fine, my friend,' he said, patting Angus on the back. 'It's my fault. I'm late for my flight.' The young man pulled up his sleeve and tapped his antique gold watch.

'Have a good flight,' Angus said as he kept moving.

Seeing Angus coming, Dom threw his arms in the air.

'Black!' he called out with warm regard. Angus slowed as he approached and pushed Dom's chest with both hands.

'Where the hell have you been?'

'Here and there,' Dom answered with a cheeky grin.

'You couldn't pick up a phone? Send someone a message?' Angus pushed him again.

'Wait, wait, none of that matters,' Cinder interrupted them. 'I have something amazing to tell you. Tor is alive, your sister is alive.'

'Yeah, I know.' Dom said matter-of-factly.

'You what?' Angus asked, pushing him for a third time.

'Stop pushing me and give me a hug,' Dom said, throwing his arms open

'We've been searching all over Europe to find you and tell you,' Angus said, ignoring him. 'How long have you known Tor was alive?'

'A few weeks.'

'Eight months you've been missing, idiot. You didn't think to call us,' Angus continued. Dom shrugged.

'I lost my phone,' Dom said apologetically.

'Idiot,' Angus said again, shaking his head in disbelief.

'Hang on, hang on,' Cinder said, putting her hand on Dom's shoulder. 'If you found out about Tor weeks ago, why didn't you come home then?'

'You know me. I met a girl.'

'So, you stayed here for a girl?' Angus asked, crossing his arms and creasing his forehead. Dom grinned.

'Yep, but it's not what you think. The girl I was staying with knows all about you two. She's the one that told me to come and find you here today.' Dom was enjoying the confused looks on the faces of his two friends. 'You know how you said you had something amazing to tell me? Well, I need to tell you the same thing,' he said, throwing his arm over Angus's shoulder.

'What do you mean?' Angus asked.

'I mean, I need to tell you the same thing. Your sister is alive.'

. . . .

Moss grew thick and green along the edge of a well-worn path. Small quartz rocks reflected the moonlight and crushed under the weight of a pair of sturdy but feminine black boots. Frogs and crickets competed with each other to be the headline act of the evening chorus. A dark figure moved to the side of the path to avoid a puddle, humming a tune into the night. She had long forgotten the words, but the melody was burned into her memory. It was melodic and repetitive but also filled with melancholy and reminded her of long-lost friends. Her long black robe swung about her ankles as it danced in the cool night breeze. As she neared the Kinnard farmhouse, she removed her hood that shadowed her face, revealing long locks of thick, auburn hair.

Someone had been following her for the past five minutes. She walked on, unperturbed. To most, her pursuer would be someone to fear, but to the woman in the robe's old eyes, she was just a child. A child that she was, in fact, looking forward to meeting again. A child that she knew with powerful emotions and by name. A child called Torry.

She stopped in the shadows of the majestic oak trees that towered over the farmhouse in front of her. Puffs of grey smoke rose invitingly from the chimney, warm orange light escaping through gaps in the curtains. The wooden front door swung open. A bearlike man with a shotgun stood silhouetted in the doorway.

'That's far enough.' His booming voice filled the night. Torry moved out from behind a tree, a long hunting knife in both hands.

'Move into the light so we can see you.' She commanded. The lone figure followed the command and stepped into the silver moonlight.

'Hello Uncle Gunn, have you got the kettle on?' she asked. Gunn stumbled backwards, the shotgun dropping to his side. With his free hand, he scribed the symbol of the cross over his chest.

'What's wrong, Dad?' Torry called out, seeing his distress. 'Who is that?'

'That's Katie,' he said. 'That's Black's sister.'

Chapter 20
The Returned

Stray hair flicked around Torry's ears, and gravel crunched under her booted feet. Her quick footsteps echoed off the stone wall as she ran through the shade of the oak trees, back to the main house. Slowing and resting her hands on her hips, she approached her father.

'The car's coming now!' she said between breaths. Gunn stood in the open doorway, his arms crossed over his broad chest and his stoic eyebrows set low over a penetrating gaze. Torry tucked the loose hairs behind her ears and turned to look back along the driveway she had just run down. 'Come on, come on!' she called out as she tapped the front-step of the farmhouse with her heel. She pulled some fluff from her top and looked over her shoulder at her father. 'Jesus dad! Would it hurt you to smile?' Gunn moved his eyes slowly to his daughter. The left corner of his mouth raised half-heartedly to reveal his teeth, then he returned his gaze to the driveway.

'Happy?' he asked.

'Sure,' Torry replied, rolling her eyes

'And don't blaspheme,' Gunn added.

'Sorry,' she said as she started walking back up the driveway. 'Oh my God, they're here!' She yelled, jumping on the spot. Gunn coughed and raised his eyebrows. 'Sorry,' Torry said again.

An imposing looking black SUV with tinted windows turned into the drive. Clouds of orange-grey dust flicked up around the large chrome-rimmed tyres as it drove slowly towards the farmhouse. Spotting a female figure in the back seat, Torry ran up beside the car and tapped desperately on the window. The tinted glass hummed as it glided slowly down. Cinder's hand appeared first, reaching out to take hold of Torry's. Then Torry could see her face. Sun-kissed, freckled nose and cheeks creased with joy and her green eyes large and bright with excitement, Cinder squeezed Torry's hand.

'Hey sis!' she yelled over the sound of the engine and tyres on the gravel. Torry danced and jogged along beside the SUV.

'AH!' was the only response she was able to make.

The car came to a stop a few metres away from the front door to the house. Dom emerged from the front passenger seat, stretching and yawning before throwing his canvas satchel over his shoulder.

'Hey, hey, hey!' he called out, slamming the car door and banging on the roof of the car with his fist. 'The prodigal son has returned.'

Letting go of Cinder's hand, Torry ran around to the front of the vehicle, sliding across the bonnet like an '80s TV detective.

'Great holy, mother!' Dom yelled as Torry jumped into his arms. He stumbled back a few steps as she wrapped her legs around his waist and her arms around his neck. 'Hey how you doin' short stuff?' he asked, kissing the top of her head. Torry mumbled something in reply, but tears muffled it and she had her face buried in his shoulder. Dom wrapped his arm around her and patted her shoulder.

'It's good to see you. I should have known it would take more than a few scratches to stop you,' he said, running his thumb over her scars on the side of her face. Gunn made a gruff, coughing noise at the back of his throat.

'Hey dad,' Dom said as he lowered Torry to the ground. Not wanting to let him go, Torry twisted around under his arm, pushing her face into his back and hugging tightly around his waist. Gunn glowered at his son, his face hard and stern. Pulling a large handkerchief from his hip pocket and shaking it out, he collected his spectacles that had been hanging by one arm from his shirt collar. After breathing hot breath on the lenses, he cocked his head to one side and began to clean the glass. Dom's eyebrows creased together. 'Are you okay, dad?' he asked, pulling awkwardly at the strap on his shoulder.

'Am I okay!?' Gunn's deep voice bellowed as he shoved his spectacles on his face and rolled up his sleeves. '*Am I okay*, he asks.'

'Dad?' Dom asked, as he and Torry took a step back.

'Do you know?... Good for nothin... Piece of slimy rubbish.' Gunn held his clenched fist in front of his face and took long strides towards Dom. 'What... What do you think this is?'

Torry slipped the satchel from Dom's shoulder and, hugging it to her chest, she backed away. Gunn took another step towards Dom, pointing an angry index finger at his face.

'Where was your head, boy?' Dom's mouth opened but none of the words forming in his mind seemed appropriate, so he closed it again and swallowed.

'It's good to be home,' he said finally.

'You good for nothin'. I oughta...' Gunn turned side on to Dom and pulled his fist back. Flinching and raising his hands to protect his face, Dom turned and shot a distressed look at Torry. Torry's face echoed his concern. Gunn lunged forward and embrace his son in his giant powerful arms. Joy, in the form of a single tear, trickled down his wrinkled cheek. 'Don't ever bloody do that again. You hear me? You hear me?' he said in Dom's ear. 'Boy?'

'I hear you,' Dom said, his arms pinned at his sides and his hands at his face. Torry dropped the satchel, ran forward and wrapped her arms around both of them.

Cinder paid the driver and Angus and she both thanked him before they exited the rear doors. Standing on one of the side steps that run along under the doors of the SUV, Cinder looked over the roof of the vehicle at the three united family members. Torry grinned and wriggled with excitement. Cinder smiled back and gave her a wink before hopping down to the ground. Angus had begun to unload their luggage. 'Isn't that sweet?' Cinder said as she came to help him with her bag.

'What?' Angus asked, looking up.

'Them.' Cinder pointed to Dom, Gunn, and Torry.

'Oh, yep. Sweet.'

'Are you with us, Black?' Cinder asked, placing her hand on his shoulder and turning him so she could look him in the eyes.

'What? Yep, they're sweet.'

'You said that already,' Cinder said, gently squeezing his bicep. 'Are you okay?' she asked with a laugh.

'Hey? Yeah, yeah. All good,' Angus replied, returning his focus to unloading the luggage. Torry skipped over to Cinder and Angus

'I'll take those. You should go inside,' she said to Angus, taking hold of the bags. Once she had a good grip on the handles, she leaned forward on to her toes and kissed the side of his face.

'Welcome back. Thanks for finding the idiot.'

'Hey Tor,' Angus said, putting his arm around her shoulders. 'He kind of found us in the end.'

'I'm glad we're all back where we should be.' Cinder said. Torry hoisted another bag from the ground and motioned with her head towards the farmhouse.

'Off you go then,' she said to Angus. Angus took a deep breath and let it out slowly.

'I, um. I'll come back for these,' he said, rubbing his hand through his thick black hair and taking a step back.

'We've got the bags,' Cinder patted him on the back. 'You just go.'

Setting his shoulders back, Angus walked slowly towards the house. Stopping just outside of the door, he wiped his palms on the hem of his shirt and looked back at Cinder. 'Go,' she mouthed and smiled reassuringly. With one more run of his hand through his hair, Angus stepped inside.

• • • •

The blinds in the family room were yet to be opened to the morning sunlight. The fireplace crackled, warm and inviting, and cast an orange glow in the otherwise dark room. Angus breathed in the familiarity of home. Usually, his first port of call would have been the fire, where he would stand warming his hands behind him. Today, however, Angus stopped, swaying gently from side to side like he had suddenly stepped onto the deck of a ship. A young woman with long red hair pulled back in a ponytail sat in Uncle Gunn's recliner. She sat with her legs tucked beside her, as she looked at the fire across the top of a mug of coffee pressed to her lips. Angus recognised that she was in a pair of Torry's pyjamas. Noticing Angus enter, she placed the beverage on the table next to her.

'Hello Angus,' she said warmly, in a voice far more mature than Angus was expecting.

'Is it really you?' He didn't need to ask. She looked different from how he remembered. Older, of course, but the fact that she looked like the perfect mix between him and their mother was unquestionable.

'Yes and no,' she replied.

'Katie?'

'Yes and no,' she said again. 'Are you going to come into the room, Angus?'

'I don't understand,' he said, taking a step forward.

'It will all make sense in time, but for now, come closer and let me see you.' She stood up and held her arms open, beckoning him forward. Angus stumbled into the room and fell to his knees in front of her, wrapping his arms around her waist.

'I've missed you every day,' he said between sobs. His powerful shoulders rising and falling in shudders.

'I've missed you too, big brother,' Katie said, running her hands through his hair. Angus dried his face with his sleeve.

'But you died,' he said, looking up into her glassy eyes.

'Yes. Yes, I did.'

Chapter 21
The Daughter

Gunn placed a fresh log on the fire, sending sparks flying and crackling up the chimney. Grunting, he pulled himself up from his knees, holding the mantle to steady himself. Torry approached him with two mismatched, steaming mugs.

'Here you go, dad,' she said, handing him one.

'Thanks, princess,' Gunn said, taking a sip and sitting on his recliner. Cinder, Angus, and Dom entered the family room, holding their own mugs. Last of all, Katie followed them in. All eyes followed her as she moved to stand in front of the fire.

'I guess I need to explain some things,' she said, looking around and noticing all eyes focused on her.

'That would be good.' Cinder said, taking a seat next to Torry.

'Only if you're ready,' Angus added, standing next to Katie.

'Yes,' Katie said. 'It's time.' She sat her drink on the mantle and stared into the dancing flames. 'I am Catherine, your sister,' she said, gesturing towards Angus. 'But,' she paused. 'I am also Sase, a centuries-old vampire.'

'You're what?' Cinder said, standing up and spilling some of her tea. Angus moved in front of her. Dom had been standing in the entranceway to the family room but took a step back towards the kitchen, eyeing a knife on the bench.

'What the hell did you just say?' he demanded.

'It's okay,' Katie said. 'I'm not my brothers.' She held her hands up in front of her submissively, trying to reassure Cinder.

'I'll decide what's okay,' Cinder said, her nostrils flaring as she pushed against Angus. Katie dropped her head submissively.

'I know what they have done to your family and to many other families like yours. I am like them in some ways, but in many ways, I am the opposite and I'm repulsed by their actions.'

'You didn't tell me that back in Romania,' Dom grumbled, taking another side-step towards the kitchen bench. 'You told me that the Red Banshee saved you. You didn't say anything about being a blood sucking monster.'

'Let her speak boy,' Gunn interrupted, raising his arm and holding his palm towards Dom. Torry sat still and straight, her eyes flashing from everyone in turn. She felt like the smoky air in their little house had grown thick and suffocating.

'Why? So she can tell us more lies,' Dom asked. 'I shared a hotel room with her, for God's sake.'

'I'm sorry, Dom.' Katie sent him an apologetic smile that looked very innocent on her childish face. 'What I told you was true. I am Katie and I was saved by the Red Banshee.'

'You never told me anything about also being a vampire.' Dom crossed his arms over his chest, pulling his shoulders up to protect his neck.

'How can you be both?' Angus asked, as he gestured for Cinder to take her seat again.

'Get her out of here, Black,' she whispered in his ear, as she reluctantly stepped back and took her seat. She glared with fierce intensity at the vampire. Watching every move as Katie continued her story.

'Like you, Cinder, I was the daughter of a Lycan queen. I was the youngest child of Vlad the Third, ruler of Walachia and the Queen Leeanna, his first wife. We were royalty, but not treated as such. In fact, we were treated less kindly than our father's animals. My mother was kept in chains, my five brothers and I, the product of her body being used for his violent and perverse entertainment. From the very beginning, it was obvious that my brothers were different. Their porcelain-fair skin would blister in the sun, so they were kept locked in dark holes. When angered, their faces would contort and deform. They were born with mouths full of teeth, teeth that would become elongated and sharpened when they were provoked. My father's men would poke them with pointed sticks for entertainment. Their only food was the unfortunate creatures that found their way into their holes or the blood and bones of my father's many enemies.'

'I differed from my brothers. As an infant, I appeared just like every other child. I was allowed to stay with my mother, and with her help, I was able to hide what I really was. I could move around in the daylight and with my mother's love and protection, I kept my powers concealed. As my brothers grew, they became stronger and more dangerous. Their pain in the daylight also increased, so they never saw the sun. They would be dragged out of their pits at night, chained like hounds, used as weapons in my father's conquests.'

'Staying with my mother allowed me to know love, to feel the reassurance of her voice and the soft touch of her kindness, a kindness that my brothers were never shown. They knew nothing of love. Their world was one of persecution, violence, darkness, and blood. I stayed hidden. The only sign of being different was that I stayed younger for longer, sparing me from my father's gaze. When I finally moved out of childhood and grew into a young woman, my father's attention shifted from my mother, who had lost much of her strength when I was born. One night, he forwent my mother's body and found his way into my bed. In her attempts to stop him, my mother was killed. Years of anger and hiding erupted inside me. In my anger, I broke my chains and freed myself. My father escaped my vengeance that night, but many of his men did not. Bathed in blood, I freed my brothers from their holes, and we left together.'

'Why would you take them with you?' Cinder asked indignantly.

'They were my family. I didn't know what they were capable of then, what they were going to become. I tried to show them the love my mother had shown me, but they had too much of my father in them. They had seen too much hatred and violence. Above all else, they desired power over others. When they came to realise that I was different, they turned on me. I was always the strongest, but I could not contend against them all. I disappeared, made myself a nobody. I lived in the smallest houses in the smallest places. I knew they would seek glory, power, and riches, so I stayed away from those things. Many years passed, but as I had in my youth, I stayed unnaturally young. My adolescent years stretching on for many decades. As people's suspicions grew, I needed to move on; only able to stay in one place for short periods of time. I tried to avoid my brothers, but I would hear rumours. Sometimes I would come across their victims. There were many stories of their cruelty and destruction.' Katie looked up at the faces around the room. Mostly, they looked on with interest. Cinder, still propped on the edge of her seat, looked incredulous.

'It's your fault,' she spat. 'You let them out.'

'Cinder!' Angus tried to shut her down.

'What?' she said, getting up. 'She did,' she added, marching out of the room. Dom gave her a wink as she swept past him.

'She's got a point, mate,' he said, turning back to Angus.

'Not you too.'

'Well, she has.' Dom added, as he sat down in the seat next to Torry that Cinder had just left.

'It's okay,' Katie said, resting her hand on Angus's shoulder. 'They are allowed to feel how they feel.'

Gunn tapped tobacco residue from his pipe into a small dish atop the coffee table beside him.

'Keep going, love,' he said, slipping the pipe into his breast pocket. Katie watched as Cinder slammed her empty mug down on the kitchen bench and took a seat at the table. Their eyes connected as Katie continued with her tale.

'After I had been moving through this world for many centuries, only then did I begin to feel old age creeping into my body. I wondered if the death I was seeing all around me would one day catch up with me. Some days I wished for it. The answer came from a news bearer that I had not expected. One humid summer night as I explored the dark streets of Paris. I was reunited with Doi, my second oldest brother. He seemed different from how I remembered, obviously much older and frail, but he almost greeted me with friendship, something that he had not done since we escaped our father. He brought news that our oldest brother, Unu, had died and not at the hands of one of his many victims. He had just simply not risen from his dark bed one evening. It was the first time that we were really aware of our mortality.' Katie paused, noticing Cinder rising from the table and moving slowly back towards the family room. Katie turned her back to the others, leaning on the mantle.

'That night, however, I learned of the new depths of my brother's cruelty. Doi explained how they had forced captives to drink their blood. First draining them of their own until they hung on the edge of existence. In extreme levels of pain, they would become desperate for the blood of the vampire and my brothers would feed them.' Katie's voice fell to a whisper.

'What you need to understand about vampires and about blood is that what we find so delicious is blood's ability to pass on memories, thoughts, knowledge, and emotions.' She turned and looked at Angus.

'You see, my brothers were draining people of their very existence.' Her voice grew louder again. 'Then filling them with their own hatred and malice and pain. My brothers called them Postea, the things that came afterwards.' She turned to the others.

'Imagine the horror of feeling life drained from your body, to then wake, and find someone else in your brain. Someone that had pushed out all your happiness to fit in there. Then imagine suddenly being filled with centuries of hate and torture and self-loathing. An adult brain couldn't handle the pain. Their victims would literally rip themselves apart, tearing out their own hair, flesh, eyes; anything to try to pull the evil out of their minds. My brother Patru was the first one cruel enough to experiment with children.'

'I met him,' Cinder said.

'How unfortunate for you,' Katie said. 'He is the vilest of them all.'

'Those poor kids,' Torry said, hanging on every word.

'What Patru did not realise until it was too late,' Katie continued, 'was that he had created a small version of himself. He kept it as something of a pet, using it to entertain my other brothers. It grew older, stronger, and more cunning. One night while Patru slept, it killed him and took his place. Eventually, my brothers saw this as a way of obtaining true immortality. They could pass on all their knowledge and power to their Postea. They treated them like their children until they were old enough to kill off their fathers.'

Cinder was now leaning against the wall at the entrance to the family room, her arms crossed.

'You must have done that to children too,' she said, failing to hide her disgust with the idea.

'I'm sure it wasn't like that,' Angus said, frowning at Cinder.

'I was almost 400 years old when I created my first Postea,' Katie said. 'I could feel death around each corner, creeping just out of sight in the ever-growing shadows around me. A plague had come to Romania, killing old, young, rich, and poor indiscriminately. Unlike my brothers, I had chosen to live among the common people and serve my neighbours as a midwife. I had no children of my own, but I had been present when dozens of them came into the world. A message came from a village two hours' ride from my home. I rushed but arrived too late. All I found was death or those fast approaching it. The mother to be was in the last stages of labour and of life, blood flowing freely from anywhere it could. I ripped the dying child from its mother's womb. As I took the child in my arms, it struggled desperately to take its first and last breaths. I realised hers was the one life in that entire village that I could save. She became my daughter that day, taking her first drink not from my breast but from my vein. Throughout the years, I have found myself new daughters. Only choosing children who would not survive otherwise.'

Cinder pushed herself off the wall and walked out the front door, leaving it open behind her. Torry followed quickly behind, tapping Angus's arm reassuringly on her way past.

'Are you okay?' Torry Asked when she caught up with Cinder.

'No, I'm not okay, not okay at all.' Cinder kicked at the orange gravel of the driveway.

'It's a lot to take in, isn't it?' Torry asked.

'I'm glad that Black has his sister back, but all I can think about is the vampire that killed my father. At least I was able to reassure myself that it died at the same time. But now I hear that they make these copies. It could still be out there somewhere, still doing horrible things to more people.'

Inside the farmhouse, Sase, the vampire inhabiting the body of Angus's sister Catherine, turned a moon pendant over inside her pocket. The pendant that she had ripped from the neck of her brother Patru.

Chapter 22
Queen of the Night

Now that Dom was back, Angus offered him their old bedroom. Cinder and Angus moved their things into the guesthouse, a situation that Cinder was happy to oblige. It was nice for them to have a space of their own with a lock on the front door. Cinder loved Torry like a little sister, but there were times when a couple didn't want a little sister walking in on them. The feminine touches in the guesthouse, left over from Torry's aunts, created a homely feel that was preferable to the broken surfboards, bikini girl posters, and dusty books of Dom and Angus's room. Most of all, Cinder was excited about the idea of no longer needed to share a bathroom. Boys, she had discovered, had a different opinion than her about acceptable levels of bathroom hygiene. As comfortable as Cinder was with the new sleeping arrangements, sleep eluded her.

That first night after meeting Sase, (everyone except Cinder was calling her Katie) Angus had fallen into a deep sleep almost immediately. Cinder lay next to him, looking up at the ceiling, listening to deep comfortable breathing. She tried to convince herself that her insomnia was because of jetlag. *Of course I can't sleep*, she told herself. *It would be the middle of the day in Europe at the moment.* She played with the ends of Angus's thick hair, Happy that he could sleep so soundly, *happy?* Yes, she was happy. She gave his hair a tug and Angus grunted and flicked his hand across his face as if he was drunkenly swatting at a fly. Cinder crossed her arms and breathed out a long sigh. Pulling the pillows from under her head, she threw them to the floor. Angus's breathing grew in intensity. When it crossed the border from breathing to snoring, Cinder threw her side of the quilt over him and stormed to the ensuite. On her return, she collected the moon pendant from the bedside table and a blanket from the wardrobe, closing the wardrobe door more firmly than she needed. Angus rolled over, mumbled something, and went back to his deep breathing.

Pulling her boots out from under the bed, a great ensemble with her silky blue pyjamas, Cinder went outside. She wrapped the blanket around her shoulders and sat on the porch. The night air was cold on her face and hands, but not uncomfortable. In fact, the chill, combined with the familiar smells of forest and ocean, was invigorating. Cinder looked lovingly around at her new home as she pulled her boots on. Sheets of translucent white clouds slipped silently across the waning moon. Silver beams of light fell across Cinder's chilled face. Power, like small sparks of electricity, shot throughout her body. The hair on the back of her neck and arms tingled and stood on end. She gripped her pendant tightly as it worked its magic to hold back any changes. The chain felt cold as she hung it around her neck, but her hand had warmed the moon-stone. With her boots on and the blanket wrapped around her, she ventured out into the night.

Cinder meandered aimlessly across open fields and along the tracks, eventually finding herself in the forest. A sense of familiarity twinged in the recesses of her mind. When the forest thinned and the canopy opened up, moonlight flooded over her body once more. The tree line stopped suddenly, a few metres back from a long drop. As she had done months ago when she had come here with Angus, Cinder walked cautiously to the edge. Leaning over, she could see a wall of smooth rock that fell at a slight angle, down to the continuing forest below. Moss, grass, and blackberries sprouted from the cracks between the rocks that gleamed in the silver light, polished clean by weather and the flow of water. The coastal lights that she once compared to the night sky twinkled and glowed in the ripples of the distant ocean.

Unwrapping herself from the blanket and draping it over her shoulders, Cinder walked along the edge of Vivien's Ridge. Arms out at her side, one foot in front of the other, like someone walking a tightrope. It was cold to be out in the open in just her sleepwear and boots, but Cinder was enjoying how awake it was making her feel. An ocean breeze rolled and rustled through the branches of the trees below, tumbling towards her. Colliding with the boundary of stone and dirt, the movement of air rushed up the embankment, rumbling in her ears and sending wispy tendrils of her hair into the air. A thrill of adrenaline coursed through her as she was almost knocked off balance, but she continued on her tightrope walk to the large trunk of a fallen tree. The last time she was here, she and Angus had laid together on this tree looking at the sky. She grinned to herself, remembering how that was the most intimate interaction that she had had with a man up to that point; unless you counted standing naked in front of her stepmother's friends, and she didn't. Approaching the fallen tree from this angle, she could see that the top section lay smashed amongst the growth of the valley below.

Reaching the tree, Cinder ran her hands along the grey trunk with reminiscent affection. The ancient timber felt hard, cold, and smoothed by time, evoking memories of touching Angus's skin for the first time. Cinder slid the blanket from around her neck and draped it over the trunk. She climbed on, laying on her back to look up at the stars. A moment later, she sat up again as a thought took shape. Untying her boots, she sat them carefully on the trunk next to her and slid down from the tree, feeling the cool moist grass between her toes. Checking that nobody was watching, Cinder slipped out of her pyjamas, placing them neatly on the blanket before wrapping them up. She sat her boots on top of the blanket and then looked around her again. She decided that the only eyes watching her would be those of noisy frogs, bats, and other small creatures of the night. Her body exploded with a covering of goose-bumps as the chilly night air rushed over her naked body and the electrifying beams of light flooded her skin. Lastly, she took off the moon pendant from around her neck and pushed it deep inside her boots. Instantly, her body began to increase in size and the hair on her arms, legs, and back grew long and coarse. Her bright green eyes grew larger, cat like. Sharp teeth like thick bone-needles formed in her mouth as her jaw and nose jutted forward into a snout. Long, black claws pushed their pointed way from the ends of her fingers and toes. When her transformation was complete, she ran.

Her body flooding with joy, freedom, and power. She ran deeper into the forest. Jumping rocks and sliding under branches, she increased her speed with every stride. Breaking her way through to a clearing, Cinder stood tall in all her Lycanthrope magnificence, arms stretched out, soaking up the power of the moon. She turned three full circles, bathing in the silver magical glow. She paused, howled, then she ran on. Running on all fours, she crashed through the undergrowth back towards Vivien's Ridge. Soon she found herself in the open again, running along the edge of the forest. The sound of water trickling over rocks made her aware of the creek running gently through the thick grass on her left-hand side. Her keen Lycan eyes spotted the tree she was looking for. She skidded to a halt on the moist ground. Standing tall again, she lent one of her giant, paw-like hands against the tree trunk. Slowly and carefully, she scratched a love heart shape around the initials that she and Angus had carved there in the summer. After stepping back to admire her handiwork, she ran joyfully back into the forest.

• • • •

Back at Vivien's Ridge, four shadows crept along the tree line. A dark figure moved forward, the moonlight shining off a pair of dark eyes. Its coat of thick grey and white fur bristled as it sniffed frantically along the edge of the forest. Picking up a familiar scent, it growled approvingly, low and rumbling. Two of the others moved from the darkness of the trees. As a group, they followed the trail along the cliff's edge that Cinder had walked earlier that night. With their moist noses to the ground, they walked in single file. Finding their way to the fallen tree, they scurried around, rubbing themselves excitedly against the trunk. All three of the beasts rose onto their back legs, placing their front paws on the fallen tree. They sniffed desperately and excitedly at the pile of clothes, boots, and blanket. A howl from their fourth companion, still hidden in the shadows, sent them all scurrying on all fours back into the protection of the forest.

Cinder the Powerful, Cinder the Lycan Queen, Cinder the Free, ran with joy and peace through shrubs, low hanging tree branches. Her large fur-covered feet stomped in the mud and crunched dry leaves and twigs. Long orange hair and fur danced and ruffled in the breeze. Moonlight penetrating through gaps in the canopy of the dark forest dappled her body, sending shivers of transformative energy and exhilaration to her extremities. She slowed, feeling a twinge at the base of her spine. With the sudden feeling that she wasn't alone, she stood tall on her hind legs, sniffing the air. Puffs of warm misty air rushed from between her sharp canine-like teeth. Her ears turned from side to side as her moist nose twitched. Picking up on a familiar scent, she stopped between the trunks of two tall and straight pines, the scented needles brushing against her hairy shoulders. Ahead, a grassy embankment declined gradually to a small clearing. The long-forgotten remnants of a timber fence ran off into the darkness to her right. Grey posts crumbled, rotting, and overgrown with thick tufts of grass and twisting blackberry tendrils. In the shadows on the far side of the clearing, branches rustled and swayed with the back-and-forth movement of unseen things. Cinder lowered her head and looked from side to side, peering into the dark. Even with her Lycan eyes, she could only see outlines of the dark objects beyond the clearing, but instinctively, she knew what they were. She walked down into the clearing and stood in the moonlight. The air grew cooler and thick with the scent of damp, rich soil.

'Come into the light,' she commanded in a deep, raspy voice. Four sets of teeth and pairs of large eyes appeared at the edge of the clearing, glowing in the silver light. Cinder clenched her oversized fists.

'Show yourself,' she said, followed by a growl that rose from deep in her chest.

Emerging slowly from the tree line, a large hairy creature walked tentatively forward on its long sinewy hind legs. When it was just out of Cinder's reach, it bowed its head and stooped down on all fours, lowering its face to the ground. Shortly after, three more creatures came and stood behind the first, also dropping their heads. The hair of the smallest one bristled in the moonlight as it trembled in fear. Cinder surveyed the four Lycan prostrate in front of her. Stepping forward, she reached her open hand towards the closest one. Raising its head and tilting it to one side, the first Lycan looked cautiously up at her face. A long, moist tongue slid from between its sharp teeth, gently licking the palm of Cinder's outstretched hand. Smiling, Cinder rested her hand on the Lycan's warm shoulder. Reaching out her other hand, the remaining three came forward. Keeping their heads respectfully bowed, one by one, they licked the palm of their queen.

'Go now, and stay out of mischief,' Cinder said. The quartet backed away slowly before turning and scurrying away once more into the darkness. Cinder could hear them hooting and howling with excitement. The Lycan queen listened as their chorus grew slowly, more and more distant. With her head tilted back to look up at the moon, Cinder threw her shoulders back and let out a great throaty howl. Far away she heard the others respond with their own acknowledging call. Stretching out her long, powerful arms, she turned slowly in the silver lunar glow. She bathed in the power that tingled down her hairs into her flesh, then coursed through her veins.

Returning to where she had left her clothes, Cinder retrieved the moon pendant from inside her boots. Hanging it over her neck, the cold of the night slowly crept in as the layer of auburn hair receded. A cool burning sensation ran up her spine and tingled down her body, like bathing in menthol. As the tingling calmed, her body returned to its usual shape and size. She reached for her clothing, sitting undisturbed in a pile on the fallen tree. With her underwear in hand, she paused, then decided to place the clothing back on the log. She lay with her back on the cold trunk, remembering the night she had shared here with Angus. Once again, she looked up at the stars. It was now long after midnight. The moon's rays washing over her flesh tingled like thousands of tiny needle points, but a magic that she didn't quite understand held the transformative power at bay. When she concentrated, she could feel the opposing forces running up and down her body. Stretching out her arms and closing her eyes, she listened to the night-time chorus of nocturnal beasts. Swirling breezes rushed through the leaves above her and also down in the valley below. There was something else, something closer. Her eyes shot open.

With a cough, a human figure stepped from the shadows at the far end of Vivien's Ridge. Cinder rolled off the opposite side of the log, pulling her clothes with her. She hugged her clothes to her chest and knelt beside the log.

'Don't let me disturb you. By all means, continue.' Cinder recognised Dom's smart-mouthed tone.

'Dom!' she yelled 'Why are you here?'

'Oh, you know, I was out patrolling. Old habits die hard, I guess.' Dom took a step closer.

'That's close enough,' Cinder said. Dom crossed his arms and swayed slowly side to side, a boyish grin on his face.

'What are you doing out here anyway?' he asked.

'I just couldn't sleep. I felt like I wanted to go for a run.'

'In your birthday suit?' Dom asked, standing on his toes and peering over the log. Cinder carefully removed one of her hands from her protective clothing and pointed to the moon.

'The other *me* was going for a run, if you know what I mean.'

'I see,' Dom said, taking another step forward.

'Alright, just stop there,' Cinder said, turning sideways to keep her naked back out of Dom's sight. 'I'm going to get dressed now. You need to turn around.'

'I'll cover my eyes,' Dom said, placing his hands over his face and spreading his fingers apart so that his eyes were still visible.

'Turn around!' Cinder made a circular motion with her index finger.

'Okay then,' Dom said, turning around slowly, keeping his eyes on Cinder as long as he could. When his back was to her, Cinder stood up and hurriedly put her underwear back on.

'So, what do you think of our visitor? *Sase* or *Katie*, or whatever she calls herself.' Dom asked.

'She has some interesting stories,' Cinder replied, pulling her pyjama top over her head.

'Very interesting,' Dom agreed, fighting the urge to peek over his shoulder. 'I don't trust her, though,' he added. Cinder paused, one foot inside her pyjama pants.

'I don't trust her either,' she said, looking over at Dom.

'I've seen what she's capable of and she could wipe us all out if she wanted.'

'You can turn around now,' Cinder said, collecting her boots and sitting on the fallen tree. Dom turned and dropped his shoulders.

'But now the fun bits over,' he complained. Cinder shot him a '*be serious*' look.

'I'm sure there are more exciting things to look at than my freckly, pale body,' she said, as she pulled on her boots. Dom looked up at the sky, tapping his finger against his chin as he walked towards the fallen tree.

'Nothing better springs to mind,' he said, sitting down next to her. Cinder retrieved a few stray locks of hair that were caught in the neckline of her top and pulled her hair into a ponytail.

'What can we do about Sase?' she asked.

'Nothing. Not without pissing off Black, anyway.'

'He's so happy to have his sister back.'

'And I get that. I know how that feels, but I think he doesn't see what she really is.'

'What do you think she really is?'

'Dangerous.'

'I'm glad you say that,' Cinder said, placing her hand on Dom's shoulder, 'because that's how I feel too.' Dom patted her hand and then stood again, walking to the edge of the ridge to look out at the ocean

'But hey,' he said, turning to look back at Cinder. 'I felt that way about you, too. And now look, we're having heart talks and a naked night-time rendezvous.' Cinder pushed herself up from the tree and strolled over to Dom.

'If you tell anyone about this, I'll kill you,' Cinder said, looking out at the forest below. Dom turned to her with a very serious look on his face.

'If anyone ever finds out that I was in the dark with a hot, naked woman and all we did was talk about our... *feelings*,' he paused. 'I'll kill myself.'

• • • •

Angus's eyes twitched behind closed eyelids. He breathed deep, rhythmic breaths. The door to the guest house creaked open, sending soft silver light across the unoccupied side of Cinder and Angus's bed. A silhouetted figure stepped into the doorway. Angus mumbled to himself and rolled over to shield his face against the moonlight in the cold air. The dark figure walked forward into the room, footsteps barely audible on the timber floor. Approaching the bed, the figure stopped, paused, and then retraced its steps back to the doorway. With one hand on the open door, the night-time visitor sniffed the air.

'You can come out Cinder, I know you're there. We should talk anyway.' Cinder could not see her face in the shadows but recognised Sase's voice.

'Why are you wandering around at night?' She called out, stepping from the shadows of the oak trees across the yard from the guest house.

'I could ask you the same thing,' Sase said, looking her up and down. 'I don't sleep at night, one of the hangovers of being a vampire. I can be out in the daylight, but it's painful.' She looked back into the guest house. Cinder had once again wrapped herself in the blanket. She hitched it up with her shoulders and jogged across the yard. Her loosely tied boots flopped against her bare ankles.

Sase squinted, running her eyes up and down Cinder's body. Cinder pulled the blanket more tightly around her body.

'What are you looking at?' she asked when she reached the guesthouse

'Everything. I can see much better at night.'

'Do you sleep in a coffin?' Cinder teased.

'No, do you eat grandmothers and hunt little girls in red capes?' Sase retorted, looking Cinder up and down again.

'You're getting werewolves and Lycan confused,' Cinder said, pushing her way past Sase and into the guest house. 'Don't worry, it's a common misconception.'

'I'm not worried. I know exactly what you are.'

'What brings you to *my* doorway, anyway?' Cinder asked, pulling off the blanket and bundling it up in her crossed arms.

'I just like to watch him sleep.' They both turned to look at Angus, his face calm and still as his chest rose and fell. Cinder threw the blanket on to the bed, and moved across Sase's view of Angus, placing her hand on the open door.

'I'm not sure how things work in the world of vampires, but in normal society, watching grown men sleep is creepy,' she said as she tried to close the door. Sase turned and rested her back against the doorjamb so that the door could not close all the way. For the third time, she gave Cinder a strange look.

'Are you having a sexual relationship with my brother?'

'Am I what?' Cinder asked, incredulously.

'Are you being physically intimate with Angus? It's a simple question.' Sase said. Cinder squeezed through the door. The hinges protested loudly.

'Angus is so happy to have you back. I'm sure that he would be happy to answer all of your *simple* questions.'

'Are you happy that I'm here?' Sase asked, looking from Cinder to Angus.

'Ecstatic,' Cinder replied.

'I see.'

'Do you though?'

'Words can be laced with sugar and spice and drip with the nectar of diplomacy, but our actions are the highway of the soul; open for all emotions to travel freely,' Sase said, turning back to Cinder and tapping her fingernails against the outside of the guesthouse.

'I don't know what you're talking about,' Cinder said, her lips thinning against her teeth. Sase studied the freckles on her cheeks before looking directly into her eyes.

'I think you do,' Sase said. 'Out of everyone, I think you are the one that understands the most.' Cinder held her gaze and shrugged.

'I don't understand keeping secrets from people you say you love, or letting them think you're dead.'

'One day you will learn that some secrets are our greatest acts of love.'

'Maybe I'll learn all sorts of things tomorrow. Perhaps I should get some sleep, so I'm ready. Good night, Sase.' Cinder closed the door further. Sase didn't move.

'You don't like me, do you?' she asked. Cinder rolled her eyes.

'I don't know you. All I know is that Angus was fine without you and he'll be fine when you're gone.'

'Gone?'

'Yes, gone. I'm sure this is all very boring for an immortal being like yourself. I'm sure you have other important business to take care of.'

'What would be more important than being with my family?' Sase asked. Cinder laughed.

'I don't know, coffin shopping, blood bank withdrawals. Whatever important things have kept you away for the past dozen or so years.' Cinder spat and motioned with her hand for Sase to move out of the doorway.

'I think I might need to stay around and keep my eye on you.' Sase said, stepping slowly from the doorway.

'You had better keep both eyes on me. Because I'm sure as hell going to be watching you.'

'As you should,' Sase said with a smile. 'Goodnight, Cinder.'

'Goodnight, Sase. Always a pleasure.' Cinder shut the door in her face.

Chapter 23
The Rumours of My Death.

Cinder had seen some amazing places during her travels with Angus, but she had forgotten how beautiful Heathcote was in the spring, life waking from the winter, fresh and green. This was the first time she had seen the farm in all its pre-summer beauty. The rolling green hills with their fresh, lush covering. Bees, heavy with deposits of pollen collected from bidens and other wildflowers that spotted the paddocks with yellows, whites, and pinks. Fragrant lavender growing in patches along the stone walls. Their long purple heads swaying in the warming breeze. Butterflies, fresh from their cocoons, fluttered about, showing off their brand-new colourful wings.

Volcanic, brown rocks felt warm against Cinder's legs where they had been soaking up the afternoon sun. She sat atop the stone wall adjacent to the front entrance, watching the movements of the world. A skink scurried out of a crack, also taking advantage of the warmth. Its silvery-brown skin camouflaged well against the rocks but glistened smoothly in the sunlight.

'Hello there,' Cinder said, watching it lying perfectly still. 'Lovely afternoon, isn't it?' A large shadow fell across the skink's sunbathing spot and it retreated to its hiding place inside the wall.

'Who are you talking to?' Angus asked as he approached from behind her.

'No one now,' Cinder said, grabbing a handful of lavender and throwing it at him. The purple flowers dissipated, carried off in the breeze well before they came anywhere near Angus. Their perfume, however, hung in the air and Angus sniffed it in.

'Did you just hurl a lavender missile at me?'

'Yes,' Cinder replied, crossing her arms. 'And I wish it hit you.'

'What did I do?'

'I was making friends with a lizard and you scared it away.'

'Please forgive me.' Angus said, holding his hand against his chest and sitting next to her.

'I don't know if I can,' Cinder said, resting her head on his shoulder. 'It might have been the beginning of a beautiful friendship.'

'I guess we'd better sit here for a bit and see if it comes back then.' Angus placed a warm hand on Cinder's leg. 'Why are you out here by yourself, anyway?'

'I'm just enjoying the sun and I was trying to give you some time with your sister.'

'I want you to spend time with her, too. I want the two of you to be friends.'

'I will,' Cinder said, sitting up straight. 'You two need some time first, I think.'

'I still can't believe she's back. It's amazing, she's amazing.'

'She definitely has some amazing stories.' Cinder said, her mouth smiling but her eyes staying fixed on the spot where the skink had been sitting.

'Are you okay?' Angus asked

'Yep, I'm good,' Cinder tried unsuccessfully to sound convincing.

'Alright what's going on?' Angus asked. 'I thought you would be happy for me.'

'I am happy for you,' Cinder said, picking another lavender sprig and holding it to her nose. 'I just think you should be careful.'

'What do I need to be careful about?' Angus asked, moving his shoulder out from under her head. 'She's my little sister,' he added. Cinder laughed.

'Oh yeah, she's all innocent and sweet.'

'What's that supposed to mean?' Angus said, standing up. Cinder shuffled back on the stone wall.

'I'm just worried that all you can see is Katie and not Sase. I literally had warnings from beyond the grave about someone coming.'

'Well, I think all you can see is a vampire, so you're not willing to give her a chance.' Angus said, his arms crossed, and his voice raised.

'I gave her a chance and I think she's strange, dangerous even.' Cinder said, standing up in front of him.

'I agree she's a bit odd,' Angus said, moving his shoulders back. 'She's been through a lot.'

'Yeah, like hundreds of years of stuff,' Cinder scoffed.

'I don't mean Sase, I mean Katie. She watched our parents die. You never know what that could do to a little girl.' Angus said. Cinder's jaw dropped, then she closed her mouth tight and dropped her head to one side.

'And I wouldn't know anything about that, would I?' she yelled. For the second time, she threw a sprig of lavender at him. This time, it hit its target, striking Angus's left cheek. Cinder turned to walk away.

'Cin, wait,' Angus reached for her. 'I'm sorry. Just come back and sit down.'

'No, I need to be alone,' she said, pushing his hand away and storming off.

Cinder walked away from the main house towards the milking shed. The afternoon sun warmed her back. With her arms crossed and her chin set forward by her clenched mouth, she stomped heavily through the lush grass of the green paddock.

'Where are you going in such a hurry, sweetie?' a familiar voice called out from behind her.

'Marraine!' Cinder ran back to embrace her godmother, resting a troubled head on her welcoming shoulder. 'Where have you been? I haven't heard anything from you in weeks,' she asked. 'I was starting to worry.'

'I've been dead, actually.' Marraine said, stroking Cinder's blonde locks.

'You've what?' Cinder pulled her head up in concern. Marraine, seeing the fear and confusion on Cinder's flushed face, flashed her a mischievous grin.

'I pretended to be dead to get *her ladyship* off my back. I had some things I wanted to do with her out of the way.'

'What things?'

'I've received some leads on more of these.' Marraine unbuttoned her shirt to reveal her moon pendant.

'You found another one?'

'No, but I'm getting close. In the past, when I've got this close, *her ladyship* has gotten in my way. This time I decided to set up a distraction first.' She pulled Cinder in again and squeezed her tight.

'So, you faked your own death? That's crazy.' Cinder whispered, pushing her face against Marraine's.

'Oh well,' Marraine said, shrugging and fluttering her eyelids. 'Sometimes you need to fight crazy with crazy. But that's enough about me.' She moved Cinder in front of her. 'How are you, sweetie?' she asked, holding Cinder's shoulders, her expression serious and stern.

'Where to start?' Cinder said, stepping back. 'I'm angry, annoyed, confused, oh yeah, and irritated.'

'Let me guess,' Marraine said. 'This is about one particular tall, handsome night surfing superhuman. Am I right?'

'YES! Sometimes I just want to punch him in his handsome, superhuman face.'

'And here I was thinking that you would be having a scandalous, dirty romp around Europe.' Marraine said with a devious wink. Cinder's face softened.

'It was nice.'

'Now that's what I want to hear more about.' Marraine took Cinder's hand. Cinder looked up into the sky.

'He told me he loves me' she cringed and looked back at Marraine. Marraine smiled.

'Do you feel that way too? Did you say it back?'

'Yes.'

'Then that's great, sweetie. So why the grumpy face and the angry stomping across the field?'

'I don't know,' Cinder said, placing her face in her hands. 'Angus is great, but he's so frustrating. One moment, I want nothing more than to be wrapped in his arms. The next moment, I feel like kicking his butt and telling him to wake up.'

'I haven't had much experience with love,' Marraine said, putting her arm around her. 'But I think that frustration is a usual symptom of your particular ailment.'

'I just...' Cinder started, but paused. 'When we were away together, everything was great. We could just be ourselves. Back here, everything's...' She shrugged. 'Oh, yeah, and now he has a vampire for a sister.' Her lip twisted, and she swept her foot back and forth in a semi-circle through the grass.

'Yes, I did hear about little sister. It seems like I started a fad. Everyone's coming back from the dead now. Walk with me,' Marraine took Cinder's hand. 'I don't like surprises.' She continued, leading Cinder away from the house. 'I don't know enough about this Sase. That's why I didn't come see you as soon as you got back. I've been trying to find out more about her.'

'I know more than I'd care to know,' Cinder said. Marraine raised a querying eyebrow. 'I had to sit and play happy families while I listened to the whole story,' Cinder continued. 'Then I caught her creeping around our room the other night and we had a... an interesting chat.'

'I know a guy,' Marraine said. 'I could have her taken out. If you want.' Cinder laughed but wasn't sure if Marraine was joking or not.

'No, it's okay. I'm not there yet. Maybe if I have to hear how wonderful she is again. Maybe then, but not now.'

They walked to the edge of the paddock and when they came to the fence line. Marraine turned and leaned against a grey, timber fence post. Cinder turned and looked back at the farmhouse.

'Angus does remember that it was one of her kind that killed your father, doesn't he? Surely that hasn't slipped out of that beautiful head of his.' Marraine said. Cinder huffed.

'Poor *Katie* is the only one that knows the pain of seeing parents die, if you ask Black at the moment. I'm so angry with him. And I'm angry with you too now that I come to think of it.'

She glared at Marraine.

'I can't believe you were dead, not dead, missing, whatever, and no one told me.' she said, shaking her head in disbelief.

'Sorry, sweetie. Next time I die, you'll bet the first one I tell.'

'I'm serious!' Cinder put her hands on her hips. 'What if something really had happened to you?'

Marraine reached out to her side and took hold of a steel wire that ran along the top of the fence, held taut between the timber posts.

'The fewer people that knew the better,' she said, strumming the wire like a guitar string. It gave a rattling twang. 'I only told Bob and Lysander because I needed them to help me pull it off.'

'So, you trusted Lysander more than you trusted me?' Cinder asked, walking to the fence and slumping back against the wire. Her torso rocking with the elasticity of the thin thread of steel.

'This wasn't about trusting people, sweetie; it was about using people. It's an important difference. I would never use you for one of my games.' Marraine tugged on the sleeve of Cinder's top.'

'But you would use Bob for one of your games?' she asked, giving Marraine a sideways glance.

'Yes, but let's be honest, Bob loves being part of my games.' She winked at Cinder. 'So anyway,' she said, changing the subject. 'Tell me all about Europe. How was that?'

Cinder took a deep breath, looking up at the sky again. The sun streaked golden-white bands across the bright blue sky, peeking out from behind fluffy grey and white clouds.

'It was so good... so good,' Cinder repeated herself, biting her lower lip and swaying from side to side. 'It was just the two of us. No one telling us what to do or where to be.'

'No having to share him with anyone?' Marraine asked.

'Yes, that's right.'

'How rude of his dead little sister to return from the grave and mess that up!' Marraine said sarcastically. Cinder's hands dropped to the hemline of her t-shirt.

'It sounds horrible when you say it like that,' she said. Marraine shrugged. 'He's been a jerk too,' Cinder continued. 'He's said some really hurtful stuff.'

'I have no doubt he's been a big jerky-jerk,' Marraine said, reaching out and pulling Cinder close. She wrapped her arms around her shoulders so that Cinder was leaning with her back to her. 'I'm just saying that I don't think there is a textbook response to finding out your loved one is still alive,' Marraine whispered, squeezing her and rocking her gently. Cinder filled her lungs, causing their upper bodies to rise in unison.

'Yes, you're right,' she acknowledged, exhaling slowly.

'Why don't you come and stay with me for a few days, sweetie? See where I've been hiding out.' Marraine said. Cinder looked out across the rolling green hills of the farm to the dark, imposing tree line of the forest beyond.

'That sounds like a great idea,' she said, reaching up and taking Marraine's hand in hers.

Their heads both turned towards the farmhouse, the familiar sound of the front door closing alerting them to movement. A few moments later, Angus appeared at the side of the building. Keeping his distance, he called out.

'I just wanted to let you know that we are going to look for Duncan.'

'Is he okay?' Cinder asked.

'I don't know. No one has seen him in weeks.'

'Alright, thanks for letting me know,' Cinder said. Angus acknowledged her with a nod and turned to go join Dom.

'Hey!' Cinder called out to him. 'I'm going to stay with Marraine for a few days.'

'Okay.' Angus sounded hurt, but he didn't protest.

'Okay...' Cinder echoed him.

'Nice to see you again, Marraine,' Angus added as he left.

'Nice to see you too, dear,' Marraine said sweetly. They watched as Angus trudged away, his chin set close to his chest. 'Well, that was very...' Marraine paused. 'Formal? Yes, formal's the word.'

'Can we just go now?' Cinder asked.

'Oh yes, sweetie. We need to make you feel better.' Marraine released her from the hug and squeezed her shoulders. She was conscious of the danger of Angus venturing into the forest, Cinder's forest, while she was still upset with him. She decided to keep that to herself.

'I'll go pack a bag,' Cinder said, walking away, her posture similar to Angus's. 'I won't be long.'

'Okay, sweetie. I'll just wait here for you.'

A breeze flicked blond locks around Cinder's face as she disappeared around a shadowy corner of the farmhouse. She pulled her hair aggressively into a ponytail and marched on. Marraine crossed her arms and leaned back on the fence post, cradling her chin thoughtfully in her hand. The breeze that had ruffled Cinder's hair continued down the outstretched fields. The blanket of green, speckled with blooms of yellow and white, rippled in a wavelike motion as the warm air moved unobstructed towards the stone-walled boundary. From the corner of her eye, Marraine spotted the movement of an object that she had not noticed before. Squinting, she could just make out a human figure sitting on the stone wall. The figure stood and walked diagonally across the field towards the tree line. As it came closer to Marraine, she could see that it was a young woman with red hair. Sase, she supposed. The young woman turned and looked directly at Marraine, watching her for a short time before acknowledging her with a slight bow of her head. Marraine responded with a two-fingered salute from the brow of her tilted head. She followed the red-haired woman with her eyes, as she paused at the forest edge, then pushing aside a branch ducked into the shadows.

Chapter 24

Mate

The familiar crack-hiss of carbonated air escaping from an aluminium can caught Angus's attention. He was kneeling next to the remnants of a campfire. His head jerked up to see where the sound had originated. Dom exited the shanty-like structure that they suspected had been Duncan's home for the past few weeks. He took a swig from the can, a large grin on his face.

'Are you helping look, or are you having a party?' Angus asked.

'Why can't we do both?' Dom answered.

'We are supposed to be looking for our friend. Something could've happened to him,' Angus responded, unimpressed.

'Okay, okay, don't get your knickers in a knot. I've got one for you too.' He produced a second can and threw it to Angus. Angus swiped the can from the air and sat it on the ground beside the campfire.

'These coals are dead cold,' he said. 'There's been no one here for at least a day or two, I'd say.'

'Longer than that, I think,' Dom said, taking another mouthful. 'There is some rank food in there. With, I don't know what grow'n on it.' Dom let out a long, thunderous burp. His explosive sounds disturbed some of the local wildlife and caught the attention of something large moving close by. A set of dark brown eyes shot in his direction. The figure moved swiftly but silently towards the source of the sound.

Dom sat on a rock that someone had rolled close to the fire to be used as a seat. He finished the drink with two long gulps. After crushing the can and wiping his mouth with his sleeve, he threw the can into the empty fireplace.

'Are you going to have yours?' he asked, eying the can on the ground near Angus. Angus got to his feet.

'Are you going to keep helping?' he asked, kicking the side of Dom's boot.

'I *have* been helping,' Dom claimed, affronted. 'We've been out here for hours. If Duncan wanted to be found, we would have found him by now.' Dom bent over and walked his hands across the ground towards the second can.

'Aren't you worried about him?' Angus pushed on incredulously.

'No,' Dom said, reaching the can and lifting it triumphantly above his head. 'Have a look around here. He obviously knows how to look after himself.' He sat up and cracked open the second beverage. Angus paced around the campsite.

'I'm not so sure. We don't even know if this was his camp.' He said, looking around.

'Come here,' Dom said, getting to his feet and leading Angus to the entrance of the lean-to. 'Look at the size of that bed roll. And then there's these,' Dom held up the can. 'How many Guinness-drinking giants do you think there are camping out here?'

'Why would he just leave all of this here?' Angus asked, ducking his head to enter the lean-to. From the outside, the ramshackle structure looked simple enough. Branches stacked and leaning at an angle against a horizontally protruding tree branch, forming a wedge shape. On the inside, however, Angus could see that someone had attempted to keep out the elements. Duncan had lined the internal walls with sheets of rusty corrugated iron, lashed together with black twine and wire. Blue tarpaulin material was draped over the supporting tree branch, offering some waterproofing. A bed ran down the centre, cobbled together from piles of leaves, more of the tarpaulin and some woollen blankets that would have looked more at home in the 1960s. Angus stepped over the bed to inspect an object at the far end of the structure. Tucked tightly in a dark corner where the tree trunk met a sheet of iron, was a blue plastic cooler box with a hinged white lid.

'If he moved somewhere new, wouldn't he take his bedding with him?' Angus asked, lifting the lid, cringing and swatting away the smell and the flies that rose from within. Dom shrugged, taking another sip.

'Maybe he got disturbed and didn't want to come back here. Maybe he got sick of sleeping rough and he's actually got himself a room at The Regent,' he said. Angus doubted Duncan would suddenly have decided to book himself into Heathcote's most expensive beachfront accommodation.

The creature with the dark eyes now stood at the edge of the makeshift campsite. As it watched Dom finish the last mouthful of his drink, it sniffed the air. Its human-like mouth opened to accommodate the increasing length of its canine teeth.

Dom tossed the second crushed can into the fireplace. 'Can we go now?' he asked. 'He's obviously not here and it will be dark soon. I'm not even sure where we are,' he added, looking around. A rustle of branches made him snap his eyes up to the tree line. A woman with red hair stepped into the clearing. Her large dark eyes set deep in a contorted brow. Long, claw-like nails protruded from the ends of her fingers, held tense and curled at the side of her body.

'What is it?' Angus asked, rushing out of the shelter.

'Your sister,' Dom said hesitantly. 'I think,' he added, taking a step back.

'What are you doing, Katie?' Angus asked, stepping towards her.

'I think that's Sase.' Dom said, taking hold of his shoulder. Sase glared at them and hissed. White fangs glistened in the dying light. In a flash, Sase ran at them, knocking Dom to the ground. Angus snatched up one of the thick sticks that formed the outer layer of the lean-to. He bent his knees and held the stick spear-like, ready to defend himself, but Sase had already disappeared amongst the trees.

'Is she coming back?' he asked.

'I don't think she was after us,' Dom said, getting to his feet.

'Why do you say that?'

'I've seen her in action. We would be in the shit right now if she was trying to hurt us.'

'Yeah, I guess so,' Angus said, lowering the stick and standing up straight. Dom dusted leaf matter and moss from his jeans.

'What do you think that was about?' he asked.

'I don't know,' Angus replied, looking around. 'She looked scary though, hey?'

'Hell yeah,' Dom agreed. A painful howl rang out from somewhere in the trees.

Masses of bark and sap flew wildly through the air as thick, dark claws flailed violently against the trunk of a tall pine. Powerful jaws snapped together, flicking putrid stings of saliva from razor-sharp teeth. Sase held a Lycan firmly against the tree. She gripped a roll of flesh and hair at the back of its neck as a dog might do to carry its puppies. Her free hand reached inside her jacket pocket and she produced the moon pendant she had taken from her brother Patru. The Lycan convulsed with fear and anger, trying to free itself from her grip. Sase pulled it back and slammed it against the tree. A second howl of pain and distress rumbled up its throat. Taking hold of one of its flailing arms, Sase bent it up behind its back. Pinning the Lycan's arm with her own, she wrapped the moon pendant around its wrist. The beast began to shrink under her grip and the coarse brown covering of its body retracted back under pale, sweaty flesh. Shortly after, Sase was holding a balding, middle-aged man against the tree. He stopped struggling and pounded the trunk, defeated, with the side of his fist.

'Why are you following us?' she demanded.

'Our queen was angry; we could feel it. We had no choice.'

'Who is your queen?'

'Cinder, the compassionate queen,' he said. Sase loosened her grip on the man.

'She was angry with Angus? Were you going to hurt him?' She asked.

'No, not Angus,' he said. 'She only feels love for him. She was angry with you.'

'Oh. I see,' Sase said, smiling to herself. 'So, were you here to hurt me?' she asked. The man looked over his shoulder at her.

'It's nothing personal. Sorry, we can't really help it. You seem nice enough. The nicest vampire I've ever met, anyway. You are a vampire, aren't you?' he asked.

'I am, as you say.'

Angus and Dom emerged at pace from the trees. Spotting Sase up against the tree, they came to a halt. From behind Sase's right hip they could just make out a hairy, white butt cheek, glistening with perspiration in the dim light. Dom shielded his eyes with his hand, letting out an exclamation of disgust. Angus took a step to the right and tilted his head.

'Is that you, Bob?' he asked, resting the stick that was still in his hand on the trunk of a nearby tree.

'Yes, just me,' Bob said. 'Is that you, Angus?'

'Yes, it's me. I've got Dom here with me, too. Do you remember Dom?'

'Yeah sure. How are you?' Bob asked, waving above his head with his free hand.

'Better than you, I think,' Dom answered. 'Why are you running around the forest in the nude, Bob?' he asked. Turning to look the other way. Angus looked at Dom.

'Don't you know about this?' he asked. 'They take their clothes off before they change into werewolves,'

'Lycans,' Bob corrected him.

'Oh, yeah sorry, before they change into Lycans. So they don't wreck their clothes.'

'So that's why she was naked the other night,' Dom said.

'Who was naked?' Angus asked.

'No one,' Dom replied quietly. Sase coughed.

'Sorry to interrupt,' she said, taking a step back from Bob. 'But do you know this man?'

'Yes, sorry,' Angus replied, still staring questioningly at Dom. 'This is my sister Katie.'

'Hi,' Bob said. 'Nice to meet you. Thanks for not killing me.'

'And Katie, this is my friend Bob,' Angus continued, turning away from Dom, who was doing his best to not make eye contact. 'You can let him go now. He's harmless.' Sase dropped Bob's arm and let go of his neck. Bob stepped away from the tree, rubbing his shoulder.

'I like to think I'm not that harmless,' he said, turning around.

'Whoa!' Dom said, turning away from Bob. 'You are doing me some harm right now.'

'Sorry,' Bob said, placing his hand over his groin. 'Your sister has one of these, too.' He held up his wrist with the moon pendant wrapped around it. Sase's eyes shot back towards him.

'What do you mean I have one too?'

'This thing,' Bob said, shaking his wrist. 'My friend, Marraine, has a few of them now.' Sase glared at him incredulously.

'Who is this woman?' she demanded. Bob opened his mouth to answer, but Sase stopped him, holding her palm to his face. She circled around, sniffing the air.

'Are some of your friends joining us?' she asked rhetorically. 'We have company,' she said, walking to Angus and resting her hand on his shoulder. 'Four of them, I think. That way.' She pointed out into the forest that had now passed from twilight into the infancy of night. Angus retrieved the stick he had placed against the trunk and beckoned Dom to move in close. A low growl rumbled through the darkness. Sase's vampire eyes could see the slow rocking movement of dark masses moving between the trees. To Angus and Dom, the forest simply appeared dark and still.

'Bob, come and stand in front of me,' Dom ordered. Bob stepped forward. Angus swivelled his head towards Dom.

'You're not going to use him as a human shield, are you?'

'No, of course not,' Dom said. 'He's not human.'

'He's our friend.'

'He's not my friend,' Dom said, crossing his arms. Angus turned and looked back at Bob apologetically.

'Just stay back,' he said. Bob stepped back again.

'Have you children finished?' Sase hissed.

'Sorry,' Angus said, returning his concentration to the forest.

The dark, moist forest floor inclined at a slight angle away from them. Moss-covered rocks, stumps and fallen limbs lay scattered amongst a bed of browning pine needles. Tall, straight trunks, densely packed together, stretched up into a thick canopy, silver and black in the moonlight. Angus peered into the growing darkness. Straining his eyes, he glimpsed the passage of one of the dark objects amongst the shadows as it advanced on their position. He tapped Dom on the chest and pointed out the movement. Dom responded with a nod of affirmation.

'Why are they here?' he asked. 'I thought we were all on the same side now.'

'They are here because of Cinder, because of her anger.' Sase said, taking a step forward.

'What did you do now?' Dom asked, looking at Angus.

'They're here for me, not him,' Sase interrupted. 'Cinder and I are...'

A mass of grey fir, claws, and teeth crashed through the undergrowth, leaping at Sase before she could finish. She suddenly looked far more like the centuries old vampire queen than Angus's teenage sister. She stood tall, fierce and solid. With lightning-fast reflexes, she snatched the Lycan out of mid-air. Stepping to the side, she twisted and flung the beast behind her like a rag-doll. In a spray of pine-needles, the Lycan rolled across the forest floor, yelping. Three more Lycan emerged slowly from the shadows, their large dark eyes reflecting the dull moonlight as they focused on the vampire. Their powerful shoulders swayed from side to side as they crept towards Sase on all fours, growling and snapping. Sase stood perfectly still, a look on her face somewhere between annoyance and disinterest. The trio of Lycan ran at her as a group. She swatted one of them away like it was nothing more than a fly, but the remaining two pinned her against a tree trunk. Dom ran forward and kicked the Lycan that Sase had swatted away. His heavy military style boot connected with beast's ribs. Yelping and howling, it retreated to the safety of the shadows.

Angus went to the aid of his sister, bringing the stick in his hand down firmly on the head of the closest Lycan. The stick shattered in the three sections and the beast stumbled backwards in a daze. Shaking its head, it turned on Angus and roared at him. Sickening breath rushed across his face, hot and damp. Still dazed and angry, the Lycan made to bite at Angus, but the last of its companions smashed heavily against it. The two Lycan crashed to the ground. Sase stepped to Angus's side.

'Are you okay?' she asked.

'Yes. You?' Angus asked in return, looking her up and down. Sase laughed.

'Of course.'

Picking themselves up from the ground, the Lycan began moving towards Sase again. Angus stepped in front of her to protect her. Sase smiled to herself.

'I can handle myself,' she said, placing a hand on his shoulder. The closest of the Lycan stopped and looked at Angus. Its large black nostrils flared as it moved its snout up and down, sniffing the air. The other Lycan stopped and watched their companion. The lead Lycan threw its head back, howling into the sky. Followed its lead, the others sent their own chorus towards the heavens. Returning to all fours, they all turned and strolled back into the forest, disappearing once more amongst the shadows.

'That was weird,' Dom said.

'They realised who Angus was. He's protected now,' Bob said. The others turned around in surprise. In the excitement, they had forgotten that he was there. Bob stood, shivering, rubbing his arm with his free hand. 'Can I take this pendant off my wrist now, please?' he asked.

'Yes,' Sase said, stepping towards him with her hand stretched out.

'Hang on,' Dom interrupted. 'Why is he protected and I'm not?'

'He's the queen's mate. They've bonded now, if you know what I mean. Her scent is all over him.' Bob replied, swirling his wrist to unwrap the pendant chain.

'How do I get protected, then?' Dom asked. Bob freed the last piece of chain and held the pendant in his hand.

'You would have to bond with the queen too, I guess.' Bob handed the pendant to Sase. Dom looked at Angus.

'It's not happening, mate,' Angus said, shaking his head.

• • • •

'Hey dad, still no sign of him,' Dom announced entering the farmhouse. He shrugged his way out of his long, dark jacket and hung it on the hook behind the door. Angus followed him. A gentle breeze whistled its way inside as they closed the door behind them.

'Do you want us to go out again later?' Angus asked, pushing his way past Dom into the living room.

'No,' Gunn said huskily. He coughed to clear his throat and pulled himself up in his armchair. 'He does this from time to time. Probably just wants to be left alone.'

'Did you find Duncan?' Torry asked, entering the room. Dom looked her up and down. She was wearing a fitted, short-sleeved, yellow t-shirt and a tiny pair of glossy dark-blue lycra shorts. Sturdy padding protected her wrists, elbows, and knees. She sat down on the arm of one of the recliners, pulling knee-length yellow and blue striped socks over her fishnet stockinged legs.

'Are we wearing costumes now?' Dom asked, looking at the black smears of war paint under his sister's eyes. 'Because I'm all for that. I'd look great in tight black spandex.'

'No,' Torry said, pulling on the second sock. 'I do flat-track roller derby now. This is me,' she said, turning to show him the writing on her back.

'Gopher Kinnard' Dom read out load.

'You get it?' Torry asked.

'Get what?'

'I'm number 7 for the Surf Coast Banshees. Gopher Kinnard. Go fark'n 'ard.' Torry winked and folded the socks down under her knee pads.

'Nice,' Dom said. 'So instead of spending your nights being chased by blood-thirsty hairy beasts, now you spend your nights being chased by blood-thirsty hairy beasts on wheels?'

'Hey!' Torry said, slapping his leg. 'They're all serious athletes and lovely people, mostly. And some of them are very attractive women.'

'Please continue,' Dom said enthusiastically.

'Sorry, big brother, but most of the pretty ones prefer the company of women.' Torry said, standing and adjusting her elbow pads. She could see the cogs turning over in Dom's head behind his smug face.

'So, do you need a ride?' he asked. 'I think this could be my new favourite sport.'

'You're a pig, you know,' Torry said, pushing past him to collect her skates and helmet. 'Can't we send him back overseas again?' she called behind her as she disappeared into the hallway. A moment later she returned with all her equipment, looking like a brightly coloured warrior ready for battle. 'So, did you find him?' she asked again, sitting back on the arm of the chair.

'No, love,' Gunn said. 'We think he probably doesn't want to be found.'

'I'm sure he's okay,' Torry said, adjusting her elbow pads.

Angus had been standing silently by the fireplace. There was no fire burning, but it felt like the appropriate place to stand.

'Where's Katie?' Torry asked. Angus smiled. It was nice to hear someone call her Katie, not Sase.

'She was helping us look, but then she said she had some other things to do.'

'What kind of stuff?' Torry asked. Dom and Angus looked at each other and shrugged in unison.

'I don't know,' Angus said. 'We didn't ask. Vampire stuff, I guess.'

'Vampire stuff,' Torry parroted Angus, looking from him to her brother. 'Boys are weird. Anyway...,' she said, standing. 'Can you give me a ride to the bluff, Black?'

'I'll take you.' Dom offered enthusiastically.

'No! No, you won't,' Torry said, pointing at him with her helmet. 'I want to talk to Black about some stuff, anyway.'

'Okay, sure,' Angus said. 'Sorry mate.' He walked past Dom, patting him on the shoulder. 'Maybe next time.'

• • • •

As Angus turned Blair's 1971 VW station wagon onto Bramley lane and turned to head towards the coast, the headlights reflected red off the taillights of a car parked at the side of the road. A few mo-ments later, they sped past an expensive looking dark sedan with tint-ed glass.

'I wonder if they are all right,' Angus mused, looking in the rear-view mirror. Torry twisted around in her seat to see the car in the red glow of their taillights.

'Probably just some tourist thinking they've found a private place to go parking,' she said, moving her head around to get a better look.

Watching as the oval-shaped taillights of the Volkswagen shrunk and then disappeared around a bend, the occupant of the dark ve-hicle reached across from the driver's seat and retrieved a small but weighty case from the glove-box. She placed the case on the passen-ger seat with care, before removing a pair of black leather gloves and closing the glove-box again with a click. She adjusted her rear-view, studying her reflection as she slipped one of the gloves back onto her right hand. The leather creaked as she squeezed her hands, checking for comfort and ease of movement. Happy with the feel, she adjusted some stray hairs before picking up the case.

A small rectangle of black glass that resembled a miniature tele-vision screen sat in the top right corner of the case. The owner of the case held her left thumb against the screen. A click from inside an-nounced that the case was unlocked. With a flick of two clasps on the front, the lid sprung open, quickly at first and then slowly, ris-ing with a muffled hiss. A bespoke hand gun sat nestled in a custom cut-out space, lined with red velvet. The words "Wilson Combat" had been hand-carved in decorative font along the barrel amongst swirling flourishes. The polished redwood handle sported an oval-shaped motif, with the letters 'WC' embossed in gold.

After pulling on the second glove, the owner of the weapon re-moved it from the case and inserted a fully loaded magazine. They reached for the door handle, but something large and dark flashed past the windscreen. A split second later, someone flung the passen-

ger door open and sat down in the passenger seat. The driver swivelled around, pointing the gun at their head.

'Put the gun away, Louvelle,' they said calmly. 'You know very
well I can move my head faster than your finger can pull the trigger.
You will just damage your car.'

'Yes, but could you dodge all fifteen rounds, I wonder?' Louvelle
continued to hold the gun at the unwelcome guest's head.

'It would be very difficult for you to continue firing with your
arm torn from your body.'

'Perhaps I should go for the heart then,' Louvelle said, lowering
the barrel to the intruder's chest.

'Nice to know you think I have one.'

'Hello Sase,' Louvelle said. 'I was wondering when you might pay
me a visit. You have had an upgrade, I see. I like the new look, but
I do feel we have our fill of supernatural red-headed bitches around
here already.'

'Haven't you heard yet?' Sase said, tapping her fingernails on the
barrel of Louvelle's weapon.

'Heard what?' Louvelle demanded, flicking her hand away.

'The girl, your ward, she's sporting flaxen locks now.'

'Flaxen?'

'Yes, as golden as the straw in the fields,'

'Do you mean that Cinder has dyed her hair blonde?' Louvelle
asked, placing the handgun on her lap.

'Yes,' Sase replied.

'Why wouldn't you just say that? You're such an infuriating
woman. I've a mind to shoot you for just using the word flaxen.' Louvelle pulled at the cuff of her glove. Sase stared at her with an unreadable expression on her youthful face.

'What can I do for you this evening, Sase?' Louvelle said, after a
moment's silence. 'I have a busy night planned and you're keeping me
from it.'

'Firstly, the girl is under my protection. She's my family now,' Sase said.

'Ha!' Louvelle laughed. 'It makes no difference what face you hide behind. I know very well who your real family is. Maybe I should tell your brothers where you are. I am sure they would love a family reunion.' Louvelle reached for her phone, sitting in the centre console. Sase watched her calmly.

'I haven't finished yet. Trust me, you will want to hear this and when you do, my brother's will be the last ones you want to tell,' she said. Louvelle placed her phone down and motioned for her to continue. 'Somehow, even without all of us,' Sase continued, as she watched the dim light in of the farmhouse flicker in the window. 'She's coming.'

'Who's coming?'

'The one we have been planning for. The reason you and my brothers have kept them all alive, Louvelle.'

'Oh?' Louvelle sat up straight.

'Yes, just when it looked like all of your grooming had gone to waste, the universe stepped in and found its own way. She is coming. The new Mother.'

'Then we must prepare.'

'Yes, we must,' Sase agreed, 'and my brothers can never know.'

'It looks like we will need to work together again... *Old friend.*' Louvelle added. Sase grimaced at the word friend.

'By the way, Cinder isn't here anyway,' she announced, as she opened the door to exit.

'Where is she?' Louvelle snapped.

'She's with the pretty one with the olive skin.'

'Marraine?' Louvelle asked, twisting the barrel of her gun around inside her tightly clenched fist.

'Yes, I think that was her name.' Sase sat one leg outside of the vehicle, then turned back to Louvelle. 'My, my, Lady Gevaudan, your wrinkles are showing,' she said, looking at Louvelle's stern face. 'Perhaps it's time for some more injectables.'

Louvelle swung her handgun towards Sase once again, but she was gone, disappeared once more into the darkness, leaving the car door swinging on its hinges.

'I hate vampires,' Louvelle said to herself as she placed the weapon back in its case. She sat with her hands on the steering wheel, glaring at the open passenger side door. 'Hundreds of years old and still lacking common decency.' She reached up and adjusted the rearview mirror so she could see her face. 'I don't know what she's talking about,' she said, pouting her lips and turning her head from side to side.

The engine roared to life, and after a momentary spinning of wheels, the car lurched forward. The passenger door swung shut violently as Louvelle sped away in a cloud of dust and pelting gravel. With one hand on the steering wheel, she tapped her phone to life and scrolled to find a number.

'Yes, my lady?' a nervous voice said through the vehicle's speakers.

'Time for Plan B,' Louvelle said, and hung up.

Chapter 25

My Hero

The crowd roared, drowning out Freddie Mercury's calls of 'Don't Stop Me Now.' Flashes of blue, yellow, black, and red whirled past exhilarated faces. The warm air pulsed with excitement, anticipation, and perspiration. Polyurethane wheels skidded, rolled and stomped across the glossy timber floor, as leather and laces strained against the force of feet and ankles. Glistening bodies weaved and collided in a crush and grind of hips, shoulder, helmets, and pads. Torry leaned with her hands on her knees, her chest rising and falling. As one of her Surf Coast Banshees teammates slid a star motif covering over her helmet, a bead of sweat ran from her hairline to her chin. Wiping the drip with her shoulder, Torry stood tall and lifted her knees to her chin, one at a time. Her teammate handed her a plastic drink bottle, and she pulled a blue and yellow mouth guard from between her teeth. She squirted a long spray of water into her open mouth. With a wet fizz, she poured the remaining water down her back. After adjusting her wrist-guards and padding, she shook out her arms and slid her mouth guard back in place. With a slap on the helmet from her teammate, she rolled back into the action.

'Go Tor!' Angus yelled from the sidelines, punching his fist in the air. Next to him, Dom stood silently with his jaw hanging open. His wide-open eyes followed the action, pupils dilated like a man in a trance.

'You okay, mate?' Angus asked, leaning in so Dom could hear him over the crowd.

'Ohhh, Black,' he said, grabbing the front of Angus's shirt. 'This is my new favourite thing. I can't believe you've been coming here for weeks and you didn't tell me about it.'

'I'm sorry,' Angus said, patting him on the back. 'I had to talk Torry into letting you come first.'

From across the other side of the oval-shaped track, Angus heard a familiar voice over the top of the rumble.

'Gopher, Gopher!' Cinder called. Watching from over her shoulder, Marraine joined in.

'Gopher, Gopher!' Shortly after, half the crowd had joined in the chorus.

'Gopher, Gopher, Gopher!'

Torry's teammate Olivia skated up alongside her, slipping a striped cover on her helmet

Olivia was a short, athletic woman in her late twenties. She had an infectious smile that creased her freckled nose, and a bubbly personality. As friendly as Olivia was, she was a fierce competitor.

'Eighteen to draw, nineteen to win, then we're in the finals.' She said, turning back and forth in tight circles.

'You know the highest I've ever got was a fifteen, right?' Torry said.

'Seems like it's a good time for your P.B. then,' Olivia teased.

'Great, no pressure then?'

'Oh, no, there's pressure,' Olivia said, smiling and pushing Torry with her hip.

'Friends, family, enemies, and enemas.' The announcer's voice reverberated off the metal roof of the East Bluff Y.M.C.A hall. 'Please welcome our last jammers for the evening. From the Sisters of Sin, number twelve, Queen Bee Atch. And, number seven for the Surf Coast Banshees, Gopher Kinnard.' The crowd erupted in a cacophony of cheers, whistles, and applause. 'And…,' the announcer continued when the noise dropped. 'Our two pivots, Olivia Neutron Bomb and Crispy-Fried-Chick Anne.' The rubble of the crowd again rose to a crescendo.

Torry lined up next to Queen Bee Atch – Bee, her teammates called her. Secretly, Torry thought the Sisters of Sin's uniform was way more stylish than the Banshee's uniform.

Red, rockabilly styled pinstriped bowling shirts, paired with a black skirt or shorts. Their numbers displayed in the centre of an inverted pentagram across their backs. With two minutes set on the clock, an air horn sounded, and the two jammers raced towards the wall of rolling and bustling bodies.

Torry made it to the pack first but crashed hard into number four for the Sisters, a wide-hipped woman with spiky purple hair. Olivia veered across the track, slamming her hip into number four. Torry slipped behind Olivia to the far edge of the track. Seeing an opening, she slipped past the pack just as she made it to the first turn.

'Go, sis!' Cinder yelled with her hands cupped around her mouth. Torry winked and pointed at her double-pistol-style as she flew past. Watching her zip around the track, Cinder's eyes met with Angus's across the hall. She waved and smiled awkwardly.

'Have you talked to him yet?' Marraine asked, leaning on her shoulder.

'I've messaged him a few times to check in, but no, not really.' Cinder dropped her eyes to the floor.

Torry, head down and arms pumping, flew around the track at break-neck speed. Her black leather skates gliding gracefully, one in front of the other as her hair flicked behind her. Olivia wrestled hip-to-hip with one of the Sisters of Sin, a tall, muscular woman with red war paint across her dark glistening cheeks. Other than Bee, who was now coming up behind Torry, the rest of the competitors had bunched themselves tightly together. Torry watched for a gap. Two of her teammates forced open a space on the outside edge of the track. It was risky to go that close to the boundary, but Torry went for it, balancing on one skate to slip around the outside and stay on the track. Her foot slammed back to the ground as she passed the pack. Four points, 95 seconds left on the clock.

'I think I'm in love,' Dom said, eyes wide and mouth hanging open. Angus shot him a sideways glance and laughed at how mesmerised he looked.

'In love with who?'

'That one,' Dom said, holding his index finger out and following one of Torry's teammates around the track. 'And that one, and her.' He continued to point out different players on both teams. 'Man, I love all of them,' he added, gripping Angus's shoulder. Torry bumped and weaved her way to the front of the pack again. Eight points, just over a minute to go. The crowd erupted, pulsing with excitement and anticipation.

'I know I'm in love, for real!' Angus needed to yell so Dom could hear him. Dom turned to him, his expression transformed. His serious face, Angus noted. He usually only saw Dom like this when they were hunting.

'That's great man, that's really great.' Dom said earnestly.

'I wasn't sure that you would be happy about it,' Angus said, taken aback slightly by Dom's response. 'I didn't think you liked her.'

'I wasn't too happy when I found out what she was, sure, but...' One of the Sisters of Sin fell to the floor, sliding on her elbows and knees right up to where Dom and Angus were standing. After getting to her feet, she gave the crowd a wink, bowed, and rushed back to the action. Dom gave her a round of applause. *Serious face gone,* Angus thought, *Dom's back.*

Two more points for the Banshees to draw. Three for the win. 35 seconds on the clock.

'You were saying?' Angus tried to regain Dom's concentration.

'Oh, yeah, yeah,' Dom said, watching proudly as his little sister powered around the track like a freight train. 'I didn't like the idea of you falling for a werewolf, but she saved your life, man.' He glanced across the track at Cinder and Marraine. 'And from what I hear, she was with Tor every day while she was in the hospital.' He watched as Torry slammed into two of the Sisters of Sin. 'That crazy kid's the most important thing in my life. Don't tell her I said that,' he added. Angus thought he saw Dom wipe a tear from his cheek. Drums and guitars erupted through the P.A. system as My Hero by Foo Fighters blasted across the anxiously vibrating audience. 20 seconds on the clock.

Marraine watched Dom and Angus thoughtfully, as she added gloss to her lips with her little finger.

'I have to admit that I don't understand how this game works.' She said, leaning in to Cinder's ear. Cinder grimaced as she watched Torry struggle to force her way past the two Sisters of Sin.

'Tor needs to get past three more players to win... I think.' Cinder's eyes widened as Torry skated past the first of her two opponents. 10 seconds to go! Cinder grabbed Marraine's hand as the yelling and cheering of the crowd grew to ear ringing intensity, drowning out the music. Torry pushed forward desperately to chase down the Sister of Sin in front of her. Their hips connected heavily, sending Torry sideways. She corrected herself quickly, but not quickly enough. A siren rang out, announcing the end of the game. The Surf Coast Banshees had lost by one point, sending the Sisters of Sin through to the finals. Torry fell to the floor, her chest heaving as sweat gleamed on her angst, flushed face. The Sisters of Sin embraced as Freddy Mercury sung, 'We Are the Champions.'

Olivia glided over to Torry, her shoulders stooped, hands resting on her knee pads. She flopped down next to Torry and rested her head on her stomach.

'We almost made it,' she said, her head moving up and down in time with Torry's deep breaths.

'I'm sorry,' Torry said, unclipping her helmet and throwing it across the floor. Olivia reached up and whacked her with the back of her hand.

'You have nothing to be sorry about, Hun. You got your P.B. we'll get them next season.'

Finishing their celebrations, the Sisters of Sin began to separate. Queen Bee-atch, rolled over to Torry and Olivia.

'Great game, ladies,' she said with a warm smile. 'You almost had us there.' She offered them her hand. Accepting the hand, Olivia pulled herself up from the floor. Both Olivia and Bee pulled Torry up to her feet.

'Congratulations,' Torry offered.

'You're a hell of a skater,' Bee said, draping an arm over her shoulder.

'Cheers.'

Sheepishly, Cinder approached the three players, carrying Torry's discarded helmet.

'Hey sis, you okay?' she asked, handing the helmet to Torry.

'Yeah, I'm fine, just stuffed.'

'You were amazing.'

'Thanks, sis.'

'Hi. I'm Olivia Neutron Bomb,' Olivia said with a wave.

'Oh, hi Olivia Neutron Bomb,' Cinder replied with a smile. 'I'm Cinder. You did an amazing job too.' she added. Olivia's flushed face turned a deeper shade of crimson.

'Thanks. You too. I mean... thank you for your support.'

'I don't know how you do it,' Cinder said, looking down at their skates. 'I don't think I could even stay upright, let alone race around that track.'

Bee lowered her arm from Torry's shoulder.

'Give her a go,' she said, prodding Torry with her elbow pad.

'Oh, no,' Cinder said, taking a step back.

'Yes!' Torry demanded 'Here put my skates on.' She sat down and begun to unlace her skates.

'Okay, but you all have to promise not to laugh at me,' Cinder pleaded.

'Oh, we're going to laugh,' Torry said, holding up her first skate. The other two nodded in agreement.

'I'll help you put them on,' Olivia offered enthusiastically. Cinder sat down and, with Olivia's help, slipped her foot into Torry's skate. She looked at Torry, twisting her lip.

'What's wrong?' Torry asked, handing over the second skate.

'They're a bit damp,'

'It's just a bit of sweat. You'll be fine.'

'Okay, but if my feet rot off, I'm blaming you.'

'Come on, put the other one on, princess,'

'Hey, I'm not a princess. I'm the queen, remember?' With Torry and Olivia's help, Cinder got carefully to her feet.

'You need to keep your knees bent to lower your centre of gravity,' Bee instructed. 'Especially when you're as tall as you are.' Cinder towered over Torry, who was already smirking.

'What?' Cinder asked, looking down at her.

'Nothing, nothing.' Torry smirked again. 'You just remind me of a baby giraffe on wheels.'

'Hey!' Cinder protested, smacking her shoulder but almost losing her balance.

'Bend your knees,' Olivia said, taking her hand and don't listen to her. You look fine.' Cinder bent her knees and Torry took hold of her hips.

'Just move one foot in front of the other,' she said, moving Cinder slowly forward.

'Alright, this is not too bad,' Cinder admitted as Torry increased their speed. 'This could be fun.'

'It's more fun on your own,' Torry said, pushing her forward and letting go.

'What?' Cinder tried to look behind her but felt her feet moving out from underneath her.

'I've got you.' Cinder felt a familiar pair of muscular arms wrap around her. She looked up into a pair of chocolate brown eyes, eyes that looked like home.

'Hi there,' Angus said.

'Hey stranger,' Cinder said, regaining her footing. Angus took her hand to help steady her. They stood in awkward silence for a few seconds. 'I...'

'I...'

'You go.'

'I'm sorry I was a jerk,' Angus said, pushing a stray hair behind her ear.

'What if I wanted that hair there?' She teased.

'Then I'm more of a jerk then, aren't I.'

'You were a bit of a jerk.'

'I know. Torry's been telling me all about it.'

'She's very direct, my little sis,' Cinder said, looking back at Torry.

'You're doing great. Keep going!' Torry yelled. Angus looked at her, too.

'She is direct. But I'm thick. I need direct sometimes,' he said. Cinder stumbled again, resting her hand on his chest to get her balance.

'I could have been a bit more understanding too,' she admitted, running her hand across his firm torso and kissing his warm lips. Angus took her face in his hand and kissed her back.

'I've been thinking,' he said, caressing her cheek with his thumb and swapping his gaze from one emerald green eye to the other.

'Oh, no, that's dangerous.' Cinder interrupted, slipping her hand around to the small of his back.

'I've been thinking,' Angus repeated, rolling his eyes. 'That we should have a night out at Paddy's for your birthday next month.'

Excitement and appreciation flooded over Cinder, curling and fluttering in her stomach.

'Thank you,' she said, pushing herself cautiously away from Angus's stabilising hold. 'I would love that. Now,' she said, changing the subject and grinning madly. 'I'm going to keep skating.' She turned awkwardly on the spot, her feet stomping against the hard floor. Holding onto Angus's hand until the last moment, she inched slowly away.

'Are you going to be okay?' Angus asked, as their fingertips parted ways.

'Yes...' Cinder said unconvincingly.

'Bend your knees!' Torry and Olivia called from behind her. Cinder glided slowly away, one shaky leg in front of the other.

'I'm skating!' she yelled gleefully, her arms flapping beside her. Angus would never tell her, but he couldn't help thinking she reminded him of a large inflatable person, flicking around in the breeze to advertise second-hand car sales or cheap electrical goods. 'I'm doing it', Cinder said, looking back at her friends.

'Yeah, you are!' Torry called encouragingly. Angus stuck two fingers in his mouth and whistled.

Olivia had removed her skates and hung them from her shoulder by looping together the laces.

'Who's this Cinder, anyway?' she asked, nodding towards Cinder as she continued to shuffle one foot in front of the other.

'That's my bestie!' Torry said, packing her pads into a large, black canvas duffle bag.

'She's gorgeous,' Olivia said, squatting next to her. 'I thought she might be your girlfriend.'

'No!' Torry said with laughter in her voice. 'She's with Black,' she pointed to Angus, who was still standing watching Cinder like a concerned parent watching a toddler. 'She's more like my sister,' Torry added.

'Well, she looks like she's a lot of fun,' Olivia said, passing Torry one of her wrist guards.

They watched as Cinder stumbled and threw her hands out to the side. Torry and Olivia both cringed and held their breath. When Cinder straightened up and continued rolling forward, they collectively breathed a sigh of relief. Most of the crowd were now moving out of the hall, giving Cinder a straight stretch of floor to roll herself along. A large, retractable frame held a basketball ring and backboard out from the end wall of the hall. Cinder cruised under the ring and continued towards the wall. She glanced back over her shoulder at Torry with concern.

'I don't know how to turn!' she yelled. In a panic, her feet slipped out from under her again. One foot after the other stomped heavily against the timber floor as they rolled violently forward, sending Cinder toppling backwards. From out of the crowd, a young man swept over to her and caught her just as her legs flew out in front of her. With one arm wrapped around her shoulders, he gently lifted her back onto her feet.

'Thank you.' Cinder said, a little surprised by the appearance of her rescuer. He would have looked more at home in the lobby of a five-star hotel or behind the wheel of an expensive sports car than in the East Bluff Y.M.C.A. Short, slicked brown hair, prominent cheek bones and a chiselled jaw under designer stubble. His clothes screamed of money. Shiny Italian leather boots, knee-length dark-grey woollen coat and an antique gold wristwatch. Some would probably find him very handsome, *if you were into that kind of thing*, Cinder thought to herself.

'My pleasure,' the stranger said in a thick European accent. *Another surprise*, Cinder thought.

'Where did you come from?'

'I was watching you skating. I hope you don't mind. It was very entertaining,' he said.

'No, that's fine,' Cinder said, blushing. 'It was a good thing you were. I might have broken something.' She placed her hands on her backside, then immediately pulling them away when she saw the stranger's eyes following them.

'You should be careful. You're very important,' he said.

'I'm what?' Cinder asked.

'You look like you are important to many people,' he said, looking around at the collection of people watching their interaction. Cinder stepped back from the man, crossing her arms and sliding one hand up to rub the back of her neck.

'Yes,' she said. 'I've got great friends. And a great boyfriend,' she added.

'Like I was saying,' the man said with a polite bow. 'You are very important.'

'Are you okay here, sweetie?' Marraine had approached from behind and placed her hand on Cinder's shoulder.

'Oh, Marraine,' she said with relief. 'Yes, I'm fine. This kind young man helped me.'

'Yes, I saw that,' Marraine said, taking her hand. 'In fact, we all saw that,' she added, opening her eyes wide at Cinder and coughing into her hand.

'I should get back to my friends now. Cinder said, squeezing Marraine's hand. 'Thank you again. Sorry, I didn't catch your name.'

'That's because I didn't offer it,' the stranger said, adjusting his coat. 'Please excuse me ladies, enjoy the rest of your evening.' He slid away, swept up once more amongst the crowd as they trundled out of the exit. Cinder watched him go, then turned to see a look of amusement on Marraine's face.

'What?' she asked.

'You really do have the whole damsel in distress thing down, don't you?' Marraine said, rolling her back towards the others.

'What do you mean?'

'I mean,' Marraine continued, lowering her voice as they came closer to Angus. 'You managed to have two attractive young men come to your aid in the space of three minutes.'

'You thought he was attractive?' Cinder asked sarcastically.

'Hot and rich. Just how I like my men and my chocolate.'

'I didn't notice,' Cinder said airily. They both laughed. 'He actually seemed familiar now that I come to think of it.'

'Of course he's familiar,' Marraine said, wrapping her arm around Cinder's waist. 'He's that guy from my dreams, you know the one?'

'Oh, yes, that's the one.' Cinder said, pushing herself forward off Marraine's arm and gliding forward into Angus.

'Who was that guy?' he asked defensively as he caught Cinder and spun her around. 'He looked familiar.'

'I thought so too,' Cinder agreed, trying unsuccessfully to spot the stranger in the crowd. 'He was just someone in the right place at the right time. I've not met him before.'

'He looked like a tool,' Angus muttered.

'Angus MacAskill,' Cinder said, poking him in the ribs with her elbows. 'He caught me as I was falling. I was glad he was there.'

'Probably trying to cop a feel,' Angus grumped.

'Maybe he did.'

'What?' Angus exclaimed

'Maybe he did cop a feel.' Cinder smirked. 'Maybe I liked it.'

'Liked what, sweetie?' Marraine asked, catching up to Cinder.

'Hello, Marraine,' Angus said, wrapping his arm around her shoulder. 'Cinder was just telling me how much she loved having her new boyfriend's filthy hands all over her.'

'Filthy rich hands, I'd say,' Marraine said with a wink. 'You might be able to catch him if you roll over there now.' She motioned towards the exit.

'No, it's okay. I've made plans to sneak out and meet up with him later tonight.' Cinder joked.

'Is that right?' Angus asked, raising one eyebrow. 'So, Marraine, it sounds like I have an opening tonight. Would you like to join me?'

'That sounds very tempting, sweetie,' Marraine said, lifting his arm from her shoulder. 'But I have been invited to a party tonight. I was hoping you could babysit this one for me.' She pulled Cinder in under Angus's arm. 'I promise she'll be on her best behaviour, or her worst behaviour if that's what you'd prefer.'

'I'm sure we can give you a ride,' Angus said, pulling Cinder close. 'Are you coming home or going back to Marraine's?'

'I'll come home with you, if you'll have me?' It warmed her heart to hear him call it her home.

'Always,' Angus said and kissed the top of her head.

Torry was hugging Olivia goodbye. Marraine pushed Cinder towards her. With bent knees and a goofy smile, Cinder cruised over to Torry, grabbing hold of her arm before she almost fell for the third time.

'Hey sis, you all done now?' Torry said, holding her steady.

'Yes, thanks' Cinder replied. 'You should get me out of these things before I hurt someone.'

'You did fine,' Torry said, helping her down on to the floor. 'I've seen plenty of people go A over T when they try for the first time.'

'A over T?' Cinder asked, untying the laces of Torry's skates.

'A.' Torry pointed to her backside. 'And T.' she cupped her breasts and lifted them towards Cinder's face.

'Okay, okay, I get it,' she said, pushing Torry away.

'I'll see you soon!' Marraine called out from next to Angus. 'I'm going now, my cars here,' she said waving.'

'Alright, I'll call you tomorrow,' Cinder said, pulling off one skate.

'Not too early, I won't answer,' Marraine said, turning to leave, squeezing Angus's shoulder as she went.

'Wait,' Torry said, slipping the skate in her duffle bag. 'Does that mean you're coming with us?'

'Yep.' Cinder handed her the second skate. Torry dropped it to the floor with a loud thud that echo around the hall, turning heads of those that remained. She leapt at Cinder, knocking her to the floor in a bear hug.

'You're coming home,' she squealed

'Yes,' Cinder struggled to say from beneath her. 'I'm coming home.' Torry rolled off her, and they sat together on the cold floor while Torry finished packing her skates away in the duffle bag.

'Did stupid-head apologise?' she asked, looking at Angus and zipping the bag shut. Cinder collected her boots.

'Yes, we sorted things out,' she said, pulling them on. Torry stood up.

'Good, he was starting to get a bald patch from where I kept slapping the side of his head,' she said and pulled Cinder up from the floor. Angus stepped forward, picking up Torry's bag and handing it to her.

'Are we all ready to go?'

'I'm all done. I just don't know where my brother is,' Torry said, hanging the bag over her shoulder and looking around. Angus pointed towards a group of people who were still lingering around the announcer's table. Dom sat on the edge of the table, his black-jeaned legs stretched out in front. He sat with his muscular torso twisted to the side while one of the Sisters of Sin girls held the back of his tight black t-shirt up at his shoulders. A group of girls from both teams huddled around him, admiring and running their fingers over his Scottish Thistle tattoo. Torry rolled her eyes and glowered at Angus.

'I told you I didn't want him to come,' she said, jabbing Angus's chest three times with her index finger.

'What?' Angus asked. 'He's just being friendly.'

'Yes, real friendly,' Torry said, turning to glare at her brother, who now appeared to be typing his number into one of Torry's teammate's phone. 'Oy, Bro!' Torry called. 'Time to go.' Dom rocked forward off the table, placing his hand on the teammate's shoulder as he handed her back her phone. He gave the gathering a casual salute goodbye as he strolled over to where Torry, Cinder, and Angus were waiting. Torry was sure she read the words, "oh my god" on one of the girl's lips.

'You making some friends?' Angus asked as Dom stopped next to him, grinning with satisfaction.

'Yep, we were comparing scars and tats,' he said smugly. 'What's wrong, short stuff?' he said, seeing the look on Torry's face. 'You still upset about losing?'

'Just get to the car,' she hissed, her face red and her nostrils flaring.

'What?' Dom said, holding up his hands.

'Just get to the car,' Torry hissed again.

* * * *

Leaning against the wall adjacent to the double glass doors that led out to the car park, the young man in the expensive boots and long coat watched Cinder. As the last of the spectators filed out past him, he buttoned his coat and turned to leave.

'I'm looking forward to seeing you naked,' he said, taking one last glance at Cinder over his shoulder. 'Again.'

Chapter 26
Choices and Blessings

For the first time in many years, Angus felt like his life was close to normal, whatever normal meant. Spring had slipped by and now the days grew longer and warmer. There had not been so much as a whisper about the Lycan roaming the forests for weeks. Cinder had been working with Marraine to focus her thoughts and calm her mind. If the queen was calm, the pack was calm and easier to control, Marraine explained.

There was talk that Louvelle might have returned to The Big House, but Angus and Marraine agreed to keep that to themselves to preserve the status quo. Until they had more information, they thought it was better to not let the others know. Cinder and Dom were still volatile when it came to Louvelle and were likely to go running off into one of her traps.

Angus still surfed, but now mostly in the daytime, sometimes with Dom, sometimes by himself, when the bikini-clad holiday makers became too much of a distraction for Dom. His nights were taken up with getting to know his little sister and with other nocturnal activities with Cinder. There was a larger share of work for everyone on the farm now that Uncle Dand and the boys were gone, but they all had more time on their hands. Everything felt calm, relaxed, happy. He had his family, his girl, and he had peace.

The peace and calm today, it seemed, also extended to the ocean. Dom and Angus had got away as quickly as they could after the morning milking and headed for the beach. They had caught a few small breakers, but mainly, they had just floated on the smooth water, talking about their time away in Europe. Dom had grown bored about an hour in and headed into town to get a coffee and watch the tourists. Angus, happy to have some time to himself, persevered.

As the day grew warmer, the beach slowly filled with more people. A small collection of swimmers and two children on boogieboards joined Angus in the water. With the sun now high in the sky, he grew hot and thirsty. Just after midday, he called it quits on surfing for the day.

Sitting on the top run of the timber steps of the dune path, a young woman in a dark hooded top had been watching him on the water, a large, black paisley satchel resting on her lap. When she noticed Angus paddling back in, she stood and slung the satchel over her shoulder. Placing her hands in the large front pocket of her top, she meandered down the steps to the beach and leaned with her back against the handrail.

Angus emerged from the ocean. He unzipped his wetsuit, pulled his arms free and folded the top down to expose the bare skin of his back to the warm summer sun. The scars from the Lycan attack he had received almost a year ago were now just faint pink lines across his shoulder blade. Faded reminders of what his life once was. With his surfboard propped under one arm, he ruffled water from his thick dark hair with his free hand and walked to where he had left a bag of clothes and a drink bottle sitting on his towel.

The centuries-old vampire who now lived inside the body of his teenage sister was waiting for him on the edge of the dunes. She bent down and picked up Angus's towel from the sand and waved it as a greeting.

'You know,' Angus said, taking the towel from her. 'I'm still not sure what to call you.'

'Well, we're here today as your sister, so Katie feels like the most appropriate title, I think,' she said, gazing out to the horizon. Angus wiped the remaining water from his hair, wrapping the towel around his body against the cold.

'It's still going to take a bit of getting used to having my sister back,' he said.

'I've fourteen years of experience cohabiting, and it still bewilders and perplexes.' Katie said.

'I'm sure it would,' Angus acknowledged.

'Will you sit with me a while?' Katie asked, kneeling down on the beach and patting the sand next to her. 'I've some gifts for you.'

'I love presents,' Angus said, wrapping the towel around his shoulders and sitting eagerly down next to her.

'Don't we all,' she said as she retrieved the satchel from under her arm. 'We give to the receiver, and we receive in the giving.'

After a moment of searching through the shadowed contents of her satchel, Katie slowly lifted a silver chain from inside. A blue moon and tree pendant identical to the pendants that Cinder and Marraine now wore hung from the end of the chain. She held the pendant up to the sun and watched the light play on the glittering surface of the stone.

'I'm sorry; the clasp is broken so you will need to replace it,' she said, as the pendant rotated clockwise first, then changed direction after a brief pause, reflecting the bright summer sun.

'Everyone seems to have one of these now,' Angus said, taking it respectfully in his palm.

'Yes, an aberration and a faux pas that demands rectification, I'm afraid.'

'What do you mean?' Angus asked, turning the pendant over in his hand.

'These were intended for the Nephilim, the seven heads of the great families,' Katie said, running her finger over the smooth surface of the stone. Angus's hand involuntarily pulled back when the pendant vibrated under her touch. 'They were never intended to be defiled by my brothers as instruments of their depravity and deception or collected like trophies by the Lycanthropes.'

'What about Cinder's one, the red one, I mean?' Angus asked.

'That was to be bestowed upon a worthy queen as a memento of peace between the Lycanthrope and Nephilim; it was returned to the families at the end of her reign. The corrupting nature of time and heart have twisted them into something they were never created to be.'

'Has anyone tried to create more of these?' Angus asked, handing the pendant back to Katie. Katie folded his fingers over the powerful object and pushed his hand back with a smile and a bow of her head.

'Some have tried,' Katie said. 'But they are very difficult to create. They require the blood of a female vampire, my blood. Something flowing through these veins sets me apart from my brothers.' She held out her arms, running her eyes over them as if she could see the flow of her blood beneath her flesh. 'It allows me to feel the warmth of the sun on my skin while they are forever cursed to walk in darkness.' She closed her eyes and turned her face skywards. 'That is yours now, as it should be,' she said, inclining her face to his and opening one eye. 'Keep it safe.'

Angus reached for his bag and pulled his t-shirt from inside. He slid the shirt over his damp skin, then wrapped the pendant protectively in his towel and stowed it carefully in the bag.

'How much blood?' he asked, sitting his bag on the sand and taking a sip of warm water from his drink bottle.

'To make all eight?' Katie clarified as she began searching in her satchel again.

'Yes, all eight.'

'All of it,' she said, turning to look at Angus. 'You can see why I have little interest in there being more of them. Besides, their ability to grant my brothers access to the light was an unforeseen and undesirable side-effect.'

'Wait,' Angus said, screwing the lid back on his bottle. 'Vampires can use the pendants to walk around in the daylight?'

'Yes.' Katie pulled something else from her satchel. 'There have been times that I have thought about hunting them all down and destroying them. So, no, I will never allow anymore to be created. We gave our body once, never will it be given again. The moment mother breathes her last, I will be with her and commit her empty crucible to the cremation flame.' The more she talked like this, the less Angus saw his sister and the more Sase was visible.

'Where is your mother?' he asked.

'She is far from here, but she is where she needs to be,' she said, holding something brown and fluffy to her chest. Like her answers often did, this response left Angus with more questions, but he could sense that she wanted to change the subject.

'What have you got there?' he asked, looking at the tattered looking object behind her arms. Katie unfolded her arms and flopped a ragged old teddy bear in Angus's lap. Angus looked down into two scratched, glass button eyes. Stuffing was poking out of a hole in the top of the bear's head, where, as a child, Angus himself had tried to give the teddy a haircut.

'It's Berry!' he exclaimed. 'But how?'

'You gave him to me to keep me company on the car ride. Do you remember?'

'No, I had forgotten all about Berry,' Angus said, caressing the time-worn and well-loved toy in his large hands. Katie rested her hand on his shoulder.

'I have watched you sometimes over the years, big brother.' She took Angus's hand in hers. 'From the outside, people see a strong, fearless warrior, but I see the frightened little boy inside. The one still waiting for his family to come home.'

'Then you don't really see me,' Angus said, pulling his hand away 'I'm not that boy. I've had to grow up and I've done it without any of you.' His argument would have been more convincing had he not been sitting in the sand with a teddy bear on his lap. 'And speaking of that,' he continued, 'Nice to know you've been checking in. Did you ever think we could have used your help?'

'Do you know what your name means?' Katie asked, looking out to the horizon once again.

'What?' Angus asked with growing annoyance.

'Angus, do you know the meaning of that name?'

'Yes, I do, but I don't see what that has to do with anything.'

'It means choice, Angus is choice, a word that epitomises you, don't you think? Irony has always delighted and riled me. My constant and provocative friend.' Her face softened. 'The fateful decision to remain with your uncle the night of your parent's passing has haunted every choice since. The burden of choice, of *Angus*, still weighs as heavily on the man now as it did the child then. The Nephilim look to you as a leader but so concerned are you with right decisions, you make none at all.'

'You know nothing about me,' Angus said, sitting the bear on top of his bag. 'That little boy you think you see died the night that his family never came back to get him.'

'I know more than most and see more than most,' Katie said, opening her satchel for the third time. 'I see you looking at that girl and I know what you're thinking. *Have I made the right choice?* Here you are again, on the edge of a decision, looking down on an uncertain future and you are too afraid to leap, too cautious to jump, too chained to death to venture into life. Too anchored to set sail.' She placed her hand on his tattoo.

'It's okay for you,' Angus said. He pulled his arm away,lifting his legs to his chest and wrapping his arms around his knees. 'You only need to worry about yourself and if you make a bad decision, you can just make a better one in the next version of yourself.' Katie closed the satchel and looked into Angus's face. Deep lines creased his brow.

'I will let you know something I have learned over my many years,' she said. 'I have stopped thinking about choices as good, bad, right or wrong. I simply ask. Will this choice make the world better for the people I care about? If the answer is yes, then that is the path I follow.'

'Cinder has made our world a better place,' Angus said, turning to look at her, his face relaxing.

'She has,' Katie agreed.

'Does that mean she's a good choice, then?'

'Like I said, it simply means that she is a path worth following. You must decide where that path leads you.' They sat for a moment, listening to the crash of the waves and the squeals of a toddler gleefully stomping on a sandcastle. Angus thought about what Katie had been saying.

'She thinks you hate her, you know,' he said, finally.

'And what makes her think that?'

'The way you look at her.'

'No need to worry about that, big brother. If I hated her, she would already be dead,' she said, flashing him a devilish smirk.

'Well, that's reassuring, I guess.' Angus picked up the teddy bear and threw it at her. 'So what is it, then? Why the tension between you two?'

'Is there tension?' Katie asked, stroking the bear's head.

'Yes, you know there is.'

'She just surprised me, that's all,' Katie said, placing Berry back on Angus's bag. 'It's not often anymore that things surprise me.' She looked down at an ant scurrying back and forth across the sand.

'She does that,' Angus said, rubbing the back of his neck. 'What about her surprised you then?' he asked. Katie turned her attention back to the satchel on her lap.

'I've already said too much. My opinions shouldn't sway your choices. You need to know that your reasons are your reasons.'

'Is this what living multiple lives teaches you, how to talk without actually saying anything? Do you ever just answer a question simply?' Angus asked. Katie smiled.

'No. Was that simple enough for you?'

'You know what mum would have called you?'

'No, unfortunately I don't,' Katie said, her smile fading away.

'A mystery wrapped in an enigma, hidden in a labyrinth.'

'I like the sound of that.'

'Do you remember them — our parents?'

'Bits and pieces, thoughts and feelings mostly. Smells,' Katie said, looking up, as if her memories were playing out across the blue sky.

'Smells?' Angus asked.

'You would be amazed by the evocative nature of scent. Memories good, bad, precious, and some forgotten until the right key is turned.' She seemed to drift off. 'Anyway,' she said after a moment. 'Speaking of memories, and at the risk of contradicting all that I have said about ensuring I am not an influential factor in your decision making.' Katie reached inside her satchel, pulling out her third and final gift. A small metallic object sat between her thumb and index finger. It sparkled gold and white as it caught the sunlight.

'Wait, is that?' Angus felt short of breath.

'Yes,' Katie said, handing him a gold ring set with three round diamonds. 'It's your mother's. Remember, I loved to play with it when I was little. I was holding it in my hand when the car crashed.'

'Then you should keep it,' Angus said, holding it out to her.

'No. I will always love you as my brother, but I am not really Catherine MacAskill. I am just the convincing actress that is playing the part of your sister in this act of your life. I'm wearing her body as my costume and I have diligently studied my part, but you know in your heart of hearts that I am not the girl you lost or the woman she would have become.'

'But I love you the same,' he said, taking her hand. Sase kissed his cheek.

'And I you,' she whispered before standing up.

'Wait,' Angus said. 'I really think you should keep the ring.' Sase shook her head.

'It needs to stay in the family. I will never have children of my own, at least not in the traditional sense.'

'It's too small for my fingers,' Angus said, sliding the ring over the end of his index finger.

'Then you will need to find a new home for it.'

'Is this your way of giving me your blessing?' Angus asked, getting to his knees. Katie shook her head.

'Fate has drawn your path and Cinder's together. Even now, fate is working to strengthen that bond. But I cannot be your guide and I have no authority to bestow such a blessing. Though our paths will cross from time to time, I have not journeyed with you to this crossroad, nor will I continue to the same destination.'

'How can you be centuries-old and still talk in riddles?'

'Time is a riddle. You have a short lifetime of choices that haunt you. I have a dozen lifetimes. It does not get easier, brother. A clear rear-view mirror may give you a better understanding of the road conditions, but it does nothing to help you avoid the potholes ahead.'

'Can you just say something... normal?'

'Cinder would not be my choice for you. But I am not you and I think you have already made your choice.'

Angus slipped his mother's ring over his little finger. It sat just above his knuckle. As he thought about what his sister was saying, he turned the ring back and forth.

'But I would like your blessing.' he said, turning back to Sase.

'My blessing? I am not who you think. I have her face, but I am just a whisper of a shadow of your sister. A parasite wearing her skin until I am ready to find a new home.'

'You have her memories.'

'I have shards of eggshells of her memories, too small and slippery to pull out. They crunch undesirably in my teeth. I don't have the right to give my blessings to anyone.'

'Why have watched over me then, and why did you keep this?' Angus asked, holding up the ring so that the summer sun danced across the glassy surface of the diamonds.

'Because sentiment is one of the hardest bits of eggshell to remove,' Sase said in a melancholy tone as she watched the light sparkle in a rainbow of colours.

'What's the hardest to remove?'

'There are two: Revenge and love.' Sase took Angus's face in her hands, bending and kissing him between the eyes. 'It's not my blessing, but I will say this about Cinder. She loves all of you. You know, she was the only one who questioned me about being here.'

'Yes, I know. I'm sorry about that,' Angus said, placing his warm hand over her cold one.

'You shouldn't be sorry. On the contrary, you should thank her.'

'Thank her?'

'Yes, it was the right thing to do, and it was done out of love. Love for you and your family. Cinder has learned not to take things at face value; something you could learn. You are all too trusting. You need someone like Cinder around.'

'So, you do like her then?'

'Like is not the appropriate word. Let us just say that I respect her and see her value. Don't start getting any ideas about us being *best-sister-in-law-friends*.' Sase said, placing her hand on Angus's stubbled cheek. The waves crashed and rumbled and a north-westerly rustled through the long, dry grass of the dunes. Brother and sister shared a silent moment.

'I guess I have a choice to make then.' Angus said. Sase took the ring from his finger. Placing it in his palm, she bent his fingers over it.

'Yes, Angus MacAskill,' she said. 'One big choice.'

Chapter 27

Growing Pains

Beads of sweat clung to the back of Cinder's neck, glistening in the light of the sultry afternoon. Her chest and shoulders lifted and fell in time with deep, rapid breaths. The thud of knuckles on leather and the grinding rattle of chain on timber echoed off the corrugated iron walls. Her bare feet shuffled and danced around the dirt floor. Thump, thump, thumpidy-thump. Skilful hands pounded a punching bag, shaking it violently. The old timber structure of the shed-come-gym protested under the strain but held firm, stretching tall and unyielding to the iron roof high above. Wiping her face on the sleeve of her t-shirt, Cinder positioned herself ready to punch the bag again, hands up at her tucked chin. As her right shoulder moved back, she stopped. Instead, reaching out with her left hand and resting in on the bag.

She dropped her hands to her side and looked around the room to check that she was still alone. *You need to cover those hands, Cinder,* she said to herself. A pair of blue, faded and cracked gloves hung from a rusty nail driven into one of the large timber uprights. After first sniffing the inside to check for cleanliness, she slipped her hand inside the protective leather. She adjusted the Velcro around her wrists and hit the bag again. Something pulled painfully in her lower back and she cringed, hissing in a breath between clenched teeth.

'What was that?' she said, stretching her shoulders up and forward to relieve the cramping and pain.'

'What was what?' Marraine had appeared in the doorway, seemingly out of nowhere, as she had a knack of doing.

'Oh, hi,' Cinder said, grimacing and peeling the Velcro open again. 'I hurt my back!'

'You?' Marraine asked, surprised. 'I thought you were a fighting machine.' She said, coming to stand next to Cinder. Cinder slipped her hands out of the gloves.

'I guess I'm out of practice,' she said, hanging the gloves back on the nail with some difficulty.

'I would give you a massage, sweetie, but you would need a shower first,' Marraine said, looking at the large wet patch on the back of Cinder's t-shirt.

'Thanks,' Cinder said, trying to smile. 'I'm sure I'll be okay. I just need to stretch it out.'

'I hope so, birthday girl. We've got a big night planned.'

'It's hard to believe it was only a year ago we were getting ready to go out to Paddy's for the first time.'

'You've had a big year, sweetie.'

'It feels like a lifetime AGO!' Cinder's face twisted as a spasm shot across her back.

'Are you sure you're going to be okay?' Marraine asked, trying not to laugh at the faces Cinder was making. Cinder exhaled slowly.

'Yep! I'll be fine,' she said unconvincingly. Marraine tilted her head to one side and raised her eyebrows.

'Are you?'

'Yes, it's just some cramping,' Cinder said as the pain subsided. 'I'll go soak in the tub for a bit.' She stretched her arms above her head, then let them drop to her side. Marraine eyed her doubtfully.

'So, birthday girl,' she said, taking Cinder's hand. 'Are you glad you came with me to Paddy's last year?'

'It's been a rollercoaster ride,' Cinder said, opening her eyes wide. 'But, yes, a thousand times, yes.' She squeezed Marraine's hand. 'You rescued me, Marraine. You're my Furry Godmother.'

'Come on, let's get out of here before I start crying,' Marraine said, leading Cinder towards the door. 'I've got some of the things of your mother's that we talked about.'

'Are you going to get ready here?' Cinder asked as they squinted and exited into the bright afternoon.

'No, I have a waxing appointment,' Marraine said. 'I feel like it's even more important now that you called me Furry.'

Cinder turned from side to side, looking at herself in the long mirror on the inside or Torry's wardrobe. She hardly recognised herself as the girl from her last birthday who was yet to meet these people. People that were now so important to her.

'I love your dress,' Tori said, running her hand across Cinder's back. 'Where did that come from?'

'Marraine gave me this. It was my mother's,' Cinder said, pulling at the dress. 'My real mother,' she added, seeing the question on Torry's face. Torry walked around her, nodding approvingly. She stopped in front of Cinder with a quizzical look.

'Have your boobs gotten bigger?' she asked matter-of-factly. Cinder crossed her arms over her chest.

'Torry!'

'What? They look big, I'm just saying,' Torry moved forward on to her tip-toes and looked down the top of Cinder's dress. Cinder unfolded one of her arms and pushed her away.

'Stop it!' she said, her cheeks turning rosy.

'Okay, okay, I'm sorry,' Torry said, stepping back and raising her hands. 'But are they bigger?' Cinder tried to look serious but couldn't help grinning at the mischievous smirk on Torry's face.

'Yes, they are, alright,' Cinder admitted. 'Are you happy now? In fact,' she continued, 'everything is bigger. That's why I'm wearing this. Most of my clothes don't fit me anymore.'

'My dad's food will do that to you.' Torry said, patting her stomach.

'Yes,' Cinder agreed, pulling at the dress again. 'And before that, I was eating real Italian food in Italy. You know how I love pasta.'

'Mmm, Italian food,' Torry agreed. Cinder moved to Torry's wardrobe and looked at herself in the mirror.

'I'm not doing hours of training every day, so that doesn't help either,' she placed her hand on her lower back. 'I'm so out of practice I hurt my back.'

'Maybe you're just getting old,' Torry teased.

'Yeah, fat and old,' Cinder said jokingly, but turned sideways and ran her hands over her stomach. 'Maybe I should wear something different.'

'No way,' Torry said. 'You look awesome.' Cinder grimaced and tried to pull the neckline of her dress further up her chest.

'I don't know. Am I trying too hard?' she asked, turning from side to side. Torry walked up behind Cinder, resting her head on her shoulder.

'Are you asking that or is your step-mother asking that?' she asked, wrapping her arms around Cinder's waste 'You are a kick-arse crazy bitch, a fricken Lycan queen! I don't think you're trying hard enough.'

Memories of running free and wild in the forest near Vivien's Ridge flooded Cinder's mind. She stood up tall and set her shoulders back. 'You're right. I can eat whatever I want, and I can wear whatever I want.'

'Yeah!' Torry agreed. 'You're the queen. You make the rules.'

'I make the rules!' Cinder yelled.

'Hell yeah! Look at us,' Torry said, looking in the mirror. 'We're so hot.' They stood for a few seconds, looking at each other in the mirror. Cinder noticed Torry's hand moving up towards her chest.

'What are you doing?' she asked.

'Can I squeeze one?' Torry joked.

'No!' Cinder squealed and ran to Torry's bed. Torry laughed and Cinder threw one of her pillows at her. She marched to the bedroom door. 'I'm going to get Marraine. I will see you soon.'

* * * *

A brush with long, soft bristles dance over a pair of proudly held shoulders. Flecks of thick brown hair fell to the floor. A young woman with dark eye makeup and black clothes placed the brush next to a pair of silver scissors.

'All done,' she said as she removed a protective smock from the young man sitting in front of her.

'Thank you.' The young man said. He turned his head, admiring his freshly styled hair. The woman in black positioned a mirror so that he could see the back of his head.

'I didn't need to do much. Your hair looked great already,' she said. The young man flashed his white teeth.

'Thank you. I get it from my father.' He ran his hand through his hair. 'I wanted to look my best. It's a special birthday tonight.'

'A special girl?'

'A very special girl. But shh.' He held his finger to his lips. 'It's a surprise.'

'I love surprises.'

'As do I.' The young man pulled up his sleeve, glancing at an antique gold watch.

'Thank you again. I had best be off. I need to ensure I am there before she arrives.'

Chapter 28
Place We Were Made.

Angus stood alone, with his back to a dark green wall. A half-full beer glass occupied one hand as the other fumbled with a small box in his pocket. He watched as a young man with a long beard and black apron, weaved in and out of a happily noisy crowd. In large white text across the back of his tight-fitting black t-shirt was the word Paddy's. Atop a tray held at the young man's shoulder, two cylindrical shaped objects wrapped in tinfoil sat nested in a cane basket. As he passed Angus, a warm, yeasty, garlic and butter smell wafted around his nostrils. Suddenly, his thoughts were back in Rome. Angus pictured himself standing on the balcony of the Hotel de la Ville, with his arms around Cinder. He closed his eyes and breathed deeply before finishing his drink. Looking impassively at the remnants of his drink, Angus swirled the few remaining drops of liquid around the bottom of the glass before placing it on a nearby table. A bead of perspiration trickle down the back of his neck as he adjusted his shirt collar.

Dom weaved through the crowd, a drink in each hand. One for himself and another to replace the one that Angus had just finished.

'Are you okay?' he asked as he manoeuvred himself next to Angus and handed him his drink.

'I'm fine,' Angus said, leaning towards Dom to talk over the crowd and taking the drink. 'Why do you ask?'

'You just look, umm...' Dom surveyed the congregation of locals and tourist mingling. 'I don't know what the word I'm looking for is.'

'Handsome?' Angus asked.

'No.'

'Manly?'

'Nope.'

'Debonair perhaps?'

'No, that's not it,' Dom said, shaking his head. 'Constipated. That's the one,' he added, lifting his index finger from his glass and pointing it at Angus.

'Constipated? What?'

'Look at you, you're all stiff and sweaty.' Dom looked Angus up and down. 'And what's going on with the hand in your pocket? Are you playing with yourself?' he asked. Angus sipped his drink.

'You want to know what's in my pocket?'

'What's in your pocket?'

'I've got something for you.' Angus said.

'Something for me?' Dom raised his eyebrows.

'Yep, here it is.' Angus pulled out his hand and held up his middle finger in Dom's face. Dom grinned, stuck out his tongue, and licked Angus's finger. Angus yanked his hand away and wiped his finger on the back of Dom's shirt.

'You're disgusting. Do you know where that finger's been?'

'Do you know where my tongue's been?' Dom asked, winking at two young women smiling at him from the bar. Angus slid his hand back into his pocket.

'No, and I don't want to know.'

'But seriously,' Dom said, nudging Angus with his elbow, 'What's up?'

Angus watched as the two women at the bar collected their drinks and started making their way towards him and Dom.

'I guess I'm just nervous,' he said with a shrug. 'It's a special night for Cinder. I just hope she has a good time.'

A long arm with freckled skin and painted fingernails snaked its way around Angus's torso.

'Who has a good time?' Cinder had appeared next to him, followed close behind by Marraine.

'You,' Angus said, draping his arm over her shoulder. 'I hope you have a good time. Happy birthday.' He kissed the top of Cinder's head. Marraine strolled casually in front and stood with her back to them, arms crossed. The two women from the bar saw the look on her face and made a beeline for a spot on the opposite wall.

'Hello there, sweetie,' Dom said, resting his chin on Marraine's shoulder.

'Oh! Hello,' she said, tuning and looking at him confused. 'Do I know you?' she asked.

'It's me, Dom.'

'Which one are you again?' Marraine asked, turning and placing her hand on his shoulder.

'Which one am I? Are you seriously saying you don't remember me?' Ask Dom.

'I'm sorry,' Marraine said. 'There's just so many of you. Are you the one that lost his boyfriend?'

'No, I'm the one that's been away trying to find my sister's killer.'

'I see. Dom was it? I'm sorry, please excuse me, I need to go to the bathroom.' Marraine turned and headed to the ladies' room. Dom slumped back against the wall.

'Was she serious?' he asked himself. He ran his hand back and forth across his chin. Pushing himself off the wall, he followed Marraine into the ladies' room.

Angus took Cinder's face in his hands and kissed her slowly and deeply.

'Hi,' Cinder said, looking into his eyes.

'Hi. Where did you two come from? I didn't see you come in.' Angus slipped his hand from her face and back into his pocket.

'There was a line out front, so Marraine got us in the back way.'

'There's a back way?' Angus asked, leaning to look behind Cinder.

'Apparently.'

'Trust Marraine to know about it.'

'Yep.' Cinder turned to look around the room. 'It's busy in here tonight.'

'Yes,' Angus agreed, watching as people weaved in and out between each other – eating, drinking, laughing, living. The mixture of the warm summer night and the music was electrifying. 'The band's great,' Angus said. Cinder looked to the front corner of Paddy's. Four young people with tanned skin and messy hair, swayed energetically under colourful lights. Drums and guitars pulsed and shone in the play of lights as a provocative melody swept out over the room.

'Yes,' Cinder agreed. They stood close together and listened as one song ended and another began.

'Do you want to dance?' Angus's voice cracked.

'What?' Cinder asked, leaning in closer to hear him.

'Do you want to dance?'

'Yes!' Cinder replied enthusiastically. Angus took her by the hand and led her towards the front of the pub, still fumbling with the object in his pocket.

As they passed the ladies' room, Dom rushed out, almost knocking them over.

'What were you doing in there?' Cinder asked when she had recovered from the surprise. Dom's face was red, and he was sweaty around his collar.

'I was in there with Marraine.'

'What?' Angus asked.

'We were umm... fighting.' Dom said, fixing his hair. 'I'm getting a drink.' He pushed past them and forced his way through the crowd towards the bar. Cinder and Angus looked at each other quizzically and continued to the dance floor. Picking a dark corner, Angus twirled Cinder around and then wrapped her in his muscular arms. Cinder's head rested against his chest, feeling at home. Underneath a pale pink spotlight, the lead singer of the band plucked away at her acoustic guitar. Her long curly black hair swayed along with the tick-tock rhythm of the drummer next to her. She smiled and stepped forward to the microphone, the light on her youthful face changing from pink to blue. She took a deep breath, pushed her lips to the microphone and sung.

They say home is where the heart is, but my heart is gone.
Left in that place where you left me alone.
I wore it on my sleeve, let it air, hung it out there.
But you ripped my shirt off, you left me bare.
How do I go home now? How do I go home now?

Angus kissed the top of Cinder's head. Cinder looked up into his chocolate eyes. They sparkled with happiness, but his brow looked tight and troubled.

'Is everything alright?' she asked.

'Everything's great,' he said, stroking her freckled cheek. 'For the first time in a long time, everything is great – perfect even.' His eyes grew wide, taking on a glassy appearance. Cinder moved her head up and pushed her lips to his.

'Perfect,' Cinder repeated back to him. Angus's hand moved from her back to his pocked.

'I have your birthday present,' he said, removing the object from his pocket.

'I love presents,' Cinder said excitedly, looking down. Angus held a small black box wrapped in a red ribbon.

'I need to ask you something first,' he said, stepping back.

'Okay then,' Cinder said, looking him up and down. Angus cleared his throat as a bead of perspiration ran down the left-hand side of his torso. He prepared to get down on one knee, but noticed that Cinder had looked away.

Chapter 29
Birthday Surprises

A clammy skinned man with yellowing complexion and flecks of white through his light brown hair sat hunched at the bar of Paddy's. His limp, inebriated hands clasped a tall glass. Warming beer dripped on his faded grey T-shirt as he watched Torry walk by. His weaselly eyes followed her like a dog watching meat on a rotisserie. Oblivious to the looks of the unwanted admirer, Torry lent on the bar next to her brother, within arm's reach of the man. The man's eyes sparkled, a drunken grin spreading across his unshaven face.

'What the hell?' Torry yelled, as the man's stubby, dirty-nailed fingers wrapped aggressively around her backside.

'How you doin' darlin?' he asked with a droopy eyed grin. The man's smile quickly disappeared. Torry's fist crashed into his round nose with a slap. The man stumbled off his barstool and dropped to the floor, blood bright and red, dripping from his left nostril. He still held his glass in his hand, but the sticky amber liquid covered his clothes.

'I think you broke my nose, bitch,' he yelled as he tried to pull himself up onto his feet.

'Oh, I'm sorry,' Torry said. 'Would you like me to punch it better?' She hit him again, just below his left eye. This time the man fell flat on his back, spread-eagle on the floor. The glass fell from his grip and spun across the timber floor. Cursing and yelling, the wet, bruised, and bleeding man groped at his face.

'I'm gonna kill you!' he yelled, stumbling to his feet and knocking over a bar stool. His blood-shot eyes searched wildly for Torry. Dom stepped forward and Angus came running. They grabbed an arm each of the drunken man, lifting him up and carrying him out, flaying and protesting, through the crowd. When they reached the front door of Paddy's, they threw him out onto the street.

The two uniformed police officers, Beccy O'Bearn and Henry Burket, were across the street from Paddy's talking to some of the locals while they waited for Detective Morgan. Beccy's hand fell instinctively to her gun belt as Torry's victim blundered across the street towards them.

'Did you see that?' the man yelled. 'You need to arrest them.'

'Yes, I saw everything,' Peter Morgan said, stepping down from the entrance to Paddy's and following the man. 'Detective Morgan, Heathcote police,' he added, showing the confused man his identification.

'What are you going to do about this?' the man yelled, pointing at his swollen and bloody face. Peter Morgan continued past the man and stood next to the other officers.

'We can certainly go down to the police station and hear all about how you sexually assaulted an underage girl and then, also how that underage girl beat you up in self-defence,' he said with a grin.

'But she broke my nose,' the man protested.

'Yes, I can see that,' Peter Morgan said, pulling a handkerchief from his jacket and handing it to the man. 'You're lucky that is all she did. You should be thankful you're still standing on two legs.' Peter Morgan turned and whispered to Beccy, 'Perhaps our friend here might need a place to sleep things off tonight.'

'Sure thing.' Beccy said, tapping Henry's chest.

Peter Morgan strolled casually across the quiet Heathcote esplanade and re-entered Paddy's. Behind him, Beccy and Henry cuffed the drunken man and wrestled him into a waiting police wagon. Torry and Cinder had joined the two boys in the doorway of Paddy's.

'Do you want to press charges, Miss Kinnard?' Peter Morgan asked.

'No, it's okay. I can look after myself.'

'I know you can, but there are others that don't or can't.'

'Okay then,' Torry agreed.

'Come to the station tomorrow. We'll get your statement then.'

'Okay. Hey Peter?'

'Yes, Miss Kinnard?'

'How did you sort out the... the stuff from the night at the farm?'

'Yes, that night,' Peter Morgan said, nodding to O'Burket. 'It appears a drug affected man went on a rampage, attacking a group of partygoers. When he broke into your farm, I had to act to protect an elderly man and his teenage daughter.'

'Thank you again, Peter. Oh, and Peter?'

'Yes, Miss Kinnard?'

'Call me Torry.'

'Yes, Torry.' Peter Morgan watched the police wagon drive away. Marraine walked up behind Dom, resting her hand on his shoulder.

'That's your little sister, right? The one that stabbed Louvelle in the leg with a branch?'

'So, you remember her, do you?'

'Oh, yes, I remember her, sweetie. She's my new hero.' Marraine turned and went back inside. Cinder turned to follow her, but as she did, she gave a cry of pain.

'What's wrong?' Angus asked, taking hold of her arm.

'I'm fine,' Cinder reassured him with a forced laugh. 'I just pulled a muscle in my back earlier and I must have twisted the wrong way then.' She held onto the door frame and stepped painfully inside. Sensing something wrong, Marraine turned back to look at Cinder. Noticing her pained face, she pushed past Dom and swept over to her.

'Is everything okay, Annabelle?' She called Cinder by her mother's name.

'I'm fine.' Cinder said, forcing a smile. 'And my name's Cinder.'

'I'm sorry, sweetie.' Marraine said, taking her hand. 'You just look so much like your mother tonight.'

'Was she always in pain?' Cinder joked.

'No, but she was a pain in the butt. Just like you.' Marraine led her to the stool that was now free at the bar.

'Take a seat here, sweetie.' As she sat Cinder down, a light flashed inside her handbag. Cinder pointed to the flashing. Angus and Torry, following close behind them, began fussing over Cinder. Marraine pulled her phone from her bag. Dom ordered himself another drink.

'I'm fine,' Cinder said in response to their looks of concern. 'Have a drink. Enjoy yourselves. This is meant to be a party.' She watched Marraine struggling to hear whoever was on the other end of the phone call. Looking concerned, Marraine walked out of the front door onto the street.

'Would you like something to drink?' Angus asked, regaining Cinder's attention.

'Yes, thank you. I think I need one.' Cinder tried unsuccessfully to get comfortable on the bar stool.

'What would you like?' Angus asked her, resisting the urge to ask her if she was okay again.

'What are you having?'

'An old-fashioned.'

'Get me one of those too, then.'

'Sure thing,' Angus said, stepping up to the bar to get the attention of the bar staff. Torry took his place next to Cinder.

'You having fun, sis?' she asked, resting her head on Cinder's shoulder.

'I was until my back started playing up again,' Cinder said, sitting up and placing her hand on her lower back. 'Not as much fun as you, slugger.'

'Oh yeah,' Torry said with a shudder. 'Getting felt up by creepy old drunk guys. I'm living the dream.' Torry looked down at her backside. 'I'm not even wearing my sexy pants.'

'You have sexy pants?' Cinder asked with a laugh that sent a stabbing pain into her abdomen.

'Hell yeah, I have sexy pants.'

'Who has sexy pants?' Dom asked as he returned with his drink. Torry performed an overly exaggerated point towards herself. Then, with a flourish of her wrist, she licked her finger and touched it to her hip.

'Me,' she mouthed more than said. Dom turned and walked away.

'I don't want to know,' he called behind him as he went. Angus turned back to the two girls and handed Cinder her drink.

'Where's mine?' Torry asked, coveting the amber liquid containing ice cubes and a twirl of orange peel.

'Here,' Angus said, handing her a tall glass of cola. Torry propped her hands on her hips and dropped her head to one side.

'That's not what I meant.'

'I know what you meant, but I'm not in the habit of supplying underage girls with alcohol.'

'Okay, so it sounds bad when you say it like that.' Torry reluctantly took the cola from him.

'Here, you can have some of mine,' Cinder said, holding her drink up to Torry's mouth. Torry tipped her head back and sipped Cinder's cocktail.

'She gets it,' she said, looking at Angus and wiping a drip from her chin. Angus shook his head disapprovingly.

'Weren't you about to give me my birthday present before we got interrupted?' Cinder asked to change the subject.

'Umm... yeah,' Angus said, fiddling with the buttons on his shirt.

'I'm going to find my brother,' Torry interrupted, suddenly feeling like the third-wheel. She moved off into the crowd and Angus stood closer to Cinder.

'What's going on with you?' Cinder asked, noticing his discomfort. Angus pulled Cinder's gift from his pocket again.

'I... umm.'

'Hold on!' Cinder stopped him. Marraine was weaving back towards them, striding quickly and purposely. Her usually cool and calm face hung heavy with concern.

'Bob's in trouble,' she said as she approached.

'What kind of trouble?' Cinder asked, standing.

'I don't know exactly. No one has seen him for weeks now and...' Marraine paused and looked at Angus. Angus nodded in unsaid understanding.

'She needs to know,' he said.

'I need to know what?' Cinder demanded, looking from Angus to Marraine and sitting her drink down on the bar heavily enough to spill.

'Louvelle's back, back at The Big House. She wasn't very happy to discover I faked my death and Bob got caught in the wrong place at the wrong time.'

'Shit!' Cinder yelled, twisting her back uncomfortably and sending a sharp pain up her left side. Many heads turned to look at her. 'Why didn't anyone tell me Louvelle was back?'

'That's a good question.' It was Dom's voice. He and Torry had seen Marraine walking agitatedly through Paddy's and followed her. 'Why didn't we know that the bitch was back?' Dom crossed his arms. Blue veins stood thick and prominent on top of his large biceps. Torry ran her fingers down the scars on her neck.

'We wanted to give Cinder a chance to get a handle on being queen before we upset her again.' Marraine said.

'I'm not a child that needs mothering,' Cinder spat indignantly.

'That's right,' Dom agreed. 'And it doesn't explain why you didn't tell me.'

'Because you are a child,' Angus said. Dom stuck his middle finger up in Angus's face. Torry moved and stood close beside Cinder.

'No one told me either,' she said into Cinder's ear. Cinder took her hand and squeezed it gently.

'We can talk about this later,' Marraine said loudly, clicking her fingers in the air. 'Bob needs our help.'

'Yes, you're right,' Cinder said, sitting back on her bar stool. 'Do you have any idea where he might be?'

'Maybe,' Marraine said. 'I tried to call him but got no answer. Then he sent me this.' She held up her phone for Cinder to see.

'At yours,' Cinder read. 'What does that mean? Would he have gone to your flat?'

'No, sweetie, I've never given him that address.' Marraine slipped her phone back into her bag. Only a trusted few have that address.'

'I don't know where your flat is.' Dom interrupted. Marraine turned to look at him, expressionless.

'That's right Dominic, you don't,' she said. Dom's bottom lip drooped. Torry laughed.

'What does "At yours" mean, then?' Angus asked.

'There is one place he could mean,' Marraine said. 'We use it to smuggle out some of Cinder's parents' things. Bob drops me off some wine that he has pilfered from her ladyship's collection from time to time. It's ten minutes away from here along the coastal road. He could be there.' She shrugged.

'But if he's there, why isn't he answering his phone?' Torry asked.

'Maybe he's hurt. Maybe he's being followed or worried he's phones tapped. I don't know.' Marraine said, her hands strangled around the strap of her handbag.

'Let's go find him them,' Dom said, placing his hand on the small of her back.

'You don't even like him,' Angus said.

'I don't,' Dom agreed. 'I think he's an idiot. But he's our idiot. Am I right?'

'Yes,' Marraine said with a smile, reaching behind her back and taking Dom's hand. 'He's our idiot.'

'Okay then, let's go,' Cinder said, but as she stood up, a wave of pain washed over her again. She leaned over and rested her hands on her knees, breathing deeply until the pain subsided.

'You're not going anywhere but home,' Angus said, as he helped her to stand upright.

'I'll be fine,' Cinder said through gritted teeth, not fooling any of them.

'No, you won't. You're no help to us like this, anyway. Go home and see Gunn. He'll have something to fix you up and then you can come and find us.'

'Okay then. Fine. But let me know when you find him.' Cinder sat back down at the bar. Marraine moved towards her with an apologetic expression.

'Sorry to mess up your birthday, sweetie.'

'Don't be silly,' Cinder said, waving her away. 'Bob is important to me, too. We can all have a birthday drink together when you find him.'

'You got it,' Marraine said, leaning in and kissing the top of Cinder's head. Torry propped one knee up on the stool next to her.

'Do you want me to stay with you, sis?' she asked.

'No, I'm just going to go home now, anyway. See if your dad can help me with my back.'

Torry, Marraine, and the two boys left Cinder sitting at the bar and weaved their way through patrons and tables back out onto the street. Cinder listened as the singer at the front of Paddy's sung a haunting tune full of sadness and sarcasm. Drinks rattled as people bustled about the pub, laughing and chatting happily. The bands' colourful lights reflecting playfully on her glass as she watched the melting ice bob up and down against a piece of orange peel. She took one more sip before sitting her glass on the bar. *Happy birthday, Cinder,* she said to herself, remembering how she had met Angus here only a year ago. No one could have predicted how that meeting would have changed her life so dramatically.

'Have your friends all left you?' someone said in a thick European accent as they took the seat next to her. Cinder looked up from her drink in surprise.

'You're the guy from roller derby. The one who caught me. Are you following me?'

'No. Would you like me to be?' he asked, getting the bar staff's attention.

'No, that would be creepy. I don't even know you.' Cinder hoped her freckles covered the blushing in her cheeks. The young man looked just as out of place here in Paddy's as he did in the Y.M.C.A. hall. The twilight was quickly dwindling, and Cinder could just see the last glow of the setting sun through the large front window of Paddy's, but there was still heat from the summer day lingering. In a room full of hot, packed together bodies, the dress code in Paddy's that night was less is best. The stranger with the good bone structure, gold watch and designer stubble, however, was wearing pants, shirt, vest, and matching knee-length jacket. The whole deal. *Somehow, he's pulling it off,* Cinder thought. *Not a hair out of place, or even one drop of sweat.*

'And here I was thinking we were old friends.' The young man said, as he ordered himself a drink.

'We've only met once before,' Cinder said. The stranger looked up and tilted his head to the side in an expression that said he didn't totally agree with Cinder's statement.

'How many times do you need to meet someone before you can call yourself friends?'

'I don't know,' Cinder thought for a moment. 'I met some new people here last year and they've been my friends ever since.'

'Well, there you go,' he said as his drink arrived. 'Perhaps this is your place to meet new friends. Cheers,' he said, raising his glass. Cinder lifted her glass, and he touched his to hers with a clink of glass and rattle of ice.

'I didn't catch your name last time,' Cinder said, taking another drink. The young man cleared his throat.

'It's.' But before he could finish, Cinder's eyes widen, and she looked across the room. Tibult, one of the two Haitian brothers who were once loyal bodyguards of Louvelle but now declared their loyalty for Cinder, was pushing his way forcefully through the packed room. 'Another friend of yours?' The young man asked.

'Excuse the interruption, my lady,' Tibult said, approaching Cinder with a scowl across his shaved head.

'My lady?' The stranger asked with an amused look on his handsome face. Cinder's face burned with anger and embarrassment.

'Just ignore that,' Cinder said, trying to avoid eye contact with the young man. She pulled Tibult away from the bar. 'I've asked you not to call me that,' she reminded him.

'I am sorry,' Tibult offered. 'Please forgive my insolence.'

'It's fine,' Cinder said, looking back over his shoulder. The young man was still watching her, his eyes twinkling with interest. A smile revealed dazzlingly white teeth between his lips. 'Why are you here?' Cinder asked the two brothers.

'I was already on our way to find you because we felt your pain and distress,' Tibult said, looking Cinder up and down. Cinder rolled her eyes 'But I received some information from my brother Lysander,' he continued, 'and we thought you would want to hear it, my queen.'

'Okay,' Cinder said, putting her finger in front of her lips. 'Let's just keep the queen stuff quiet. What's the information, and why is it so important to be interrupting my birthday?' Tibult stepped back, bowing his bald head in submission, expecting retribution. 'Stand up, stand up,' Cinder said, looking around. 'Everyone is watching.' This wasn't true. The only person in all of Paddy's interested in them was the young man in the expensive clothes. He appeared to find the whole interaction entertaining. 'Just tell me the information.'

'We received word that one of the Nephilim is being kept captive by Lady Gevaudan.'

'Where?'

'She has him imprisoned underneath Berkley's Manor. In the place where you were forced to train.'

'In the old wine cellar, my gym?'

'Yes, that's the place.'

'Do you know who it is?'

'The giant one.'

'They are all giants,' Cinder said, rolling her eyes.

'His head is as naked as my own, but he has a thick beard covering his wide chin.'

'Do you mean Duncan?'

'Yes, I believe that is his name.'

Cinder swept back over to the bar. With an apologetic smile, she sat her hands on the empty bar stool next to the young man. 'It was nice to see you again,' she said. 'I have to go now. There is some business I need to take care of. I hope we meet again sometime.' The young man reached forward and sat a chilly hand on Cinder's shoulder.

'I'm sure we will,' he said, looking into her eyes. Something in his voice made Cinder shift back uncomfortably. Something definite and certain, even hungry. She had no time to think about it more. She turned, collected Tibult, and headed for the door. As she passed the young stranger, she called to him.

'Goodbye. Next time, you'll have to tell me your name.'

He smiled again. 'I can't wait to see the surprise on your face when I do.' he said to himself as he watched her leave.

Chapter 30
The New Mother Cometh

Usually, on a Saturday evening, there would be a team of people in the kitchen of The Big House. As Cinder, Lysander, and Tibult walked quietly past the stainless steel benches, there was no one, not even a pot of water boiling on the stove. In fact, it appeared there was no sound or people at all in this wing.

'We are fortunate we are alone,' Lysander said.

'I'm not so sure,' Cinder said as she peered around the door that led to the hallway.

The entrance to the gym was via the east wing. Cinder, wanting to avoid her step-mother, chose not to enter through the front door. At the side of the house, next to the rose garden, they was a service entrance to the kitchen. They had expected to see half a dozen of the staff busy with cooking or cleaning. The pain in Cinder's back was growing. As was her anxiety.

'I don't like it,' she said. She had never known The Big House to be completely empty of people.

They made their way out of the kitchen quietly into the hallway, looking both ways before turning left towards the steps that led down to the cellar gym. As Cinder placed her foot down on the first step, pain shot across her back. She tried to stifle a moan with her hand, but it echoed off the stone walls. There was no hiding it in the eerie silence.

'Are you okay, my queen? Tibult asked, placing a steady hand on her shivering shoulder.

'Yes, I'm fine.' She shrugged away from his hand. 'I will be better when you stop calling me Queen.'

'As you wish, Miss Cinder.'

Lysander went ahead. He pushed the solid timber door of the cellar open and checked the room before indicating for Cinder to proceed. Tibult and Cinder followed Lysander in and closed the door behind them. In the centre of the room, just in front of Cinder's old tattered boxing bag, sat a large man hunched over in a timber chair. Black straps held his arms and legs in place. His wrists were red-raw with abrasions and splattered with dry blood. A black hood covered his head, but Cinder could tell it was Duncan.

'Get him out of here,' she ordered. Obediently, the brothers ran forward and began to undo the straps. A muffled shuffling noise above made them stop and look up. Cinder came to help them. 'We need to move quickly. There is someone up there.'

The door to the basement gym rattled on its hinges and dust fell like tiny brown snowflakes from the rafters.

'What was that?' Cinder exclaimed, watching her old boxing bag swing, the chain creaking against the timber.

'That dear,' came a spine-tinglingly familiar voice from behind her. 'Was an annoyance being dealt with.' Cinder swivelled too quickly, sending shock waves of stabbing pains through her injured muscles. Louvelle stood in the basement's doorway, looking as im-maculate and dangerous as ever; a look on her face like an older sib-ling who had just eaten her little sister's last cookie and gotten away with it. Manicured fingers held her handgun extended and steady. The barrel aimed straight and true at Cinder's heart.

'There is really no need to be sneaking around down here,' she said, eyeing her two former bodyguards. 'This is still your home too, dear.' She looked back at Cinder and took a step into the room. Cin-der stepped in front of Duncan. 'Thank you for bringing her back to me, dears.'

'Were you two in on this?' Cinder said to Lysander and Tibult. 'Did you know she was going to be waiting here for me?'

'No, my lady,' they said in unison.

'The only one to blame here, my dear, is yourself,' Louvelle said as she moved her aim from Cinder's heart to her head. 'I have to say, I am a little disappointed. I thought I taught you better than this. This is one of my more obvious traps.' She looked down at the floor. 'But don't worry.' Her eyes shot up again. 'You don't need to question the loyalty of your people. These two follow you now, not me.' She dropped her shoulders in exasperation. 'Oh, well.'

Two gunshots rang out, deafeningly loud in the enclosed space of the basement. Cinder was screaming, but could not hear her own voice over the ringing. Something wet and warm had hit her in her face. She wiped her chin, and her fingers came away red. Her legs felt like concrete pinned to the floor. Lysander and Tibult lay on the floor, blood pooling around what remained of their faces. Cinder screamed again. Her hearing returned. There was another warm, wet feeling running down her legs. A pool of clear liquid was spreading across her shoes and onto the floor. *I've wet myself,* she thought. *I got so scared I wet myself.*

'Oh my God, mother!' she yelled. 'You killed them. You killed them and I've wet myself.' Her body was shaking uncontrollably. Louvelle placed her gun down on the bench next to the door.

'You didn't wet yourself dear,' she said, stepping towards Cinder. 'The new mother is coming.'

'What?' Cinder yelled in anger and confusion. She stepped back from the wet substance on the cobblestone floor, glistening in the florescent light.

'The new mother is coming,' Louvelle said again. 'Your waters just broke. You're having a baby.'

Chapter 31

Little Chapter, Big Bang.

Dom reached his hand inside the opening of a blue door that sat ajar. Finding a switch on the inside wall, he clicked it on. A single light bulb hanging in the middle of a small room flickered to life, casting dull light over the contents. Dusty cardboard boxes sat amongst items of furniture and racks of clothing covered in plastic. In the far corner, something moved.

'Bob!' Marraine said, drawing in her breath. Someone had tied Bob to a chair and gagged him. As Marraine pushed the door open, he started shaking his head frantically, looking behind the door. That's when Marraine smelled something out of place. She grabbed Dom, pushed him back out of the door, threw him to the ground, and jumped on top of him.

'Wow,' Dom said, looking up into Marraine's face as it hovered centimetres from his own. 'You know I'm always up for fun, but shouldn't we...'

BOOM! Dom didn't have time to finish. A deafening roar and heat rushed past Marraine's body. Shards of plaster, timber, and brickwork cascaded and flew all around them. Marraine grit her teeth and squeezed Dom's shoulders as something sharp and hot grazed across her outer thigh.

Chapter 32
Baby Blues

'A baby? How can I be pregnant? I mean, Angus and I... We used protection and... we only. I mean, it's only been 7 or 8 months since.' Cinder was still standing in the middle of the cellar, frozen with confusion. Surely Louvelle must be lying. But it all made sense now. The nausea that she passed off as jetlag. The weight gain she thought was because of her change in diet, and the pains she had been feeling all evening.

'It's not a human inside you dear.' Louvelle said calmly, taking a step closer.

'Okay, but I thought Lycan babies needed nine months to grow.' Cinder's head spun. Was she dreaming? Was this one of her nightmares? No! This must be one of Louvelle's sick plans. 'Was this you? Did you do something to me?' She screamed.

'This is all your own doing child, don't blame your promiscuity on me.' Louvelle said calmly.

'Promiscuity!' Cinder yelled incredulously. 'Black is the only man I've ever been with.'

'Then the Nephilim boy is the father. You got here all by yourselves.'

'But how?' Cinder ran her hands over her stomach.

'My dear, dear girl, you really aren't comprehending, are you? Please sit down.' Louvelle reached for Cinder.

'Take your hands off me. Stay back. You won't hurt my baby!'

'Hurt her? You two are the most precious things in my world.'

'Precious?' Cinder laughed 'You tried to kill me!'

'Kill you? Don't be so dramatic, dear.' Louvelle interlaced her fingers and rested her hands in front. 'Why would I clothe, feed, and house you for years, just to kill you as soon as you became interesting?'

'You tied me to an anchor and flung me off a pier.' Cinder's freckled cheeks burned with anger and pain.

'Yes, and if I had wanted you dead, I would have just had Lysander break your skinny little neck. What do you think I am, a bond villain?'

'You know I can't swim.'

'Yes dear. That's why I waited until you had two dashing young surfers there to help you. You really should be thanking me.'

'Thanking you?' Cinder dropped her hands to her knees.

'Yes. Thanks to me, you got to be the damsel in distress, like the ones in the silly stories your father would read to you.'

'You are an evil and insane woman.' Cinder spat. Louvelle held her hands over her heart.

'I am what I need to be for our people.'

'You killed my mother!' Cinder yelled. Pain flooded her body.

'That was regrettable yes, but necessary' Louvelle stood beside Cinder, looking with revulsion at the liquid at her feet.

'Necessary?' Cinder asked incredulously.

'To save you. To save all of us. Your mother was good to me. She took me in when I needed help, but she was a foolish child who would have seen all of us killed, or worse, enslaved.'

'My mother wasn't a fool!'

'She was a fool, and younger than you are now when she gave up her power for you. The fate of our kind was to be left in the hands of a stupid human child. What was she going to do when the vampires came for you? Bat her eyelids at them while she played with her pigtails. I warned them that the vampires were coming, but no one listened. She wanted to make a truce with our enemies, sit and eat meals with them, work together as equals against a common foe, or some rubbish. I thought your father would know better, but he was poisoned by Annabelle's ideas. I had to sit across the table from their smug Nephilim faces, as their infant propelled food and drool all over my tablecloth; you and your father swooning over the little beast. I dealt with them swiftly.'

A look of disbelief and nausea flooded over Cinder's face as she looked away from Louvelle and swallowed hard.

'You're talking about Angus's parents and the car accident, aren't you?' Cinder shook her head. 'Ha, accident.' She repeated to herself.

'Well done, my clever girl.' Louvelle said proudly. Sweat beaded on Cinder's anguished brow.

'I'm not yours and my baby won't be yours either. You're personally responsible for the death of three out of four of her grandparents.'

'It was all for you, my dear.' Louvelle said, stroking Cinder's head. Cinder pushed her hand away and tried to move to her sofa against the wall. She only made it part of the way before the pain was too great.

'Why are you here?' she spat through gritted teeth, her chest rising and falling quickly.

'You need my protection now. What are those gym-junky, dairy farmers going to do for you? Give you milk if your breasts don't work?' Louvelle pointed towards Duncan. Noticing him flinch, Cinder turned back towards him. 'Don't you see? This is perfect,' Louvelle continued. 'It's the only way the two of us won't end up killing each other. You need me to be the queen now that your powers will be gone, and I need you to be the mother of our next queen.'

Cinder's body went tight, and she closed her eyes to ride through the next contraction. 'How do I know you won't kill me as soon as I have given birth?' she asked, as she dabbed perspiration from her hairline with the back of her hand. Louvelle retrieved a hand towel from the sink and handed it to Cinder.

'I think we can both agree that you will be a better mother than I was.'

'I couldn't be worse.'

'No, I guess not.' Louvelle smiled 'And to be honest, I hate babies. Can you imagine me feeding? Changing? Cuddles? Thank god your father was there for all that.'

'Thank god.' Cinder agreed.

Pain, unlike what she had ever felt before, shuddered through Cinder's body. She moaned and doubled over.

'I need to get out of here!' She screamed, pushing Louvelle out of her way and stumbling to the door.

'Just wait dear, I'll get someone to help you into my car.'

'Really?' Cinder asked in surprise 'You are going to let me in your car like this? What if I make a mess?'

'It has leather seats and I need a new one, anyway.' Louvelle cautiously sidestepped Cinder and exited. Her heels echoing as she ascended the steps. Cinder leaned against the doorjamb as her contractions subsided. She could hear mumbled voices above. There was no way that she wanted to stay here with her stepmother any longer, but she needed to catch her breath before she attempted the stairs.

The sound from above slowly grew from an inaudible murmur to a cacophony of angry yelling and screams, the sound of smashing glass as a crescendo. Not caring what the cause of the sounds was, Cinder saw it as an opportunity to make her escape. She had made it two-thirds of the way to the top of the stairs when the next contraction hit, bringing her to her hands and knees. Deciding that standing would take too much strength, she continued on all fours. Just as her hand reached the cold stone of the top step, a loud thud came from the cellar, followed by muffled calls.

'Duncan!' she moaned as the wave of pain subsided. She was desperate to go, but she couldn't leave Duncan behind. Turning over to sit on the steps, Cinder wiped her forearm across her brow, and took a beat to catch her breath. 'I'm coming, Duncan,' she said, more to herself than to him.

• • • •

Duncan blinked. His eyes, two bloodshot pools sunken deep into dark-ringed sockets. He rubbed the red-raw and blood-speckled bands around his wrists and pulled himself up into a sitting position. With his eyes adjusted to the harsh white glow of the humming fluorescent tubes, he turned slowly to look behind him. Cinder stood behind him, pale and clammy. She held the black hood and restraints in her trembling hands.

'You filthy, slimy werewolf pieces of scum,' he hissed between clenched teeth.

'What?' Cinder asked, startled

'You!' Duncan yelled, taking hold of her neck and dragging her across the floor. As he stood up, Cinder's feet lifted off the ground, dangling and flailing. She dropped the hood and restraints and took hold of his wrists.

'Duncan, please!'

Chapter 33

In Pieces

Angus lay flat on his back, looking up at the dark night sky. The stars twinkled through the thin sheet of clouds, but at the corners of his vision, other lights flickered and sparked. He blinked and tried to rub away the flashing, struggling to remember where he was. Rolling himself over on to one side, his head pounded and his ears rang. He remembered them all leaving Paddy's. As they did, they ran into Detective Morgan. Explaining the news they had received about Bob, Peter Morgan offered them a ride in his police wagon. Dom and Torry had played best of three rock paper scissors to decide who would ride in the cage. *Where are they now?* Angus thought to himself, looking around.

'Torry, are you okay?'

'I'm here, Black,' she answered, her voice trembling. 'I'm fine. Peter pulled me behind his wagon.'

'I saw some wires above the door as Dom opened it,' Peter Morgan said. 'Sorry, I didn't have time to warn everyone.'

'What happened?' Angus asked, looking down at his dusty and torn clothes. Small patches of blood were growing around dozens of cuts and scratches on his arms. He moved his limbs to ensure nothing was broken.

'There was an explosion.' Peter Morgan said, walking forward and offering Angus a hand. Dust and debris fell from Angus's clothes and hair as he stood up.

'We were here for Bob,' he said, the fog starting to clear from his mind. 'Is that right?'

'Yes, that's right,' Peter Morgan said, looking around. 'I hope for his sake he wasn't in there.'

What remained of the roof lay at an angle amongst the debris, smoke, and flames. The front wall and the side wall that was furthermost from where Bob had been sitting were intact, supporting one corner of the collapsed and broken roof. The explosion had reduced the other two walls to scorched, smoking piles of brick and plaster. Dom, still underneath Marraine, started yelling and cursing, his voice muffled by her chest. The others hurried forward and dragged them away from the heat and the debris still falling from the damaged roof. Marraine let out a cry of pain. Torry noticed blood trickled from her left hip, soaking into her dusty and ripped clothing. Running back to the police wagon, Torry grabbed Peter Morgan's jacket. 'Here, hold this against your cut,' she said, handing the jacket to Marraine. Dom rolled away from Marraine and pushed himself up on to his knees. He looked around at the damage, his mouth hanging open like a clown-head carnival game.

'Great holy mother father,' he said as he got slowly to his feet, dusting himself off.

'You okay?' Angus asked. Dom rotated his shoulders and cracked his neck from side to side.

'Yep, I think so. You?'

'I hit my head, I think.' Angus touched the back of his head and checked his fingers for blood. They came away clean. 'My memory's a bit fuzzy. Did we find Bob?'

'Yes, he was in there,' Marraine said, sitting up gingerly. Dom limped around to the other side of what remained of the building, tripping on some of the rubble that was hard to see through the smoke and dust.

'I found Bob,' he said. Marraine jumped to her feet and ran towards Dom.

'Is he okay?' she said, stopping to grip her hip and grimacing.

'Stop. Wait there.' Dom said, holding up his hand. 'I should have said I found *some* of him,'

'No, no, no,' Marraine said, as she tried to move inside the destruction, but the intense heat pushed her back. 'I've got to find him.'

'There's nothing left to find,' Dom said, waving smoke out of his face and moving back to Marraine. 'You need to look after your leg.' Blood was running down Marraine's leg and even under all the dust, Dom could tell that she was turning a lighter shade of her usual olive complexion. 'Come and sit down,' he said, wrapping his arm around her and leading her to the police wagon

'But I have to find Bob,' she said, looking back.

'It's okay, Marraine,' Angus said. 'I'll get him.'

'Did you hear that?' Dom asked gently, sitting Marraine down in the back of the wagon. 'Black is going to find him.' Marraine nodded, then rested her head against the inside of the wagon.

Angus stepped his way carefully through the rubble, shielding his face from the fire that was building in intensity inside. When he came to the place where Dom had found Bob's remains, he regretted having that last cocktail at Paddy's. The sweet tasting alcohol was trying to force its way back into his mouth for an encore performance. The charred and bloody remains were definitely part of a body, but he couldn't be sure what part he was looking at. Holding his fist to his mouth, he turned away. Torry moved towards him, but he waved her back.

'You don't want to see this,' he said, shaking his head. Thoughts of his parents' car accident invaded his mind, and he needed to move away.

Peter Morgan came over and stood next to Torry. He took his phone from his pocket, but just as he was about to dial, a shadowy figure zoomed past him, moving unimaginably fast towards Angus. Peter Morgan dropped his phone and reached for his gun. Torry reached across his body.

'It's okay,' she said, putting her hand over the gun. 'It's his sister, it's Black's sister.' Sase came to an abrupt stop next to her brother.

'I heard the explosion. I came as quickly as I could,' she said, looking around 'Where is Cinder?' she asked in a panicked tone, spotting Bob's grotesque remains amongst the rubble.

'Back at Paddy's, she wasn't feeling well,' Angus said

'You left her alone?' Sase asked in alarm.

'Yes, she was having some back pains.'

'This was a trap, wasn't it?' Marraine called from the back of the wagon. 'To get us away from Cinder?'

'Yes, I think so,' Sase admitted. 'You should all go back to Cinder immediately.'

'She's gone home to the farm.' Torry said.

'Good, good,' Sase said, bending down to inspect Bob's remains. 'Who is this unfortunate?' She asked matter-of-factly. Marraine stood up, pushed her way past Dom and limped/hopped her way towards Sase.

'That's Bob, and he's a friend of mine,' she yelled. Sase looked up and cocked her head to the side.

'I meant no offense.'

'Well, offense was taken. Everything about you is offensive,' Marraine limped closer, her eyes wild with rage and poised with tears. Dom ran to help her, but she pushed him away. She was just about to yell something more when her phone vibrated. She pulled it from her bra. 'It's a message from Lysander,' she said. There were only three words in the message. She read them aloud, 'big, house, Cinder.' Sase turned and ran.

'Meet me at The Big House as quickly as you can,' she yelled behind her.

'Wait for me,' Angus called out to her.

'No, I can't. I will move much faster without you.' Sase disappeared in a flash of dark clothes and red hair.

'Let's go.' Torry said, taking hold of Detective Morgan's arm and dragging him towards the car.

'No,' Angus said, running after her. 'You need to go home.'

'What?' Torry asked, her eyes wide and fierce

'You need to go home.'

'But if Cinder's in trouble, I want to help.'

'I know you do, but someone needs to check on your dad, see if he's okay.'

'Here, you take the wagon,' Peter Morgan said, throwing his keys to Angus. Angus snatched them out of the air.

'Are you sure?' he asked, looking from his hand to the police wagon.

'Yes,' Peter Morgan said, pulling his phone from his pocket. 'I will organise someone to get us and go check on Mr Kinnard. Will you come with me?' he looked at Torry. 'Please, Torry.'

'Okay, but I'm only going home because Peter asked me,' Torry said, looking around at the others. 'He's saved my life twice now.'

'Duncan, wait,' Cinder choked and pleaded, pulling at his giant fingers as they tighten. With her head held high above the floor, so high that she almost bumped her head on the rafters of the low basement ceiling, Duncan walked towards her father's old leather couch against the wall.

'You took Blaire from me and locked me up in this stinkin' hole. And now you've got another of you filthy beasts growing in your belly. I'm gonna rid the world of two of ya in one go.' Duncan said, his eyes fierce, crazed, and determined.

'Duncan... Please... It's me,' Cinder forced out between desperate breaths.

Slow, purposeful footsteps tapped their way down the steps outside the door. Cinder and Duncan turned to see a young man in a long, grey woollen coat enter the doorway. With one eyebrow raised, he unbuttoned his coat and smoothed down his thick, dark hair.

'I wouldn't do that if I were you,' he said in his European accent, looking Duncan up and down. 'I've come an awfully long way to meet the expected child. I would be quite annoyed if you took that opportunity away from me.'

'I don't give a damn if you're annoyed. I'm pretty annoyed myself.'

'I completely understand,' the stranger said, removing a pair of brown leather gloves. 'But trust me, my friend, you don't want to see me annoyed.' He slipped the gloves into the inside breast pocket of his coat.

'I'm not your friend,' Duncan spat.

'I don't care,' said the stranger. 'But if you don't let her go, you'll see just how unfriendly I can get.'

Duncan let go of his grip around Cinder's throat. Cinder dropped to the couch, gasping and rubbing her neck.

'Let's get better acquainted then,' Duncan said, striding towards the young man.

'Don't worry Cinder, Louvelle isn't going to have your baby,' the man said, ignoring Duncan's approach. 'I'm here to help.'

Duncan's stubbled and emaciated face twisted into a scowl. He reached aggressively for the young man but, with what seemed like no more than a flick of the stranger's wrist, Duncan fell, spread-eagle, on the cobblestone floor. The young man grinned smugly. Cinder coughed, trying to catch her breath.

'Stop, please!' she called out hoarsely.

'Yes, you should listen to the Red Queen,' the young man said, walking towards Cinder. Duncan rolled up on to one knee then leapt at the intruder. The young man snatched Duncan out of the air, spun to his left, and catapulted Duncan into the opposite wall of the cellar. Duncan grunted as he crashed into the wall and dropped face-first to the floor.

'What on God's green earth are you?' he asked, as he lifted himself onto his hands and knees. A chunk of masonry fell from the wall next to him.

'STOP NOW!' Cinder screamed, grabbing hold of her stomach as the next contraction took hold of her. Duncan looked down at his left arm. Halfway between his wrist and elbow, his arm bent at a sickening, unnatural angle, almost like he had an extra joint in his forearm. Cradling his broken arm against his stomach, he stood and walked slowly to the door.

'This isn't over,' he said in a deep, purposeful voice, glaring at the young stranger.

'I look forward to our next encounter,' the young man retorted, with a bow of his head.

Breathing through the pain, Cinder watched Duncan disappear out of the door and listened as his heavy footsteps sounded on the staircase.

'Thank you,' she said to the young man. 'This is the second time you've saved me.' The young man moved to Cinder and helped her to her feet. For the first time, she got a clear look at his watch. Behind the hands sat a blue moon stone nestled in the branches of a golden tree. 'Are you a Lycan?' she asked, her voice raspy. The young man smiled.

'No, not quite,' he said, wrapping his arm around her and helping her towards the door. 'But my mother was. She was a Lycan queen, just like your mother.' Cinder looked at him quizzically.

'But...' Cinder didn't finish. The unmistakable tapping of high heels distracted her. A moment later, Louvelle re-entered the cellar.

'Hello Louvelle,' the young man said, tightening his grip on Cinder. 'It appears that you dispatched with my associates more efficiently than I had hoped.' Louvelle strolled to the basin against the wall. Turning her back on Cinder and the man, she turned on the tap and washed her hands. She cleared her throat and spoke calmly.

'Good evening, Patru.'

Chapter 34
The Stitch Up

'Cessez de vous disputer!' Dom said.

'Excuse me?' asked Marraine. She was laying across the back seat of the police wagon, resting against Dom.

'It means stop arguing.'

'I know what it means. I'm just surprised that you know what it means. You haven't been practising French just to impress me, have you, Dominic?'

'No,' Dom said, turning away and pretending to be interested in the door handle next to him. 'I was stuck on a ship for a month with French-speaking sailors. I picked up a few things.'

'I'm still not going to the hospital, no matter how good your French is,' Marraine said indignantly. 'They ask too many questions.'

'There's just a lot of blood,' Dom said, gripping the head rest as Angus took a sharp corner at speed, the tyres squealing in protest as they struggled to hold the vehicle to the road.

'Dom,' Marraine said.

'Yes?'

'You're going to have to pull my dress up.'

'What?' Dom's eyebrows shot up. Marraine giggled and then cringed with pain.

'Don't get too excited. I just mean that you will need to pull up the side of my skirt to see the cut on my hip. I want you to tell me how bad it is before I look.'

'Oh, yeah, right.' Dom reached down and tried to find a section of the hem that wasn't soaked in blood and caked in dust. Finding a spot that looked okay, he pinched the material between his thumb and index finger. Pulling the bottom of Marraine's dress away from her body, he gently lifted it up over her hip, tucking it under her back to keep it out of the way.

'Is it bad?' Marraine had turned away to avoid looking at her injury.

'There is a lot of blood, but no, it's not too deep.' Dom said, squeezing her shoulder. Marraine turned to look at the gaping hole that ran from the top of her thigh to just above her hipbone.

'Not too deep!' she exclaimed, the colour draining from her face again. 'Dominic, I could keep my phone in there. I think I saw bone.'

'Sorry, I just didn't want you to panic. At least it's not the other side. It would have ruined your tattoo.'

'How do you know Marraine has a tattoo on her thigh?' Angus asked, looking at Dom in the rear-view mirror.

'You just worry about driving,' Dom said with a grin.

'Dom,' Marraine said, reaching behind her and grabbing one of Dom's large, bulbous biceps. 'You're going to have to stich it for me.'

'What?' Marraine felt his muscle tense under her grip.

'I'm going to bleed out Dom, you will have to stich me up.'

'But I can't, how? What with?' Dom tumbled over his words.

'There must be a first-aid kit in here somewhere.'

'I don't know what to do. I...' He stopped when he felt Marraine wobbling against him. She was giggling.

'Looks like the only one getting stitched up is you, mate.' Angus said from the front seat.

'Oh, yeah, real funny.' Dom pulled the bottom of Marraine's dress out and threw it back over her thigh. 'That's the last time I try to be nice to you.'

'I'm sorry, Dominic,' Marraine said, patting his shoulder. 'You were being very sweet, thank you. I heal fast, I should be fine. I will probably have a scar. My days of wearing string bikinis might be behind me now.'

'Why didn't you say so before?' Dom said, looking around. 'Where is that first aid kit? No one told me we had a bikini emergency.' They all laughed.

As they climbed up away from the ocean around a long, sweeping bend, the lights of The Big House came into view. It loomed unwelcoming atop its rocky prominence, warding off visitors like a lighthouse keeping oceangoing vessels from the coastline. Silence fell over the vehicle except for the hum of the engine and the rumble of the tyres against the coastal road.

'I'm sure she will be alright,' Marraine said, with a touch of uncertainty in her voice. 'She's tough, and she knows how to take care of herself.'

'Yes,' Angus agreed, his brow furrowed. 'I'm sure she's fine.' His foot pushed more heavily on the accelerator.

• • • •

Louvelle turned off the basin tap. Picking up a thick cotton hand towel, she methodically dried her hands before she collected her handgun.

'What did you call him?' Cinder demanded, pushing herself away from the young man.

'What did she call you?' She glared at him. The young man looked at her but said nothing.

'I called him Patru.' Louvelle said, turning to look at them. 'You have met him before. You know his sister, of course, – Sase.'

'You've had the displeasure of the company of my little sister?' Patru asked. 'You have my condolences.'

'But how can you be Patru?'

'Oh, yes, the new body,' Patru said, pulling open his coat and turning around slowly. 'It can get confusing, I know.'

'I know you steal and defile the bodies of children.' Cinder spat in disgust. 'But you said that your mother was a Lycan.'

'Yes,' Patru said, taking a step towards her. 'That's how it works. She was the first mother and now the new mother is almost here.' Pain radiated around Cinder's body. Pain that came with the undeniable desire to push. She got down on her hands and knees and tried to steady her breathing.

'Why are you here?' Louvelle asked, walking over and placing her hand on Cinder's back. Cinder swatted it away angrily.

'I'm here for the new mother, the child that was promised.' Patru removed his coat and threw it across the room to land on the leather sofa. 'It looks like I came just at the right time.'

'What do you want with my baby?' Cinder said through gritted teeth as she crawled towards the door. 'Why would you need a Lycan child when you're just going to empty it out and fill it with your evil?'

'Empty it out!' Patru laughed. 'She doesn't know, does she, Louvelle? Haven't you taught her anything?' Cinder paused and looked up at Louvelle.

'What's he talking about?'

'Nothing,' Louvelle said, shaking her head. 'He's just trying to hurt your baby. Don't listen to him.'

'Hurt it?' Patru moved with lightning speed and knelt down in front of Cinder. 'Your baby is the most important thing that has happened to the vampire. I have been sent to protect it with my life.'

'Get away from her!' Louvelle yelled, moving forward.

'No!' Cinder said. 'I want to know why.' Patru wiped a bead of sweat from her cheek. Cinder tried to swat his hand away, but he grabbed her by the wrist.

'Did my sister tell you how the vampire came into being?'

'Yes,' Cinder spat, trying to pull her arm free. 'She told me that your father was a monster who raped and tortured your Lycan mother.' Patru let go of her wrist. He pushed his fingertips together to make a pyramid shape with his hands, resting his chin on the apex.

'My sister lies,' he said, looking into Cinder's eyes. 'My father was a great man, an emperor, and a powerful warrior. He honoured my mother by looking past her affliction and humbled himself by joining with such a woman. For his sacrifice, he was rewarded with five powerful heirs.'

'He locked you away in pits and used you as weapons!'

'He protected us from the burning sun and trained us to protect ourselves from those who would intend to destroy us. Now come,' he said, stretching his hand out to her 'Let me get you somewhere more comfortable.' Cinder could taste her cocktail from earlier in the evening. She tried to swallow, the bitter orange flavour burning her throat.

'I'm not going anywhere with you,' she said, pushing past Patru and crawling to the door. 'I'm getting out of here.'

'I can't let you do that.' Patru swivelled on his heels and clamped his powerful hand around Cinder's ankle. 'My brother has plans for this child.' He tried to pull her back, but Cinder pushed her fingertips between the gaps in the cobblestone floor and held tight.

'Why me? Why my baby?' She yelled.

'Because,' Patru said, taking hold of her other leg. 'This child is the new mother. The one that we have been waiting for. The one your mother promised us.'

'That's enough Patru,' Louvelle said, stepping forward. 'Let the girl go. The new mother will stay with me, with the Lycan.'

'What is this new mother rubbish, anyway?' Cinder yelled, struggling to get her legs free. Patru kept hold of her legs but turned to look up at Louvelle.

'You told me she was smart, Louvelle, but she still hasn't figured it out.'

'Figured what out?' Cinder asked as she got one leg free. She kicked desperately at Patru's hands, but Patru simply laughed.

'Don't you see?' he said. 'Your child is the new mother. The off-spring of a Lycan and a Nephilim.'

'Patru, no!' Louvelle yelled. An arrogant smile crept across Patru's face. He yanked Cinder along the floor. Her nails scraping across the stones as she slid next to the vampire. Patru leaned his face close to hers. His breath was cold and salty, like a winter breeze off the ocean.

'The child you carry is not a Lycan or a human. Who did you think your mother had been parading you in front of all these years, if not vampires?' he whispered. 'Louvelle was very proud of her good breeding stock.'

Cinder couldn't hold back the flood anymore. Her mouth filled with sickly-sweet, burning fluid. She shook her head in denial. With satisfaction, Patru saw the look of realisation in her tear-filled eyes. He put his icy lips close to her ear and spoke triumphantly.

'Your baby is a vampire.'

At the word vampire, the floodgates opened. Everything exploded out of Cinder. Anger, pain, hatred, and pre-digested alcoholic cocktail. Patru recoiled as the body-temperature projectile liquid splattered over his expensive pure-wool suit. Cinder's fist connected with his stunned face, knocking him backwards. Louvelle took the opportunity to launch herself at Patru and sent him skidding across the floor. The two Lycan queens ran for the door, slamming and locking it behind them before they leapt to the top of the stairs. Cinder collapsed to her knees in pain and exhaustion.

'Get up,' Louvelle ordered. 'This is no time to lay about. That door won't hold him for long.' Cinder looked up at her stepmother in disbelief, thinking of what she would do to her if she had the energy. With a moan, she pulled herself up on the corner of the wall at the top of the stairs. The overwhelming urge to push was stirring inside her again.

'This thing's coming,' she said, leaning with one hand against the wall. Cold perspiration pooled on her neck and dripped from her hair.

'Here, take this. It's a gift for the child.' Louvelle held out Cinder's red queen pendant 'I overestimated the power this would hold over your followers. Even without it, they still chose you. It will be much more use to her than to me.' Cinder took the gift, confused but too exhausted to ask questions. 'Now go,' Louvelle ordered. 'I will find whoever is still alive to help hold Patru off. You need to get as far away from here as you can. Find Sase.'

Cinder used a trembling hand to steady herself, leaving a smudged trail of glistening perspiration on the eggshell-white wall. She moved as quickly as she could towards the nearest exit. A succession of violent thumps rattled the cellar door and echoed up the stairway behind her. She crashed through the kitchen door and collided with a cupboard, clattering the crockery inside. Blurry, dark shapes like clouds, grew at the edge of her vision. Rapid heartbeats pounded in her woozy head. A humming noise was intensifying in her hot ears, but she thought she heard a crashing noise and angry raised voices. The fresh, warm air was a temporary relief as she tumbled out the exit at the other end of the kitchen.

Slamming the door behind her with such force that she cracked one of the glass panes, she dropped to her hands and knees and crawled into the shadows of The Big House. *This can't be happening*, she thought to herself. *I'm not ready to be a mother and not here in the dirt.*

'I'm sorry you need to wait,' she said aloud to her stomach in a pleading tone. The cold brick wall held her upright as she slid her knees and trembling hands across the stale-scented moist earth. A cobweb flapping in the mild summer breeze fell across her agonized face. The sticky silk tendrils clung to her hair and the long eyelashes of her right eye. As she wiped at the webs, disgusted and exasperated, her supporting arm gave way and she fell to the ground. Defeated, she moaned and rolled over. Laying on her back on the cold grass, behind a row of sweet smelling rose bushes. She was alone, and her baby was coming. There had been many lonely moments in her life, but this was the first time she could remember feeling utterly alone. She wished Angus was here, or Marraine. Then she thought about Louvelle. She hated the woman – no question – but she was also the only mother she had ever known. As the next contraction took over her body, she twisted in pain.

'Mother? Mother, please!' she called out as she stretched her hand out towards the light from the kitchen door.

• • • •

Patru looked with revulsion at the vomit down his front. He pulled off his vest, as he stepped over the split and broken remains of the cellar door, crumpling it and tossing it to the corner of the stairway landing. Breathing deeply through his nose, he smoothed his thick, dark hair back into place. After unbuttoning the top of his shirt, he slid his hands into his hip pockets and climbed casually up the stairs. Two Lycan greeted him at the top. Their large hairy bodies taking up most of the hallway. They watched him with bloodshot, brown eyes. Low, rumbling growls escaping between their razor-sharp moist teeth. Louvelle stood behind them with two more bodyguards, still in their human form.

'What's this all about?' Patru said, with his head to one side. He pulled a hand from his pocket and pointed with disinterest at the two Lycan.

'The Child is one of us. It will stay here.' Louvelle said.

'The new mother belongs to my brother. You promised him the first-born child, Louvelle. Don't tell me you've grown a heart after all these years.' Patru leaned against the wall, his ankles crossed.

'My heart has always been for my people. I have always done what is best for the Lycan. The child will stay with her mother.'

'If you do not let me take the child, I will pull your Lycan heart from your chest and fertilise your rose garden with it.'

The Lycan closest to Patru took a step towards him.

'Stay!' Patru said, holding his index finger up at the Lycan. 'There's a good doggy.' He smiled, showing that his canine teeth had doubled in length. The Lycan's shoulders hunched forward, and it retreated two steps.

'Don't let the blood sucker intimidate you!' Louvelle commanded. 'Leave now Patru and tell your brother that there has been a change of plans. Leave now and I will guarantee your safety.' Patru looked down at his feet, laughing to himself.

'I like you, Louvelle,' he said with a grin. 'Usually, I can't stand your kind, but you... You've always had a certain je ne sais quoi.' He slid his left hand from his pocket and made a flourish in the air. The gold of his watch flickered in the glow of the down lights set in the high ceilings of the hallway. Keeping his head tilted down, he slowly rolled his eyes up to meet Louvelle's. 'I'm only going to say this once because I'm growing bored with this and because you should already know. My brother gets what he wants, and he doesn't do, *change of plans*. Now get out of my way, Lycan.' He spat the word Lycan from his mouth like it was a rotten piece of meat.

Louvelle pulled her handgun from behind her and shot. A hole appeared in the wall where Patru had been standing, but he was no longer there. In a blur of grey, he had moved behind one of the Lycan. Wrapping his arm around the Lycan's hairy neck, Patru squeezed and yanked the beast's head upwards. With a sickening crunch, the Lycan's body convulsed and then went limp. Patru dropped the lifeless heap to the floor with a thud. As he did, Louvelle let off a volley of more shots. Her two bodyguards wrenched firearms from beneath their jacket and joined her. There was an ear-ringing cacophony as they repeatedly discharged the three weapons in the confined space. Plaster board, paint chips, and dust exploded from the walls as they were peppered with bullets. Caught in the crossfire, the remaining Lycan tried to get out of the way. Tufts of hair flew into the air and blood splattered walls and roof. The Lycan howled in pain, unable to escape. Patru darted behind the injured Lycan, using its body as a shield. The two bodyguards lifted their fingers from their triggers but Louvelle continued firing, putting three rounds in the Lycan's chest before she hit Patru in the shoulder.

'Don't stop!' she ordered, sending a second bullet through Patru's neck.

The bodyguards resumed firing. Soon both the Lycan and Patru were full of bloody holes. Patru stumbled backwards and fell, pulling the beast down with him. Even as he fell, Louvelle continued to fire until she spent her last round. Her bodyguards looked to her for instruction.

'Keep going,' she said, taking a step back from the blood-soaked bodies. They continued until they had also drained their weapons of ammunition.

'I think he's dead, my Lady,' one of them said, kicking Patru's lifeless arm.

'No,' Louvelle said, tossing her emptied revolver to the side with a clunk on the polished timber floor. 'That will only slow him down. Reload. I'm going to find my daughter.' Under the bloody, hairy mass, Patru moaned.

• • • •

Duncan slumped to the ground in the shadowy darkness of the trees that bordered the sprawling lawns of The Big House. Grunting and cursing, he awkwardly and painfully removed his shirt. Employing his good hand and his teeth, he fashioned the shirt into a makeshift sling for his broken arm. With gritted teeth, he slid his giant frame across the leafy ground and rested with his back against a tree. Flashes of Blair came to mind. The last time Duncan saw him alive, he had been sitting like this only a few hundred metres down the hill from where he was now. Duncan shook the thought from his head and rolled over onto his knees. He had just placed his good hand on the tree trunk, ready to get to his feet and walk away, when he heard Cinder cry out in pain. He looked between the tree trunks back towards The Big House, but couldn't see any movement. Cinder cried out a second time. Louder and full of desperation. Duncan turned and looked down the slope at the distant lights of Heathcote flickering warm and inviting through the trees. Turning back to The Big House, towering above him in the night, he cursed under his breath and got to his feet.

Moving as quietly as he could with the shooting pains in his slung arm, Duncan crept back towards the kitchen. As he crouched next to the door, glass from the shattered pane cracked loudly under his heavy boots. He cursed silently to himself again. Trying not to put his face in the light flooding out of the kitchen door, he bobbed his head back and forth, checking that there was no one inside. Hopeful that the room was indeed empty, he pulled the door open slowly and slipped inside. Across the room, he spotted what he was looking for. A large wooden knife block stood prominently next to an industrial sized stove top. Keeping low, which was not easy for someone so tall, Duncan stalked across the kitchen, grimacing at the pain caused by each step. His head swivelled from side to side, constantly checking that the room was indeed empty. Crouching next to the stove, he reached one of his large hands towards the knife block. That was when the first gunshot rang out. Instinctively, Duncan pulled his hand back. The sudden movement sent waves of pain vibrating through his injured arm. Red faced, he growled through gritted teeth. More gunshots exploded in the hallway outside the kitchen. Without worrying if there was anyone to see him now, Duncan grabbed a knife from the block, sending the remaining knifes falling and rattling across the bench before tumbling to the floor. With the knife clenched firmly in his fist, he ran for the exit, crashing through the door, back out into the night.

Behind the rose bushes, a small but welcome cry announced the arrival of a new life. In a mixture of laughter and tears, Cinder pulled her slippery, newborn daughter up on to her stomach. The child was far smaller than she thought a newborn would be, but her lungs sounded fit and powerful.

'Hello, little one,' Cinder said, checking all the tiny fingers and toes. A few metres away, the external door from the kitchen flew open. Her eyes met Duncan's, keen, purposeful, and determined. Then, gripped tightly in his massive hand, Cinder saw the knife.

Chapter 36

Get Away

The light streaming from the kitchen fell across one side of Duncan's face. Beads of perspiration glistened on his bald head and unkempt beard. Cinder could see a single eye glaring at her, wide, wild, and bloodshot. She had always thought of Duncan as resembling a big teddy bear, but now, with a long-bladed knife grasped in his shaky hand, he looked like something from a slasher film.

'No, Duncan. Please, she's just a baby.' She pleaded. Duncan took a step forward.

'Don't worry, lass, I'm not going to hurt you or your little one.'

'Oh god, thank you.'

'I'm sorry for how I acted back there. I think I lost my mind a bit.'

'I understand,' Cinder said. 'My mother has that effect on people.'

Duncan knelt next to Cinder and handed her the knife.

'Here you go, lass,' he said, placing the handle in her hand. 'You'll need to cut the cord.'

'I'm not sure I know how,' Cinder said, looking down at her baby.

'I've birthed my share of calves in my time. There's nothin' to it. I'll help.' Together, they cut the umbilical cord and Duncan moved the child up onto Cinder's chest 'She's a beauty,' he said, wiping his cheek. 'She's got her dad's thick black hair.'

'Are you crying?' Cinder asked, looking up at him.

'Must just be a trick of the light.' Duncan put his hand gently on the baby's head. 'Sorry I left you back there, lass,' he offered.

'You're here now. Now when I needed you. We needed you.'

Noticing that the gunfire had stopped, Duncan picked up the knife again. He cut a strip from the bottom of Cinder's dress to wrap the baby. 'We need to get her out of here,' he said, handing Cinder the strip of dress and getting to his feet. 'Can you stand?'

'I think so,' Cinder said, wriggling her toes. She wrapped the baby and lay it gently on the ground next to her. Using the wall of The Big House to steady herself, she got to her feet. She leaned for a moment against the cold bricks to catch her breath, her head spinning. The baby let out a cry and pushed one of its tiny hands out of the wrapping. Cinder bent down painfully and picked her up. In the dim light coming from the kitchen door, Duncan could see how pale and clammy Cinder's face was. She took a few steps before pausing and swaying from side to side. Duncan wrapped his good arm around her.

'Are you going to be alright?' he asked, holding her steady.

'I need to be. We need to get out of here.'

The light from inside shuddered as a shadow moved across the glow. Battered, exhausted, and with a newborn baby in tow, Duncan and Cinder tried to run. They took a few stumbling strides when Louvelle blocked their way.

'Get out of our way!' Cinder yelled. Duncan let go of her and pulled out the knife. Louvelle stepped back and raised her palms towards them submissively.

'I'm not here to stop you,' she said calmly. 'I'm trying to help. You need to go to the hospital. You can take my car.'

'I still can't believe you are going to let me in your car like this,' Cinder said, looking down at the dirty, putrid mess on her legs and torn dress. Louvelle's blood-red lips twisted.

'Like I said, I have leather seats. They'll come clean,' she said, clenching her hands into fists.

'I don't trust her,' Duncan interrupted gruffly.

'I don't either,' Cinder said, taking hold of his arm. 'But I don't think we will get far without a car.'

'Yes, that's right, dear,' Louvelle agreed. 'The child is important to me. You can trust that. Now come. My men won't be able to hold off Patru for much longer.' She held her hand out to Cinder.

'Okay,' Cinder said, marching forward. 'But you can keep your hands away from my daughter.' She glowered at Louvelle's outstretched hand. Duncan followed closely behind her.

'I'm keeping this,' he said, showing Louvelle the kitchen knife.

'Of course, dear,' Louvelle said with a practised smile. 'Would you like the entire set?' she gestured back into the kitchen. Duncan walked on wordlessly, keeping his eyes fixed on Louvelle.

A long, low building constructed of large grey bricks ran along the tree line at the southern boundary of the property. Three double-wide roller doors fronted the windowless structure. Louvelle held her thumb to a small screen next to the first roller door. A moment later, the screen turned green and a number pad illuminated. She entered a code and the roller door rumbled to life. A slit of cool-white light appeared at the bottom of the door, growing wider as the door rose painfully slowly. Duncan crouched low to check that there were no surprises awaiting them on the inside. When the door was high enough, he ducked under and surveyed the inside of the building.

Two rows of large pendant lights ran the length of the ceiling, their light changing as they warmed. For a moment, Duncan forgot to keep a watch on Louvelle. He stood with his mouth hanging open and his eyes wide. He knew little about cars, but even so, he recognised that there was a king's ransom worth of vehicles around him. Immaculately polished paint, rubber, and chrome glistened in the warming light. At a quick count, there were a dozen vintage and new vehicles he could see. Duncan recognised the names. Ferrari, Mustang, Harley Davidson.

'Wait! What's that for?' Cinder called out behind him. Duncan spun around to see Louvelle pulling a handgun from a metal cabinet.

'Don't worry darling, this isn't for you.' Louvelle said, collecting a set of keys from another shelf.

'I'm not going anywhere with you if you've got that.' Cinder said, holding the baby close to her chest.

'That's fine darling,' Louvelle walked towards Duncan. 'I'm not coming with you.'

'That's close enough,' Duncan growled, holding up his knife. Louvelle laughed and waved the gun above her head.

'This works across the room. Honestly, dear boy. You would already be dead. Yes?' she continued towards Duncan. Duncan lowered the knife and nodded. 'Can you drive?' Louvelle asked.

'Is it auto?' Duncan asked, adjusting his sling.

'Yes.'

'Should be fine.'

'Good.' Louvelle unlocked her car and pushed the keys into Duncan's good hand. As she did, she ran her thumb across his. 'I will miss our times together.' Duncan's eyes burned with rage. He pulled his hand away but said nothing.

'If you're not coming, what are you doing then?' Cinder asked. Louvelle walked briskly back to her and opened the rear car door.

'I'm going to finish off the vampire.'

'By yourself?' Cinder asked, climbing into the back seat. 'He'll kill you!'

'Better me than my granddaughter,' Louvelle said, looking down at the baby. Cinder glared at her.

'She's not your granddaughter!' Cinder stroked the baby's thick, black hair. 'Is it true? Is she one of them?'

'She's whatever we make her.' Louvelle said. Cinder slid to the other side of the car.

'Stay away from us,' she said quietly. Duncan opened the front door and manoeuvred awkwardly into the driver's seat. After some adjustments, to accommodate his long legs, he turned to Cinder.

'Ready to go, lass?'

'Yes, let's get out of here.'

'Go! Go now,' Louvelle called out, holding her weapon in both hands and looking back towards The Big House.

With the turn of the key, the engine roared to life. Duncan awkwardly slid the car into drive. With a screech of the tyres on the concrete floor, they drove out through the roller door past Louvelle. Before they had made it halfway to the front gate, gunshots rang out. Cinder ducked down low on the seat, pulling the baby close to her and covering its head. Duncan floored the accelerator and fumbled around to find the headlights. As two beams of light appear at the front of the vehicle, something dark flashed past the now illuminated front gate. More gunshots fired, and Cinder saw a cloud of dust as a bullet ricocheted off the fence. They were metres from the gate when a large crash sent them sliding sideways. The passenger side windows exploded at the impact and the car swerved off the driveway and into the grass. With a second crushing thud at the front of the car, they spun, leaving them facing the opposite direction. The engine stopped.

Cinder had fallen between the front and rear seats. She had managed to keep the baby held to her, and she felt they were both unhurt, but the baby was screaming.

'Are you okay?' she called to Duncan, trying to soothe the baby. Duncan gave a muffled moan from inside the air bag that had engulfed his face. His broken arm had come free of the makeshift sling. Pulling the kitchen knife from his pocket, he stabbed at the airbag. It deflated with a pop-hiss.

'What the hell was that?' he asked, loosening the seatbelt that was constricting his chest. 'Did she shoot our tyres out?'

'No, I think something hit us, something big. I saw something moving in the darkness just as you turned the headlights on. I think...' But she didn't get time to finish. A deformed, bloody, and

twisted face appeared at Cinder's window. She recognised the hair
and the eyes as belonging to Patru, but the rest of his face was different. He looked somehow serpent–like, with sharp teeth and a sunken
in nose.

'Give me the child,' he ordered. With only a slight effort, he
forced his fingers into the cracks at the edge of the door and ripped it
from its hinges. Duncan leaped from the car. He slashed the knife towards Patru, but Patru simply moved the door between them. Metal
scraped against metal. Patru slammed the door into Duncan, sending him sprawling across the grass. Cinder kicked frantically against
the door on the other side of the car.

'Leave me alone. You're not getting my daughter,' she yelled. Patru grabbed her by her hair and started pulling her from the car. Cinder took hold of the back of the driver's seat and held on with all
her strength. She slid the baby into the front passenger seat and took
hold of Patru's wrist before he pulled a chunk of her hair out. She slid
from the car and flopped to the ground. Patru pulled his wrist free,
but as he did, Cinder spun around and kicked him hard in the groin.
Patru bent over in pain but recovered quickly. He took Cinder's arms
in a vice-like grip and lifted her into the air.

'Let her go or the New Mother dies.' Louvelle was standing on
the opposite side of the broken and crumpled vehicle. In one arm she
held the crying baby, the other hand held the handgun pointed at the
child's head.

'You wouldn't,' Patru said.

'Have you ever known me to make idle threats?' Patru pondered
this for a moment.

'Very well then,' he said and threw Cinder aside like a discarded
piece of rubbish. 'Now give me the child, as was agreed.' Louvelle
lowered the gun from the baby's head and took a step back towards
The Big House.

'No,' she said firmly and sent her remaining bullets at Patru's head. Patru moved to the side but not quickly enough to avoid the first round. His left ear exploded in a shower of blood, flesh, and cartilage. Gripping his ear, he leapt at Louvelle, screaming with rage. Louvelle twisted her body to keep the baby safely away from her attacker. Further enraged by Louvelle's defiance, Patru slashed at her with sharp fingernails. Three deep cuts opened up in the pale flesh of Louvelle's shoulder. What began as a scream of anguished pain grew into a deafening growl. Louvelle's long fingernails thickened, turning grey, elongating into sharp, pointed ends. Her pupils grew and formed two long slits. Sharp, wolf-like teeth filled her mouth. Cinder got to her feet and ran towards the wrestling pair.

'Get away from my baby!' she screamed. Patru swatted her away.

'It's my baby,' he said with a scowl 'she's coming with us. She's one of us now.'

Cinder got wobbly to her knees, hands shaking. Louvelle had now grown several inches and thick orange hair was showing through rips in her shirt. She kicked at Patru with a powerful leg, sending him crashing into the car.

'She is ours. She will stay with me and her mother.' Louvelle growled. Patru smeared blood from the side of his head.

'We left you alive, Louvelle, and the deal was that we would have the first-born, female child.'

'I'm changing the deal,' Louvelle said.

'Patru! Leave the child!' a young but commanding voice yelled. Patru turned to see Sase emerging from the tree line.

'Sister, dear, it is always lovely to see you,' Patru said, tilting his head to one side. 'I hear you killed me.'

'Hello again, Patru,' Sase said 'Not soon enough it seems.'

'On the contrary,' he replied. 'Your timing was perfect; I was planning to burn that old shell myself. You saved me the trouble of all that unfortunate business.'

'That's me, always cleaning up after my brothers.'

Patru straightened his clothes, dropped his head, and glared at Louvelle from the top of his eyes. 'If she's not coming with me, then no one will have her.' He flew at Louvelle again and she struck out at him with her clawed fist. Quickly, he ducked under her arm and punched her in her snout. With a nauseating crack, blood exploded from Louvelle's face. She stumbled back, almost dropping the baby. Regaining her composure, she turned and ran. Cinder had never seen her stepmother run. It amazed her to see how quickly Louvelle moved towards The Big House. Patru was faster – moving so fast, it was like his feet didn't even touch the ground. He was in front of Louvelle in a matter of seconds.

'Get away from them!' Cinder yelled, trying desperately to get to her feet, but there was nothing she could do. Louvelle tried to fight Patru off, but with her injuries and one arm occupied with protecting the child, Patru was too quick and too desperate. Cinder watched from a distance as her stepmother fell to the ground.

'Why are you just standing there?' she asked, turning to Sase. 'Help them!' Sase walked forward and helped Cinder to her feet.

'Cinder is not my queen, nor is Louvelle,' she said. 'I will make my own choices about my actions.' Cinder turned on her, speechless and incredulous. 'I will ensure my brother does not leave with the child.' Sase continued. Cinder glared at her before turning and running to rescue her baby. 'Wait for Angus!' Sase called after her. 'You can't do this alone.' Cinder yelled a collection of curse words and continued running. Her body felt so tired, heavy, and unresponsive. Her legs simply refusing to move as quickly as she wanted them to. Louvelle remained motionless on the ground. Patru lifted the baby off her, holding it up in front of him by one of its tiny legs. The torn-dress swaddling fell and floated to the ground.

The roar of an engine and the skidding of tyres across the blue metal driveway announced the arrival of Angus, Marraine, and

Dom. As the car slid to a stop, Angus flung the door open and leapt from the driver's seat. Cinder had fallen to her knees next to her stepmother's body. She held up her hand to Angus, warning for him to stop. Angus skidded to a stop in the moist grass of The Big House's lawns, surveying the scene in front of him.

'What's he holding?' he yelled to Cinder.

'It's a baby – our baby.'

'What do you mean?' Angus took a few steps closer, his hands on his head.

'Cinder has given you a beautiful baby girl,' Sase called out from behind him.

'And now I'm going to take her away,' Patru added with a mischievous smirk, stepping closer to Cinder.

'What?' Angus yelled, bewildered. Sensing that he was readying once more to run to Cinder, Sase called out to him.

'No, Angus stop! Come to me,' she pleaded, holding out her hand to him.

'That's right boy, go to little sister,' Patru goaded. Cinder got to her feet.

'He's got our baby, Black,' she yelled. Patru wrapped the naked, crying baby in his left arm. Cinder reached for her daughter, yearning to hold the child, desperate to keep it safe. Patru pulled the baby away and kicked Cinder in the stomach. She fell back to the ground with a sickening cry. Ignoring his sister's warning, Angus ran to help her. Patru turned to face him. With his free hand, he smacked the side of Angus's face. Angus stumbled sideways, but kept his footing. He swung his fist towards Patru. With implausible speed and flexibility, Patru ducked backwards under the blow. Angus faulted and Patru slapped the other side of his face.

'You should have listened to your sister, boy,' he said. Cinder rolled on the ground, moaning through gritted teeth.

'Give her back to me!' she screamed. 'I'll kill you.' Black dots danced across Angus's vision and a metallic taste pooled in his mouth. Stumbling back a few steps, he spat blood, then ran at Patru again. He swung wildly, but Patru simply sidestepped every punch.

'I like this one, sister,' he called out. 'He has some fight in him.'

'Black! Come to me,' Sase yelled again. Angus ignored her. In one swift motion, Patru slipped behind Angus, grabbing him around his neck. Now within inches of the baby, Angus pulled desperately at Patru's arm, trying to free it. Patru's arms were like metal bars, unmoving. Satisfaction swept over the vampire's face as he looked down at the two creatures in his arms.

'Take your hands off me, stupid child,' he said. 'It's no use.'

Furious, Angus pulled harder. Veins pumping in his skull and arms rippling with sweat. He wrenched at the vampire's grip, desperate to free the child that he had never met, but already loved completely. Gradually, Patru's arm moved. A smile twisted the corner of Patru's mouth. He raised his eyebrows.

'Yes, yes, good,' he said with malicious laughter in his voice. He turned to look down at Cinder, still on her hands and knees on the ground. 'He's very strong. You chose a suitable mate.'

Dom had emerged from the car and was holding Marraine up on her feet. Marraine pushed him off.

'Go help him, I'm fine,' she said, waving him away. Dom ran to help but before he could get to Angus, Patru swivelled around and pushed Angus hard in the chest with lightning speed. Flying across the lawn, Angus crashed into Dom, sending both men sprawling in the grass and soil. Angus rolled off Dom.

'Get Cinder,' he managed to say between gasping breaths.

Patru leapt on to the side of The Big House, the baby crying under his arm as he scaled the wall. In agony, feeling her power draining from her body, Cinder stumbled to the wall. Reaching up, she pursued Patru, climbing the wall that Dom himself had climbed almost a year ago. Dom reached out to Angus.

'Are you okay?'

'Just help her,' Angus wheezed, wrapping his arms around his chest. Dom looked to The Big House, raising his hand to shadow his face from the moonlight.

'How did he get to the roof so fast and what's he holding?'

'I think he's a vampire and I think he's holding my daughter.'

'Great Holy Mother Father!' Dom sprung to his feet and ran to where Cinder was climbing. When he reached the wall, Cinder was already at the top floor windows. Dom cursed under his breath, recalling his fall from this very spot last year. He positioned the toe of his boot in a good foothold and began the ascent once again.

Cinder had to stretch out at a precarious angle to reach past the eaves. Metal guttering ran the length of the roof. She took hold of it tightly in one hand, pushing away from the wall. She swung and dangled by one arm until she could steady herself. With a groan, she swung her other hand up to grasp the gutter. The metal twisted and protested under her grip but held in place. She couldn't see Patru, but she could hear his heavy footsteps on the roof tiles. Terracotta chipped and cracked and a fist-sized piece rolled from the roof, hitting Cinder's shoulder. A hand, unnaturally cold and clammy, took hold of her wrist and dragged her onto the roof. Lifting her by her throat, Patru dangled Cinder over the edge, her legs kicking frantically in the air.

Below, Sase had helped Angus from the ground and was moving him closer. He turned to her. 'You need to help them, not me.'

'What does your name mean?' Sase asked.

'This isn't the time for your riddles,' Angus said, pushing himself away from her and stumbling towards the house. 'Help them!' he yelled. 'You're the only one that can.'

Patru held the baby out next to Cinder.

'If I see my dear sister move, I'll drop them both. Just let me leave with the child and you can have Cinder back.'

'Do something!' Angus pleaded.

'I can't save them both, and I cannot be the one to choose,' Sase said calmly. 'The decision is yours. Cinder or the child?'

'I can't.' Angus gripped his hair in his fists. 'There must be another way.'

'Black,' Cinder said hoarsely from above, looking down at Angus. 'It's okay,' a smile spread across her face. 'Don't worry, Black, I've already decided.' She pulled at Patru's vice-like fingers. Managing to get her fingers between his grip and her neck, she pulled his index finger into her mouth, biting down hard. Reflexively, Patru pulled his hand away and as he did, Cinder lifted her legs and kicked hard against his body. She watched her baby's face drift away. The gap between them widening as she pushed away from Patru, his finger still trapped inside her triumphantly grinning mouth. Her unnamed child's face disappeared behind the wall of The Big House. As she fell, she spat the finger at Patru's anguished face.

Dom had climbed to the top floor. He reached out to Cinder and the tips of her fingers wrapped around his. As she swung below him, Dom tried desperately to hold on, but Cinder was too exhausted. Their fingers slid apart. Cinder gazed up one last time at the twinkling stars before her body slammed into the cold earth.

Patru glared with anger and disbelief as blood oozed from the stub remains of his finger. Lifting the baby over his head, he made ready to toss the child down at Cinder in furious retaliation. With the silence and speed of a gust of wind, Sase was across the lawn, up on the roof, her hand at Patru's throat. Tiles cracked and smashed as she forced him down against the roof, sending great shards falling from the side of The Big House. Sase snatched the baby in her other hand, folding it securely to her breast.

'Let me go, bitch!' Patru yelled, flaying about, sending more broken tiles over the edge and crashing to the ground. 'You know the child will be better off with her own kind.'

'These are her own kind — her family.'

'Please,' Patru scoffed. 'These are arrogant, immature children, squabbling amongst themselves. What do they have to offer her?'

'They have love.'

'And what does a vampire need with love?' Patru asked, as his nails grew into long, black claws. He dug them into the flesh of Sase's arms. Unflinching, she squeezed his neck tighter. Then, placing her knee on his chest, she spoke.

'I loved you once, brother,' then she pulled Patru's head from his body.

Angus rushed to Cinder's side, joined shortly after by Marraine. Moaning and coughing blood, Cinder lay with her arms and legs twisted at abnormal angles.

'Is she safe?' She asked, twitching and trembling, her eyes rolling back in her head. 'Is our baby girl safe?' she spluttered and began to convulse.

'She's safe now,' Angus said, kneeling next to her and taking her shaky hand. 'Katie has her. She's safe.' He pulled the hair away from her face and stroked her cheek.

'I don't want her to touch our baby,' she stuttered.

Dom hurried down the wall and dropped the last few metres to the ground.

'I'm sorry, I couldn't hold her,' he said, kneeling next to Angus. Cinder fell still and quiet.

'Hey,' Angus said, tapping her lily-white cheek.

'No, no, no.'

He placed his ear to her chest. All he found there was terrifying silence and the realization of Cinder's mortality.

Marraine limped past Dom and fell beside Cinder's broken and twisted body. 'Can you hear me, sweetie?' She took Cinder's other hand.

'She's not breathing!' Angus said, taking her face in his hands. He pushed his lips to hers and breathed. Cinder's chest rose and fell in time with his breaths. He lifted his head and looked at Marraine, but she simply shook her head. Forgetting the pain in his own chest, Angus placed his hands over Cinder's rib cage and forced it down, pumping her heart with all his love.

Sase dropped to the ground next to Dom, still cradling the baby. Marraine looked up at her in rage and sorrow.

'Give her to Dom.' she ordered. 'Cinder doesn't want you touching her.'

'As you wish,' Sase said, holding the baby towards Dom.

'No, I'm no good with babies.' He took a step back. The baby opened its eyes and smiled. Dom watched as her tiny fingers twisted in her thick black hair. His lips twisted into a smile of affinity with hers. 'Okay then,' he conceded, taking off his top to wrap her in. 'Hey there, little one,' he gushed, as Sase slid her into his arms.

Angus grunted as he continued the compressions. Sase stepped to him and rested her hand on one of his powerful shoulders as they rose and fell rhythmically.

'She's gone Black. Her body was too broken.'

'No!' Angus yelled, shrugging her hand away.

'Black,' Marraine said softly, placing her hand over his. 'She's done fighting.'

Angus stopped to look at the surrounding faces, his eyes hot and damp.

'This can't be,' he said and then rested his head on Cinder's chest. 'Don't go,' he begged in a whisper, as his tears soaked into her mother's dress. Marraine held Cinder's cold, lifeless hand and kissed it gently.

Angus turned to his sister. For the first time since her return, he could see that she looked much more like the vampire Sase than she did his little sister Katie.

'Save her,' he said. Sase knelt next to him.

'It's too late. She's already gone.'

'Make her like you. Bring her back like you brought Katie back.'

'She is too old. She has seen too much pain and sorrow. She won't be Cinder; she will just be a tortured shell filled with a half version of me.' Angus sat up so that his eyes were level with Sase's.

'You keep telling me I need to be the one to make the decisions, well this is what I choose. Bring her back.'

'Mate, are you crazy?' Dom interrupted. 'You can't do that. How many vampires do we want running around? And besides,' he continued, 'Cinder would hate that. She hates vampires.'

'It's the only way,' Angus said, glaring at him.

'No, I won't let you,' Dom stepped towards Cinder's body.

'Maybe you should have caught her, and this wouldn't need to happen.' Angus spat. Dom paused.

'I'm taking the baby to the hospital,' he said, then turned and walked away. 'Do what you want.'

'Dom, wait,' Marraine called behind him, but he ignored her and continued on his way.

Sase took Angus's trembling hand in hers. 'If this is the path you're choosing, big brother, I will help you, but you must be sure.'

'Yes, of course I'm sure I can't live without her. And we have a daughter now. She needs her mother.'

'The child will have all the love it needs.'

'I need her!' Angus said, tears streaming from bloodshot eyes. 'Do it.'

'There may be a way,' Sase said, leaning over Cinder's body. 'She will need blood, a lot of blood.'

'She can have mine.' Angus offered his wrist to Sase.

'She will need more than that, and it must be a combination of Lycan and Nephilim blood. I will need the two of you,' she said, looking at Marraine. 'The two who knew her most intimately.'

'Whatever she needs,' Marraine said.

Sase pulled Cinder's bloody and dirty hair away from her neck.

'Are you sure?' She asked one last time. 'I can make you no promises. Are you willing to face the consequences and pay the price?' Angus and Marraine nodded in unison. Sase's four canine teeth elongated and sharpened into needle like fangs. Leaning over, she gently pushed her teeth into Cinder's freckled neck with a pop. Blood trickled from the wounds, but Sase's lips quickly covered the holes. As she sucked, Cinder's fingers began to twitch.

'Wait,' Angus said, sitting up straight. 'She's still alive.' Sase paused and turned her head to face him.

'No, she is becoming undead. If I stopped now, she would be an empty crucible. Teetering on death's precipice until she finally falls.'

'Like a zombie?' Marraine asked.

'Worse still than that. There will be nothing of her left, an empty shell. Without the knowledge that she needed to feed and a body that refuses to pass on. She would remain in an animated state until her body crumbles to nothing.' Sase used her thumb to wipe away the blood running from the punctures in Cinder's neck, then continued sucking. Marraine shuddered at the thought of an undead Cinder wondering around Heathcote until her body rotted away.

'I hope this works,' she said, looking into Angus's red, puffy eyes.

'It has to,' he said, taking hold of one of Cinder's twitching hands.

• • • •

Still cradling the baby tight in his arms, Dom approached the waiting police wagon. Bruised and battered, Duncan sat propped against the rear tyre, padding blood from his forehead with his good hand.

'Is the little one okay?' he asked, seeing the bundle in Dom's arms.

'Yeah, I think so. I'm taking her to the hospital.'

'Good,' Duncan said, moving his body uncomfortably. 'I think I should go there too.'

'You look like shit,' Dom said, offering him a hand. Duncan grunted as he pulled himself up.

'Are the others alright?' Duncan limped to the front of the wagon.

'I'm not sure how to answer that,' Dom said, opening the front passenger door for him.

'Well, did they get the bastard that did this to me?'

'Heck yeah,' Dom said as Duncan sat down. 'Black's sister pulled his head off.'

'Nice!'

'Yeah, it was.'

'That's good then. Why aren't the others coming with us?'

'They're too busy making more vampires.'

'What?'

'I'll explain on the way.' Dom handed the baby to Duncan and shut the door.

• • • •

Blood dripped from Sase's wrist. She had sliced it open with her own fangs. A second drop fell on Cinder's lips, red and dark against her snow-white skin. As the third drop hit, Cinder's eyes shot open, unfocused but intense.

'It's time,' Sase said, holding her hand over her bloody wrist. 'You need to let her drink, but as she does, you must focus on thoughts of her. This will not be easy. She will want to suck away all your joy and happiness and you must let her. You will be taken to the point of despair, and for Cinder's sake, you need to go there willingly and even beyond. Keep your mind always on her and let her take what she needs. Do you understand?'

'Yes,' Angus and Marraine said together.

'Give me your hand,' Sase said, taking Angus by the wrist and holding it to Cinder's mouth. 'This may hurt a bit.'

Angus could feel cold lips and warm blood against his skin. Pain, mixed with a feeling like warm running water, shot up his arm. Fangs concealed in Cinder's mouth sunk deep into Angus's wrist. Her eyes rolled back into her head as she sucked enthusiastically.

'Keep her here and here,' Sase said, touching Angus's head and chest.

Chapter 37
Blood of My Blood

Angus and Marraine sat with their backs against the cold bricks of The Big House. Their clammy washout faces hung heavy with exhaustion and sadness; their cheeks smeared with dirt and tears. The dying embers of hope flickered in their eyes as they fought to keep them open and focused on Cinder's motionless body. Sase wrapped makeshift bandages around their wrists, fashioned from strips of Angus's shirt.

'I need to go before she wakes,' she said, tucking away the loose end on Angus's wrist.

'What?' he asked drowsily, only half aware of what she said.

'I'm going. Believe me, she won't want to see me when she wakes.'

'But she's still not moving. What if it didn't work?'

'She is breathing,' Sase said, turning to look at Cinder. 'It is too shallow for you to see, but I can see.'

'Will she be alright?' Marraine asks. Sase looked up to the sky, pausing before she answered.

'Only time can answer that now. What is done is done.' She stood and walked away.

'So that's it? You're just leaving us now?' Marraine said, watching her go. Sase did not answer and disappeared into the shadows of the forest.

Marraine's eyes fell on something else just on the edge of the light flooding from the kitchen door, another body laid out on the ground. Realising for the first time that it was Louvelle, she smiled.

'At least something good came out of this godforsaken night.'

With a loud gasp, Cinder sat up. The bones in her limbs had set themselves back in their correct positions. She ran her hands up her arms and over her face. Angus and Marraine crawled towards her.

Cinder's eyes, oversized and vivid, turned towards Marraine.

'Oh Sweetie!' Marraine exclaimed apologetically, seeing Cinder's face hanging heavy with confusion and betrayal. 'I'm sorry,' she added, her eyes welling with hot tears. She placed her hand over her mouth, as if to hold back the flood of emotion. Cinder looked from Marraine to Angus, pulling at her clothes as she shuffled backwards. Marraine crawled closer, reaching out a reassuring hand. Cinder swatted her hand away, a moan of painful confusion tumbling from her blood smeared lips. Marraine pulled away, holding her hand to her heart.

'It's okay, sweetie, you're safe. We're here. We're both here for you,' she said. Cinder shot her another heartbreaking look of betrayal. Marraine sat back on her legs, holding her hand out pleadingly towards Angus behind her. Angus crept forward, taking her hand.

'Cin,' he said, moving cautiously towards Cinder. 'Cin, it's me. It's Black. Do you know who I am?'

'I know?' Cinder asked, turning her hand over and over in front of her face.

'Yes,' Angus said, moving closer 'Do you know who I am?'

'Who I am?' Cinder repeated.

'You're Cinder, remember? And I'm Black.' He placed his hand on her shoulder. Cinder's eyes darted to his hand and then back to her own.

'I'm Black,' she said.

'No,' Angus corrected her. 'I'm Black. Do you know who you are?'

'I know.'

'You do?'

'I know,' Cinder repeated, tapping her head with her index finger and grinning as if remembering something amusing. 'I know, sweetie,' she said, stretching out her arm and staring at her finger as if she had never seen it before. 'I know,' she said a third time before tapping her finger against Angus's furrowed brow.

'Good,' Angus said, taking hold of her other hand. 'I'm glad you're alright.'

'Alright?' Cinder pulled her hand away from his. 'Alright?' she repeated, taking hold of Angus's face and moving his cheeks around, squeezing them comically in on his lips.

'Cin?' Angus said with concern, as she squeezed harder.

'No,' she replied, squeezing harder still. 'I know what you did.'

'You're hurting me, honey.' Angus took hold of her hands.

'Hurting you? I'm hurting him, did you hear that?' she said, turning to Marraine. 'I'M HURTING HIM!' her yell reverberated off the walls of The Big House. A darkness flooded across her eyes, like black ink in a pool of white.

'You need to let him go, sweetie,' Marraine said.

'Let him go, sweetie,' Cinder mimicked her. 'Yes! Go, go, go, go, go!' she yelled, getting clumsily to her feet. Then, without warning, she ran. In a blur, she disappeared into the forest.

• • • •

Gunn stood on a grassy rise about 100 metres north of the farmhouse, turning his unlit pipe over in his large hand. He had heard the explosion. In fact, the entire district must have heard it, he had thought to himself. He had been half asleep in his armchair when the sound rumbled around the farm, rattling the windows and the empty whiskey glass on his coffee table.

He slid the pipe into his mouth and pulled on the thick woollen coat that he had draped over his arm. Even with his ageing eyesight, he could see the tell-tale red glow of a fire on the clouds, as they drifted slowly over Tallo's Bluff. Keeping his eyes on the glow, he fumbled in his breast pocket for his tobacco and matches. As he prepared his pipe, flashes of red and blue on the clouds indicated the arrival of emergency vehicles. A small flutter of concern grew in his stomach. He had not heard from anyone all evening. But he consoled himself with the thought that they were all out at Paddy's and nowhere near the Bluff. They're all probably just having too much fun to think about calling me, he thought to himself. Feeling reassured, he stood watching, more out of interest than concern.

"'Tis a perfectly pleasant night for a pipe outside anyways,' he said to himself as he lit the match. The night was mild and still, but he cupped around his pipe to nurture the small flame, keeping it alive long enough to spark up the tobacco with a familiar crackling glow. He let the match burn down towards his thumb and index finger for a moment more before dropping it to the ground and suffocating it between the brown soil and his boot heel. Drawing the beloved smoke into his mighty lungs gave some relief to his concerns. It was a comfortable temperature for night gazing, but still cooler than his warm living room. Holding the pipe in his teeth, he folded up the collar of his well-loved and hard-working coat. *This old thing has seen better days*, he thought to himself as he noticed a hole in one sleeve and a threadbare patch on the other. Taking another puff, he watched the smoke rise and disappear amongst the starlit sky. The lights of Heathcote twinkled below him, just as naïve and ignorant as ever, and the ocean beat out its never-ending crashing of waves, the constant reminder of time passing. He made a sound of disapproval at the back of his throat, reminded that he had less time ahead of him now than what was behind. And then he thought of her –Emily, his wife.

On nights like these, they would have walked along the beach, their fingers interlaced, their free hands carrying their shoes, swinging back and forth. They would lean in close, watching their toes dig into cold, wet sand. She would talk about her day, their past, and their dreams of the future together. He would listen, watching her and drinking her in. Gunn could listen to her for hours and never get bored. She would always have something fascinating to share.

Deciding that the evening's excitement was over, he emptied the ashes from the end of his pipe, kicking them around in the dirt. As he placed the pipe in his shirt pocket, something else caught his attention, something closer to home. It was very quiet, but he was sure that he heard glass smashing, and as he often reminded his family, he may be losing his eyesight, but his hearing was still as sharp as ever. He paused and strained his ears. This time, he was sure. Glass smashing louder, and somewhere close by. Gunn hastened back into the farmhouse, retrieving his shotgun and knife from beneath his bed.

At the west end of the milking yard, a small wooden building sat nestled under a sprawling oak tree. The little door that was usually locked hung open, rattling from one bent hinge. The second hinge lay on the timber deck, bent screws still protruding from their holes. Approaching cautiously, Gunn could see a large figure moving about frantically amongst the shadows inside. Bracing the butt of the shotgun against his shoulder, he edged closer. A sound somewhere between crazed laughter and a cry of misery filled the night. The hairs on Gunn's neck stood at attention.

'You best come out of there now,' he said, taking a step back.

The figure of a tall, young woman appeared in the doorway. Gunn recognised her immediately, but something about her didn't sit right with him. Her eyes shot from side to side, not staying focused on anything for more than a second. Then Gunn saw her mouth. Lips twisted with rage, gaped open, exposing two canine teeth extended beyond their natural length. Cinder ran from the doorway, stopping a few metres in front of Gunn. Blood dripped from broken containers held at the ends of her loosely hanging arms. She swayed on the spot as she looked around the farm and up to the sky. Gunn could see more blood dripping from her lips and covering the front of her clothes. He took another step back, lowering his weapon and holding his hand in front of him reassuringly.

'It's just me,' he said, trying to remain calm. Cinder twitched and lurched towards him. Instinctively, Gunn grabbed for his knife, hidden in the back pocket of his jeans. Cinder paused, a flicker of recognition behind her tortured eyes. Gunn looked at the containers of blood as they dripped from her trembling hands. With one hand stretched out reassuringly in front of him, Gunn took a step forward.

'It's just me, love. It's Uncle Gunn,' he said, leaning the shotgun against the trunk of a nearby tree. 'What have they done to you?' he asked, looking at her, blood dripping from her chin, glistening in the moonlight. 'Oh, sweet child,' he sighed in realisation. 'They've turned you, haven't they? You poor thing.'

Cinder's eyes, blazing with fierce intensity, dropped to the blood-filled containers in her hands. The fingers on her left hand slipped slowly apart, and the container dropped to the ground with a sloshing thud. The container on the right followed shortly after, tipping onto its side. Thick blood glugged out of the small opening and pooled around Cinder's dirty feet. Listlessly, Cinder raised her hands towards her face, spreading her bloodied fingers in front of her unsettled eyes. With a shuddering moan, she dropped to her knees, her shoulders slumping forward as though something inside her chest had broken and collapsed in on itself. Cautiously, Gunn walked forward and placed a large, warm hand on her shoulder. Cinder trembled beneath his touch, folding further in on herself. Turning her head to the side, she looked at Gunn's hand and reached slowly for it. As her blood-soaked hand moved shakily into view, she jerked her head backwards, pushing Gunn away. Her eyes shot wide open, all pupil and white, none of their usual green. She hissed at Gunn with pointed teeth.

'Cinder!' someone called out from behind Gunn. Torry was running along the fence at the side of the milking yard, followed closely by Detective Morgan. Torry vaulted the fence and ran to her father. Detective Morgan pulled his weapon from his hip and propped himself on the fence. Gunn held up a hand to warn Torry to stay back. Cinder pulled at her stained and tattered dress.

'Cinder,' she said to herself with a laugh.

'Sis, what's wrong?' Torry asked. Cinder turned to look, her face hanging heavy with confused misery. She shrugged, then with a heart wrenching cry, she sprung to her feet and ran into the darkness. Torry ran forward to follow her, but Gunn stood in her path.

'Leave her be,' he said, taking hold of Torry's arm. 'We need to let her find herself before we can find her.' Torry pulled her arm free and continued forward. After a few steps, she paused and looked back at her father.

'I don't understand,' she said, placing her hands on her head.

'I'm not sure I do either, princess.'

Peter Morgan came to stand next to Gunn, holstering his weapon.

'Are you alright, Mr Kinnard?' he asked. Gunn looked over his body.

'I'm uninjured, if that's what you mean.' Gunn placed one of his large, calloused hands on Peter Morgan's shoulder. 'But no, I'm not alright. I would feel much better if I knew what was happening with my boys.'

'I'll find them for you.' Peter Morgan said with a nod.

'Thank you. Be careful.'

As Peter Morgan walked away, Torry slumped to the ground. She sat cross-legged, pulling at a tuft of grass. Gunn collected shards from the broken containers and made his way to the little storehouse. After inspecting the broken windows and the door hanging loose on the frame, he moved inside. He replaced some of the unbroken containers back on their bench.

'What have they done to you, girl?' he asked, as he pulled a handkerchief from his pocket, wiping the remnants of blood from his old hands.

Chapter 38
A Mind So Complex

A kiss of life, a kiss of love, a kiss to raise the dead. One kiss to rape, re-move, and plunder. You're still inside my head.
The shadows cast across my heart, they creep, entwine, and cage. When even hope is snatched away, all that's left is rage.

Three days. They woke in the morning and they worked the farm, but for three days no one saw Cinder. They prepared meals and ate them together. Three breakfasts, three lunches, three dinners, but no place set for her. *What would she be eating now, anyway?* For three nights, Angus went to an empty bed and tried to sleep.

Gunn had found a crib that had been Torry's, in the dark recesses of one of the sheds. He lovingly cleaned away the dust and stitched together a temporary mattress from some unused pillows. Once he was over the initial shock of the yet to be named child, Gunn had fallen madly in love with her.

'I know I'm not your grandfather, but you can call me Poppy,' he said as he took her from Angus's arms, tears of pride in his eyes. To everyone's relief, Sase had explained that the baby didn't need blood. In fact, cow's milk would do until they could get her some baby formula, something that was not in short supply on a dairy farm. The days dragged on, hot and muggy with a stagnate sadness. On the third night, the heat broke with a storm. Towering grey-black clouds rolled in from the east, turning the ocean molasses-black. Pelting rain on the tin roof and the distant rumble of thunder kept Angus from much needed sleep. Countless hours passed as he lay awake in his lonely bed, waiting for sporadic flashes to light up the room. In the crib next to his bed, the baby slept undisturbed. The storm seemed to have a calming effect on her. Eventually, he fell asleep, but not for long.

In the early hours of the fourth day, Angus woke with a start. Something or someone was moving around on the deck outside. He wrapped a blanket around his shoulders and checked on the baby. She stirred at his approached but remained sleeping. Unlocking the door, Angus pulled it open a crack. Once his eyes had adjusted to the dim morning light, he saw someone with matted hair and dirty scraps of clothes sitting on the edge of the deck.

'Cin, is that you?' he asked, blinking.

'No,' the figure said without turning to look at him. 'But I am a close approximation, I guess.'

'It is you,' Angus said with relief. He opened the door and came to sit with her.

'No, no, it's not,' Cinder said, turning to look at him. Her green eyes burned with new intensity. 'What is closer to the truth of things is that I'm you,' she said, tapping his shoulder.

'Are you... Are you okay?'

'Better than okay, I'm perfection, sweetie.'

'Good.'

'Is it though? Is it good, Black?'

'You're alive.'

'That I am,' Cinder said with a nod. 'I can see a dozen shades of blue in the sky. I can hear the difference between the warm air and the cold air. I can taste your desire for me floating on the breeze, and I can feel the vibrations of your heartbeat. Everything is loud but crystal clear. And not just the sounds, but the colours and the tastes. Mmm, the tastes. Everything tastes amazing and blood most of all. Don't worry, I can control my desire,' she said, seeing the look of concern on his face. 'I don't feel like I need to drink, but I can certainly understand the appeal. It's warm and sweet and tastes of emotion and memory and nostalgia. And the energy! I feel like I could run and keep on running. Never having to come back to this place.'

'You're scaring me a bit,' Angus said, pulling at the blanket around his shoulders.

'I know,' Cinder said, looking him up and down. 'I can smell your fear and it is making me feel sick. I remember that about myself, how the smell of fear sickens me. I don't blame you, though you should fear me.'

'I'm not afraid of you. I'm scared of losing you?'

'I died. Cinder is dead. You lost her when that happened. This is just some sick, twisted Angus-Marraine hybrid.' she said, looking down at her body. 'All that is left of the girl you knew is all the nightmares.'

'Then I will learn to love your nightmares.'

'Oh, you will, will you?' Cinder asked, raising her voice. 'You're just going to choose to do that? This coming from the scared little man who can't make any decisions for himself. Well, good for you that you can decide something about my nightmares because I can't!'

'That's harsh, Cin,' Angus said quietly. Cinder sprung to her feet.

'*That's harsh* he says,' She glared at him. 'You think I'm being harsh? Do you remember what my nightmares are about? Those nightmares that you are going to love?'

'I remember,' Angus said, his eyes moistening.

'My nightmares!' Cinder was yelling now. 'The only things that I know are really mine are my memories that I hate vampires. I hate this!' She ran her hands up and down her body, ruffled her messy hair, and then slapped her face. 'You made me into my own personal bogeyman.' Her eyes burned with rage, like two fiery green pits in her bloodstained and dirty face. Angus wiped a tear from his cheek.

'Please, Cin. Please, just sit down before you wake the baby.'

'It's here?' She asked, her eyes darting to the doorway.

'Yes, she's sleeping inside. She doesn't have a name yet. I was waiting for you to come back.' Angus stood and reached for Cinder's hand, the blanket falling from his shoulders. 'Do you want to come see her?'

'Keep that thing away from me.' She moved away from him. 'In fact, you all need to stay away from me.'

'Stay away? But we love you. We have a daughter now who needs her mother.' Angus turned to look inside. When he turned back, Cinder was gone. He held his hands on the back of his neck, looking around for Cinder but not expecting to see her. Away on the horizon, the teal blue ocean danced with streaks of orange, yellow, and magenta. The semicircle sun burned without compassion at Angus's sad and sore eyes. His heavy heart beat strong and painfully behind his bruised and broken ribs. The chill of the morning breeze made him uncomfortably aware of his other injuries. Picking up the blanket, he pulled it across his shoulders once more and slumped down on the deck, resting his face in his palms.

A short time later, a small cry from inside the guesthouse alerted him to the fact that the baby was waking. He kicked at the dirt and took a deep breath.

'I'm coming,' he said, rocking forward onto his feet. The floorboards creaked as he walked barefoot across the room. He dropped the blanket on the end of the bed and flicked on his bedside lamp. The baby squirmed and squawked, pushing a determined hand out from under her blankets.

'Hey, baby girl,' Angus said, picking her up. 'Your mother was just here.' He rocked her gently in his arms. 'She wasn't ready to meet you yet. I guess I will have to give you a name myself. I was thinking, Annabelle. Do you like that?'

'After Cinder's mother?' Sase had appeared at the door. Angus looked her up and down, then looked back at the baby. 'We're getting all sorts of visitors this morning. Mummy and now Auntie Katie. Aren't we lucky?' he said in a babyish voice.

'I knew Annabelle,' Sase said, entering the room and ignoring Angus's sarcastic tone. 'She was a nice girl, naïve, but nice.

'We haven't seen you for a couple of days. I was beginning to think that you had left for good' Angus said, stroking the baby's cheek.

'I've been keeping my distance,' Sase said, extending her hand and letting the baby wrap its tiny hand around her finger. 'I've actually just come to say my goodbyes.'

'Goodbye. What do you mean goodbye?' Two thick lines formed between Angus's eyebrows.

'I must go. This little one will need her mother. My presence here will only keep Cinder away.'

'I'm sure we can work something out,' Angus said, bobbing up and down to stall the cry that was forming on the baby's face. Sase shook her head.

'There has never been two different female vampires. She most likely blames me for what she has become. One of us will kill the other, then where would that leave you?' I told you that the price would be excessive. This is the price.'

'So, I have to lose both of you?'

'To keep both of us, yes, you have to let me go for now. You do have to appreciate the poetic irony of it.'

'Appreciate it? I'd like to take all the irony of it and shove it up its poetic arse. That's how much I appreciate this!' Droplets of spit shot from his dry, cracked lips. 'Will I ever see you again?'

'I have a niece now. That's something new. I will definitely be around if she needs me.'

'Well, Aunt Katie, I think we need you now.' Angus held the baby up to his nose and screwed up his face. 'She needs to be changed.'

'Oh no,' Sase said, backing away. 'I really must go. I have important vampire business to attend to.'

'No, you don't,' Angus said, passing her the baby. 'That's the excessive price you need to pay for leaving me.' Sase smiled and held out her arms.

'I concede that is only fair. Are we calling her Annabelle?' She asked. Angus nodded. 'Come to Aunt Katie, Annabelle.' She took Annabelle in her arms and kissed the top of her head. 'Where should I change her?'

'Her things are in there,' Angus pointed to the bathroom. When Sase had left the room, he slid open his bedside draw. He pulled a small dark object from the draw and turned it over in his hands.

'Happy birthday, Cinder,' he said, before dropping the object back in and slamming the draw shut again.

Chapter 39
Unsaid But Not Unheard

The little beach town of Heathcote sat still and quiet. In a few hours' time, the shops along the esplanade would open. For now, however, the blinds were drawn on Mac's Butchery. The sign on the door of Ocean Views Ice Creamery was turned to closed, and Bartlett's Surf and Fishing was chained and padlocked shut. Up the hill, on the side of the hospital road, Mr Loo's A-frame sign was out and chained to the telephone pole – he started early. A greasy sheet of paper that had been pulled from a bin by seagulls looking for discarded fish and chips, tumbled along the gutter; other than that, there were no signs of movement. The summer was coming to an end. Most of the holidaymakers had left.

The calmness of the morning extended to the ocean. It lay flat and still, like a giant mirror reflecting the turquoise and cyan hues of the cloudless sky. The sun sat just above the horizon, adding a band of orange-red shimmer to the watery canvas. Even the most devout of the local surfers were taking advantage of the conditions and staying in bed. Only one figure stood on the otherwise empty beach. A tall man with broad shoulders, dressed in black. His long shadow stretched away behind him, up the sand and into the grassy dunes.

Angus stood at the ever-changing edge, where ocean met sand. His bare feet inviting the waves as they inched closer and closer, trying to find skin. As the water finally found his toes, he bent down and rolled the bottoms of his dark jeans. Standing again slowly, he slid his hands inside his jacket pockets. A black hood covered his grim face. Bloodshot unfocused eyes peeked out from the shadows. Sea spray, whipped up by a gentle breeze, chilled his face, but he stood still, unresponsive. The full moon was still visible, like a ghost against the blue. He had been out here since it was bright and white against the star-speckled blackness. Once upon a time, a time before Cinder, he might have spent the night on the ocean with his friends, but last night he was more alone than ever. Walking further into the shallows, he slid a small package from his pocket, rolling it around his hand. *How can something so small contain something with such emotions?* Angus thought to himself. As he looked at it now, the packaging seemed insignificant and inappropriate for the precious cargo inside. A small black cardboard box held closed by a cheap red ribbon. With a small tug of his large fingers, the ribbon slid free and fluttered down to the water, carried away, twisting and bobbing into the dark sea. He gently removed his mother's ring before crushing the box remorsefully in his powerful fist. Now, even though he held the ring in his hand, Angus didn't feel like it belong to him. The ring belonged to Cinder. He was going to give it to her for her birthday, the day she died. Holding it up to the sun, Angus watched the light play on the polished gold band and the diamonds, expertly cut to sparkle with every slight movement. How could this ring that contained memories of such happiness and joy be causing such anguish and sorrow at the same time? What should happen to the ring now? These few ounces of gold and diamonds, dug up from the ground and crafted into something beautiful. Who should it go to? Did it belong to anyone? The questions twisted around Angus's mind like the ribbon on the ocean that was now drifting out of sight.

* * * *

High in the dunes, hidden in the shadows of the dark arms of the tea trees, a pair of bright green eyes blinked glistening tears from their corners. The creature who had once called herself Cinder watched as the dark figure of the man whom she both loved and hated held something up to the light. Her new eyes, cursed with the ability to see everything, saw the gold and the diamonds. As she wiped the tears away with the back of her chilly hand, a wave of recognition flooded over her. That ring was for her, or at least the woman she once was. Raising her fingers to her mouth, Cinder could taste the ocean's saltiness as she ran her tongue along her lips. The memory of Angus's delicious blood flooded her mind. A thought that both excited her and sent a thrill of disgust through her whole body.

Finding the strength to go to him, Cinder wiped her eyes once more. But as she rose, she saw something that stripped away the last piece of hope, the last twist of the betraying knife that had torn open her broken heart. She crept from her shadowy hiding place, but fell to her knees after only a few steps, hardly able to believe what she had just seen was true. Angus had thrown the ring into the ocean.

Cinder sat, digging her hands into the cool sand. Misery wrapped around her, pulling her into darkness as an unknown portion of time passed. What did time mean to her now, anyway? She waited until Angus had left the beach, listening to his footsteps on the timber steps, and waited until his intoxicating scent dissipated on the breeze. When she was sure he was gone, she slipped silently down to the beach. Tracing Angus's footprints, she walked to the edge of the wide, terrifying dark waters. Standing just beyond the water's reach, she stared out at the white crests of the waves as they turned and rolled, ceaselessly reaching out for dry land before being pulled back by the unyielding currents. 'Such is life,' she said to herself. Her eyes glazed and heavy, Cinder turned slowly towards The Big House and walked away from the water's edge. She drifted away along the beach like one more piece of dry weed tumbling in the ocean breeze and her broken heart sank like a once precious and loved belonging, tossed into the dark cold depths of the sea.

Epilogue
Cinders and Black.

A flurry of bright orange sparks escaped; a warm updraft lifted them into the dark cavernous chimney. With one hand on his knee to steady his aging body, Gunn prodded the embers and turned over a half-charred piece of firewood. He hung the poker back on its hook beside the mantle, and with a look of satisfaction, he added another log to the fire. The days still held some remnants of the summer warmth, but the nights in the draughty farmhouse were growing cold. Gunn had suggested that it would be better for Angus and baby Annabelle to move inside and take Torry's room. Torry was happy to move to the guest house and have her own space. 'I'll move out again when Cinder gets back,' she had made a point of saying.

In the kitchen, Angus cradled Annabelle with one arm as he tested the temperature of her formula on his wrist. Convinced that the liquid was not too hot, he wiped his wrist with a cloth draped over his shoulder and joined Gunn in the living room. As he sat down, the front door opened. Dom and Torry stuck their heads in before entering.

'Is she asleep yet?' Torry asked.

'No, I'm just giving her her bottle before I put her down.'

'Oh, let me.' Torry said excitedly, skipping into the living room.

'Sure thing.' Angus said, passing Annabelle into Torry's waiting arms.

'Come to Aunty Tor,' she said, taking the bottle and sitting on the sofa next to Angus.

Dom shut the front door and sat in the armchair next to his father. He had his guitar with him. Since Gunn had agreed to stop smoking inside while Annabelle was in the house, Dom had been using music to pacify him. Dom plucked a few notes to check if his instrument was in tune.

'Hang on, I'll get Mildred,' Gunn said, getting quickly up from his chair. Mildred was the name Gunn had given his banjo. He jogged from the room. The others laughed at his excitement.

'What do you want to play, Dad?' Dom asked when he returned.

'See if you remember this one,' Gunn said as he took his seat. His fingers moved with dexterity across the instrument. A familiar, nostalgic melody filled the little room. Dom recognised it after the first stanza, he had heard it many times throughout his life. Father and son played together, their feet tapping in time. Then, as though they had rehearsed it, Gunn and Dom started singing.

Rest ye head, still ye heart. Be stirred not by wake or fright.
Lamp is a-lit, the door's a-bolt. No wolf can howl or bite.

Gunn sang the melody, deep and raspy, while Dom added the harmonies.

The day was long but night hath fall'd rest ye now and sleep.
Wrap ye tight in a lover's arms and safely there you'll keep.

The warmth of the room soothed Angus's exhausted body, and the music calmed his troubled mind. He closed his eyes and lay his head back against the sofa. Soon he was asleep.

• • • •

Mars hovered, small and red, against the dark backdrop of the night. Cinder wiped the eyepiece of her telescope, her moist eyelashes determined to hinder her view. Picking up a small piece of red chalk, she pushed it into her bedroom wall. Moving her hand frantically in tight circles, she scribbled a red dot until the chalk gave under the strain, snapping and falling to the floor. Pulling her sleeve over her hand and clasping it in her fist, Cinder slowly rubbed the words and pictures off her four walls. With the walls empty save for the red dot, she sat on her four-poster bed and watched the smoke creep under her door. As her bedroom floor become flooded with the thick grey cloud, she lent down to search for something. The floorboards felt hot to the touch. She picked up a piece of discarded chalk and scratched one last phrase onto the black walls.

Three simple words now hard to do. That word that fits with I and you.

. . . .

That sound? Angus's eyes shot open. Somewhere in the night, he thought he heard someone cry out in pain. Clearing his mind and listening, he realised he could hear a siren. He rose and walked to the window. On the hill far across the valley, above the quiet and sleeping town of Heathcote, something glowed orange. The wispy clouds reflected red and ochre as the light cast flickering spectral shadows through the trees.

'Cinder,' he exclaimed, running for the door. 'What have you done?'

Coming soon: Anchor and the Moon Book 3.
Name and Number.

Find out more here:

If you want to keep up to date with Maxx Victor's books and have access to exclusive content, Sign up to the *Hello From Heathcote* newsletter at www.maxxvictorbooks.com[1]

---

1.   http://www.maxxvictorbooks.com

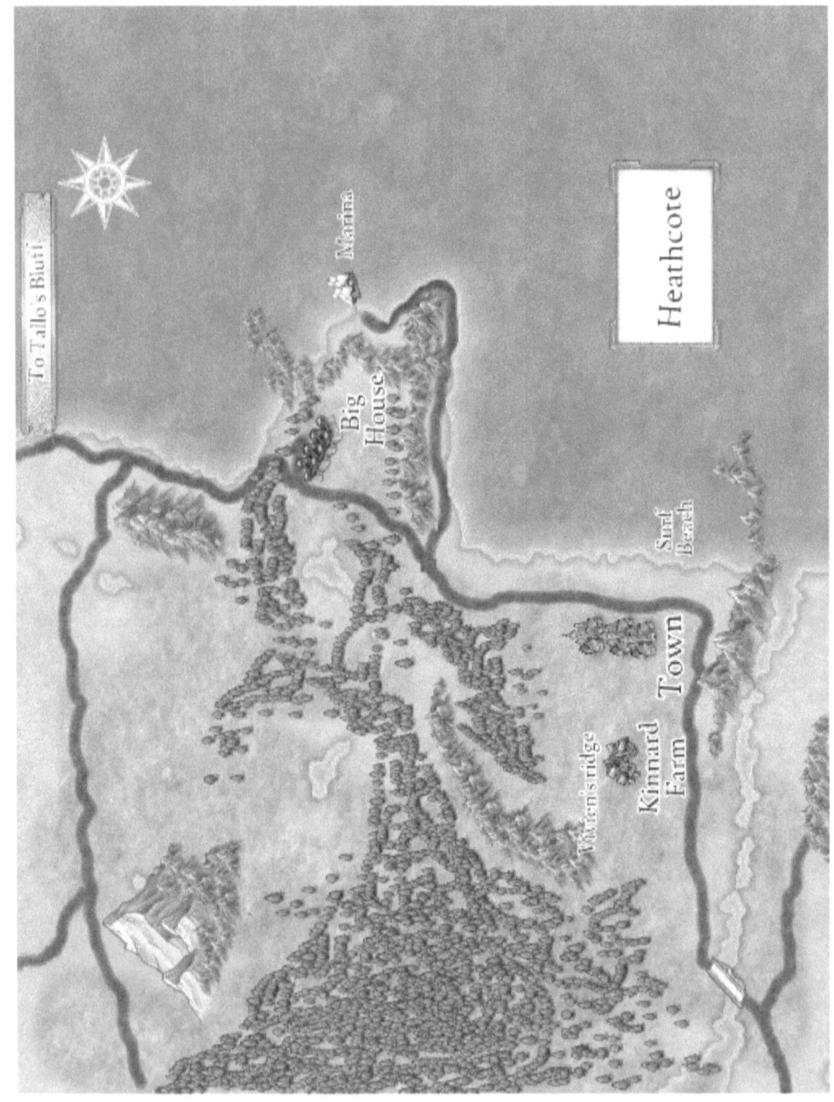
To Tallo's Bluff
Marina
Heathcote
Big House
Surf Beach
Wren's ridge
Kinnard Farm
Town

REWARD
The Maikranz Method

In 2009 author D. Eric Maikranz, offered a reward to readers of his novel "The Reincarnationist Papers". This novel has now gone on to be the inspiration for the Hollywood movie "INFINITE" by Paramount Pictures. You can read full story at https://eric-maikranz.com/

This was the reward offered by D. Eric Maikranz.

As the author of this work, I offer you the reader, the opportunity to redeem a cash award for introducing this work to any literary agent, publisher or producer that offers an acceptable contract to the author for this work. The reward offered is 10% of any initial book advance or option contract for film or television series up to a maximum of $10,000.

Via this reward, our mutual goal is to introduce this work to literary/publishing professionals or producers. Many are likely familiar with the term "6 degrees of separation," the theory that anyone on the planet can be connected to any other person on the planet through a chain of acquaintances that has no more than five intermediaries. This is what I aim to accomplish here with your help

With his blessing I now offer you the same reward. Please send any leads or contacts to maxxvictorbooks@gmail.com.

Thank you and happy hunting,
Maxx Victor

About the Author

Maxx Victor is an Australian author, musician, and secondary school science teacher, who has achieved award winning success with his short stories. A dedicated husband and proud father of two, he is also highly involved in his local arts community; performing in bands and producing and directing amateur films.

Maxx's author journey began at a very young age. As a child with dyslexia, reading and writing were a constant struggle. To help, his father implemented the nightly routine of reading Titin and Asterix comics and Biggles books to Maxx and his brother; installing a lifelong passion for reading. Maxx's mother also encouraged him to write stories (some which he has kept to this day).

During his secondary school years, Maxx unearthed a love for music. He regularly wrote poetry and song lyrics, as well as scripts for plays and short films. Something again sparked the curiosity for writing stories when Maxx's children were toddlers. He frequently created impromptu, twisted fairy-tale bedtime stories, with his family members as the main characters. Maxx now writes teen fiction and hopes that his writing can inspire young people to be defined by their passions and talents, not by the things that the world will tell them are impairments.

Acknowledgements

Thank you to my wonderful family for all your support on my author journey. To my wife Amanda, who keeps the real world running at the times I am lost in my imaginary world. Harvey and Alex, thank you for being the first fans of the Anchor and Moon series, even if you had no choice. To my extended family, thank you for your ongoing feedback and words of encouragement and, most of all, for instilling a love of reading and writing. To mum, even though you will never read my words, they would never have been possible without your love.

To Paul Mah, thank you for your amazing cover designs. You effortlessly turn my scribblings and vague descriptions into works of art. Thank you also to my editors, Steph and Jenn, for polishing my words and making them palatable for my readers. I learn something new from you all the time.

Thank you to my ARC team for helping to shape this book into something better than it would have been. Ben, Treece, Steph, and Troy, my creative life coach. The Fenkins crew, thank you for helping to keep me sane and for giving me limitless inspiration and content for my stories.

To the Instagram writing community and those that have supported the Indie Author Maxx podcast, your kindness and help have made this journey far more enjoyable. #supportindieauthors. Thank you also to the bookshops who have taken a chance on an unknown and stocked my books. You have made one of my dreams come true.

A big thank you to those that sing the lyrics, strum the strings, and bash the keys and skins. Your music forms the pictures in my head that become the words on these pages. The world has lost some of you over the years, but your art lives on.

And lastly, thank you to you, the reader, for spending some time in my imagination. I hope you enjoyed your time there and will come back again soon.

Praise for Maxx Victor

I think the prologue did a great job at setting the scene for this story, with Black strolling along the French Quarter of New Orleans.

As well as being labelled a paranormal romance, I would also say this story has the undertone of a rom-com. Some of the scenes were very comical, and the banter between characters literally had me laughing out loud.

I must say, this story was completely unpredictable, and I was left trying to guess what the big secret was the whole way through. I definitely wasn't expecting the ending I got!

If you're looking for a fun paranormal romance with an added mystery, you should definitely give Cinder and Black a read. - **Nikki Minty, Author of the NYC-Big-Book winning, "Zadok" series.**

• • • •

After reading the blurb, I was so excited to get my hands on a copy of Cinder and Black. Maxx has done an amazing job bringing the story of Cinder and Angus to life. Throughout the story, I could almost smell the salty air, and hear the washing of the waves against the night-cooled sand of a dark beach. Most of the book had the vibe of a gorgeous, sleepy seaside town just sailing along, but with an undercurrent of danger that most of its inhabitants remained oblivious to. Learning about the world through Cinder's eyes, and that of the colourful and amusing cast of characters was a real treat. If you like shifters, YA, a little hint of darkness, some good teenage angst, and budding romance, this is the book for you. - **Liv Evans Author of "Derivates Rising" trilogy.**

• • • •

If you enjoyed this book or any of my books, I would love you to leave a review on Amazon or Goodreads. If you would like to know more about my journey as an indie author or about my indie author friends, please check out the Indie Author Maxx podcast on Spotify. As always, thank you and happy reading.